# SHALLOW GRAVE

# KAREN HARPER

## SHALLOW GRAVE

*mira*

ISBN-13: 978-0-7783-1922-1

Shallow Grave

For questions and comments about the quality of this book, please contact us at CustomerService@Harlequin.com.

MIRABooks.com

BookClubbish.com

**Printed in U.S.A.**

Recycling programs
for this product may
not exist in your area.

To all our Naples, Florida, friends
and, as ever, to Don for thirty lovely winters there.

# SHALLOW GRAVE

# CHAPTER ONE

*Naples, Florida*

Claire had never been more content.

"I'm glad we don't have to be scared anymore," her daughter, Lexi, said on their usual night walk around their neighborhood. "'Specially now that I'm almost five. Even in the dark 'cause it's October now."

She was holding hands between Claire and her stepfather, Nick, skipping along on the cul-de-sac circled by their large, new house and four others. It was just after 6:30 in the evening. Nick carried a flashlight but hadn't turned it on since the houses and pole lights, as well as the sharp slice of moon in the sky, made it light enough to see.

Nick, a criminal lawyer and senior partner of a big law firm, had told Claire he'd been at his desk and conference table all day and needed to clear his head before a late dinner for adults only. Claire had fed Lexi already.

She thought the night was so lovely with its soft air and welcome low humidity when they'd been living in air-conditioning for months. She was glad for a walk, because she was almost five months pregnant with their first child, and mild exercise also helped with her narcolepsy. She was fighting to keep the disease under control with the addition of herbal remedies instead of relying only on hard-hitting meds. Although her ob-gyn had assured her the prescriptions would do no harm, she was worried about having a healthy baby.

All they'd been through over the past number of months had made her anxious about things somehow going wrong. Still, she had no intention of putting up walls around herself or her family. As ever, she'd found reaching out to help others helped her. To that end, she was still tending her website *Clear Path*, using her forensic psychology training as a consultant for companies hiring staff or even consumer fraud issues—all by laptop or phone, since she was planning to stay home for the foreseeable future. Her only in-person outreach was with her sister to help a group of at-risk youngsters.

"Nope, nothing is scary anymore," Claire assured her daughter. "But remember what we were saying about looking carefully both ways before crossing any street, even a quiet one like this? You said your teacher talked about that, so it's important."

The child nodded, but the skipping stopped. Claire had to admit she'd gone easy on her lately, especially since their archenemy had died and they'd felt safe to come home again.

Even before she married Nick, it had been a dangerous roller coaster ride with him. At least they and Lexi's father, Jace, had come to an understanding about sharing the child. Lexi had even adapted well to calling Jace "Daddy" and Nick "Dad." Claire did worry, though, that since Jace had a serious female friend—whom she and Lexi both liked—that she'd someday have to share Lexi for longer periods.

"You okay with this walk, sweetheart?" Nick asked Claire. "Not too tired?"

"I feel fine," she insisted, and smiled at him in the glow of a neighbor's post light. She wished he'd turn on his flashlight, but she didn't want him or Lexi to know she suddenly felt jumpy.

No streetlights illuminated this newly developed area south of Naples off Collier Boulevard, not far from the fringe of the wilderness and the Everglades. It was sad, she thought, that developments like theirs were pressing against the Glades, because that meant wild animals sometimes encroached on the neighborhood. Or, the truth was, humans were encroaching on them. That reminded her that they were going to a petting zoo tomorrow.

She and her sister, Darcy, were overseeing a trip there for the children in their charity, Comfort Zone, an organization for kids who had endured violence in their homes. Nick was going along this time, so she was pleased about that. They would visit the Backwoods Animal Adventure, which locals called the BAA. Its logo was a sheep, but there were plenty of more exotic animals, including birds such as parrots and flamingos, not to mention an abused tiger the BAA owners had taken in.

Claire gasped as Nick jerked her and Lexi behind him.

He clicked on his flashlight. The beam sliced through sharp shadows to palmetto and dwarf palms, which seemed to leap at them.

Before anyone said a word, he slanted the beam to the side. It shone on a bright yellow sign the Save Our Wildlife group had put in. The sign had bold print and a drawing of a Florida panther—an endangered species that inhabited South Florida and was quite secretive and stealthy, moving mostly at night.

"The sign?" Claire whispered. "What?"

"Shh. There!"

She glimpsed a sleek shadow slink across the street toward the thicket on the other side. A blur of beige fur, gleaming gold eyes, a rustle of leaves, and it was gone. Neighbors had claimed to see the big cats crossing nearby, but they were elusive.

"Wow! It ran fast, but I saw its eyes!" Lexi cried, clinging to Claire as if it would attack. Nick put his arms around Claire with Lexi pressed between them.

"No one will believe we actually saw one," Claire whispered. "Some call them ghost cats. The newspaper says that claims to see them usually turn out to be something else."

"We did see one," Nick said, "but let's head back."

But for a moment, the three of them still stood tight together, staring at the sign that read Crossing Danger above the outline of the beautiful beast.

Before Nick and Claire had supper that night, they let Lexi stay up so Nick could help her research Florida panthers and tigers on the family laptop while Claire called her sister. Lexi had already taken the phone from Claire to tell her cousin Jilly, who was going to the BAA with them tomorrow, that they had seen a Florida panther—a real big one with big eyes.

Now Nick could hear Claire back on her cell phone, talking about a kid nicknamed Duck, one of the Comfort Zone children she worried about because his father had committed a murder and was still on the run. Ex-con Irv Glover had come home drunk to find a male social worker talking with his wife, Marta. She was asking him how to get a restraining order. He'd beaten both of them in a rage, while Duck hid under a bed, and the social worker had died from his injuries. Irv had not been seen since.

Marta and Duck had moved, but money for them was being mailed to their old address with postmarks from Tennessee, where Irv had lived once, so the authorities were looking for him there. Still, Marta Glover was barely making ends meet. More than once Claire and Darcy had taken a food basket to them. Nick knew details of the boy's life because he'd helped to prosecute his father years before for aggravated vehicular assault stemming from a road rage incident, for which he'd served time.

"I'm going to call Duck by his real name Duncan from now on," Claire was telling Darcy. "He needs to have his self-image and confidence built up. The other kids still snicker over 'Duck,' and that doesn't help anyone recover from an abusive situation."

He watched Claire pace as she talked to Darcy, her only original family member left. Darcy and Steve lived closer to town with their two kids, a boy, Drew, who had just turned seven and Jilly, who was Lexi's age. The two girls were as tight as Darcy and Claire.

While Lexi looked at pictures on the screen of Siberian tigers like the one they would see tomorrow—man, he didn't know tigers were endangered from hunters, poachers and loss of environment—he looked away to watch his beautiful wife.

Unlike most native Floridians, Claire had light skin, red hair and green eyes that could haunt a man—and had him from the first. She was tall at five-ten, slender but sturdy looking, even carrying the baby, his baby. Like an idiot, his eyes filled with tears he blinked away. When he'd first met Claire, he'd hired her because he'd seen how good she was in court, testifying as a forensic psychologist expert witness. Thank God they had both lived through three harrowing murder investigations since then, and he had vowed never to put her on the stand or in danger again.

Life was good. He was thrilled with Claire, loved his stepdaughter and hoped for a son, though he'd be happy with another girl. Lexi was all in for a sister, though Claire tried to explain that she'd be a "big" sister to the new baby since she'd be five years older. When they'd had the ultrasound recently, they had told the doctor they didn't want to know the child's sex ahead of time. Lexi had been furious over that, but Claire had wanted it that way—"the old-fashioned way." Yeah, if that meant family values and Claire just pursuing her career online, at least until the baby was here and a bit grown, that was fine with him. Besides, she had a big house to oversee now, even with a nanny's occasional help. He smiled at Claire as she ended the phone call and came over to sit beside him on the couch.

He put his arm around her, and she leaned against him. Lexi was listening to a narrated piece about tigers in Thailand, and she'd turned the sound way up, but they still whispered.

"Everything set for tomorrow?" he asked as he gave her a squeeze. "I suppose Jace's girlfriend, Brittany, is going to be there, the 'tiger talker.'"

"Darcy and I like her, thank heavens. You know, it's nice that Jace likes her family too—her father, at least. A navy flyboy and a marine, they get along great. I don't think I ever told you that Jace feels his own father loved his marine recruits more than he did him, so I'm thinking Brittany's dad, Ben, is more or less a father figure to him."

Nick said, "That's my favorite psychologist, always probing and assessing."

"Anyhow," she went on, "Brit, as Jace calls her, is going to give us the tour and a little lecture about their new tiger they've named Tiberia. Clever, huh, the *t* in *tiger* mixed with 'Siberia'?"

"I can see her allure for Jace. He's passionate about flying—now about her too."

"True," she said, frowning. Sometimes Nick worried Claire still cared too much for Jace and vice versa.

Just then a single-engine plane roared overhead. "If that was him saying good-night," Nick said, "glad he missed the roof."

"I hope it wasn't Daddy after dark," Lexi put in, turning down the laptop volume. "His plane has lights, but sometimes he flies over water, and I told him to remember what happened before."

Nick just shook his head. Sometimes Lexi sounded so much like Claire.

Claire's ex and Lexi's father was supposedly flying a citrus orchard crop-dusting plane, and/or a Zika virus mosquito–spraying plane. But Claire and Nick knew that regardless of whatever logo was painted on the fuselage, he was actually working for the FBI in its Stingray program, which could track persons of interest and criminals by their cell phones. Stingray wasn't top secret anymore, but it was still in use by the government. Jace was glad to be flying again but longed to return to international jets, so good luck to the "tiger talker" Brittany Hoffman if she wanted to tame Jace.

"Time for bed, sweetheart," Claire told Lexi. "Your dad and I are going to have a late dinner, and then we'll be going to sleep too."

"'Cause you are eating and sleeping for two," Lexi said, and gently patted her mother's stomach when she got up from behind the laptop.

Nick put his hands behind his head and stretched as he watched Claire rise—still somewhat gracefully—from the leather sofa. He loved their new house, especially this spacious great room with its calming neutral colors and touches of light blue and green. The high, domed ceiling fan still turned lazily, though it was finally cooler outside. Their swimming pool, just beyond the patio, glimmered from its lights below the surface. After all they'd been through, Nick would have worried about the expanse of glass and the darkness outside where someone could be watching and lurking, but surely not anymore. Yet sometimes he had to work hard to convince himself they were safe now.

"Night, Dad," Lexi said, and went over to give him a kiss on the cheek. He hugged her. "Sleep tight, and tomorrow is tiger day—and all those animals you like to pet."

"But I still love my pony Scout the best," the child told him, her pert face so serious as she referred to the horse she met during their adventures on Mackinac Island. "Remember, you promised that no snake's gonna hurt him, even if he's staying at a place on Rattlesnake Road. Glad it's not in the Glades where those real big snakes get caught."

"Everything will be okay," he promised. "Claire, I'll heat that lasagna in the microwave. It wouldn't hurt me to turn in early too, after the day I've had."

"And the life you've had," she said. "But things, like Lexi's said more than once, are going to be 'all better' now."

For one moment she thought she glimpsed a figure outside in the shadows behind the patio, but surely that was just her own reflection in the glass. She would not worry Nick with her fears and certainly didn't want to upset Lexi. After all, their enemies were dead.

# CHAPTER TWO

"I've decided I'm going to call you Duncan, your real name," Claire told the thin, quiet nine-year-old boy the next day as the group walked from the BAA parking lot to the zoo's entrance. "It's a good and strong name."

"I don't know," he said, tugging on the brim of his too-large, beat-up Miami Dolphins hat. It hid his eyes and made his brown, shaggy hair spike out the back. He always walked with his head slightly down, and she'd love to change that too. "My dad might not like it. Duck's his name for me," he added so low she almost couldn't hear him.

"But he's not home now. What will your mother think?"

"She'd be okay, I guess, 'cause she used to call me that—Duncan. Till he said no. But why's it a strong name? 'Cause I'm kind of skinny."

"You will fill out and get stronger as you get older. It's a strong name because it's a name from a great country called Scotland, and there was even a King Duncan of

Scotland. It's a somewhat unusual name for a young person, so it's very special. If you don't want me to call you Duncan, I won't, but Lexi, Jilly, Darcy and I would like to call you by your real name—also because you are a friend and good person to us."

He shrugged his skinny shoulders under a stained shirt that was not quite warm enough for the day. "Then okay," he muttered. "Just for now, but if my dad comes back, don't say it in front of him—and hide from him, 'cause I will too."

Claire's eyes filled with tears. To have seen all this child had…to be so afraid. Her own child had been through terrible times, but she could have stood right there and sobbed for this little boy and the others along with them today.

Claire and Darcy had discussed more than once whether the motto for their Comfort Zone program for children affected by domestic violence should be Children Need Both Roots and Wings or There Is No Rainbow without Rain, so they used both. So far, through social services and contacts from Darcy's church, they had nine children they met with weekly to take to some sort of experience where they could learn, have fun, and feel safe and appreciated. Darcy's elementary education background and Claire's psychology degree gave them the skills to cope with deeply damaged and sometimes endangered children—at least they hoped so.

Darcy's husband, Steve, who oversaw a construction team in South Florida, couldn't come today, but it was a rare treat to have Nick along for this visit to the Backwoods Animal Adventure. Nick and Claire had picked up three of the children; Darcy and Jilly had arrived in the

small parking lot with three; and Nick's employee Bronco
Gates and his girlfriend, Nita, had picked up the other
three. Nita had been Lexi's nanny and was now their bab-
ysitter. She was going to work for them part-time when
the baby was born.

The ages of the Comfort Zone kids ranged from eight
to eleven. Claire and Darcy had gone through the paren-
tal permission routine or interviews with their guardians,
which gave them a chance to better understand their difficult, sometimes dangerous home situations. Two of the
kids were in foster care.

Claire wasn't sure why she especially gravitated toward
this child everyone called Duck, except that, before she
knew Nick, her husband had been the lead prosecuting
attorney in the trial that had sent the boy's father to a state
prison for four years. That was for running his truck into
and then brutally beating a guy who pulled in front of him
in a car—road rage at its worst. The boy, who had been
in the truck, had testified through a child advocate, and
his horrendous tale of spousal and child abuse had helped
to convict his father, though the defense lawyer had tried
to get all of that thrown out. After being released for just
a few months, Duck's dad, Irv Glover, beat up his wife
and killed a social worker. Glover had disappeared, but
his child and wife still suffered.

Claire saw the boy flinch when Brittany Hoffman, their
host for this visit, nearly jumped out from just behind the
small ticket and information building where her mother
sat. Claire put her hand on his bony shoulder.

"Welcome to all of you!" Brittany shouted. "We are
going to have fun and learn a lot today!"

They had already been welcomed in the small parking lot by both of the senior Hoffmans, Brittany's parents, but they'd returned to their duties, and Brittany was a bit late meeting them. She looked tired, with dark circles under her eyes. Too little sleep? Claire wondered. Maybe she'd spent the night with Jace. Despite looking tired, she was animated and almost gave off sparks.

"I'm Brittany, the daughter of the owners of the BAA. We're so happy to see you! Don't worry, because all the animals that bite are in special cages or behind fences. We want to show you all our farm animals, our Florida animals and tropical birds—even our snakes and alligators—which we do not pet—and especially our new tiger who is here because he was treated badly at his first home."

Sally, a Comfort Zone child and victim of sexual abuse, who seemed so much older than her years, whispered to Claire, "What's new about that? Let's welcome that tiger to the club."

Nick was pleased to see how well Brittany and Claire got along, considering that Brittany was Claire's ex-husband's girlfriend. More than once when Jace had picked up Lexi for a visit, a couple of times with Brittany in the car, Jace had joked that Brit was really good at taming wild animals. Nick wondered if they'd tie the knot—and if that mattered to Claire.

Brittany Hoffman was cute rather than beautiful, although she didn't work much at it and looked a bit blitzed today. She had sharp blue eyes and a glossy mane of sandy-colored hair she wore pulled back in a big ponytail. Minimal makeup, though she hardly needed it with her healthy color. She was petite but shapely, toned and tanned. Of the Hoffman family who owned this place, she was really the only one with credentials for working with animals, as Claire had said she had a BS from the University of Florida in zoology and animal management.

As for the rest of the family, her parents, Ben and Ann, just plain loved animals. After military service, Ben had sold advertising for the local newspaper, but said he'd wanted to get away from the "rat race." He'd told the kids when someone asked, no they didn't have rats to pet here.

The man was tall and muscular, as if he could wrestle some of the gators they had here. Jace had mentioned he really liked the guy, an ex-marine to match his own navy pilot career. Actually, Jace had met Ben before Brittany, at a Veterans of Foreign Wars event, and it was Ben who had introduced them.

The Hoffmans were probably in their midfifties while Brittany was midtwenties. Ann Hoffman, a bit overweight with an animated face framed by sleek silver hair, seemed gracious and outgoing, whereas Ben appeared solemn and distracted, despite being a solid, salt-of-the-earth kind of guy. Since the Hoffmans were trying to make a go of what was basically an animal shelter and amateur zoo—though the State of Florida had deemed them worthy of taking in the tiger since they had built a good cage facility—Nick had insisted on paying for everyone's ticket, even though they had offered to let the group in for free.

The only other Hoffman child was a son, Lane, a violinist with the Naples Symphony Orchestra—the black sheep of the family. Nick knew who he was from the days he attended social and charity gatherings, but couldn't really say he knew him.

The Comfort Zone kids were given sno-cones, and their group spent almost a half hour next to the tiger cage while the poor beast paced back and forth glaring at them. As good a job as Brittany did talking about tigers, he could tell Claire was glad when they moved on to more cuddly, placid animals that meant hands-on action. Man, he thought, if that tiger got out, it had a gourmet dinner waiting just across a small moat where llamas, goats, sheep, calves and even a baby camel awaited the kids. Tiberia could probably smell dinner on the breeze.

Nick had to admit, though, that the Hoffmans were brave to try to establish the BAA here, as its fifteen acres were wedged in between the big ranch to the west and orange and grapefruit orchards to the east on this road. A nine-foot wire fence surrounded the property, and they were still making improvements on cages and refreshment stands. Obviously, it was their dream to help animals, big and small, and teach youngsters to love them as they did.

He was grateful that they'd let the kids in an hour before general admission today, though he wondered how many families would actually show up. At least Ben Hoffman had skills from his old career to arrange for advertising for the place; Claire had said she'd seen ads in both the newspaper and online.

Nick glanced back to see Ben Hoffman had appeared near the cage with a big box of something, maybe to feed the tiger. Good thing the kids didn't stay to see a carnivore eat dinner, but at least there was no kill involved.

Near the petting cages, Nick settled down on a bench,

holding a white rabbit while the kids tentatively, then more assuredly, petted, held and even talked to the animals. Duncan seemed the only one to want to pet what Brittany had called a rare mulefoot hog piglet, a squirmy little thing that looked both muddy and ugly.

Besides Brittany moving from child to child, Claire was everywhere, comforting, praising, suggesting, especially watchful of Lexi and Duncan. Nick smiled to see his former bodyguard, big Bronco, now man-of-all trades, petting the animals too. Nita, Bronco's very significant other, was smiling and speaking Spanish to the anteater, who seemed to be the only antisocial creature of the bunch.

After about fifteen minutes, Jackson, the man Brittany introduced as their "jack-of-all-trades around here," joined them with two pink flamingos that elicited oohs and ahhs. Though the guy was a maintenance/custodian type, Nick noted he seemed great with the animals—and kids too.

Jackson, however, introduced himself as the zookeeper. He was a tall, lanky African American around sixty, almost bald, with a big smile. He lived on the grounds, he said, helped to feed the animals and was going on an errand to get fresh vegetables for the flamingos to eat so they would stay pink.

"Because that depends on what they eat," Jackson told the kids. Nick was impressed when he went on, "What you eat makes you colorful too—so remember to eat your veggies, okay?"

The kids nodded or responded, and waved to Jackson as he guided the flamingos back toward the small moated area labeled Flamingo Isle where he disappeared into the foliage.

"Not only our keeps-things-together genius," Brit told them, "but a longtime friend of my dad's."

Duncan laughed loudly, not at that comment, but at the little piglet he was hugging.

And then—

A screech, a roar and a scream pierced the air.

"Tiberia!" Brittany yelled, and took off on a dead run.

"Watch the kids!" Claire shouted to the other adults, and headed across the moat after Brittany.

Damn! Why had he married a take-charge, bleeding-heart woman?

"Bronco, you're in charge. Keep the kids here!" Nick ordered, and thrust the rabbit into his hands. That cry had been fierce, feral—but he was sure he'd heard a human scream too.

Claire broke into a run over the wooden bridge spanning the moat. She hadn't run for weeks, and she was quickly out of breath. Couldn't see the tiger cage from here because of the curve in the walk and a small building blocking it. Brittany...out of sight ahead. Had that restless tiger just roared at someone, maybe someone too close to its cage, then the person screamed?

Surely no one would get too close. They'd have to climb a fence first.

But that scream had been first low, then shrill, blood-curdling.

She tore around the corner of the small glass enclosure that held beaver and otters in two separate displays with small water pools. When she turned the next corner, she saw only horror.

# CHAPTER THREE

Brittany had climbed the four-foot-tall restraining fence and was right up to the bars of the tiger cage, shouting, "Tiberia, back, back! No! Nooo!"

But the big cat seemed to just be standing. Growling. Eating something. Brittany had told the kids it was almost feeding time, but someone else would do it today. Claire had assumed that she didn't want the children to see a carnivorous animal tearing into its meat.

As she came closer, Claire saw a man, face up, grotesquely sprawled under the cat in a pool of blood. Brittany's father! The tiger lowered its jaws to the big man's ravaged, red neck and gave his limp body a hard shake.

"I'll call 911!" Claire shouted at Brittany, who, now sobbing, clung to the bars of the cage.

Nick ran up, his cell phone already out of his jeans pocket. He was talking into it, asking for help, paramedics, the police. He put an arm around Claire, hugging her hard to him.

Brittany, hysterical, kept screaming at the beast. She began to rock against the bars as if she'd pull them from their moorings. Then she turned away, climbed the fence again, and tore around to the door of the interior part of the display where she'd told the kids there was a "tiger bedroom" and supplies. As she ran in, the door behind her caught and stood ajar. A red fire extinguisher was mounted there.

Ann Hoffman appeared, running, gasping. "What?" she cried, and then she saw. Nick hurried toward her. Unlike her daughter, the woman didn't scream, but fastened her fists in her hair and stared aghast as if in shock.

"Do you have a gun here?" Nick asked the distraught woman. "Ann, do you have a gun? Tranquilizer darts?"

She just stared. Dear heavens, Claire thought, this was a nightmare. If Ben Hoffman wasn't dead already, they'd never save him now.

Surely Brittany didn't intend to go into that cage. This was no metropolitan zoo with protocols and stun guns. But that fire extinguisher gave Claire an idea.

She rushed to the door where Brittany had disappeared and shouted, "Brittany, come back! The fire extinguisher will stop him!" She lifted it from its holder attached to the inside of the door. Heavy. She staggered back with it. Nick ran to help. Good thing, because she realized she had no idea how to use it.

Leaning forward over the restraining fence, Nick yanked a ring on the metal extinguisher, pointed the hose and nozzle, and pulled the lever just as Brittany ran back out toward them with a long metal gaff. She must have meant to use it to shove the tiger away from her father, but the chemical spray hit the cat. Some of it bounced back toward them, and Nick aimed it better.

"Brittany!" Claire shouted. "Help is coming!"

"He'll bleed out by then! Dear God, why did you do it this way?" she screamed into the cage.

*Why did you do it this way?* The tiger? Her father?

Again, Brittany climbed the restraining fence and threw herself against the bars again, gripping them, thrusting the gaff through the bars. What if the big cat rushed her too?

Ann Hoffman had collapsed to her knees and began to wail. Nick climbed the fence too and aimed the extinguisher through the bars, pinning the big cat back in a corner of the cage where it roared as if in pain. Finally, after an eternity—but then they were outside town on a county road—they heard sirens screaming. Claire hadn't realized she was crying. She was hyperventilating, shaking.

"We need to get the kids home—out of here," she told Nick as the spray fizzled out. "What if that tiger had escaped?"

In that deep, calm lawyer voice of his, Nick said, "Go tell Darcy to divide up the other kids, with Bronco and Nita, and take Lexi too. They should leave right now, but we'll have to stay here to help Brittany and Ann."

Ann! Claire thought. She'd been so intent on the cage. She turned to see Ann Hoffman still on her knees, her body racked with sobs, her face in her hands.

Claire turned back to Nick. "Yes, we might have to answer questions since we were kind of first responders. Should I call Jace to help Brittany?"

Nick shook his head. "Only if you want him to parachute in and try to take over. Go on, sweetheart, tell Darcy, and don't run. Maybe Brittany and her mother will need a lawyer. This extinguisher's out of spray, but the tiger looks like he's staying put. And find out where Jackson went, their custodian."

On her way back to the kids and their chaperones, Claire saw two police cars pull into the parking lot outside the entry, but the EMR vehicle drove right in through the open gate. She pointed out the direction they should go but realized they'd never get over the moat bridge in the vehicle. She hurried to get the Comfort Zone kids away.

Comfort zone. Had Ben been so comfortable with the tiger that he'd walked into that cage, or had something or someone made him enter? No one else was around. And what had Brittany meant by why he did it *this way*? Was she screaming at the tiger, or at her father?

Claire stared at the chaotic, tragic scene. Ben Hoffman had been pronounced dead by the Collier County Medical Examiner. Ann Hoffman was in such a state of shock that the medics, who had been called and arrived before the ME, had attended to her too. Brittany was pacing just as fiercely as Tiberia had earlier, only outside the fence surrounding the cage where the cat now lay limp from tranquilizer darts.

The tiger had been darted by workers from the Naples Zoo so that the medics and ME could get to the victim and the police could more closely survey the scene. The police had strung their neon yellow CRIME SCENE DO NOT CROSS tape and cleared the area, except for the owners/family and eyewitnesses who were first on the scene.

The body, at first covered by a tarp, was finally taken away by the ME in an official van. Unfortunately, the media had picked up on the tragedy already, and a curious crowd was beginning to gather at the front gate, now closed, where Claire spotted two TV vans with satellite dishes on their roofs. Others who had intended to visit today at the regular opening time—it looked like some grandparents with kids—still milled around, trying to learn what was going on.

Also, Nick had said that a few picketers for *the humane treatment of cats*, no less, were already walking back and forth outside with signs, chanting. Jackson, who had gone to run a short errand, was back now and had more than once tried to disperse the crowd. The police had briefly questioned him, but as he hadn't been on-site, he'd just gone back to guarding the front gate. Nick had seen the guy had tears in his eyes. After all, Brit had said he was friends with her father. Jackson kept shaking his head, stunned about how this could have happened.

"Counselor Markwood," a policeman who recognized Nick called from inside the taped-off area, "you here as a guest, or you representing someone?"

Nick rose from the bench where he sat with Claire and walked a few steps away to talk to the officer. "I'm a guest, at least for now," Nick told him. "My wife and I brought a group of charity kids here today before regular opening hours. We didn't see this happen but ran over when we heard the noise. I don't think anyone knows why he did that—the deceased."

"Yeah, especially since he evidently didn't enter with the animal's food," the officer told him. "A box of it was dropped just inside the enclosure but wasn't taken in or thrown into the cage. Real weird if it was an accident, but the detectives will check security protocol when they get here, and we'll have to wait for the ME's report. It was suicide to go in there. He should have known that. His wife and daughter are too shaken to explain things so far, and his son's playing in a concert uptown. His phone's off right now, according to his wife, so we don't have all next of kin notified. Wish the media buzzards wouldn't circle," he added with a glance at the growing crowd at the gate.

With a tap of his fingers to the bill of his cap, the officer went back to his position by the cage. Despite sitting, Claire's legs were shaking as she watched and listened. Observation and analysis were in her forensic psych blood. The only time her brain wasn't spinning with *what, how, who* and *why* was if she slept or messed up her meds and had a narcoleptic nightmare. But a nightmare this was.

Nick came back over to her. "You still doing okay? You should carry your pills even when you rely on herbal tea."

"I thought we'd be home by now. Nick, I know your ears perked up when you heard him say accident or suicide, but who would choose that dreadful way to kill himself and horrify his family and others when he could just jump in the Gulf or get a gun?"

He nodded as they huddled together on the wooden bench. "You know, this all hits close to home. I'd really be all in if this had any implications of being a murder like with my father, but you can't charge a big cat with that."

He put one arm around her and gripped her knee with

his other hand. He was shaking too. She knew how hard he'd struggled to cope with the supposed suicide of his father when it had turned out to be murder, one that had taken Nick years to prove and to bring the killer to justice.

That early loss had so impacted his life that he'd founded the private South Shores investigation company. With its small, secret staff, he kept it separate from his law firm, and most of the cases managed to fly under the radar. Through South Shores funding and legal expertise, he helped others who had lost a loved one by mysterious means. He was especially drawn to cases where the cause of death was undecided and unproven: accident, suicide or murder. And had they walked into another tragic situation, or would Ben's family have an explanation of how or why this happened?

Brittany's frenzied words still haunted Claire: *Why would you do it this way?*

Jace Britten brought the Zika virus mosquito– spraying plane into the Marco Island airport and, after waiting for an old Piper Cub to land behind him, taxied toward the small hangar. What a far cry from his navy pilot days landing his fighter jet on a carrier at sea or flying solo missions over endless, blazing sand in Iraq. As much as he longed to take to the skies again in an F-35 or a big commercial Airbus loaded with lives he would die to protect, this was it for now.

But, he had to admit, he kind of liked this assignment to spray for those hellish mosquitoes that caused women to deliver babies with congenital birth defects. Zika danger had hit not only Southeast Florida but now threatened here, Southwest Florida too. And his ex-wife was pregnant with her new husband's baby. As much as he had issues with Nick and Claire sometimes, they were good for his daughter, Lexi, and he hoped like hell that Claire would have a healthy baby. Maybe this spraying would help.

But he was serving above and beyond that too, since he was tracking the whereabouts not only of drug dealers but other criminals for the government. It was a new endeavor for him, but one that at least made things more interesting and still helped the US fight its enemies. He figured he was still serving his country as he had once. And he needed the job after leaving the airline.

"Roger that," he responded to final directions from the small control tower. "Over and out."

He steered the plane, which the FBI secretly owned, toward the hangar where a contact he'd met only once would service the plane, actually electronically "debrief" the recordings from his latest Stingray mission. The camera and tracking device mounted under the fuselage were worth about $400,000 of government money, and there were other pilots in the air like him, especially along the Mexican border. The Stingray aviation surveillance program relied on a tracking system that acted like a cell phone tower, one that recorded locations and could photograph events. If it had to, a Stingray plane could first focus on an area or neighborhood, then pinpoint a person and snap quite a clear picture—if they had a cell phone on them, and who didn't lately?

The FBI had wanted him to take a desk job in DC, overseeing Stingray, but he hadn't wanted to leave Naples, Lexi—and now Brit. Nor had he ever gotten flying out of his blood. He needed some excitement, the kind that gave him a new lease on life. And Brit—whom he'd actually met through her father, an ex-marine who had been in special ops—was a very intriguing woman both in bed and out. She had a good sense of humor too. She'd joked from the first that he had to marry her so that her name would be Brittany Britten.

He rechecked the controls, unlatched his seat belt and popped the door. He was barely off the concrete hangar floor and out into the sunny, windy afternoon when his cell sounded—the "Marines' Hymn." Yeah, he was a die-hard leatherneck, always would be.

The caller ID said it was Brit.

"Hello, tiger girl," he said.

"Don't. Don't say that."

"What's the matter? You're crying. Where are you?"

"Jace, believe it or not I'm with Claire and Nick at the BAA."

"What hap—"

"My father went into the tiger's cage—somehow. I mean I know how. Jace, it mauled him, killed him. The police are here and—"

He felt like he'd been hit in the gut. Ben. That big man dead? In the tiger cage! He'd—he'd gotten so close to him so fast. He couldn't be dead! Jace had liked the older man from the first. He'd kidded him just the other day that it had been a long time since he'd had a wingman, and Ben was like that to him.

"Brit, I'm so sorry. Is Lexi still there? Is she okay?"

"No. I mean, yes, the children are safe. Everyone is gone, even the paramedics. They took his body to the medical examiner for an autopsy. Why cut him up when he's a mess? I—I need to talk to the police now, keep the press away. It ruins everything—this place, my plans, our lives."

He felt like throwing up, but his military training kicked in. Assess. Keep calm. React.

"Slow down, honey. Breathe. I'll come right out. I just landed on Marco. Will they let me in?"

"I guess. Nick's still here. I'm going to ask him to represent Mother and me if we need it, and—"

"Listen to me. The damn tiger killed him, you didn't! I'll be there ASAP. Listen, if it comes to needing legal help, Nick's firm is the best. You need other support, you got me."

He punched off the phone and broke into a run across the tarmac toward his car.

# CHAPTER FOUR

Claire and Nick finally had permission to leave. With Jackson's help, they had just run the gauntlet of media and curious onlookers outside the gate. With microphones thrust in their faces, Nick had made a brief statement that the accident was under formal investigation and they had no other comment. Claire was upset that cameras rolled and the newspaper photographer took several shots. After all they'd been through, she had no desire to be back in the glare of publicity and the peril it could sometimes lead to.

Things had been going so well, and now this tragedy. She and Nick had both given statements to the Naples detective who had arrived. Ann Hoffman had been interviewed briefly since she had not been in the immediate area nor even seen the tiger that day. Besides, she was in shock. Brittany had told Nick that Jace had suggested he represent her, at least for now, so Nick had sat in with her for a lengthy interview with Detective Jensen.

When they were in their car in the parking lot, Claire exhaled hard and said, "Whew. The last time I was on TV, it brought our enemies to our front door. I just hope there won't be criminal charges against Brittany or Ann. And they can hardly charge a dead man with criminal negligence."

"Or his own suicide. But as you said, no one would try to kill themselves that way. And I think—from the fact Jace admired Ben Hoffman so much—with a group of young kids nearby, it couldn't be suicide."

"You're not thinking it could be murder?"

"As I told the media mavens, I'm sure there will be an investigation. I may help out right now, but after all we've been through, we're not getting involved in this. Listen," he said, reaching over the console to put a hand on her knee, "let's sit here for a few minutes to see if Jace drives in so we can brief him before he goes inside."

"Okay, fine. But Brittany was in charge of that tiger. Could the State of Florida at the very least accuse the BAA of inadequate safety procedures or something like that?"

"Her father's the one who went in the cage. Thank God it wasn't that the beast got out. She's still adamant that the tiger was only doing what came naturally. She told the police that the cat should not be punished, not be put down, and she wanted to be there to watch when it regains consciousness. But about your question—yes. The Florida Fish and Wildlife Conservation Commission and even the US Department of Agriculture might get involved, but for a private, small zoo—not sure. There's Jace's car. I'll go snag him."

Nick got out and hurried over to where Jace parked.

Claire had to admit, despite trying to keep it together in front of Nick and the police, that she felt emotionally drained and exhausted. Feeling revved up could actually slow her responses, and her narcolepsy was kicking in to make her want to sleep on her feet. In the chaos, she hadn't taken her herbal stimulant, Country Mallow, on time either. It was at home with her other herbals, which is where they should have been by now. Timing was the problem with herbs, at least hers, so maybe she needed to start carrying a thermos of two kinds of herbal tea around with her.

At least talking on her cell earlier to Lexi and Darcy had calmed her some. Her sister still had Duncan because his mother had not yet been back from her job. Darcy said they had decided not to tell the children what had happened, only that there had been an accident, but Claire figured Darcy was waiting for big sis psych major to explain. And in case they heard about it elsewhere, it was going to be best to tell them the truth.

Claire watched Nick flag down Jace as he parked. She got out and walked over one lane and several spaces toward them as the men walked toward the gate. They evidently didn't see her.

The only two men she had ever loved seemed so different from each other. Nick was dark-haired with silvering at his temples and gray eyes—her brilliant silver fox. He was several inches taller than Jace, who was more muscular. At age forty, Nick had a sexy, deep voice and tightly coiled but smoothly controlled body and demeanor. He was a deep thinker, with deeper emotions, who had helped many people—mostly without fanfare. Jace was thirty-four, blond with a broad face and blue eyes, still navy-short hair, sharp movements, a modern day Viking with a swashbuckling aura. His feelings were usually all on the surface and sometimes likely to explode.

"What's with the crowd?" Claire heard Jace ask Nick. "Can't they leave a tragedy alone? It's worse than rubbernecking at a car wreck. I—I really liked Ben. Hell of a thing."

Claire could tell even from this distance that Jace's face looked ravaged, as if he'd been crying or trying not to. His body language showed he was not only tense but angry.

As she joined the men, she saw Jace study her also, narrow-eyed as he always did, a quick check of her belly. Awkwardly, at first, instead of looking at each other, the three of them turned to look at the people milling around by that entry gate. Their chants swelled, and some held signs picturing lions, tigers and the Florida panther. The original ragtag bunch must be getting more organized.

"Save big cats! Don't be rats!" they recited over and over. And, once in a while from another group, "Keep the wild in wildlife!" Claire wondered if those people could be from the Save Our Wildlife group Darcy had recently joined, but no time to think about that now.

"Lexi's all right?" Jace asked her, raising his voice over the noise.

"The kids are all safe," she told him.

"Thank God. Gotta get to Brit. But why would her dad go into a tiger cage?"

"Good question," Nick said. "I hope she or the BAA won't need representation, but she's asked for it, just in case. I didn't want to get involved but I told her sure. If it gets sticky or drawn out, I can always assign a partner."

"Good. I told her you could help."

Jace extended his hand, and the two men shook. Despite some rough spots in the past, they'd worked together to live through worse than this. They had been on edge with each other at first, but they had saved each other's lives since. What was that Chinese proverb, Claire thought, that if you saved someone's life, you were somehow responsible for them?

"Be safe," Jace said with a lift of a hand as if he were blessing them. But he turned back. "Does Lexi—the other kids—know what really happened?"

Claire shook her head. "I asked Darcy and Bronco to tell them there was an accident, but they don't know details—not that anyone really does. I'm going to explain as best I can."

"Tell Lexi that I—we—love her. Gotta help Brit," he threw over his shoulder and jogged toward the crowd at the gate.

Nick took Claire's arm, and they were starting toward their car when a sleek, black pickup truck pulled up to them. The door was emblazoned in gold with the words TROPHY RANCH, NAPLES, FLORIDA, HUNTER'S HEAVEN. A rugged-looking, handsome man with a mustache, wearing a Western hat, leaned out and called to them, "I'm the neighbor. Just heard what happened. Hope I can help. You're Nick Markwood, right? We've met before."

"Right. I recognize you, Stan Helter," Nick said and reached toward the driver's window to shake hands.

"Nothing to do now, I think, unless you can get rid of this crowd—or want to be interviewed by the media."

"Even for free publicity, hell no. Don't need our future guests getting gun-shy over an animal killing a man. Big ex-marine shoulda had a gun on him. As for the crowd, coupla blasts with a hunting rifle in the air might clear them out."

Claire figured that was his idea of humor, but she wasn't so sure when she saw he had a gun rack mounted in the back cab window, one obviously not for show since it bristled with rifles, some with big scopes attached.

"They gonna keep the killer cat alive?" Helter asked Nick.

"It wasn't really theirs. A refugee, kind of a ward of the state they took from some old woman who couldn't keep it and shouldn't have had it. Its BAA keeper insists the killing was instinct, not intent."

"Brittany Hoffman, you mean, the beast-loving blonde. But they're sly and crafty—big cats. Hope I can help the Hoffmans later somehow. Listen, Markwood, come visit us someday, almost always something doing. Bring our mutual friend Manfort with you. See you, Counselor. Ma'am," he said, giving Claire a good once-over before he drove off.

"Someone who works at the Trophy Ranch?" Claire asked as they headed toward their car again.

"Its mastermind and owner. That place is big business. I met him once at a Save the Glades charity event. A friend of mine from way back, Grant Manfort, introduced us. I think Grant's a shareholder in the Trophy Ranch."

"But they shoot big game there, don't they? Those 'save

big cats' protestors should go picket his spread. And he asked what they were going to do with the tiger as if he'd like to get his hands on it."

"I think they hunt everything there from gators and wild boars to who knows what else."

"I noticed—maybe he did too—that you didn't introduce me."

"Not the type of guy you'd like to know. Grant says he's savvy, but a rough character and a real womanizer." He opened the car door for her, and she got in. "Sweetheart, let's just go get Lexi before either of us starts cooking up suspicions or strategies about Ben's death. Besides, you look like you need your meds before a bad dream hits."

"This is already a bad dream. Yes, let's go try to tell the kids a version of what happened before we go home."

Inside the tight quarters of the BAA administration trailer, Jace held Brit close. He'd had to talk his way in through the cop at the gate. Brit had said her mother was heavily sedated and lying down in the back room, just staring at the ceiling. Brit hugged him back hard, but he was amazed she didn't cry. Tough cookie. Or else she was in shock, like her mother. He knew damn well from combat experiences that horror sometimes took a while to be real, let alone to heal.

"The tiger had already mauled him and bitten through his carotid artery," she said against his shoulder. "There was blood, blood, blood all over. Jace, just when the tiger was bringing more people in, and our family was getting on better. Wait until Lane hears. He'll go ballistic. He hated the idea of the BAA."

"Yeah, you got a brother who's a far cry from the rest of you. But back to what happened here," he said with a sniff as he pictured an apparently healthy, happy Ben having a beer with him just last week. Had he known the guy at all? Had he liked him too much too fast? Damn, but he regretted their recent argument. Trying to keep his voice steady, he asked, "Did Ben go in to feed Tiberia?"

"He was going to feed him since I was with the kids, including Lexi, but he knew better than to go into the cage for that—for anything, especially at feeding time. He knew just to shove the food through the hatch and then push it in closer only with the long gaff pole. The food box was not in the cage—but he was." Her voice broke again.

"Maybe he just stepped inside because he thought the animal was secure in that holding area—what you called the bedroom, separate behind the cage. Maybe Tiberia was hiding in that little cave you made so he could get out of the sun, and then—"

"Jace, I've been over it all with an officer, then a detective with Nick Markwood there!"

"Sure. Sure," he said, kissing the top of her head through her wild hair, then pressed his lips there. "Just a mystery, then, one we may never have the answer to."

"He hadn't been himself lately. Kind of depressed and inwardly angry—more than usual, that is. That scares me."

"You mean that he might have been secretly sui—"

"I don't know. I don't know! Now I have to decide whether to admit Mother to the hospital where they can keep an eye on her or whether I can take her home."

She suddenly exploded in sobs. He held her as tightly as he could, sat down in the swivel desk chair and pulled her onto his lap. If only Claire had been like this when they were married, telling him everything, trusting him, clinging even.

Claire, Nick and Darcy sat the four children down in Darcy's living room. Lexi perched on a leather hassock between Nick's legs. Duncan was sitting cross-legged on the floor with Darcy's son, Drew, and Jilly leaned against her mother's shoulder on the couch. Still fighting exhaustion, Claire sat in a chair, facing everyone.

In her steadiest voice, feeling a bit better since Darcy had brewed tea for her, even if it didn't have her herbals, she began, "I know you are all wondering about the accident at the BAA today."

"It was a loud scream and scary," Jilly said.

"It was real bad," Duncan added. "Like someone getting beat up and real hurt."

"Okay, that's all true," Claire put in, feeling it wouldn't take much for this to "go over Niagara" as her father used to say. "Remember that Brittany, the tiger talker, told us that tigers are wild animals. When they live in the wild, they have to kill to get meat to eat."

Nick nodded in encouragement, and Darcy bit her lower lip. Claire still didn't know how she would have survived her own childhood without her younger sister, when their father took off for parts unknown and their mother became such a recluse, escaping reality through books. Sad that the two men Claire had cared for had father issues too. And what was the truth about Ben Hoffman's relationship to his daughter and son—even to Jace?

"Well, Mr. Hoffman, Brittany's father," Claire went on,

struggling for words, "the man we met in the parking lot, made a mistake when he went to feed the tiger its meat. Somehow he didn't know Tiberia was in its cage and he walked inside, and the animal thought it was still in the wild, and he hurt Mr. Hoffman. Sadly, he died."

Drew asked, "You mean the tiger or Mr. Hoffman?"

"It was a terrible accident, but Mr. Hoffman died."

Lexi said, "Then isn't the tiger a murderer, not just a hungry big cat?"

Claire tried to keep her voice steady. "But you know that's how animals are. They aren't like people, who decide whether they will hurt or kill someone. Animals don't know right from wrong like people do."

"Bronco sometimes kills gators and those big snakes that are out in the Glades," Lexi said. "Is he a murderer? And do you mean that Tiberia ate Mr. Hoffman—like—like—for dinner?"

"My dad hurt and killed someone," Duncan said, "and that's why he ran away, but the tiger's in a cage and can't go anywhere."

Questions, protests followed, some rational, some off the wall. Lexi and Jilly cried. Claire and Nick, Darcy too, tried to calmly, carefully explain animal instinct and carnivorous vs. herbivorous to the children. Though she'd thought she could handle this, Claire scolded herself. She could have done better actually testifying before a hostile lawyer in court right now.

Besides, in the middle of this terrible day, Claire remembered that last week she and Nick had invited their friends and South Shore team members Heck and Gina, Bronco and Nita for dinner in—she glanced at her watch—three hours. At least the women were bringing dishes to go with salmon steaks on the grill. She bet, with all this going on, Nick had forgotten too.

But despite it all, she refused to cancel the dinner because it was going to be a big night for Bronco, and he had wanted those closest to him there. He was planning to announce his engagement to Nita after he proposed to her out by their pool, under the gazebo he had built for them. No going back to reschedule, since Bronco had picked this date because it was also Nita's birthday and, he'd said, there would be a full moon tonight.

Full moon. Perfect! Wasn't that when people supposedly went crazy?

# CHAPTER FIVE

"Welcome," Claire told Bronco and Nita as they came in the front door. "So glad to see you under much better circumstances."

Bronco nodded. Nita carried a basket with a salad. Little did she know that she'd be going home this evening with a diamond ring. Surely she'd accept Bronco's proposal. All they needed was more upheaval of any kind today.

Bronco and Nita had fallen in love when they'd first worked for Claire and Nick. They had known Bronco longer, ever since the first South Shores "murdercide" case they had worked together. They had hired Nita as Lexi's nanny when their family was endangered, so they had been blessed to have both Bronco and Nita as aides and friends.

Bronco was a big, burly guy with the proverbial heart of gold, one who used to make his living hunting gators and the huge constrictor snakes that bred in the depths of the Everglades and, like other animals, were encroaching on civilization. Nita was a young widow, a pretty Hispanic woman who was cousin to another of Nick's employees, his tech guru Hector Munoz, called Heck, who was just getting out of his car in the driveway with his girlfriend, Gina.

Bronco was telling them, "Nita said we should cancel since we all been through too much today—'course, next to the Hoffman family, it's nothing. But it's her birthday, and we can be happy as well as sad."

Nick took Nita's basket while Claire and Nita hugged. "I agree," Claire told them. "I think friends need each other at times like these."

Bronco looked so nervous. She hoped that was from planning to propose, not from the terror earlier today. Much too up close and personal, she'd seen Bronco snap under pressure once, and she didn't wish that on Nita or herself again.

Nick took their guests to the great room, where Claire had laid out appetizers and wine on the big glass coffee table surrounded by the grouping of leather sofas. Lexi was still up, but she'd agreed Nita could put her to bed tonight, "just like the old days," as if the almost-five-year-old were ancient.

Claire held the door open as Gina and Heck came in, Gina with the coconut cake she'd made for Nita's birthday. More greetings and hugs all around. Both Heck and Gina were of Cuban heritage and looked great together, though Heck had been in the States much longer. Sadly, he was more in love with Gina than she was with him, but Claire prayed things would work out for them.

They didn't know about Bronco's surprise for Nita tonight, so maybe that would spur on Heck and Gina, Claire
thought, though Gina was starting med school in Miami
in January. Both Nick and Heck were helping to finance
that. Gina was living with a friend of theirs who had recently moved to South Florida from Michigan, Liz Collister, and Liz's elderly father who had Alzheimer's. Gina
helped to tend him in exchange for living there until she
left for med school.

Claire kept an eye on her baking scalloped potatoes,
which Lexi had helped her fix after they both took a nap
earlier. It hadn't really refreshed Claire because she kept
seeing the cage, the tiger—all that blood. So how must
it be for poor Brittany? At least, like she had Darcy, Brittany would have her brother's support soon.

Claire steadied herself with her hands on the granite
counter of the kitchen island before joining the others just
in time to kiss Lexi good-night as she disappeared with
Nita down the hall to get tucked in—after being promised that they'd save a big piece of birthday cake for her.

Claire sat on the sofa next to Nick and picked up a glass
of sparkling water, forgoing the wine.

"Bad day to have someone lose his life when I'm just
starting a new one," Bronco said, digging into the taco
chips and spinach dip. Although Nita had left the room,
he kept his voice low.

Gina, bright as ever, tossing her long, black hair, picked
up on that. "Are you two going to make a big announce-
ment?" she asked, lifting her wineglass as if in a toast.

"Hope so, but don't you let on," Bronco warned. "Got

the ring here," he said, patting his jacket pocket. "After dinner. In the gazebo."

"She'll say yes," Gina said. "You're her perfect catch."

Heck said, "Like a fish or one of those denizens of the Glades he catches?"

Before Heck could make things more tense as he always seemed to lately, Claire put in, "Like a good man is hard to find, and Bronco's a good find."

"Sure. That's what I meant, right, boss?" Heck asked Nick. "So you gonna end up taking this BAA case, if it comes to charges?"

"I don't think it will, not serious ones anyway. I was just on scene—sadly—so I wanted to help out if I could. I can't imagine a case against the family. I think Ben Hoffman must have somehow been distracted and made a big mistake—a fatal one."

"Or," Gina added, "it might have been an intentional one, suicide, but I can sure think of better ways to die."

"Don't say that," Heck said, reaching out to take her wrist. "I'm just glad things are improving for us, after we've all been through hell and back. I'm sure Nita and Bronco's future plans will only make things happier."

"I couldn't have said it better myself," Nick said, leaning forward and lifting his glass.

Nita came back to join them and sat on the end of the sofa next to Claire near Bronco's chair. "I can't wait until your baby comes and I am back to help you with both Lexi and baby too. So hard to wait for good things you want. And yet I'm so very sad for the Hoffmans, as they are in mourning. I—I understand that."

Nick said, "You're right, Nita. It's a shock when the

world shifts so suddenly, terrific or terrible, but tonight, we'll focus on the terrific. Agreed? Here's to your birthday, the future Markwood baby and whatever else great comes along."

The clink of glassware was the only sound for a moment, as the six of them toasted quietly, each, Claire assumed, with his or her own thoughts of love and loss. She sent up a silent prayer that Ann, Brittany and her brother, Lane, would get through their family tragedy together, as well as the setback for the animal sanctuary.

You never quite knew what was coming next in life, she admitted to herself, even if you thought you had things all planned out. Nita, whose first husband had died young in a fall from a roof, had no idea she would have the opportunity to start a new phase of her life tonight. Claire had never fathomed she'd marry Nick when she'd testified as an expert witness against one of his clients. Meanwhile, the little things in life went on as well as the big ones.

A strange, yet shared, moment of silence followed before real life set in again. Claire got up to be sure the salmon steaks were marinated enough, with Nita and Gina coming into the kitchen behind her while the men went out onto the patio to tend to the burning coals in the barbecue pit.

Exhausted, Brit had fallen asleep on Jace's lap. His arms ached from holding her, but he sat still in the desk chair, listening to muted animal sounds outside. Brit had said the detective had questioned Jackson, who was like an overseer around here, then let him go back to tending the BAA denizens, so at least someone else was on the property besides the one keeper from the Naples Zoo who had stayed behind to keep an eye on Tiberia. The tiger was still lethargic from being drugged.

To Jace, this kind of felt like being in the jungle, not that he'd ever been. He longed to get up and turn on more lights, to get Brit and her mother out of here, take them home. But they were waiting for Brit's brother to arrive after being told of the tragedy. Brit had talked to Lane's wife who said he'd be here soon.

And Jace was aching with an almost physical pain over his friend's tragic and weird death. He felt a sudden kinship to Jackson, the ubiquitous guy who oversaw the place, since he'd known Ben much longer. Jace wanted to sit and commiserate with him sometime. Misery in losing a good friend could love company.

Ben's death just didn't fit with the man he knew, the man who had befriended him and thought enough of him that he'd introduced him to his daughter and encouraged their romance. Ben was long retired from what he'd done in the marine corps, but he was mentally sharp and physically well trained and basically still in shape.

Jace admired that Ben had been in an elite section of the service, spent time on the Fleet Anti-terrorism Security Team, known as FAST. He'd been part of a fast-deployment team, armed and combat trained, ready to be sent around the world if there were threats. Ben had served in Panama in 1989 and in Desert Storm before he retired. And the guy had been so proud of his banner in the den at their house that read MARINE GRUNT: NO BETTER FRIEND, NO WORSE ENEMY. For sure, in the few months he'd known Ben Hoffman, despite one big upheaval, the man had been no better friend. And a guy who was fit and had served in a FAST unit—why in hell hadn't he gotten fast out of that cage and why had he gone in there in the first place?

Jace, still holding Brit, blinked back tears, then wiped them away with one hand when he finally heard fast footsteps, then feet on the metal treads to the trailer. The door burst open, and Brit's older brother Lane stood there, in shirt and tuxedo slacks but no jacket. It was a shock to see someone so dressed up here—a loosened bow tie and long-sleeved white shirt with cufflinks, no less. It was strange that Lane didn't resemble his parents or his sister. He was blond but long-faced with a thin nose, but that all kind of went with his artistic look.

Brit came instantly awake and got groggily to her feet. Jace stood too, steadying her as he leaned against the desk and she went around it. He expected the two of them to hug, but they stopped ten feet apart.

Brit said, "I can't believe it took you so long to get here."

"Since Dad was dead, the orchestra manager made the decision to tell me after the concert. After all, I am first chair and key to everything."

He peered around Brit. "Jace. Brittany, I see you had someone to comfort you anyhow. Where's Mother?"

"In the little bed in back. She's sedated. The tiger was too. Shock, of course—for Mother."

"Yeah, well, we're going to help her through this, but this just goes to prove what I said more than once, and none of you listened to me. This kiddy zoo was ridiculous from the get-go."

"Not now, Lane, please," Brit said. "And keep your voice down."

"I'm not going to let her blow any death benefit money from Dad's will or insurance on spiffing up this grade-C sideshow, so I'm serving you notice."

"Death benefit money? Life insurance? On Dad? If he had that, it must have been recent. Anyway, not now. Let's just sign a truce to get Dad's body back from the medical examiner and help Mother make funeral arrangements."

Jace was no whiz at insurance policies, though he'd sure seen and known fellow pilots who needed them. He'd made out a will in his midtwenties in case he never came back from the Middle East, let alone when he became co-pilot on international flights and had a young family. But if Nick did go further with this case, wouldn't a big insurance policy taken out recently on a soon-to-be-dead man seem suspicious?

Coming around the desk, Jace said, "Brit, unless I can help you with something, I'll head out, now that big brother's here. Sorry for your loss, Lane, whatever your feelings about the BAA."

"I'm sure they told you I think it's nuts. Well, they weren't exactly behind me when I majored in violin in college, paid my own way, playing for weddings, gigs in an Italian restaurant, things like that. They could have been at the matinee performance today where I had the solo, since I'm now first chair, and this wouldn't have happened. They could have seen Lane Benjamin Hoffman playing Leopold Hofmann's *Symphony in A major.*"

"Mother and I were coming Sunday afternoon, while Dad oversaw things here...oversaw..." she got out before her voice broke and she collapsed in sobs. Jace held her again, glaring at Lane over her head.

"Well," Lane said, "since you haven't taken Mother out of here yet, I'll take her home in my car. Come along if you want. She obviously needs someone with her tonight. I'll stay there for a while, and you'd better try to help her instead of all your pets here, especially that killer tiger you were so enamored with. I can't believe Dad went into that cage on his own, can't believe it." His voice cracked, and he clamped his hand over his mouth either to stop from saying more or to keep from sobbing.

Finally, Jace thought, this jerk was showing some emotion. He'd obviously been hurt either as a child or lately—or both. Yeah, he understood a son being let down and damaged by his father, knew that up close and personal, so maybe this guy wasn't so bad, just grieving in his own way.

Lane lowered his hand and went on in a shaky voice, "Maybe Dad was just going to shove the food in and fell in—or the cat grabbed him, pulled him in. He wouldn't be drinking on a Saturday morning, would he?"

"Of course not," Brit insisted, and blew her nose. "I'll go see if we can get Mother up and moving. She wanted to stay here rather than go home before, wanted to be here where they were living their dream."

"Your dream too," Lane said under his breath as Brit opened the door to the smaller room and tiptoed in, closing the door behind her.

Jace felt torn about Lane. He came off as a self-centered, snobbish SOB, yet maybe Brit had been Daddy's golden girl. Lane hadn't taken more than a few steps into the room. He hadn't hugged his sister. He sounded much more angry than grieved.

And, Jace thought, as the two of them stared at each other, though he was no forensic psych like Claire or a law genius like Nick, hadn't this guy just spewed out at least two things that would suggest Ben Hoffman's death wasn't an accident? That maybe Ann Hoffman—Brit too—had benefited from his demise financially, and Lane himself emotionally?

Though it had been a hellish day earlier, Nick broke out a bottle of congratulatory champagne to toast Bronco and Nita. Claire and Gina kept fussing over her engagement ring.

"Pretty, huh?" Nick overheard Heck ask Gina. "You want one like that?"

"Maybe someday," she told him with a tight smile and a toss of her dark hair.

Nick liked Gina, their Cuban refugee. She was bright and perceptive, which he was used to in Claire. Gina had picked up on the fact that Claire was wavering with exhaustion and had taken over hostess duties, insisting Claire stay put and telling the radiant Nita this was her special night and she should sit still while Gina brought in the goblets for Nick to pour the champagne.

Then Gina put dishes in the dishwasher while Claire and Nick said good-night to the newly engaged couple.

"So romantic, so *bonita* in the moonlight by the gazebo he built," Nita was telling them at the front door.

Nick had his arm around Claire's waist, in a way propping her up. He had to get her late-night meds into her, get her to bed. But he should have known his sweetheart had insisted on walking Bronco and Nita to the door for a special reason. He wasn't surprised that she brought up a plan they had discussed recently.

"Nick and I would like to offer our gazebo, backyard and home for the wedding, if you want," Claire told them.

"Right," Nick put in. "You two talk it over and let us know. Or, if you want to be married in a church, the reception could be here. Just if you want—no pressure either way."

Nodding madly, Nita started to cry again. "Lexi, she can be a flower child," she told them.

"Flower girl," Bronco whispered, his arm around her waist. "It would be a great honor—a great gift to us, but we buy the food and drinks, sí? If you two would stand with us, best man and best lady of honor, it could be here. You both already been so good to us. We'll say yes now, 'cause we got reminded today that life can be over fast, bad things hit people they don't see coming. Joy in life comes to you, but maybe teeth and claws too."

As Claire and Nick went back inside, Nick said, "Pretty profound from Bronco." Heck and Gina were heading toward them, holding hands. They said their goodbyes, then, when they were finally alone, Nick told Claire, "Now let's get you to bed."

"You'll take the case if they ask you, right? It will be cut and dried, obviously an accident."

"Just don't you get involved. *Obviously* is a dangerous word in the practice of law."

"And for forensic psychs who need to rely on observations, not feelings. I'm just so tired I'm not thinking straight—obviously."

He kissed her, locked the front door behind them and led her toward the master bedroom, thinking with relief that there could not possibly be another day like this one.

# CHAPTER SIX

Claire stepped into the room that had bars all around it. She was trapped and afraid. Ahead in the cage were two identical doors. She had to protect herself, save Lexi and her new baby. Where was Nick?

The bigger question was—where was the tiger?

Her mother was reading a story out loud to her called *The Lady and the Tiger.* The tiger was behind one of the doors, and Nick was behind the other. She was being forced to choose by the king in trial by ordeal... If she chose the door with Nick, she was safe. If she chose the one with the tiger...

She heard a rumbling roar, but where did it come from? She was certain she had seen the tiger kill someone already. Why did Mother always have to read them books for adults when they were little? Some were scary and hard to understand. Why did she bury herself in books after Daddy left? Their parents had let her and Darcy down. Now that dead man in the cage had let his wife and children down.

But Claire loved to read to Lexi too, so maybe she was like her mother. She wanted to hide so she and her family would not be hurt anymore. They had almost been killed by a human predator, Nick's enemy. Mother was at the end of the story, and Claire had to choose which door. She pointed toward one. At first, she was sure that Nick would come out to help her. Maybe Jace was behind the other one. Trial by ordeal…

But no—in the darkness outside their house a big cat crossed in front of her and turned toward her with burning eyes. It had clawed a man and there was blood, but then it leaped at her and she screamed…

"Claire. Claire, sweetheart, you're having one of those dreams." Nick's voice. Was he behind the other door? "You cried out and screamed."

Nick holding her. In their bed. Dizzy. Crazy. Was this real?

"A t-t–tiger…" she stammered in a whisper.

"Yes, I can see why you'd be dreaming of a tiger, but it's not real. You were just having a narcoleptic nightmare. You're here with me. You're safe. Maybe you'd better go back on your regular meds, not try to get by on those herbal teas."

"I just got off the timing today, with everything that happened."

He sat up with his back against the headboard, pulled her to him and held her tighter with his chin on the top of her head as she nestled against him, her face pressed to his warm neck.

"Then for sure we're not getting involved in this," he said. "We'll take the flowers and food to Brittany and her mother tomorrow, but I'll pass the case on to someone else at the firm, if they still need help."

Her head began to clear. The image of the animal, the fear began to fade. Yes, they were in their bedroom. She could see the wan glow of the nightlight from their bathroom. Safe here. Safe in their new home. Still, she held on to Nick even tighter.

In a stronger voice she told him, "But if Brittany and Ann still need help, especially if there's a question of whether it was suicide, that's what you do, give help. And me too. I help you."

He kissed her damp forehead and smoothed her tousled hair back from her face. "You *do* help me. You—Lexi too—are the best thing that ever happened to me, and I will protect you both with my life. The new little one too," he added, and his voice broke as he put a gentle hand on her rounded belly.

Her head was clearer now. Clear enough to know that, despite her horrid dream, Brittany and Ann were the ones in a cage and they had to help them.

Sunday afternoon, while Jace took Lexi to the stables for a riding lesson on her beloved pony Scout, Claire and Nick took a basket of gourmet food and a big bouquet of flowers in a vase to the Hoffmans. They had called their house, but when they heard they were at the BAA, decided to go to see them there. Brittany said the gawkers and media were gone now. Claire told her they didn't plan to stay long.

"I've heard that Trophy Ranch just beyond is huge," Claire observed as they drove for several miles on the narrow dirt road toward the BAA, a speck in the edge of Everglades land.

"Grant said it goes deeper back than what appears along the road, with hundreds of primitive acres. He said it has cabins for hunters to stay in, a lodge and lots of terrain to hunt. I think they guarantee all kinds of kills for big money there. That reminds me, I want to see Grant soon. It's in the back of my mind that he said something about wanting to buy up the surrounding land, that the orchard owners might sell, but the Hoffmans never would."

"Sorry for suspecting anyone and everyone right now," she told Nick, "but that could mean Stan Helter is not such a good neighbor. Like maybe he wants their few acres, but they've refused to sell. Maybe he put pressure on them, maybe had words with Ben Hoffman or even Brittany. His voice had a tinge of disdain and anger in it when he referred to her as the beast-loving blonde. You said he was a womanizer. Maybe he came on to her, and she turned him down."

"Sweetheart, don't get carried away with fiction. Let's avoid the 'maybes' unless we have to. We don't need more nightmares, asleep or awake. I think we decided last night that I'd pass this case on to a colleague if it gets sticky."

"But we agreed that you help people, and I help you."

He sighed and nodded as they turned into the now nearly deserted BAA parking lot. A big Lexus sat there with a Going for Baroque decal on the back window and a bumper sticker that read STRINGS ATTACHED.

"I'm not a betting man, but I'd say Lane Hoffman's here," Nick said.

But they also saw hand-printed signs at the entrance to the lot and the gate that read TEMPORARILY CLOSED UNTIL FURTHER NOTICE. Someone had also tacked a piece of paper to the entry gate that read *RIP, Benjamin Hoffman*. And another—Claire swore it looked like Jace's handwriting, quite large, that read *Semper Fi!*

As they approached the closed gate—Brittany had told them to knock and Jackson would let them in—their gazes snagged. Claire tilted her head. "I hear a violin. Lively music."

"Maybe Lane's playing to lift their spirits."

"I wish he'd lift ours."

Jackson let them in, still shaking his head as if he couldn't believe what had happened. A frown made his dark face sag. "Don't make a bit of sense," he told them. "Sure, Ben had problems like all of us, but to be off enough to do something like that? No way. 'Preciate it if you can help out Miz Brittany and Miz Ann," he told Nick, shifting his head shakes to nods. "Now, Lane, like you can hear, he got his own way of dealing with things."

With a nod toward the music, Jackson locked the gate behind them and headed quickly away, soon lost to their view in the foliage behind the now empty ticket office.

"I suppose in a way it was best that neither Ann nor Jackson saw it happen," Claire said, taking Nick's hand. "Remember, Brittany said Jackson and Ben were friends from way back. It was bad enough for Brittany to see her father attacked just before we got to the cage."

They found Ann Hoffman standing in the petting

zoo, stroking a small, nervous ostrich, which had a collar around its long neck. The violinist—likely Lane—seemed lost in his own music and didn't seem to see them at first, even when Ann nodded and gestured them over. At least the new widow was calm now, though she looked ravaged and haunted. Maybe the music and the animals would help her. Brittany was not in sight.

Claire jumped when the violin screeched out a sound that was a hee-haw, then one she was certain was a roar. Lane lifted his violin, then swept it down to his side and made a flourish with the bow.

Lane Hoffman looked the part of a musician, Claire thought, though she instantly regretted her stereotyping. He wore his blond hair to his neckline and straight; it shifted when he played with such emotion. He had a light brown, perfectly clipped beard. Unlike many Floridians, he had pale skin. He was not really thin, but seemed, well, *graceful* for a man, or was that just the effect of the music on her?

"I heard you were coming and that you helped yesterday," he said. "The family appreciates it. You know, this was the most apropos piece I could think of, *The Carnival of the Animals* by Saint-Saëns."

"Glad to meet you," Claire said, and Nick echoed that, though Lane began to play again with a mere nod. "As you can see, we come bearing gifts," she told Ann.

But it was Lane who spoke while playing. His moving chin bounced the violin a bit, but he didn't miss a note. "Again, greatly appreciated. Brittany's with the tiger— which, I hope, will be leaving here soon one way or the other."

"We can take these things over to her."

"Oh, let me take them into the administration trailer," Ann put in. "This is all so kind of you. I'll be right back."

"I'll go with you," Claire said. "The basket's heavy."

She took it from Nick and went toward the trailer with Ann. Though she seemed calm and was on her feet, she was a bit out of it and slow-spoken, so maybe she was on tranquilizers.

As they went up the steps into the trailer, Ann said, "I'm sure it was a shock to you—seeing it too."

"Yes. I'm so sorry. I was worried for Brittany."

"She loves big cats. Wants to work with them forever." She cleared her throat and put the vase of flowers on a cluttered table, then began to empty things that needed to be kept cool from the basket into the small refrigerator in the corner.

"It's a huge mystery, of course," Ann said, bent over, not looking at Claire who found herself studying Ann's body language since she couldn't see her face. "He left a legacy. He had his problems, but don't we all?" she asked, almost defiantly, as she stood and faced Claire. "As you can well observe, the fact we were all at odds with Lane—well, that was something that haunted Ben. At least Lane's here today, playing happy music, wouldn't you know."

Before Claire could delve into that mixed message, Ann abruptly rushed past her and headed back outside, so Claire followed.

Pulling a broken strand off his bow, Lane said to Nick, "I understand my sister or my mother might have mentioned something to you about needing representation and you sat in with them for the police interview."

"In case state or national agencies levy a fee or some charges, they may need counsel. I expect their rulings will blame your father and not the BAA."

"We all appreciate your advice, but surely an inquiry or possible charges will come to nothing. As far as I'm concerned, if the state wants to take that tiger, the sooner the better. Brittany loves the damn thing, but it's pretty obvious they were all in over their heads keeping it here after it had been abused by some old woman. That made it more likely to strike out, I'd say."

"You do realize this might reach beyond the State of Florida. The ultimate authorities are not only the Florida Fish and Wildlife Conservation Commission, which will no doubt investigate, but it could go to the US Department of Agriculture. A bizarre death like this is national news."

"Been looking into it already? I would like to get my father's cell phone back, though. The cleanup crew found it wedged way back on the floor of the cage when he must have dropped it or maybe thrown it, and the police have it."

Nick saw him shudder. As cold as Lane Hoffman seemed to him, maybe the man did have feelings for his father. But, damn, his attorney antenna said this man was covering up something.

"I can look into that," Nick said. "As a favor for Brittany."

The two of them stared at each other. A lamb baaed, and the ostrich Ann had been petting strutted off. Nick was amazed to see a flamingo sprint by with Jackson chasing it. Despite the tragedy here, this place had a certain strange charm, something Lane obviously didn't get despite his *The Carnival of the Animals* music.

As Claire and Ann came back, Nick said, "If you two don't mind, we'll just go see Brittany before we leave. She has my number in case you need any advice. I'd be happy to help with anything, minus which music to pick to calm the savage beasts around here."

"You know a lot of people misquote that," Lane called after them. "It's correctly said, music to soothe a savage *breast*—of people, that is. And some of us need that. Evidently my father did, and—as usual in his life—went about it entirely too gung ho."

# CHAPTER SEVEN

As they walked over the moat bridge, Claire observed to Nick, "No wonder Jace said Brit doesn't get along with her brother. I'll cut him some slack since he's no doubt shocked and grieving."

"Maybe in the orbit he travels, he was ashamed of them and this little place and feels guilty now."

"I read anger in him covered by flippancy. And I read avoidance in Ann."

"Lane may not want me on the case, but I see you're working it already."

"Not really. It's just me, curious but cautious. Look, Nick," she said, pointing, "both of them are pacing."

They stopped when they turned the corner by the otter and beaver display. The tiger was stalking back and forth again as it had before, and Brittany was pacing with it, though she could hardly keep up, on the outside of the bars, but as fiercely and seemingly just as caged.

Claire had to call Brittany's name to break the spell. She jerked her head around and frowned.

"Oh, glad you're here. I'm just trying to calm him down. And myself too, of course. I think Darcy said you're a shrink," she told Claire as she left the edge of the cage, climbed the restraining fence and came closer. "I could use that as well as a lawyer, I think."

"Actually," Claire told her, putting a hand on the woman's shoulder—she was shaking—"I'm a forensic psychologist, someone who works in the area where the law meets forensics. I observe and analyze people, advise lawyers, sometimes testify in court."

"I hope it doesn't come to that," she said, leading them to the same bench where they had sat a long time yesterday. At least the police tape had been taken down. Brittany ran her hands along her scalp as if she could squeeze her brain, raking her hair upward until some stood on end.

"Frankly," Nick said, "we just spoke to your brother, and he doesn't think anyone needs legal advice."

Brittany gave a little snort. "He's not the one in charge of—and in love with—that poor tiger. Tiberia's been abused, lonely... Well, that's no excuse for what happened, but it was carnivore nature. Human nature maybe some can control, but not that. I hate to say this, but I hope the investigators' ruling will censure my father, not the BAA."

"From my checking it out, I think you're probably right," Nick said. "I found a similar ruling that 'the zookeeper did not follow established safety procedures.'"

Brittany heaved a sigh. "Or common sense, and that scares me. He did have common sense."

"You said something yesterday I didn't understand,"

Claire told her, leaning closer. "You asked either Tiberia or your unconscious father, 'Why did you do it this way?'"

"Did I? I must have meant that he went in the cage at feeding time when he knew better," she said with a quick shrug. "But listen, I do have notes from the ME about the autopsy, if that helps, Nick—if you end up defending me or this place we had such hopes for. Here. It was so long and formal I scribbled notes from it. We'll have the official death certificate in a few days. I know you could get all this anyway, and the police evidently have Dad's cell phone. The newspaper's trying to make the autopsy public. Well, how do they think a wild beast is going to attack someone, with a knife or gun? I could have written this about his wounds."

But another paper fell out too, no, an envelope with bold handwriting on it. "Oh," she said. "A condolence card with a note. For once this guy's in our corner, at least, after he's been wanting to buy this land." She picked up the envelope but didn't take the card out, just kind of waved and pointed with it.

She went on, "Stan Helter of the big ranch next door has offered us baby alligators and baby wild boars, no less, when we reopen. As if we have the money to build new venues for them, but I'm going to take him up on it. You know, I hear his employees, maybe his worldwide rich clients too, call him Big Cat. Ironic, huh?"

"Very," Nick said with a look at Claire that she read as *Don't follow up on that right now.*

Brittany opened a sheet of paper she had jammed in her jeans pocket with the envelope, spread it open on her knees and said in a shaky voice, "I'm translating some of the medical lingo here. Cause of death, accidental. No heart attack or stroke. Victim's skull was broken so uncertain if skull was struck by exterior force because skull was partly crushed and degraded in jaws of animal...severed facial nerves...eardrum and eye punctures on left side...bites to neck and fractured spine...several arteries and right jugular vein torn...claw marks on chest, shoulders and arm...victim bled—bled out..."

Her voice broke into a gasping sob. She crumpled the piece of paper between her knees. "He was just doing what he should—should have. Tiberia, I mean, not my dad."

Claire leaned closer to Brittany and put her arm around her back.

"I swear," Brittany choked out, "I—this place—we are going to need a lawyer. We're running on financial fumes here, but we'll pay."

"Don't worry about that now," Nick told her, crouching in front of the two of them. "My interest in this case would not be only to help you, as a good friend of Jace, and therefore of ours too, but to protect the BAA from state or federal fines or bad publicity. The firm has done pro bono work before. Brittany, I know the ME has ruled the death accidental, but for some reason, your father entered a tiger cage, knowing it was certain death. Or else he was forced to enter. That interests me too, not only for professional reasons but personal ones."

"Forced to enter? That's crazy! By whom?" she cried, lifting her tear-streaked face. "He had to be alone here!" she went on, gesturing so wildly Claire shifted a bit away. "You yourself saw the place was deserted when we took the kids away, and people can't just fly in here. We have that fence—a double fence, counting the one from the ranch where those gun-happy people kill animals!"

"Look, I get your frustration and anger," Nick said. "My father was once found with a bullet in his brain and the gun in his hand. But he didn't kill himself. Someone else did. It took me years to prove it. I'm not saying it's the same, but something's wrong here. And if you trust me on this—and Claire will help too," he added with a nod at her, "I'll need access to your father's laptop, his correspondence, his desk, and I don't think your brother, maybe your mother either, is going to be thrilled about that. I'd need all that soon in case this turns into something worse than it is, and the police or other authorities confiscate all that."

Claire stared wide-eyed. Nick Markwood at his determined best, and after he'd told her to avoid getting involved. But he probably still meant that his law office would oversee things, not that he—and she—would stay involved. Although, he'd just volunteered her to help too.

"I guess, then, we'd better move fast," Brittany said, bouncing up as Nick stood too. "Dad's death is more than newsworthy, as his *Naples Daily News* advertising friend warned me on the phone earlier today. This is all going to blow up. I've already been contacted by the American Zoo Safety Commission, as well as state authorities."

Nick said, "I think OSHA, you know, the Occupational Safety and Health Administration, might get in the mix too."

"All I wanted to do was educate children to love animals and save more abused big cats. Yes, I'll be sure you get those things from Dad's office here right now and from their house tonight. Give me your address, and I'll get them to you, or send Jace with them. I know he's with your daughter right now, but I'll see him later. He's been a big help and—except for you two—my only support right now, and that counts my brother, Lane. Who needs outside enemies when there's a traitor in the family?"

Nick told her, "I want to assure you that your legal team can be your biggest supporters. Claire and I admire what you're trying to build here."

"Thank you! Thank you for that," she said as the three of them began to walk toward the administration trailer. "Nick," she rushed on, still gesturing wildly, "I'll come into your office and sign whatever I need to. At all costs I want to save and build the BAA through all this, not sell it to be more citrus orchard land or part of that big game ranch. Mother will trust me on this, though I'll have to buck Lane. But he's taken himself out of control of this place, so he doesn't have a legal or financial leg to stand on."

Claire couldn't resist that opening. "Despite the fact he's here today, I take it Lane and your father didn't see eye to eye, on this place, or Lane's chosen career."

"Well, Dad was wrong about that, but he was such an outdoorsman that Lane's violin passion and career was like—like a foreign language, and it made them kind of— at odds sometimes."

"I can understand that," Claire said, and then stopped since Nick cleared his throat as if to say *enough for now*. But everything she saw and heard here made her feel all in for helping Brittany. Who knew that this wasn't help- ing future family if Jace and his "Brit" stayed together?

As if he'd read her mind, Nick said, "Is it okay if we call you Brit the way Jace does?"

"Yes—yes, fine."

"Claire," he went on, "all right with you to come alongside as a support person, as long as you can work from home or the office?"

That last comment was rather pointed, she thought. But maybe a cause and mental work was exactly what she needed until the baby was born. But staying home through it all?

"We can discuss that later," she told him, "but I want to help."

"Good. Brit," Nick said, "our first goal is to keep this local and hope that it won't explode to more."

She seemed to deflate. She stopped walking, and her shoulders slumped. "Oh, I did forget to mention something you should know. Not only did we receive an offer of baby animals from Stan Helter—maybe as a smoke screen of kindness, if you ask me—that envelope you saw also contained a big check. Twenty thousand dollars for our father's burial and a memorial, his note said, and there would be another hundred thousand if we wanted to sell this acreage and move to some other place with better memories. Well, you know when someone dies, the bank freezes all their assets until they see the death certificate, so this is—is really needed, so it's tempting."

"Glad you told us that too," Nick told her. "So Stan Helter's extended an olive branch, but with a sword attached."

Brit said, "The Lord giveth and He taketh away and so does the lord of all he surveys next door, that greedy wretch Stanley J. Helter, as the signature on the check reads. I wanted to tear it up, but Lane wouldn't let me. We started to argue but with Mom there—we just put it unendorsed in the safe. It's made out to Mother, not me or Lane."

She seemed to wilt even more, almost to stagger.

"Did you get any sleep at all yet?" Claire asked, putting her arm around the woman's shoulders.

"Only a nap on Jace's lap before Lane came busting in yesterday. Then some in bed last night with— Oh, sorry, Claire, I—"

"It's all right. I think you two are good together."

"Oh, no!" Brit cried, squinting into the sun past Nick's shoulder.

"What?" he said as all three of them turned.

"Somehow she got in!" Brit muttered as they saw a wiry, tanned, very old-looking woman run at them, swinging a long wooden pole with a hook cutter on the end of it. Two beefy, bald men ran behind her, both out of breath, either trying to catch her or help her. They lugged a big, dark plastic sack between them. In their free hands, one carried a hatchet, the other a butcher knife.

"It's Gracie Cobham," Brit shouted, "the woman the state took the tiger from! Run!"

# CHAPTER EIGHT

The old woman shouted to the men with her, "Cut 'em up, boys!"

Claire sucked in a huge breath. Did these people intend to maim or kill them with the hatchet and big knife?

Nick yanked her with him faster than she could run. He fumbled for his phone. Brit, just ahead of them, tried to jam a key from her ring of them into the door that led to the back of the tiger's cage.

Claire saw they were trapped by the tall, double fences of the BAA and Trophy Ranch. If Brit still had that tranquilizer gun or if the fire extinguisher had been replaced— In her haste, Brit dropped the ring of keys and scrambled for them as Claire darted a look back at their pursuers. But were they pursuers? The two men had dropped their big, gray garbage sack and were slicing it open. What looked like two dead possums fell out of it.

"Fresh roadkill, Thunder," Gracie Cobham crooned to

the tiger. "Possum's nice and fresh, just the way you like, poor boy. They the ones been treating you wrong, not me. That's my Thunder, that's my baby boy."

"Nick, wait!" Claire insisted and put her hand over his as he started to punch in 911. "She meant cut up the possums."

It was true. The two "boys"—who must be in their sixties—were skinning and cutting up the dead animals, and Gracie was picking up chunks of the bloody meat and tossing them against the bars of the cage. Tiberia/Thunder was pawing them inside and devouring them, not with a roar or growl but with what sounded like a loud purr.

Grabbing the key ring from the ground, Brittany was noisily raking through keys for the one she wanted. She whispered, "I've still got the tranquilizer gun in here. I'm calling the cops again, if you aren't. She's trespassing at least, and I have a restraining order against her for trouble before."

"Could they have been here on Saturday?" Nick asked Brit. "They'd have a motive to hurt your dad."

"I don't know how in hell they got in, but they can't feed Tiberia that roadkill. It could mean maggots—rabies. I'm going to get those Florida crackers arrested."

But some instinct in Claire told her that gun plus cops was not the way to go here. She'd seen people of all kinds in psychological distress before. Her heart was still pounding from exertion and shock, but she peeked around Nick, who was blocking her against the building, and called to the old woman, "Was that your name for the tiger, Ms. Cobham—Thunder?"

Nick swore under his breath, and Brit finally got a key

to work. She quickly disappeared inside the dim enclosure. Nick tried to push Claire in behind her, but she'd seen Gracie's look of pain and determination on other faces before. And for an old woman to take in a tiger and baby it—and to boss around those two big louts who were probably her sons...

"Nick, we'll never get anything out of her on this case if we get her arrested," Claire muttered and shook his restraining hand off her shoulder. To make things worse, Claire saw Jackson on a dead run across the bridge, and he had a gun.

"Sure was his name," Gracie called to Claire. "Still is, first name he had. I read in the paper 'bout the accident. It's s'posed to be Tiberia now. But his roar sounded like distant thunder to me, 'specially when he was small, so Thunder it is and will be till the cows come home."

"A very good name," Claire said, careful to take only one step past Nick so he wouldn't pull her back. She had to act fast before Brit came out with the tranquilizer gun she'd mentioned or Jackson used his gun. The "boys" had only used their potential weapons to tend to the meat so far. "So, how did you get Thunder in the first place?" she asked, taking several more steps.

Gracie threw the last big hunk of meat at the bars, then wiped her bloody hands on her jeans. "Told all this to the wildlife officers who stoled him," she said, coming closer to Claire.

"Careful, Ma," the larger of the two men said. "We did what we come to do. Paper said they won't kill Thunder."

At least, Claire saw, Jackson had stopped where he was on this side of the bridge. He kept edging close, but he hadn't raised the gun. She thought to hold up a restraining hand, but then the Cobhams might react to him and the gun. Her heart beat so hard she could hear drums in her ears.

Trying to keep her voice steady, Claire said, "Brittany argued with them when anyone tried to talk about putting Thunder down. She loves him too."

"'Put him down.' Pretty way to say kill him, right?" Gracie challenged.

Up this close, Claire noted the woman's sun-bronzed skin was tight yet webbed with wrinkles. She looked wiry, strong and emanated stubbornness. Talk about endangered species: this woman and her boys were remnants of "old Florida," either the best or the worst of the fading past. Behind the Cobhams, Jackson kept shuffling slowly closer.

"You part of the Hoffman family?" Gracie asked, squinting at her. The sun was not in her eyes with that billed cap she wore, so she evidently needed to see Claire better.

"Just a family friend and friend to Thunder. We brought some children here the other day to admire him, and they thought the big cat was really beautiful and impressive."

"And he's in mourning. Not for the captor he kilt. For me. Paces all the time," she insisted, though Claire had no idea how she'd know that. "See how calm he is now?" Gracie challenged, pointing, as Brit came back out, thankfully, with no tranquilizer gun in sight. "It's my voice, my being here, calms him."

Brit challenged, "You're not even looking at him, so how do you know what he's doing?"

Claire wished she'd change her tone of voice. She wasn't close enough to elbow her. Surely, despite all she'd been through, she knew not to upset this woman and her sons. Evidently Jackson had assessed things correctly, though, since he had stopped and moved behind a big gumbo limbo tree.

"I know him, my Thunder," the old woman said, and it was true. Lying down, the tiger was calmly washing his paws with a huge tongue. The appearance of the Cobham clan, despite the movement and raised voices, had seemed to calm the beast.

"No one listens to me 'bout I know best for him," Gracie went on, cutting off another comment from Brit. "Got him as a kitten from a real phony, but I'm not. So wrong to steal him from me, give him to someone goes to school to learn about him," she said and spit on the ground in Brit's direction. Gracie crossed her arms over her flat chest and stomped once on the ground. "Real tired of peeking at my Thunder through the fence. Glad someone fin'ly listened to me," she added as she glared at Nick and Brittany, nodded at Claire and turned away.

"Clean up that mess," she muttered to her sons, who jumped to obey, then scurried to follow her out the way they had evidently come in. She didn't look back.

"She's trouble," Brit whispered, and walked behind them, evidently to be sure they left. Claire noted that when Jackson saw the intruders were on their way out, he held his gun to his side and followed them ahead of Brit.

Nick and Claire started to walk out too. Yes, the Cobhams were gone and Jackson was asking Brit why no one told him they'd gotten in. "And how did they get in?" he asked her, his voice rising. "Thought it better they just leave, or I'd have confronted them on it."

"You know, Nick," Claire told him, putting a hand on his arm to halt his steps for a moment, "Gracie let slip that she was tired of watching the tiger through the fence. Through what fence?" she asked, looking around at the perimeter of the BAA. "Could she have a hiding place just outside to spy in here? Even to slip in? And Jackson—if he's so in charge, how does he keep missing all the action?"

"As for Jackson, it's a big enough place with lots of sight barriers. Probably chance or bad timing, but what a character the old woman is, one we may have to watch."

"A real frontier woman," Claire insisted. "If I question her again—on her turf—who knows what she might tell us about the tiger or if she resented Ben Hoffman. Those 'boys' of hers would probably do anything she asked."

"You mean sneak in here like storm troopers, hit Ben on the head and shove him in the cage, and not be noticed? Wouldn't they be scared that Momma only wants her Thunder to have possums, not humans? But, yeah, she sure calls the shots. And no, don't even suggest you're going anywhere near Everglades backcountry to question some old woman or those two with her."

Claire heaved a huge sigh and leaned against him. "I think we're both back on a case—accident or murder or suicide—aren't we?"

"I guess I am, but you're pregnant."

"No kidding. And don't be sexist. If I go anywhere dangerous, I'll take Bronco or Heck—or even you—with me."

"Let's just get Ben Hoffman's stuff and get out of here before something else happens. I'm starting to think I need some of that calm-down herbal tea of yours."

★ ★ ★

Nick had their master bathroom so steamed up from his shower Claire could hardly see in her vanity mirror to take her makeup off. Sitting in the low-backed padded chair, she leaned closer to the glass. "You know," she said as he stepped out of the shower to dry himself off, "this tiger cage case we're working on now—"

"It's not an official case. It doesn't mean we're all in for it."

"Nick, you said different earlier today. What if that old woman gets blamed for harassment or even murder? And Stan Helter wants the BAA land, maybe at any cost. Lane didn't get along with his father, and also wants his family out of there. We have plenty of places—people—to start with. Anyhow, I was going to say that Ben's murder—if it's murder—is kind of like a classic locked room mystery. You know, like Poe's 'The Murders in the Rue Morgue' or Agatha Christie's *And Then There Were None.*"

"Haven't read those," he said, tying a dry towel around his waist and quickly running his electric shaver over his day's growth of beard. Her antenna went up. They hadn't made love for a while, and he usually didn't shave until morning. So why was he being difficult if he had that in mind? In general, she was learning to pick up on his actions and body language, so why couldn't she figure out what he was really thinking about Ben's death? She had to keep prying and prodding.

"Well, I haven't read them either," Claire told him, "but my mother's years-long mania reading instead of taking better care of Darcy and me means I know all about them. You know, a locked room murder would fit this—the cage was locked, and anyone who got in to murder Ben would have been attacked too, and why would he go in there on his own? The place is double fenced, and the entry wasn't open that morning except for our group. Nick, we've got to find some serious reasons and answers, and it can't be something stupid like the Poe story where a woman was murdered in a closed upper room because an escaped ape got in there with a razor and killed her."

Nick looked at her in the blurry mirror where he was now combing his wet hair back. "You're kidding," he said, straightening to face her. "An ape with a razor? Next we'll be thinking the tiger jumped through the bars and pulled Ben in because it was missing roadkill possum."

He tossed his comb on the counter and leaned stiff-armed on the marble sink top while she began to smooth moisturizer on her face. The intensity of his perusal of her made her feel she wasn't wearing a nightgown and her terry-cloth robe.

"Sorry for that," he said, straightening and coming over behind her to put his big hands on her shoulders. His thumbs stroked the back of her bare neck. Every muscle, every thought, began to go lax. He whispered, "The thing is, I'm still torn about spending time on this case with the baby coming, and now that we're finally safe to have family time."

"Maybe Heck will ferret something out of Ben's records you gave him. He often does."

"And you're itching to ferret out something about Ben—if he had an enemy hateful enough to kill him—from talking to people he knew. But enough of all this right now. Let's go to bed. Talking about locked rooms,

I think I'll lock ours for a few minutes so we don't have Miss Lexi in here asking me why I'm kissing Mommy places besides her cheek or mouth."

A jolt of lightning shot straight to Claire's belly. She might be pregnant, she might be married, she might have made love to Nick Markwood for months now, but it was always like that first time on the yacht when she gave herself so totally to him—and, she believed, conceived this child. When he bent to kiss her throat, she twisted in his arms and kissed him back hard and hungry.

He loosed the towel around his hips, helped her out of her robe and nightgown, and lifted her into his arms. In their bedroom, he bent to click the lock on their door, then laid her on the bed and got in beside her.

Everything fled—disappeared—except Nick when he touched her, when he took over like this.

"I'll be careful," he said, keeping his weight off her.

"Yes. Tonight, but also with getting too involved..."

Her words weren't making sense.

"I'm always too involved with you," he murmured in her ear as he slid his tongue from her neck to her breasts.

She shut out everything except their love, but when he had her purring, she thought of that tiger again and went so crazy with passion that she accidentally scratched his back.

# CHAPTER NINE

The next day, Nick called Grant Manfort and asked to meet him for lunch at the Chops City Grill in downtown Old Naples. As he sat at the bar, waiting for Grant and glancing at the menu, a chill ran down his spine. Not from their prices for aged beef but at the tagline on the menu: "A steakhouse that's a cut above."

He was still nervous from the almost-attack by butcher knife and hatchet from that wild woman and her backwoods sons yesterday at the BAA. If he was going to look into what Claire was calling the Tiger Cage Case, she was right: they needed a lot more background on possible perps.

His techie Heck's combing through Ben Hoffman's laptop and paper files was one thing, but Nick needed some insider info about the Trophy Ranch's Stan Helter. As far as he could guess at this point, Helter had the most to win if the Hoffmans were forced to sell the BAA land.

Of course, if Gracie Cobham was out for revenge, she'd
be a possibility too. But Ben's son, Lane, as a suspect? As a
son who had adored his own father, Nick couldn't get his
brain around that. Besides, Lane had a very public alibi,
though, of course, Nick had seen overly smart and entitled
guys like him hire people to do their dirty work for them.

"Grant, good to see you," Nick said, and got off the
stool to shake hands with him when he entered.

The few times he'd seen Grant lately, Nick had always
been impressed with how in charge the man seemed. He
looked strong yet almost ascetically lean. The guy was a
runner and extreme hiker, the type who probably ran ten
miles to get here and would eat the Paleo caveman diet,
though he'd be a pretty polished-looking one with his
business suit and his dark brown hair slicked back. No
wonder he'd built his company, Florida Gulf Coast Life
Insurance, into a profitable behemoth. To sell insurance,
you had to look like you knew what you were doing but
also have a comforting, friendly persona. The insurance
biz was a murky mess to Nick, but then law was like that
to most people.

Actually, the company had not been Grant's from the
first. Just as Nick had eventually taken over his deceased
father's law firm, Grant had taken over Florida Gulf Coast
Life from his mentor. That was another reason Nick had
always felt a bond with Grant: Nick had lost his father,
then carried on for him as Grant had for his lost mentor.
The older man had gone fishing with his granddaughter, a young woman Grant was dating. Some accident on
board had taken her and her grandfather. The boat was
found but no trace of the two on it despite an extensive

coast guard search. From a beginning insurance salesman, Grant had quickly stepped up to build the company after that tragic double loss. Grant was evidently crushed and had never married.

Nick didn't really believe in lawyer's lunches à la booze, but he recalled that Grant liked to drink—an exception for a health nut—and Nick could understand why with the double tragedy in his past.

"Haven't seen you in ages," Grant said as they were seated at a table. An old habit from when he was being stalked, Nick sat where he could still see the front door. "And," Grant went on, "I hear, another professional bachelor bites the dust, but congrats on that. Someone said you were out of the country for a while too."

"All business—except for my marriage. Beautiful wife and I inherited a lovely little daughter, and we have a baby on the way."

Grant nodded, looking unsurprised, as he ordered a dry martini with an anchovy olive. "So did you ask me here to talk about family coverage life insurance?" he asked Nick.

"Actually, I've had heavy coverage for years. Can't be a criminal lawyer without it these days. It's a career in which one makes loyal friends but, on the other hand, makes some very bad people very unhappy."

"Gotcha on that. With my passion for high trail hiking and mountain climbing, I believe in insurance, insurance, insurance, so I'm fully covered too. Last year I climbed Kilimanjaro in Tanzania. Hell of a climb—fantastic experience. Just call me the Hemingway of our times. Ever read his short story 'The Snows of Kilimanjaro'?"

"No, but I'll bet my wife has."

"I'd like to meet her."

They managed some talk about local events. Nick hoped he could get Grant to open up about Stan Helter or at least finagle an invitation to the ranch through Grant. Although Helter had invited him, he didn't want to suddenly go waltzing in there alone without one or two people he could trust. He had the strangest, angsty feeling about that vast place.

But right now, he figured he'd better try to make an end-around approach when the small talk was over and they got down to it. They ordered salads and steak sandwiches. Nick told the server to put it on one check.

"We're currently planning a wedding on our new property," Nick told him. "You know—talk about adventures—the groom is an employee of mine who not only has hunted gators but was part of the team that caught the escaped Burmese pythons in the Glades. Any of those monsters encroaching on your property out in the Vineyards?"

"Hunts gators? No kidding!" he said, wide-eyed. "And those huge snakes too? Nothing around my place like that yet, but Stan Helter says they're here and there on the ranch. He said a thirteen-foot python scared some rich desert-sheikh-type guy out of his mind a couple weeks ago."

"Speaking of Stan, I saw him just the other day, and he mentioned you. He said to come to the ranch as there was always something going on. He had stopped by the BAA where his neighbor died in the tiger cage."

"I read in the paper that you and your wife and some kids were there, made statements to the police. Anyhow, yeah, I made an early investment in the Trophy Ranch and consider Stan a friend. I think of the place as protecting a huge stretch of Florida wilderness. I'm big on that as you know from our time on the Save the Glades committee. I hate to see pristine land eaten up by new developments, the animals too. The ranch is a bulwark against that—a wall, a fence of its own kind."

"Yet animals are hunted and killed at the ranch."

Grant's dark eyes darted away. "At least their animals are bred and live in the wilds. When I was in Tanzania for the Kilimanjaro climb, I also went on safari. Saw amazing, exotic—some endangered—animals. Animals should live free that way, not be in tight, fake places like petting zoos or even some of the best zoos in the world. They're still trapped, still prisoners, and I can't stand that. I think we can all agree on that."

So he didn't like petting zoo places like the BAA? Or even big zoos. But Nick couldn't argue with him on some of that, despite how much it educated humans about the natural world.

"At least the Africans," Grant went on, "are waking up to their shrinking heritage and trying to protect wild animal turf, kind of like the defensive line in football. You follow the Miami Dolphins or Tampa Buccaneers?"

As they talked pro football and tucked into their salads, Nick thought, Bingo! He felt he'd scored two points already. He'd managed to open the topic of Helter and the ranch without being too obvious. And wasn't that a sign that he—as Claire kept insisting—was meant to work this as a South Shores case? It made him feel lucky and a little reckless.

"Actually, I do have an insurance question," he told Grant.

"Shoot."

"Not a lawyer question about insurance fraud, at least I don't think so."

"Rampant these days. All kinds, mostly by customers, not the companies—not mine, for sure. People can trust the company and me to be completely trustworthy in more ways than one."

"Years ago when my father's death was ruled a suicide—I was just a boy—his insurance company had language in his life insurance contract about death benefits. Suicide canceled those, and the company never paid my mother, who is now deceased. But since his death has finally been proved to be murder, can there be restitution?"

"Check the old contract for a time limit. Insurance firms have to watch cases where someone sets up big bucks for death coverage, then actually kills himself or hides out so next of kin can collect the money, maybe share it with the so-called deceased. It's called pseudocide. I looked into that when I lost my friend and boss Steve Rowan, but no one benefited from his death since his heir evidently died that day too. Or sometimes a spouse or child takes out a policy on their supposed loved one, then knocks that person off to get the funds. So that's really why you asked me here today, right—for info about that?"

"And I appreciate it," Nick told him, not quite answering the question.

But that mention of a family member cashing in on a victim's life insurance made him think of Claire's comment about Lane resenting his father. Lane was prickly and pompous, but they'd need to look into that father-son relationship too, despite the fact that Lane was twenty miles away in front of hundreds of people when his father died.

Grant was saying, "I'll bet, clever lawyer like you could find an escape clause on that suicide-murder denial. You and your firm manage to take some big public cases, and the last thing insurance firms want is bad cred in the media or on the streets, believe me. It was a nightmare for the firm when Steve and Leslie died and their bodies were never found," he said and his voice broke.

"Thanks, Grant. That helps and earns you dessert."

"Not me, pal, thanks. But your hosting me today earns you an invitation at the Trophy Ranch. I'll see what's going on there and let you know next time I'm going."

"Maybe I could bring my snake-and-gator guy with me. I wouldn't be interested in a hunt, but I'd love a tour."

He wouldn't be interested in hunting wild game, that is, Nick thought, but he admitted he was now on the hunt for human game in a new South Shores case, and he couldn't wait to tell his warrior woman Claire.

Claire and Nita were having a great time, planning the wedding and reception. Lexi, back from afternoon preschool, was so wound up about being the flower girl, getting a fancy "princess" dress and walking in with the rings on a pillow, that she was driving them crazy.

"I'm good at that, Nita, really," Lexi assured her former nanny, "'cause I was at Dad and Mommy's wedding too. That was kind of scary, but it was pretty," she added with a slanted glance at Claire. "And you both said you and Dad might have another little wedding here in Naples, right? Then different people can come who like us."

Those childish comments sobered Claire a bit. Although they had been very much in love and would have likely had their own wedding eventually, she and Nick had been forced to marry when they did by Nick's nemesis. He'd wanted to threaten her and Lexi's lives if Nick didn't go along with his nefarious plans.

"We thought about it, but with the baby on the way, not for a while," Claire said. At the least, they might have a much delayed reception, but no time to explain all that now. "Lexi, how about you just listen to Nita and me for a minute while we figure out how many guests we can put out by the gazebo in chairs."

"I'll go out and make a count—a guess," she said, and darted away.

"And do not now or ever get near that pool without me or Nita or Dad there!" Claire called after her.

"I won't, even if I can swim!"

"Now," Claire said, doing another rough sketch because it helped Nita to visualize things better, "I think we'll want to have the tables with the cake, sandwiches, et cetera in this room." She looked out the patio window to watch Lexi. "We'll move these couches out, have the two buffet tables over there in front of the hearth, the card tables with tablecloths for seating in here and some on the patio if the weather's good that day."

Nita gently grasped Claire's wrist with her hand as Claire glanced outside again. Good. Lexi was heading back in.

"I—both of us—can never thank you so much for this," Nita said. "For all you do for us."

"Nita, *mi amiga*, you both do a lot for us too. We are proud and grateful to have you work for us. I could not have made it this far without your care of Lexi, and Bronco has been our friend since our first South Shores case in St. Augustine. He's come a long way since then and so have we all."

"You see his good heart?" she asked, frowning. "He seems all rough, but he is so—well, sweet."

"Of course he is. We're happy for both of you. We want to make the wedding in the gazebo and the reception here and in the back as lovely as—"

They both jolted stiff at a screeched "Mommy! Mommy!" from the back door. "Mommy, is that gator here visiting from the BAA place?" Lexi shouted. "Are we taking care of it for a while?"

Claire leaped up from the table so fast she almost fell. The child had a great imagination, but could an alligator have come into the yard? They were sometimes seen on golf courses and came through big drainage pipes.

She tore outside with Nita behind her.

"I didn't go near it, just saw it," Lexi cried, pointing into the pool.

In the deep end floated a good-sized alligator, five feet at least as it surfaced and glared, dead-eyed, at them.

It wasn't just dead-eyed—it was dead! Claire pulled Lexi back behind her.

"Is it sick, Mommy?"

"Maybe he got lost and fell in," Nita said, her voice

shaky. "Then he drowned. Bronco, he would know what to do."

"Nick should be home any minute, or I can call him to ask but—"

When, slowly, the dead animal turned belly up, Claire saw its pale throat had been slashed into red ribbons of flesh. No, not slashed—clawed.

# CHAPTER TEN

Nick and Bronco arrived in separate cars about the same time. Nita stayed in the house with Lexi, who kept asking how the gator scratched his neck, and Claire led the men outside. On their way through the house, Nick tossed his suit jacket, ditched his tie and rolled up his shirtsleeves but he still looked in lawyer mode to Claire—until he saw what was in their pool.

"You've got to be kidding!" he shouted when he saw the dead animal floating belly up.

"Man, oh, man!" Bronco said, kneeling on the raised concrete near the edge of the pool to look down into the water. "It's no accident this beat-up guy wandered in here, no way."

"And no accident that it got those claw marks on its throat," Nick said, his voice hard and angry as he pointed at the large, lurid scratch marks. "I'm glad it's dead, since Lexi found it."

Claire said, "Could it have been nearby and was attacked, then more or less fell in the pool? I'm thinking of that Florida panther we saw down the street last week."

Nick shook his head as Bronco said, "Panthers don't like a fight. Some call them ghost cats, they're so loosy. That the word, Nick?"

"Elusive," Nick said. He tugged Claire down on a lounge chair and perched on the end of it, knees spread with elbows on top of them and chin on fists, as he glared into the water. "I don't know whether to leave it like that or if we should pull it out. The retrieval net for leaves and stuff is over there—it's not big enough for it, but we should at least put the net around part of it so it doesn't sink. I'm going to call the Fish and Wildlife Conservation Commission number." He pulled his cell phone out of his pants pocket.

"Did you represent that group?" she asked him. "It seems like everyone owes you a favor."

"Only the ones who aren't out to get me for sending them to prison. No, I just know that's who you call if there's a dead wild animal. Here's their website. Call 'nuisance wildlife, FWC-GATOR,'" he read off the screen, then punched in the number. He got up and walked around the pool as he talked, peering carefully behind the crotons, blooming hibiscus bushes and clusters of dwarf palms as if another beast would jump out.

And maybe it would, Claire agonized. Her stomach must hurt from nerves, because she hadn't missed her meds or her herbal tea. Oh, maybe it wasn't just nerves. She distinctly felt the baby move. When she'd noticed it before, Nick had put his hand on her stomach to experience the thrill too, but this time the little one really moved as if upset, as if trying to tell her something. She crossed her arms gently over her belly as Nick finished his circuit of the backyard and Bronco netted the gator to draw it slowly over to the side of the pool.

"Since it looks like the gator's been attacked," Nick said, "and they told me on the phone they doubt it would have been by a panther, they're sending over a couple of their law-enforcement officers. If it had just been an untouched dead one, they ask the property owners to dispose of it."

"That's a good one," Claire said. "Like put it down the garbage disposal or out in the trash? I'm going inside to see how Lexi's doing. If she asks one more time why the gator scratched his own throat, I'm out of clever answers."

Nick walked to the back patio door with her. He told her, "Before the wedding and reception—and before you or Lexi are out in this yard again—I'm going to have a fence put up. The foliage will hide it, especially when it matures a bit. Don't worry. We'll get one to fit the decor, not some plain wire thing."

"The tall fences didn't help with the tragedy at the BAA," she said, turning to face him before they slid the glass door open.

"You're thinking this may be tied to the tiger clawing Ben somehow?"

"Aren't you? Or is it just that, like you've said before, you still have enemies out there you've prosecuted? And I felt so safe in our new neighborhood."

"You know, I just said more or less the same to Grant Manfort when I saw him for lunch today. I'd just write the whole thing off to edge-of-the-Glades living if it wasn't for those scratches. Maybe someone thinks I'm going to take the tiger case—"

"Which you are. If so, is it a message to steer clear of it? Or are we just being paranoid because of all we've been through?"

"You know what I'm afraid of? That the answers are 'yes' and 'yes.' But I still say we need to carefully question what the cops like to call persons of interest surrounding Ben's death."

He kissed the tip of her nose. "Bronco and I will wait for them out here. Meanwhile, I'm making a second call and ordering a sturdy, tall backyard fence."

"Robert Frost had a line that said something about fences making good neighbors."

"I'm just hoping fences at the BAA meant maybe Ben Hoffman did die from an accident or even suicide. If someone got in somehow and hit him over the head, then shoved him in the cage—that someone likely wants to stop anybody from looking into that."

It took the two Florida Fish and Wildlife Conservation Commission officers only about an hour to arrive, but it was starting to get dark. Nick had turned the pool and patio floodlights on. Claire had sent Nita out with soft drinks and sandwiches. Bronco had downed his fast, but Nick could hardly eat, knowing what was weighing down the net Bronco kept an eye on. Without the buoyancy of the water, the net and gator might have gone straight to the bottom. Nick was also shaken by the approximate price of the fencing he'd just been quoted on the phone.

When the two FWC officers arrived through the side

gate, he thought they looked a bit like regular police in their drab olive military uniforms. The younger of the two sported a firearm in a side holster.

"It would be really rare for this alligator to have tangled with a big cat," the older of the two men told them as he played his flashlight over the wounds of the gator, still in the water and the net. "The way an alligator would fight back would not tend to expose its throat to be raked by claws. 'Course the blood could have washed away, but those cuts look deep and would have bled. My guess is it's been dead awhile, since you say the pool water didn't look tinted. Contrary to folklore around here, gators do bleed red and not green."

"A Florida panther was spotted in the neighborhood," Nick told them.

"Nah," the younger guy said, shaking his head. "*Puma concolor coryi*, to use the Florida panther's scientific name, would run, 'less it was protecting kittens. Like I said, can't see a wrestling match between a big feline and a gator."

"So, we'll report this," the senior officer told them, tapping a message onto the screen of his phone. "I'll take a coupla photos. Then the four of us can haul him out. We can drag him on a tarp to our vehicle, get him up our ramp, take him back with us for a necropsy, if they want, then disposal. He's pretty big to bury in a backyard, and the refuse guys don't want any part of even a dead one."

"Nor do we," Nick said. "Thanks, and let us know if you figure anything else out."

The younger officer took a camera out of their gear and bent over the side of the pool to take photos. The camera's bright flash seemed to explode in the water, making Nick see colors.

"Let's get him out, and I'll get better pics on the pool deck," the officer told them.

Nick glanced at the back of the house before he helped them drag the net up, then roll the gator out onto the tiled surface. Claire had closed the patio drapes a while ago so Lexi wouldn't keep staring out. He could see vague silhouettes moving inside. He just hoped that someone else wasn't watching them in the darkening night.

"Sorry I was late, boss, and missed all the action," Heck said in the house after they'd told him what had happened. The wildlife officers, as well as Bronco and Nita, had left. Nick had finally changed his clothes.

"There wasn't much action from the gator," Claire put in.

"I didn't fall asleep or nothing like that," Heck explained. "I just didn't want to leave Gina earlier. She's on another guilt trip over leaving her parents in Cuba since her brother's dead and they got no one else. *Caramba*, the truth is she's scared about starting med school in Miami when her training's all been Cuban. She needed me," he explained, his voice breaking as he blinked back tears. "I needed to hold her, not go for my phone to call you."

"Just glad you could help her," Nick told him. "She needs you more than that, Heck, and she'll figure out how much. Just give her time."

Claire's eyelashes were wet. Nick, the counselor and comforter. Maybe he was taking that softer approach from her. She thought Heck looked exhausted and emotional, but weren't they all? It had taken her a lot of talking and hugging to get Lexi to relax and go to sleep tonight. She could have used some protective hugs herself, but at least she was going to get something done right now. This was to be a preliminary report on what Heck had found on Ben Hoffman's laptop, because the police had his phone and Nick was going to look through files from Ben's desk himself.

"Thanks," Heck said as Claire brought him a cup of coffee. "*Sí*, a few interesting things on his computer. One, Ben Hoffman still freelanced some for his advertising agency he s'posedly retired from. Must've needed the money. He actually borrowed some cash—which he paid back—from that Jackson guy, their fix-it man at the BAA. The guy's run a janitorial service for years and is really handy. Retired, 'cept he loves being outdoors and does all kinds of stuff at the BAA for his buddy Ben—his dead buddy Ben."

"The BAA needed money in general," Nick put in. "Brittany said she was hardly taking any salary there."

"*Sí*. Or maybe Ben, he used his moonlighting or this Jackson's money to pay for his insurance package, an expensive one. His wife and daughter the sole beneficiaries of it—no mention of his son. Bitter waters run deep."

Nick asked, "Did you see if there was any info in the insurance contract that his death had to be accident or murder—not suicide—for the beneficiaries to collect? Of course, so far the coroner has ruled the cause of death 'accidental.'"

"Just skimming documents, no, but we can check that out," Heck said, taking a long drink of his coffee, then pulling a digital backup USB stick out of his pocket. "Just in case the authorities do look more into cause of death and we have to hand stuff over, I thought we'd better keep the info."

"The insurance company wasn't Florida Gulf Coast Life, was it?"

"No. Another name, can't recall, but that wasn't it."

Nick nodded. It wasn't like Heck to let any detail slip through that brain of his, but the guy was really shaken by Gina. Yeah, he could understand that, he thought, as he glanced at Claire. She was leaning forward, listening intently, but she looked tired and more pale than usual. He had to get her to bed.

"What about this zoo overseer, Jackson?" Claire asked. "What's his full name?"

"James Jackson," Heck said. "What about him?"

"I don't recall the police questioning him. He showed up after we'd petted the animals awhile, but he no doubt had the run of the place, and who knows what he saw earlier before he left to run an errand when Ben was killed— and can he corroborate that errand?"

"Good point," Nick said, "though he's supposed to be a long-time friend of Ben's. I'll make a note to talk to him. Better that than asking Brit everything."

"I went through stuff pretty fast," Heck admitted, rotating his coffee mug in his hands. He handed the USB to Nick.

"So what else did you find?" Nick asked, grabbing a notepad from the coffee table.

As if he'd taken his finger out of a crack in the dam, Heck talked so fast that Nick could hardly jot notes to keep up. "Ben left money to his female relatives, but he and his son got along like oil and water. Picked that up from a lot of negative emails back and forth, from his laptop. Other thing, though don't see how it relates to a murder—though maybe to carelessness that could cause a fatal accident—Ben Hoffman drank enough to belong to an online Alcoholics Anonymous group. Oh, yeah, he'd had some back and forth emails with the guy that runs the Trophy Ranch too."

"Bingo," Nick said, writing STAN HELTER LAND GRAB? in big letters under the names of the dead man's family members, as well as GRACIE COBHAM and JACKSON, just as the doorbell rang.

"I'll see who it is," Claire said, getting up.

"Not alone—not after all that's happened tonight," Nick said, and jumped to get ahead of her to the front door. He turned on the porch light and looked out to see who was there.

Jace. This late? He must know Lexi would be in bed. For once he didn't have Brittany with him, but then surely she was with her mother planning Ben's memorial service, since the ME had released the body.

"Jace. Everything okay?" Nick asked after he unlocked and opened the front door and they shook hands. Jace stepped inside.

"I should have called but I was nearby," he told them. "Whose car is that in the driveway?"

"Heck's here updating us on some things Brit gave us. Come sit down."

"No, gotta get going. But glad Heck's on it. Listen, I found out a couple things from Lane Hoffman being so damn hard on Brit after all this. I—oh, Claire, thought you'd have turned in by now, baby and all," he said when he saw her in the entryway behind Nick.

At least, Nick thought, Jace was smart enough not to go down memory lane right now about the two of them sharing Claire's first pregnancy. Or had he been away on international flights a lot then? That had been one of their problems, Nick recalled.

In the awkward silence, he said, "We're still all wound up from finding a dead alligator in our pool out back— one with what looked like deep claw marks on its throat."

"Hell, no one needs that! Lots of idiots around these days. Be extra careful then, but I know you're both good at that by now. I just have some things I wanted to tell you in person. I guess I'm still paranoid of tapped phones after our earlier adventures. Just file this away in that lawyer brain of yours, since you've promised to help Brit if worse comes to worst."

"We do want to help her," Nick assured him.

"We, meaning Claire too? Well, sure—good. I know you guys are a team, and our ladies seem to like each other."

Nick just nodded.

"For one thing," Jace went on in a rush, "Lane let slip and Brit explained later that her father was a recovering alcoholic and had some wild friends in his good old drinking days. Also, Lane let on that there was some big life insurance policy on Ben's life. From the way Brit reacted to that, I don't think she knew. I hate to say this about the guy—Lane, not Ben—but he's a jerk, to put it nicely," he said, with another glance at Claire. "I get it that guys can hate their fathers—I had problems big-time with mine—but he still carried on about it shortly after he learned his dad was dead."

"And then gave a violin lecture and performance at the BAA the next day," Nick put in. Damn, did everyone he knew have father problems that still haunted them as adults?

"Listen, Nick—Claire, you too. If you guys get into this, which I'm glad to hear you will—Brit had nothing to do with this mess. She loved her father, but she also loves that tiger, wants to help wildlife of all kinds, especially big cats."

All that sent Nick's suspicions spinning back to Stan Helter again, the guy he'd heard had the nickname Big Cat. He had the weirdest feeling—call it criminal attorney's intuition—that Helter was as dangerous as some of those trophy animals he bought and bred so they could be killed. And one of the things the ranch advertised it had for anytime hunting was gators.

# CHAPTER ELEVEN

"I think the hand signals lesson—and from a scuba diver in full gear—will make a great program for the Comfort Zone kids this weekend," Claire told her sister as they headed out to Darcy's car. They had to talk loudly since workmen were installing the new fence in the backyard.

"And he said he'd teach it in your pool. That's handy—after the lesson we can have them practice with us and each other."

"It's possible this will be more than just fun. If one of the kids is being threatened or abused, someday hand signals could be a way for them to ask for help without saying a thing. I keep thinking how awful it must have been for Duncan to be out with his dad somewhere, to want to get help for himself and his mother, but be afraid to say something in front of him. Which reminds me, I've been telling Lexi it's a big secret that there was a gator in our pool. She has promised not to tell the other kids anything about that, though we can hardly forbid tiger talk."

Darcy hefted a basket of food they were taking to Duncan's mother, Marta, and Claire carried a clear plastic sack with some new clothes for the boy. They skirted the workmen's two trucks in the driveway and walked to Darcy's minivan parked on the street.

"Actually," Claire shouted, "with all that noise, we could use some hand signals right now. And it might come in handy for me to tell both Lexi and Nick sometimes when they should cool it or too much is just too much."

"I know what you mean. I could scream when Drew and Jilly keep hounding me for something. I hope there's a cut-it-out-right-now-or-else sign for weary moms."

The shrill sound of drills and pounding hammers from the backyard did not let up. Bronco was there during the construction, which Nick somehow managed to plan to have completed in one day.

They smiled at each other as they got in the minivan. Sometimes the two of them could finish each other's sentences. Claire was happy that she and Darcy resembled each other facially, because physical similarities stopped there. Claire's hair was long and red compared to Darcy's blond pixie cut. Darcy was much thinner, even when Claire didn't sport a baby bump. Claire was older, but they had depended on each other for years.

As she snapped on her seat belt, Claire thought that maybe a bad father and tough childhood was another reason she felt so attached to Duncan. He'd be at school today when they visited his mother on her day off from work, but this food and clothing would help him anyway.

As they drove out of the cul-de-sac, Darcy nodded at the panther sign. "That Crossing Danger warning reminds me of something I meant to tell you."

"Sorry, but I don't have time right now to help out on your Save Our Wildlife committee, though I think it's a great cause—especially lately."

"No, not that. Maybe after the baby comes and you start getting house fever, you can join. But I was going to tell you there's a better new way to warn traffic when Florida panthers are near. It's a motion detector with wireless sensor networks. When the detector spots a large, low, moving form, the road signs blink BEWARE! BEWARE! Pretty cool, huh? Installation would cost a fortune, but it's saved lots of wild cats out west."

"Wish Nick and I could have something like that installed around our property instead of a tall wood fence."

"At least things are looking up now," Darcy said, and reached over to touch her arm. "We are already doing something else to help save the panthers. You know, for years Florida has done flyovers to monitor the radio collars they put on the cats to locate and document them. Telemetry flights, they call them. Small airplanes have to cover over twenty-six thousand acres, and they could really use help from expert pilots."

"Jace, you mean? He's doing double duty now with Zika virus and citrus spraying. Besides, he's not mine to suggest things to anymore, and with Ben Hoffman's death, he has plenty on his mind."

"Is he going to work with you and Nick to help Brittany and the BAA?"

"I'm sure he'll just focus on her and not get involved

with the legal end of things, if there is a legal end, which we're hoping there is not."

"Good. After all you've been through, best if none of you get pulled into a 'death by tiger' case."

Jace had been tempted to call in for a personal day off to be with Brit, but he had more than dedication to his job in mind today. After swooping low to spray acres of grapefruit and orange trees east of Naples—and track some guys who might be bringing in drugs—he headed toward the big citrus grove inland, the one that abutted the Backwoods Animal Adventure.

But that wasn't his real goal either. He'd already seen the BAA from the air, had even taken Brit up in a brief fly-over before they soared over the Glades. Maybe he should have proposed to her that day. He'd been thinking about it lately, but with this mess now—not the time.

Today he planned to do an aerial recon of the Trophy Ranch, because Brit had mentioned that the owner/over-seer, or whatever his title, had been putting pressure on her father to sell BAA land. The monster ranch not only abutted the BAA, but looked, even from the ground, as if it could swallow the little place whole. Ben had been stubborn about selling, and Jace wanted to take a survey of the ranch—to do something to help out in Ben's honor. If he had to make a list of suspects who wanted to hurt Ben, the people behind the ranch would be at the top.

"Huge!" he muttered, as he circled the contours of the vast property, following the tall wire fence below, doubled up where the land abutted the BAA. He noted that the entry gate to the ranch, which on the road seemed a ways from the BAA parking lot, was really quite close to the BAA land since the ranch road curved. There was a small building near the ranch entrance, maybe a guard house or service center, though it might be hidden from the road.

The magnificence of the sprawling wilderness awed him. "Man, the boundaries stretch clear to the Glades," he said aloud, wishing he had someone here to tell. "Looks like footage I've seen of Africa."

After passing above the clustered roofs of small and large buildings and a swimming pool near the ranch entrance on the road, he was once again over grasslands, some standing in shimmering water in the sun. He saw a pack of wild boar running free near a stand of slash pines. And near the road, he glimpsed the distant cell phone tower, which seemed to stick out like a sore thumb in all this natural beauty. He figured that would work for calls at the compound, but not many miles back into the wilds.

He dipped lower, then realized too late he'd spooked about twenty whitetail deer that fled from a small woody area, chased by the shadow of his plane. He tilted his wings to skim a lagoon that appeared to be loaded with alligators, looking like scattered tire treads, lying along the banks in the late-afternoon sun. What must be a flock of wild turkeys took flight beneath him, so he went higher to avoid a collision. Surely black bears and even Florida panthers roamed down there somewhere under the sporadic cover of thick, green foliage. And, of course, those damn, dangerous breeding pythons Bronco used to hunt.

He noted on the farthest inland reaches of the ranch there might be shooting platforms in trees, called stands. He'd seen those for snipers in basic training years ago. Or were those the wooden roofs of buildings under trees or even in the trees?

He banked again and headed back toward Naples. In the stripes of sunlight on cypress and sawgrass below—did he see two zebras? No, that couldn't be. It was just that the shading and his speed made him think that what must be wild horses were zebras. A lot of these Florida ranches used to herd cattle by horseback, and some still did.

He soared even higher when he saw what looked like a swamp buggy break from the trees. So that was what had scattered the deer and horses. He glanced back to see three men in the open-sided, canvas-top vehicle with the huge balloon tires. Yes, they were chasing the deer herd. Two men in the back seat stood to shoot. He saw a glint of gun barrel in the sun. One antlered stag crashed down, two, then three. Their huge racks of horns made them topple into grotesque shapes.

He made a quick turn but not before he saw huge vultures just below him, circling, just like he was. Not looking back again, muttering, brooding, he headed for the Marco Island airport.

He had never been a hunter, except of America's enemies in Iraq. Hunting animals for sport made him angry. Besides, he couldn't help but think that poor Ben must have gone down as fast as those poor deer. Only a bullet hadn't brought him down. Had he been hunted and surprised just the same, though? Ben had been well trained. Could someone have sneaked up on him? Jace would bet it wasn't just a tiger and somehow—though he didn't intend to tell Nick or Claire so they would warn him to steer clear—he was going to prove it.

★ ★ ★

Marta Glover and her son, Duncan, lived in a trailer park, one ridiculously called Paradise Acres. Darcy drove into the area, which had nothing "paradise-y" about the single-or double-wide trailers crammed in on streets with names such as Sunset Court and Palmetto Lane. But she could see why Marta, for more than financial reasons, had wanted to move from the house where her husband had beat her and killed her young social worker guest while Duncan hid under a bed.

"I hope," Darcy said as they parked a short walk away, "she doesn't take this wrong—like it's a guilt-gift or a handout, especially since Nick helped send Irv to prison for that road rage attack."

"I don't think she will. She's grateful we want to help bring Duncan out of his shell, and she knows there are other kids involved, so it's not just charity for one boy."

"You think you can get her to start calling him Duncan? You're pretty good at manipulating people."

"Not manipulating, sister mine, but encouraging them to change!"

"Okay, okay. I guess you've managed to ditch Lexi's bad-seed imaginary friend—and you did help raise me. I hear loud music, even though the front door's closed."

Claire climbed the three metal steps and knocked on the door. Duncan's bike, a beat-up-looking two-wheeler, leaned against the side of the trailer, and some *Star Wars* figures were scattered nearby. The dish-towel curtain flicked as someone evidently looked out, and the music stopped.

"Oh, hiya!" Marta called when she opened the back

door so only the screen door stood between them. "I know the weather's good today, but I keep it locked up anyway." She unlocked the screen door too. "Got to teach Duck to use his key, not leave things unlocked, not after what we been through. Come in!" she said, gesturing, and her light blue eyes went wide when she saw the food basket and clothing. She whispered, "Oh, my!" and ran her hand through her frizzy, long blond hair as she stepped back to let them in.

They gave her the gifts and tried to ignore the fact she cried silently as she put the food in the fridge or single kitchen cabinet and the sack of clothes on the countertop. She wore cutoff jeans and a T-shirt that read GIVE BLOOD! American Red Cross, so maybe she'd been the recipient of help from that organization.

GIVE BLOOD snagged in Claire's brain. Poor Ben Hoffman and all that blood... Then those clawlike cuts on the alligator's throat in the pool...

Sitting around the small table, after the three of them had chatted a bit over cups of tea, Claire didn't even have to bring up Duncan.

"The boy says you all wanta call him Duncan, 'stead of Duck."

"Yes, I hope you don't mind, Marta, but I thought it might remind him of better times, and that he has a very fine real name and doesn't need to be defined—I mean labeled—by his father. The kids sometimes tease him for the nickname—'quack, quack' and all that."

"Hard to not say Duck, for a coupla reasons," she told them, biting her lower lip. "Used to it, plus his daddy insisted. He's still out there, see. Even though he sends us near fifty dollars every two weeks from Tennessee, he—well, it feels to me like he's still out there."

"You haven't seen him, have you?" Claire asked. "Or any sign of him?"

Marta shook her head but shrugged, kind of a mixed message. But Claire figured, as scared as Marta and Duncan were of Irv Glover, they'd be on the run if they thought he was near.

A chill racked her, but, trying to sound upbeat, she said, "I heard about the money from Tennessee going to your old address and that the post office and police are nice enough to be sure you get it." She reached out to cover the woman's hand with her own. She could see Marta had not only chewed her fingernails, but she'd been picking at her cuticles and several were bleeding. GIVE BLOOD, the words on her shirt seemed to shout again.

Darcy put in, "It shows he does have a conscience, some feeling for you and the boy—the money he sends."

She nodded jerkily. "Never want to see him in the flesh, nor his name in the paper ever again. But you're right, least that helps pay the rent—that and my Taco Bell job. He was so diff'rent when I met him, handsome, big talker, had a steady job at that Trophy Ranch near where you took Duck—I mean, Duncan—last Saturday, where Gracie Cobham's tiger hurt that man."

"Your husband used to work at the Trophy Ranch?" Claire asked, sitting forward. "And—do you mean you also knew or know Gracie Cobham?"

"Why, sure. Irv, he worked there years ago, driving a swamp buggy for guests out hunting. Didn't pay much, so he left. But Gracie—seen her off 'n' on for years, eighty

if she's a day. My momma knew her. I carried an orchid
from her little backwoods store when we got married,"
she said, and started to cry more openly. "You know, years
ago she used to sell Glades orchids when it was legal from
her little place out near the Seminole Village, past the road
to Marco. Now she just grows her own. Why, just saw her
and her boys at Taco Bell the other day. She said she'd be
at the craft show Saturday at Cambier Park, and I should
come by and she'd give me one. Don't quite know how
selling orchids mixes with that tiger she had, but this is
the crazy wilds of deep South Florida."

As if that said it all, Claire thought as she exchanged a
sharp look with Darcy.

Nick took the phone call at his desk when his secretary
said it was Grant Manfort.

"Hey, career criminal counselor," Grant said, "how
about a jaunt to the Trophy Ranch this Saturday?"

"You going out there?"

"I am now. Talked to Stan who said, sure, bring you
along. He's got some German guests, and some Japanese
investors are next on the docket, but we're welcome to the
clubhouse, a swamp buggy tour of the grounds, though
not the far reaches of the spread where there's supposed to
be some sort of private goings-on this weekend."

"Sure. Should I come out to your place or meet you
there?"

"Meet me there at the gate. We'll make a day of it.
Might want to wear boots in case we get out and walk
around. You want to bring your snake-and-gator guy, go
ahead. Actually, those pythons—and fire ants—are what

the boots are really good for. See you bright and early at
8:00 a.m. at the gate."

"Thanks, Grant. The place just looks so intriguing."

"More than an outsider could imagine. See you there."

# CHAPTER TWELVE

After dinner that evening, Lexi was so exhausted that she fell asleep on the couch with a rerun of *Dora the Explorer* on the TV. Claire and Nick tiptoed outside to the patio, where they could look through the glass doors and watch her. They sat cuddled on a wide lounge chair, admiring their new oak fence.

"The yard's safer," he said.

"I agree. But, you know, I'd like to buy some native orchids and hang them from the fence to soften the effect, to make it more natural."

"In other words from Gracie Cobham on Saturday, where you would just happen to talk to her about the tiger and who knows what else."

The minute he'd walked in the door, Claire had told Nick about the two interesting facts she'd inadvertently gathered from Marta Glover. Not that she thought they were really important, except for the fact that she now had a chance—a great excuse—to interview Gracie Cobham in a public, controlled setting, a downtown park, where she'd be selling her "homegrown" orchids.

Nick had been adamant that Claire not get near the volatile old woman and her crazy sons, but he'd okayed her plan since it seemed the safest way to approach her. She would go to the park when the craft show opened at 11:00 a.m. before heading home to host the Comfort Zone kids at her house where a friend of Darcy's would teach scuba diving hand signals in their newly walled backyard pool. Nita was bringing the snacks for after the kids splashed around in the shallow end of the pool.

"But still take someone with you to the park," Nick told her as the daylight faded around them on the patio. Claire craned her neck to check on Lexi again; she hadn't moved. "Take Nita maybe, since Darcy can take care of Lexi then. Bronco's going to be with me at the Trophy Ranch. Safety in numbers for both of us, okay?" he added and took her hand.

"Okay, boss, as Bronco and Heck always say. You know, it's a start on questioning Gracie at least. Who would imagine that tiger-loving, tough old woman would grow orchids? But then, as Marta said today when I told her I was surprised about her knowing Gracie and that Irv had worked briefly at the ranch, 'this is the crazy wilds of deep South Florida.' I guess you just never know who knows who or is going to turn up where."

"True," he said and squeezed her hand, then lifted it to his lips to kiss the back of it. "At least this eight-foot fence will help keep the wilds out of our backyard and give us more protection and privacy, even this close to the house." He sighed and shifted closer to her, pressing his hard thigh to her hip. "I hated to order the fence and apologized to both of our next-door neighbors, but they understood, with Lexi and the baby coming. As for the gator in the pool, I did not tell them it was dead on arrival with its throat slashed."

"At least we don't have a third neighbor behind us to worry about too."

"Yeah, but with that empty lot back there, I'll bet that's where someone hauled in that gator, right through the thicket of ficas and invasive melaleuca trees. I should take Bronco in broad daylight and see if there are drag marks through there."

"I just hope nothing weird happens at the memorial service for Ben on Thursday. I'm sure Brit would like to put a fence up around that to keep out the press and the gawkers."

"And I hope we'll be able to be a buffer for her. I know Jace will. After my visit to the ranch, I'm tempted to ask him to do a flyover, especially if I note any parts of it that seem to be off-limits when Bronco and I visit. There's a lot of thick foliage cover out there, but Jace might spot something from the air."

"Like illegal animals?"

"Exotics? Maybe. It seems to me Stan Helter must be nervous about protecting its privacy to offer such a good price for the small acreage of BAA land. Maybe he's really afraid that people so close would spot something illegal. Right now, I'm clutching at straws, but I'm going to keep my eyes open for any sign of illegal immigrants he might have working there. It's more common around here than we think. The place seems to have a lot of perks to bring in the German visitors Grant mentioned today, and the desert sheikh guy earlier. So you just be careful with Gracie, and I'll watch myself with Stan. And let's keep our eyes and ears wide open at the memorial service."

"I was thinking, as nice as this new wooden wall is," she told him, gesturing with her free hand, "the one at the BAA, the bars of the tiger cage too, didn't keep danger out."

"Claire, it's going to take a tall ladder or a ghost to get over or through that fence."

"I know, I know. But I had a dream about a ghost cat—like the one we saw down the street—getting in the house."

He turned to her, frowning. "Then you'd better get your narcolepsy meds recalibrated. We're going to be careful, and we're safe here now. Gated and locked fence, locks on doors and windows, state-of-the art security system, and Bronco, if we need him. So stop worrying."

Yet his tone of voice and his frown showed he was worried too.

The memorial service for Ben Hoffman was held in the small chapel of the First Baptist Church in North Naples. It was a good thing, Nick thought, that the place had a big parking lot, once he saw the cars parked there. Maybe Ann and Brit should have asked for the large auditorium on the site. As they went inside, he hoped the numerous guests really knew the Hoffmans. At least the ushers had kept the media out of the building, though they'd seen vans with their satellite dishes in the parking lot and reporters with mics practically accosting people—which they'd managed to avoid by hurrying inside.

"Obviously, it will be a closed casket when they bring it in," Claire whispered as they slid into a padded pew about halfway back. Bronco sat on one side next to Nick, and Darcy was next to Claire as if they were guarding them. Heck was hanging around outside; Gina was tending her Alzheimer's patient at home; and Nita was staying with Lexi.

Nick nodded and said quietly, leaning closer, "That was the medical examiner I spoke to in the hall. I knew him from his testimony on one of my cases. He says Ben's death is going to remain ruled accidental. They got enough tox tests back to tell that there was no alcohol, drugs or poisons involved."

"Poisons? But—"

"Shh. They have to check everything. He admits the skull fracture could indicate that Ben fell and hit his head on the concrete—or not."

"A blow to the head *before* he fell?"

"As I said, or not."

"Well, at least no one's claiming suicide like they did with your father. Granted, there's no weapon. Look, there's Stan Helter, sitting way up in front."

"Yeah, with Grant."

"So that's your friend and contact."

With a nod, Nick glanced around at people who were seated or coming in. Jackson came in with a younger African-American woman, probably one of his daughters. Nick had learned the BAA's manager was a widower with two daughters and some grandkids. Brit had said he was content to live on the grounds in an apartment attached to their storage building, now that his wife was gone. Nick bet his grandkids loved to visit Grandpa. Nick had also learned that Jackson had been questioned by the police the day Ben died and had taken it hard since he'd known the man for years. Ann and Brit thought a lot of Jackson, relied on him. Perhaps he'd be a good person to talk to, though he hadn't been at the BAA when Ben died, having gone out to run an errand.

They all stood as the casket, covered by an American flag, was rolled in by pallbearers while Lane and Brit followed with Ann between them. Lane's wife and two children, Nick assumed, walked at the end of the procession. Sandra Hoffman was beautiful, nicely dressed and made up. She nodded and smiled to people she evidently knew. The boy looked to be about twelve and the girl a little younger, both serious as could be, maybe even a bit embarrassed. They all sat in front where Jace was already waiting for them, so they must consider him to be a part of the family.

Lane immediately rose again, holding his violin. Standing at the head of the wooden coffin beside a vase with a spray of tropical flowers, he lifted the instrument to his throat with a flourish and began to play.

Nick glanced down at his memorial program, which had a photo of Ben at the gate of the BAA, then saw the listing of musical pieces under it. *Funeral March* by Chopin was the first solo, which they were listening to now. *A German Requiem* by Brahms would be next, and at the end, Handel's *Dead March*.

So was Lane giving a miniconcert here? It seemed the focus was on him, not his father.

The pastor preached a sermon that fit the occasion,

about Daniel in the lion's den. "There are some things worth going into a dark den for, a terrifying cage, in this life," he was saying. "In the Old Testament, Daniel went in because he believed in the true God despite living in a pagan land. Daniel believed, despite enemies accusing him of breaking their laws, that he could do good. For a reason known only to God, Ben Hoffman went into a tiger cage. He believed in the beauty of wildlife and wanted to share God's creation with others, despite those who disagreed the Backwoods Animal Adventure could do any good. Ben is now on a much bigger adventure than he could ever have had here in an earthly paradise..."

Nick was impressed with the message, yet his mind wandered. Why had Grant shrugged more than once at Stan, who was whispering to him? Why did Brit have her arm around Jace's shoulders instead of the other way around? Darn, but Claire's continued reading of body language was rubbing off on him. He was anxious to ask what she thought of all this.

And poor Ann Hoffman looked absolutely wilted; yet when they filed out by rows after the service to greet the family, she motioned to him and Claire and stepped out of the reception line. She led them into the shadowy alcove by the double doors to the sanctuary.

"I found something," she said, tears in her eyes. "I don't want Lane or even Brittany to know yet—maybe ever—but I have to tell someone."

"Some sort of evidence?" Nick asked. "Something that sheds light on Ben's state of mind?"

"Exactly. But first, are you going to help us if we need it?"

"If it's in my capacity as a legal counselor, yes, both of us will help the BAA and you as well, though if it comes to some sort of legal action, I may assist one of my partners. Is there a legal problem?"

She bit her lip and shook her head. She suddenly looked more scared than sad. Her red lipstick had run into the cracks around her mouth, and she blinked back tears.

"I can't believe it, of course," she said. "Ben must have been more depressed than I thought—angry, even bitter. I got out his family Bible, thinking Brittany or Lane could do a reading from it today—something uplifting. I love the Psalms, '*Yea, though I walk through the valley of the shadow of death…*'" Her voice caught.

She darted a look between his and Claire's shoulders where they hemmed her in as if they were protecting her. And maybe they were.

"It isn't something that implicates anyone, is it?" he asked.

She looked even more frightened. Claire reached out to steady her, a hand on the older woman's shoulder.

"It's—it's almost a suicide note," she whispered, "though one not meant to be found. I hid it, but I want you to see it. It scares me to death—to death."

Nick fought to keep calm, to nod in understanding. But he felt the way Claire sometimes described her narcoleptic nightmares, like walking through a thick fog where hands reached out to grab you, and a huge hole opened up and the black, deep earth swallowed you, and—

For one dreadful moment, he saw again the gun near his father's hand and all the splattered blood and the back of his head gone, and he was young again and—screaming, "Dad! Dad! Dad!"

He felt Claire grip his arm as if she were holding him up too, pulling him back. This woman needed help like his mother had, and he'd tried so hard to fill his father's shoes.

Claire said, "Ann, if you want to keep that private right now, do you want to bring the document to us, or shall we come to you? You don't have it with you, do you?"

Nick felt the earth settle under his feet again. The reason he'd dedicated himself to his private South Shores endeavors flooded back, his crusade to help others who lost a loved one under strange circumstances.

"No, I—I hid it. Only one other person knows where it is—Jackson."

Nick said, "We completely understand if you don't want to bring it into a law office. As Claire said, we can come to you, unless—"

"Would you mind coming to the BAA tomorrow?" she asked, looking up at him and dabbing under her eyes with a wadded tissue. "Brittany has a morning meeting in town, but I'll be there. We very much—in Ben's honor—want to keep things going, despite some financial woes."

"I understand. About ten o'clock then? Claire will come too."

She nodded. "I'll be waiting. I thank you both for—"

"Mother, there you are!" Lane interrupted and almost shouldered Nick aside with his black leather violin case. "For heaven's sake, people are looking for you. I was about to send Sandra into the restroom. You certainly don't need an attorney for any reason—does she?" he asked Nick. "Especially not a criminal attorney."

"A lawyer might help, depending on the complications of the will," Nick said.

"Ah, yes, the will. Everything to the two women in his life who went along with his 'Daniel in the lion's den' experience of building up the BAA. If we need counsel, we'll find it. Mother, come on. The car is waiting to take us to the *private* graveside service," he said and took her elbow to guide her—to practically pull her away.

"I'd like to break that expensive violin over his head," Nick muttered as Lane led his mother to the exit.

"He's so deeply hurt and angry. I guess I can see why. He's kind of odd man out in the family, and that must hurt."

"I'm trusting you to read between the lines of whatever document Ann is going to show us. Oh, I see Jace must be going to the cemetery with Brit," he said, watching Lane and Ann join Brit and Jace as they headed for the outside door. After filing through the family reception line, most guests had left the building.

"Even if Ben was depressed," Claire said, taking Nick's arm as they moved toward the door, "that doesn't mean he went into that cage deliberately. As I've said before, there are a lot easier ways he could have taken his own life if that was his intent."

"Yeah, but to a guy who loved animals—"

"No, he would have seen that Tiberia might be blamed then, and that it would cause a lot of problems for Ann, Brit and the BAA. They could lose the tiger, the entire place, so he would not have killed himself that way."

"With a son like Lane, maybe he was tempted—just kidding. But people considering suicide often have that one tenuous, black moment when they can do it, and if it passes, they won't. I realize we have to be careful not to let the fact Lane's a jerk color our suspicions, though it wouldn't be the first time a bitter family member set up someone's death when he himself had a perfect alibi. But who then? Who hit that big man on the head and put him in the tiger's cage and then just disappeared into thin air?"

# CHAPTER THIRTEEN

"We're getting to be the BAA's biggest attendees," Nick told Claire as they got out of their car in the familiar parking lot the next morning.

"And not for the right reasons," she said, taking his arm as they walked toward the entry gate. "Poor Ann and Brit, not only to lose their loved one that way, but the BAA is a dream deferred if not threatened. I hope we can help them, even if Ben left a suicide note."

"Ironic. I asked Grant Manfort about my mother not getting my dad's death insurance settlement because there was a clause in there about it being negated if the cause of death was suicide. Of course, it wasn't," he said, his voice hardening, "but it took me years to prove it. Ann and Brit are already worried about this little place not having enough funding to keep it going. In honor of their father and husband, they would do about anything to keep it from being eaten up by Stan Helter's ranch. In short, I hope that is not a suicide note."

"You're not thinking that Ben might have taken out that big insurance policy that Jace overheard about from Lane to save this place? Okay, I mean, Ben tried to make it look like a natural death—albeit by tiger—so Brit and Ann would get a lot of money, not to mention publicity, for the place."

"You ought to write fiction, sweetheart. Let's not jump ahead but see what the document actually shows. And," he said, as they let themselves through the gate that Ann had phoned to say she'd leave unlocked for them, "if I get the chance, I want to question Jackson. He evidently knew Ben well, and it's obvious Ann trusts him since she left the letter with him for safekeeping."

"I hope the handwriting can be substantiated as Ben's and be dated as fairly recent. If we can borrow it from her, I can put my forensic document examiner skills to work. I haven't needed any of that since our first case in St. Augustine."

"There would be no reason for Ann to forge it. Especially if it does hint at suicide or even depression, she and this place could have a lot to lose."

As they closed the gate behind them, they passed exhibits and glanced into cages and through fences. The place suddenly seemed like a modern, miniature Eden to Claire. The sound of muted, distant splashing water lured her. Tabebuia trees were just starting to break into golden bloom. Tropical foliage trained over a trellis dripped bloodred hibiscus. Birds chattered. Adam and Eve must be somewhere in here, but where was the tree of the knowledge of good and evil? They needed answers and now.

She jumped when they passed a cage where a rainbow-hued parrot screeched, "Who—are—you?" as if he were the area watchman.

"There's that little mulefoot pig Duncan liked over there," she said, pointing as they headed for the administration trailer. "He seems like an imaginary or prehistoric animal, several of them put together."

"That pig's a strange little dude, but so's Duncan. Maybe that was part of the attraction for him."

She jumped again when a deep human voice called out from the Flamingo Isle area, which was surrounded on three sides by a shallow moat: "Heard you were coming!"

It seemed Jackson had been hiding in the foliage. He suddenly appeared, walking toward them through the moat that served as a pond where six long-legged, pink birds waded and preened. Several eyed him warily, but they were obviously used to his presence.

Nick told him, "Brit said you are a Jackson of all trades around here. I see what she means."

Jackson let himself out through the chain-link gate and came around to walk with them. He was wet to his knees and left a trail of footprints. "The flamingos, they're my favorite," he told them, his voice and face so serious. "Beautiful, almost heavenly, but need lots of earthly tending—make me feel needed. Feed them only the best, fresh veggies, some shrimp, not that chemical additive canthax-anthin that big zoos use now to keep them pink."

"You've got them in a beautiful setting," Nick told him.

"You know, that little hidden isle there in the middle's

the highest place on this property. It's an old Calusa Indian mound, I bet, though some call it a hammock hill like out in the Glades." He shrugged and shook his head, maybe at some distant memory. "Meanwhile," he said, clearing his throat, "gotta do my best to pick up more duties around here with Ben gone." He kept shaking his head slowly as if in disbelief. "Huge loss to this place. Can't believe it happened."

"As much as he knew this place and the animals, do you think it really was an accident?" Claire asked.

Nick cleared his throat, an obvious hint not to pursue things right now. He had just said he wanted to talk to Jackson, so maybe he thought she was overstepping, but weren't they a team?

Jackson shrugged. "Can't believe no one saw it, 'less he planned it that way. It's not like him, even if he was down in the dumps lately, and I don't mean this place is a dump. Looking good compared to when we opened up. Anyway, so you want to see Ann first, or I can get you that letter she asked me to keep."

"How about Claire can go in to see how Ann's doing, and I'll go with you to get the letter. It's on the grounds, right?"

"In the storage shed. Sure, come along if'n you want to see my best hiding place right smack-dab in the mess of birdseed and paint cans."

Claire headed toward the trailer while the men veered off toward a small concrete block building set back in a corner of the fence. She saw a wooden building was attached to it, probably where Jackson lived now. She thought the storage building looked large and sturdy, not like what Jackson had called a shed. A wheelbarrow loaded with big bags of feed and a golf cart were parked outside.

She was a little annoyed at Nick taking Jackson off like that. It made her all the more anxious to question Gracie Cobham on her own, and didn't Nick realize she wouldn't be afraid to psych out Stan Helter? Nick seemed to be keeping her from observing him, even from being introduced to him. If the owner of the Trophy Ranch was that dangerous, Nick really should be looking at him—suicide note or not—as someone who had harmed Ben. But then, maybe that's exactly what he planned to do tomorrow.

"You do keep a lot of things in a small space here," Nick noted as he scanned the interior of Jackson's storage building, which was lit by hanging bare light bulbs. Metal shelves went floor to ceiling in tight rows, something like a small hardware store. Nothing was labeled. In his dark work outfit with his dark skin, Jackson almost disappeared when he went to the end of a row. Nick noted that taped to metal dividers and dangling to the shelf below were several photographs of Jackson with his wife and two daughters—and one of Ben and Jackson deep-sea fishing, both grinning and holding a big tarpon together.

"Only kind of animal he'd ever hurt," Jackson muttered, seeing where Nick was looking. "Truth was he threw even good eatin' fish back in after he caught them. Loved animals from the day he was born, he said."

Nick watched as Jackson lifted a large can from what looked to be a row of paint cans and removed a flat, zipped plastic sack from under one. A white piece of paper lay within. Nick was pleased to see Ann or Jackson had thought of preserving what might be evidence. There could even be fingerprints or DNA on that paper.

"You should see my filing system," Jackson said, replacing the can. "My banking system too. Got more than one thing stashed in here, including a weapon I got me a permit for—the one I would have used to corral that Cobham clan if I'd needed to. If I'd been here when that big cat attacked Ben and could have gotten to the gun—well, Brittany woulda killed me for it, but I woulda killed that cat."

"You and Ben go way back."

"He was 'bout the only one treated me like I had a brain in my head when I first met him. Ran things by me for my opinion when I was custodian of the first advertising company he worked for. Drinking buddies after work."

"And did he still drink—maybe too much?"

"Not if you mean he was too drunk to realize he was stepping accidentally in Tiberia's cage—no way."

Realizing that was not quite an answer, Nick regretted not bringing Claire with him. Since that day he'd seen her shot, he'd been protective of her, especially with all they'd been through. But now that she was pregnant, was he being overly defensive about her?

"So," he said as Jackson handed him the plastic envelope with a handwritten note in it, "did Ben run anything by you to make you think he was feeling low lately?"

"Feeling worried," he said, nodding. "Sure, about this place. But, I'd say, something deeper. You can read it in the lines there and between the lines."

Nick thanked him and went out into the morning sunshine. Strangely, he felt chilled despite its warmth. Claire was trained to read between the lines, but, unfortunately, this letter had been printed, which he knew was harder to evaluate.

He glanced through the tall BAA wire fence and the ranch fence at the dense foliage edging Helter's property. And had the feeling, when the palmetto leaves shuddered in the wind, that someone had just been there, watching.

Claire leaned over Nick's shoulder as he read the letter aloud through the plastic bag. She could read it from here, though, as it was quite neatly done in large, handwritten print with black ink.

DEAREST ANN: I WANT YOU TO KNOW I RESPECT LANE'S OPINION. HE BELIEVES THAT HIS RIGHTFUL LEGACY HAS BEEN GIVEN AWAY TO BRITTANY BY OUR BUILDING THE BAA, BY OUR SQUANDER-ING HIS INHERITANCE ON HER. I REALIZE I HAVE MADE MISTAKES WITH HIM, BUT HE CAN'T ACCEPT THAT OUR DREAM IS THIS PLACE, AND IT IS NOT ALL FOR BRIT-TANY, BUT I SEE IT'S BEEN WRONG THAT WE FAVORED HER.

I SUPPOSE HIS ARTISTIC TEMPERAMENT, EVEN THE EMOTIONAL, PASSIONATE MUSIC HE IS MOST DRAWN TO, DICTATES HIS PERSONALITY. I REALIZE NOW THAT BRITTANY'S INSISTENCE ON THIS PLACE AND HER LOVE FOR THAT TIGER THREAT-ENS OUR FUTURE FINANCES. AGAIN, I RE-GRET I HAVE MADE MASSIVE MISTAKES

AND BLAME MYSELF FOR SO MUCH THAT
I WISH I COULD MAKE UP FOR IT ALL BY
JUST ENDING

Nick turned the paper over.

"Nothing on the back," Claire observed. "Did he imply ending his life? It's as if he was interrupted, though the sentence could end there. No period, though, when the earlier punctuation is obvious. Maybe something or someone interfered, and he quickly stashed the paper in the old Bible where Ann found it.

"Ann," she said, turning toward her where she sat in the chair, gripping her hands together on the desk, "did Ben always print like this?"

"Not really. I thought of that too, but maybe he wanted to be sure it was legible. It's written carefully and the letters are big."

"But this is such an emotional outpouring, and people usually write quickly to get that out."

"Well, his handwriting's gotten worse, like mine, and, like I said, he didn't usually print. And the Bible—well, it wasn't kept in a public place in which he'd be interrupted. A drawer in our bedside cabinet. I've gone through all the pages, and there's nothing else but my notes in the margins."

"Is there anything here to date the note?" Claire asked. "Anything in what he says about Lane that sounds current?"

"No. All those problems have been ongoing," she said with a sigh. "From when Lane first liked to stay indoors to practice and was afraid of animals. See, the boy accidentally closed a house cat in a door one time and hurt it something awful. It yowled and cried so bad. Ben took it to the vet, but it died. I guess that might have—what's the word—terrified him. Ben was pretty upset about it."

"Traumatized?" Claire asked, and Ann nodded, though she was now blowing her nose.

"And Lane thought his father blamed him?"

"Lane never liked cats big or small after that, no animals, really. And there was a long string of sad things between Ben and Lane. I guess I should tell you about the car exhaust," she said with a huge sigh. "Last spring, Lane left our car running in our attached garage one night when he drove me home in our car from a concert. His wife followed him, picked him up from there and he hurried away with her. But then he always was so absentminded about—well, about practical things."

"So, obviously, no carbon monoxide poisoning," Nick said. "Is that what you were going to say? How soon was the running car exhaust discovered?"

"Not until Ben went out to the kitchen to have a nightcap and heard something in the garage. He turned it off, opened the garage door to air it out, had a real row with Lane the next day. Like I said, Lane was absentminded."

"Any other unusual incidents?" Nick asked, handing the letter, still encased in plastic, to Claire. She wondered if Ben had forgotten about it or had died before he could retrieve it. She planned to study it closer since Ann had said they could take it with them for now, as long as they returned it eventually.

"Not really unusual incidents," she went on, almost drawling her words as if hesitant to share more. "Well, distracted driving when he was with us once, but then he would have been hurt too, so we didn't think much of it. That was always Lane, head in the clouds, hearing music, not watching where he was going. But—but he did yell at his father just last week, that—I know this is dreadful and I don't mean to accuse him of anything, really... He had an argument with his father and said he could go to hell, and he wished he were dead."

"He wished Ben was dead, not he wished himself dead?" Nick asked.

She nodded and started to cry. "It's one of the reasons I nearly collapsed when I saw Ben in that tiger cage. Thank God Lane was miles away in front of a big audience. Brittany deeply resented Lane too, but I can't—I can't believe I could even think that he would hurt his father, no matter what their differences."

"So Brittany knows all this?" Nick pursued. "The car exhaust, the distracted driving with you in the car?"

"She told Lane to shape up or else."

Or else what? Claire wondered. But what was also bothering her was a forensic document examiner case she recalled from college where a murderer had printed a fake suicide note for his victim because he knew he could never replicate the victim's handwriting. Lane might have been miles away when Ben died in that cage, but could he have really wished his father dead? And then, as smart and talented—and as bitter and angry—as he was, somehow arranged just that?

"Baby, wake up," Jace said, rolling over in bed and reaching backward for Brit in the bright daylight. "Clock says almost eleven."

The other side of the bed was empty. He heard the shower going in his bathroom. He's the one who should be waking up, he thought, stretching and groaning. They'd made crazy love last night, and it had nearly knocked him out, and here he had to fly at one o'clock. But she'd been so needy—desperate, grasping—and that wasn't like her, though he understood why she felt that way right now.

He rolled out of bed and grabbed for his shorts and T-shirt on the floor. He'd just hop in the shower with her and hope that didn't lead to something more. He felt a stab of guilt that she'd been here last night with him instead of with her mother, but Ann had told Brit she finally felt she could sleep and wanted peace and quiet.

He knocked on the bathroom door, then went in. The place was steamed up, and he felt like he was fighting through a fog. "Mind some company?" he called to her, then realized the sound he heard was not just the jet shower spray. Was she crying? Sobbing in there?

"Brit, honey?" he said and knocked on the glass shower stall. It was frosted glass, and he could only see her outline, a bent elbow, hands to her head like she was scrubbing her face or washing her hair. He gasped as she seemed to slip and fall.

He shoved the shower door open though the steam and spray splashed out into the room. She was soaked and sobbing, curled into a fetal position on the tile floor with water pounding her and swirling down the drain. This was not like this woman—no matter what had happened recently.

"Brit, honey, talk to me."

He sat on the shower floor, holding her in his arms

while she clung to him. He could hardly hear what she was saying at first—broken gibberish in the crash of water.

"I—the last time—we talked… I—you know Dad and I had a huge fight. But you'd gone out to your car for something—maybe didn't know or overhear it all. I told him we could lease the land back from Stan Helter after he paid big for it. Keep the place, run it for Dad's lifetime… Make Helter sign, ask Nick to take care of the legalities. But he refused."

"You mean you went to him without your dad knowing? When I came back in, I knew you were both upset, but why didn't you tell me why?"

She choked out, "I didn't think you'd understand either, my dealing with Helter, but it was a way to keep the BAA going, build it up. But Dad flipped out at me, just because I brought it up as a possibility. He didn't know I had already seen Helter about it."

"I hear he's a ladies' man. You tangled with him?"

"I bargained with him!" she shouted and tried to pull from his embrace. He let her, steadying her so she wouldn't slip as she struggled to get up.

He got to his feet. He should talk, he knew. He hadn't told her that he and Ben had a near knock-down, drag-out fight right after she left the house. He thought Ben was drinking too much and was scared what that would lead to. Ben became an almost different person then—not only drunk but dangerous. The water pounded on them, at them. His thoughts, mingled with new fears, pounded on him too.

# CHAPTER FOURTEEN

When Bronco and Nick followed Grant's Jeep through the tall wooden gates of the Trophy Ranch early Saturday morning, it seemed they left the civilized world behind. As the stockade gates swung closed automatically behind them, Nick saw a heavy dew glistening on the grass and trees where pelicans and ibis roosted, ready to fly away for the day's fishing. No dust on the road with the recent rain. Expectation hovered in the air.

"Bet we could drive half the day and still be on his land," Bronco said as he steered his new truck down the road. "Hey, look, boss, vultures on the carcass of that big boar. Think someone shot it and left it?"

"I don't know the rules around here, but we're about to find out." They passed the vultures stripping the carcass bare on the berm. The big birds didn't even move or look up as the vehicles passed close by, but Nick craned his neck to look back. "Maybe there's a worker coming to clean it up," he told Bronco. "I see a bearded guy wearing camouflage watching either us or the vultures. I think I glimpsed a guard station hidden back in that foliage, so maybe he's the same guy who controls the gate."

They parked about a half a mile in where Grant pointed when he got out of his Jeep, its top and sides zipped up today. They all got out to shake hands. Nick saw a horse-shoe-shaped cluster of buildings dominated by a sprawl-ing lodge that looked like it was made from cedar logs. Some buildings appeared to be wooden cabins. He spot-ted—and smelled—what might be a big smokehouse. A kidney-shaped swimming pool sporting a tiki hut bar with palmetto roofing glinted at them—rustic chic in South Florida. Two dark-haired women were washing off the poolside lounge chairs.

Another bearded man wearing camouflage—so that was the uniform of choice around here—waved to them and motioned them over toward the lodge. "Stan's wait-ing," he called, and moved his arm in a windmill motion. "Come on in. How ya doin', Grant?"

As they walked toward the lodge, Nick noted a dark green swamp buggy pulled around to the side, maybe one to take them on the tour he'd been promised. With their big balloon tires, the motorized, ramshackle-looking ve-hicles could slog through any swampy terrain. Claire had said Irv Glover had worked at the ranch years ago, driv-ing a buggy to take hunters to shoot the game featured here. That had been news to Nick. It hadn't come out in the trial where he'd helped get Glover sent to prison for aggravated assault.

Inside the lodge, he saw what he'd call rustic grandeur.

Lots of leather couches and reclining chairs, walls heavy with the heads of mounted game such as big rack stags, boars, and more than one gator head or just toothy, jagged jaws. Last night when he'd studied the ranch's website, he'd seen a photo of a guy who had shot a stag with a massive 46-point rack that was worth more than $100,000. Big money here, one way or the other.

Also, the website had boasted that guests were guaranteed a gator kill anytime of the year on private land, despite that the state-wide hunting season for them on public land closed yearly on November 1, in just a few days. He might have been a lawyer for years, but Nick hadn't known about that. Evidently, rules were to be broken here. He couldn't help but wonder if that applied outside the boundaries of the fence—like maybe those who opposed Stan Helter were always open season too.

"Hey, glad you could spend some time with us," Stan told them, appearing from a back room beyond an open area with tables for both eating and gambling, and an extensive bar that was not staffed now. Grant must be familiar with it, though, since after greeting Stan he went over and poured some tomato juice—then grabbed the vodka bottle, evidently to make a Bloody Mary. He plunked himself in a leather chair and put his feet up on the ottoman as if he owned the place.

Stan wore jeans, a Western-style shirt and denim jacket. He extended his hand. Nick shook it and introduced Bronco, then they shook hands.

Stan said to Bronco, "I hear you're a retired gator guy who's also snagged those bastard pythons that were mating like crazy."

"Yes, sir. Working for Nick now. Getting married soon."

"Congrats on that! So, we'll have to talk. At the least, maybe you could come in sometime, train some staff about handling gators, but especially those honker snakes. They hide out in armadillo holes and wreak havoc on deer and other game. Like to knock off every last one of them, cut them up for gator food."

So, Nick wondered, were all animals here fair game? What about the human ones who got in the way?

The Saturday craft fair at Cambier Park near downtown Naples sported booths around the edge of the tennis courts and public area. People wandered here and there, some leaving with purchases in their arms, while others came in from parking or walking from uptown.

As nervous as Claire was about facing Gracie Cobham again, she was keeping an eye on how Gina and Heck interacted with each other. Not being nosy, of course, but after all, she was trained as a people watcher. So far, it seemed they were touchy with each other—both kinds of touchy. Holding hands, eye contact, quick little pats, but they seemed also on edge as if they were just getting over an argument.

When they passed kids sitting at tables, learning crafts like decoupage, origami and macramé from instructors, Claire wished she'd brought Lexi, but then this was serious business, and Lexi was happy at Darcy's for now. At least at this busy, crowded venue, she didn't have to worry about being in a dangerous, isolated situation with Gracie and her "boys."

"If I'd been onto this event earlier," she told Heck and Gina, "I could have brought the Comfort Zone kids here to learn crafts and kept the scuba diver hand signals lesson for another day."

"You'll find something like this hands-on fun for them again," Gina said, patting Heck's shoulder. "Right, *mi hombre?*"

Talk about hand signals, Claire thought, as she watched the two of them exchange a deep-soul glance at the mention of "hands on." It made her miss Nick. Why were these two sending mixed signals right now?

"Some good wood carvings of wild birds over there," Heck noted, clearing his throat and tearing his gaze away from Gina to look around.

"That artist, he carves fish too, see?" Gina said. "Makes me think of *mi padre*, fishing all alone in Cuba now. So sad my brother died. So you said the woman who is the tiger tamer, she has a brother too, Claire?"

Claire nodded as she picked up a brochure at the information booth and skimmed it for anything about orchids. Yes, this had to be it: Home Grown Orchids, booth 37.

"Let's go this way. Yes, Brit has a brother she doesn't get along with and vice versa. Different goals in life, some of the usual sibling rivalry, I guess," she told them, hoping that was the extent of it. Jace really cared for Brit, and she'd hate to have his future wife upset by not only losing her father but having to continually deal with an embittered brother.

Claire had to admit she was disappointed in the let's-understand-and-forgive-Lane letter, but she'd told Nick that she'd never seen a so-called suicide note that was so difficult to deal with. First, that it was printed so she couldn't compare it to what was called a "standard" script handwritten document by Ben, since Ann had only been able to show her Ben's cursive writing.

Second, its ending was vague. Had Ben just been worried about their retirement finances, or did he really mean to kill himself, hoping his death looked like an accident so Ann and Brit could use his insurance policy? Had he meant to leave a more specific suicide note and that one was a draft? Had he finished it? Why hadn't he signed it? This entire Tiger Cage Case was going everywhere and nowhere.

"Oh, look, so cute, Heck," Gina was saying, tugging him back toward a table where an artist was drawing caricatures of people who were lined up to pose. The sketches he had displayed were simple pen and ink, but they captured the essence of his subjects.

"Listen, you two," Claire told them, "I see the woman I want to talk to over there, and it might work better if I did it alone. But, Heck, just keep an eye on me, okay? If I put a hand on top of my head, come on over."

"Sure. *Sí*. Nick said to watch you close. Guess this is close enough. He said if two big lugs come around, time for you to leave."

Claire thanked them both and headed for the booth that did not need a sign. Its frame was draped with lovely, multihued orchids, most in wire baskets lined with sphagnum moss. If the plants weren't in baskets, they dangled from what looked to be colored strings or fishing line strung from post to post. Swaying in the breeze, they looked so lovely, so innocent. Some were shaped like butterflies, others like dancers, slippers or even spiders. Claire waited while Gracie made a sale to two women who each walked away with a plant.

"I know who you are," Gracie Cobham said, folding her thin arms over her flat chest. "Don't have your friend tiger-girl with you, I hope."

"Hello, Mrs. Cobham," Claire said, trying to sound calm and even cheery. "No, I'm here with two other friends."

"So you are friends with her."

The word *her* dripped venom. Claire didn't want the conversation to go that way. Those sharp blades her sons had were only to cut up dead possums, but she could yet recall the glint of them in the sun.

Claire plunged on. "I was delighted to hear there was to be an orchid display here, and what a coincidence it would be yours. You see, we just installed a tall fence around our backyard, and I could use some advice and some plants to soften the effect."

"Glad to help," she said, her wrinkled face softening a bit. "You just remember one thing. Orchid plants are not fragile and delicate, like they seem. Sure, they got to be treated right to bloom, but they are tough and strong."

As she said that, she put both hands on her hips. Was she talking about orchids or herself? This woman was more clever—more tough and strong—than she had seemed to Claire at first.

"I see," she told Gracie. "I really do see."

"Good. Thunder was raised up with all kinds of orchids just outside his cage so he'd be calm and not riled. Fetched them in and out of my greenhouse every day for him. I bragged on him too much, and the park rangers come and took him—said that BAA cage was bigger and better for him."

"I'm sorry. I know you tended and loved him."

"How 'bout we can make some kind of deal," she said, glancing in both directions as if they were about to commit espionage. "Free orchids—real pretty native ones I grow myself, since it's been years the Glades orchids are off-limits—and you convince that girl at the BAA to feed my boy more possums."

Claire wasn't sure whether to laugh or cry. "Perhaps something can be worked out, but I think Brittany learned in her college studies of wild animals that carcasses like that can transmit diseases to an animal."

Gracie cussed under her breath and spit on the grass. Darn, just when she thought they might be coming to an understanding, this wasn't going well again.

"There's a natural curse on folks what mistreat animals," Gracie said. "See what happened to the owner of that place? Wasn't Thunder's fault he went in that cage."

"No one at the BAA is blaming Thunder. Now, it's so exciting to think that your orchids originally came from the Glades."

"Used to be able to just take them, before the fancy State of Florida laid down laws in the '50s about don't touch. The gov'ment thinks it can run our lives, you know. But I had a lot of orchids by then, was breeding and growing my own. Here. Here's some you might want for your fence."

Gracie came around the table and proceeded to point out and describe orchids, some with unusual names like Shadow Witch. "Now off-limits," she put in. "Them gold and white with the purple tongue are butterfly orchids, and that big one's a Cowhorn, and you can see why with those two big, curved stems. Now this one here's a spider orchid, rare even by the '50s, but its red and yellow stripes always made me want to call it a tiger orchid."

"They're amazing. I can see why you've spent years growing them—saving them, if they're endangered now."

She nodded and seemed to sniff back tears, though she still looked steely-eyed. "Just like I was trying to save Thunder 'fore he got off-limits. And someone done paid for that."

Stan drove a swamp buggy—a really nice one with a camouflage exterior—and Nick sat beside him while Grant and Bronco sat in the back.

"Proud to say we have our own taxidermy shop here, run by a really talented guy," Stan told them as he gestured toward a good-sized wooden building.

"Always wanted to see how that was done," Nick said. "I suppose you do mostly gators."

"Some deer and wild boar too," Stan said, "though I think our 'artist in residence' longs for something bigger."

"Let's stop for a minute and let them meet Drew," Grant suggested, so Stan U-turned and parked at the back of the building. An air conditioner not only sat there but was running on this cool day. The building had quite an extension out the back, but it had no windows.

They got out and tramped around in front. Rather than just going in, Stan knocked. "Drew Hewitt, like I said, is an 'artiste,' but I can't argue with the great work he does. We cut him some slack, lots of perks to keep him here rather than where he'd like to be doing exotic game."

A slender man with wispy blond hair and pale blue eyes—maybe in his forties—answered the door and, after introductions, gestured them in. "And what trophies shall we preserve for you gentlemen?" he asked. His voice was gentle and a bit high-pitched, almost like a girl's. Nick reminded himself never to stereotype people, since he'd expected some big, strong guy who could heft animals around, skin them, mount them.

Except for the sharp smell, it was like a gallery in here, only with mounted heads staring from the walls instead of framed art. "Polyester resin scent," Drew told them as he pointed out some of the projects he was working on. Creepy, yet the end results were amazing.

Bronco was fascinated by the gator mounts, especially the ones with open jaws jammed full of terrible teeth. "Glad I never got snagged by one of those when we were hunting," he told Nick.

"So, more of these in your big back room?" Bronco asked.

"Strictly storage and a state-of-the-art freeze dryer, a new trend in preservation. It absolutely mummifies small animals, often used for pets because it keeps the features and form intact. I do some household pets on the side, but those clients never come here—I go to them."

"Couldn't quite afford someone this talented if I didn't let him moonlight a bit," Stan added after they thanked Hewitt and went out to the swamp buggy. "Though we have well-heeled guests here, the upkeep of this much land and our accommodations is expensive, so we're always grateful to nature preservationists like Grant who underwrite us."

★ ★ ★

"You did what?" Heck said as he and Gina helped Claire carry armfuls of hanging orchid pots to the car. "Boss ain't—isn't—gonna like that."

"It's my job to psych people out. She's eccentric, she's upset, but I trust her. I insisted on paying her for these. And yes, I told her where we live, and she's coming out next week to bring some other orchids and help me arrange these."

"*Caramba*, wait till he hears Gina and me was getting our caricature done when you did that."

"I can explain to him. Now, let's get back. We'll just hang some of these on the fence before the kids arrive. The scuba diver friend of Darcy's is coming early. Several of the parents are coming too, because I think this is going to be a great lesson for everyone. The responsible parents—like Duncan's mother, Marta—will learn the hand signals too. Talk about endangered orchids. Those kids still can be too."

Gina turned around in the front seat to face Claire as they pulled out of the parking lot of a nearby elementary school. "It's true. I think it is so great what you are trying. The whole family suffers when one of the kids is sick. And home violence is worse than being sick. I'm glad some of the parents are coming today. I will stay and help. You helped me, you believed in me, and it kept me going when we had to leave Cuba. I am on your side even if Nick, he gets upset."

"Thank you for that vote of confidence, Gina. We women know how to stick together and support each other, wherever we come from, whatever our ages or crazy passions—like tigers and orchids."

Claire saw Heck shake his head and knew he was thinking Nick would be upset with him and her. But she was being careful. Nick had hired her in the first place for her good instincts and people-savviness. She'd finessed a bad start with Bronco. Things were much better between her and Jace. She felt sure of herself right now, carrying this baby she was so excited about. Tough and strong, like Gracie's orchids.

# CHAPTER FIFTEEN

Jace landed the plane, grabbed a late lunch and headed for the BAA. He wanted to see how Ann and Brit were doing, but he had to talk to Brit alone after her morning meltdown. He could accept she'd be emotionally strung out with all she'd been through. But she'd said she'd gone to see Stan Helter and had been hiding that from him—maybe from Ann too. She'd been too distraught for him to have it out with her this morning.

He found her at the tiger cage, alone on a bench, eating a granola bar, just staring—maybe glaring—at the cage where Tiberia seemed content to sit and yawn, then put his head down on his big paws to doze. Not a care in the world, that natural killer.

"I can't believe you're here now," Brit greeted him, sliding over so he could sit.

He didn't hug or kiss her, but threw one arm on the

back of the bench behind her shoulders and crossed one ankle on the other leg, with his knee almost touching her.

"Too preoccupied to fly this afternoon."

"You? After your Middle East battles, the war you've been through?"

"Are we at war now, Brit?"

"What?" She turned to face him. Her lids were swollen and her eyes red-rimmed. She sounded stuffed up. "What are you talking about? I need your help and support and—"

"Then tell me the rest about the battle plans you must have cooked up for keeping this place afloat. Undercover bargaining with the enemy?"

"Okay, okay. I met Stan Helter on neutral ground, at the Cracker Barrel near the I-75 entrance to Alligator Alley."

"Without your parents' knowledge? Or mine. Obviously, it was before the tragedy."

"Yes, it was a few days before Dad died. But I could tell he was so worried about finances, about losing the BAA. It was my parents' dream as well as mine. So I figured I could make a long-term deal with Stan Helter. He would agree to own the place, because the land deed was in my name, so they wouldn't have to sign or even know. But Helter would have to promise not to control or absorb the land into the ranch until both of my parents were retired or—or gone. It sounded so good on the surface. I could tell them I got a research grant with the money, dole it out so it didn't look like so much. He was agreeable—he offered a lot, but then, since Dad died soon after..."

She sucked in a big breath and blinked back tears. "I realize now I might have—might have made a mistake trusting Helter. What if he was afraid Dad would find out or make me renege on the deal?"

"And why, since Helter has so much land already, is he so set on owning this fairly small piece? Just because it sits up a little higher here than his water lands? I realized after I did a flyover that might be it. But what I really want to know is did the bastard want you to go beyond meeting at a family restaurant and sign on the secret dotted line to settle this deal?"

"You—you mean his reputation with women? I've seen women being driven into the ranch, but they're staff who clean and cook, so I've heard. No, he didn't make that kind of move. But didn't you hear me? What if Helter decided to make sure that he only had to bargain with me—and not deal with Dad—by harming him? And that would be absolutely my fault—like I gave him that fatal shove."

He'd figured she was guilt-ridden over her final fight with her father, but he felt pain too for the same reason. Could Brit's argument with Ben, then his right after that, have triggered the man's suicide? Ben became such a different person when he drank that who knew what he could plan or do?

He hugged her sideways to him. "Brit, don't torture yourself like this. As for the Helter-as-killer theory, you mean he flew over the fence, shoved Ben in, then flew back over the fence, actually two tall fences?"

"That's it—I mean, that's the catch, one of the holes in my theory. I just pray Dad didn't know I went behind his back, that Helter didn't tell him and cause him to step into that cage to get the insurance money so I wouldn't sell to Helter. Dad had to have done it himself in that case, but I still think Helter could have triggered it somehow. Maybe the fact I was so—so desperate to keep this place at any cost scared Dad. I didn't tell Mother, I didn't tell anyone—but now you…"

She dropped her half-eaten granola bar on her lap, covered her face with both hands and sobbed so hard she shook him too when he put both arms around her.

Though Claire was only able to quickly hang a few of the orchids along the fence before the Comfort Zone kids arrived, she loved the look of it, the way it softened the area and seemed to draw the foliage from the empty lot behind their property inward. But she had little time to admire it since she had to greet their scuba diver guest and speaker, Sean Armstrong. He looked to be in his late twenties, a tall blond with spiky hair and a friendly face.

"So any of these signs you want me to emphasize with the kids?" he asked as he sat in a lounge chair by the pool to unpack his gear. "Here, a list of them with sketches."

She studied the laminated plastic sheet he handed her. So many of them, so it would be best to select just a few. *Standard Diving Hand Signals*, they were called. "Since these are at-risk kids," she told him, "we definitely want the signals that indicate distress or 'I need help.'"

"Okay. That would include the wagging finger one for 'something is wrong.' Also the big arm sweep for 'distress' or 'help.'"

"Good. 'Come here' and the 'watch me' ones could be useful too. If you have time, maybe this double-pointed hand one that means, 'you lead, I'll follow.' I told you several of the parents, foster parents or caregivers will be here, so keep that in mind if you mention circumstances where children might need help."

"Got it. Will do. This is a good idea about silent signals for abused or endangered kids. You ought to write it up or post it online or something like that."

"Well, let's see how it goes first."

Darcy arrived with two of the children who did not have an adult coming, and with Jilly and Lexi, who ran inside to change into their swimsuits. Claire was glad to see that Marta had come with Duncan, who was already eyeing the pool and talking to Sean about trying on his mask.

"I wish I had a mask to hide sometimes," Claire overheard him confide to Sean. But she could tell the boy felt safe here. For once, he didn't keep glancing around as if looking for someone.

When everyone had arrived, Gina and Heck came back to the pool from greeting the guests.

"I wish Nick was here to see this," Claire told them.

Heck rolled his eyes. "I s'pose him and Bronco'll be back soon from the Trophy Ranch. Hope he doesn't have my head for a trophy when he hears the old tiger woman's coming here. She say when? What if she shows up during this lesson, now that she has your address?"

"Heck, calm down," Claire told him. "I'm sure he'll be glad to have Gracie on our territory instead of the other way around. And nothing bad happened."

Heck nodded, but it annoyed her that he rolled his eyes again, as if he was expecting something to go wrong. She left him to Gina and hurried back to the edge of the pool to help keep an eye on the kids.

★ ★ ★

After a great brunch served in the lodge, Bronco, Nick, Grant and Stan ventured out over what Stan jokingly called "the back forty"—vast grasslands, swamps and glades. They saw animals, sometimes spooking them to move or even groups of them to stampede. But they stopped at a sign that said STAY OUT.

"What's so special about the land beyond this sign?" Nick asked, lifting himself out of his seat to survey it in the bright, crisp October air.

"It's kind of like a high rollers hunt club," Grant answered for Stan. "Special privileges to stay or shoot here on more-or-less virgin land. There is some fencing back a ways to be sure prime game stays in there."

"Certain guests stay there?"

"There are two treetop cabins, specially built," Grant said. "You know, the price you pay for private paradise. There are four German industrialists there now, with guides, valets and drivers."

So, Nick thought, as Stan drove them away from the verboten area marked only by that crude wooden sign, that might bring in a fortune from people who had a fortune. Deepest Africa in the heart of Florida.

They came upon the half-eaten carcass of a white-tailed doe. Actually, the corpse looked more dissolved than eaten.

"See—pythons at work, right, Bronco?" Stan asked.

"Looks like it to me. You'd think something that could run away wouldn't end up like that inside a slow-moving snake, but, yeah. Ten to one, there's a big Burmese python or more than one nearby. The snake would have squeezed it to death, then ingested it—part of it anyway. I saw some armadillos back there, and the snakes like to hide and mate in their burrows. With armadillo protective plates, the snakes couldn't digest them anyway, but this—for sure."

At the largest of the gator holes they approached, to Nick's surprise, Stan stopped the buggy and climbed down. "I want to show Bronco one heck of a big boy, since he's familiar with gators," he said. "Sit tight. We'll be right back. I haven't let anyone bag the gator I call Big Mac, because I'm kind of proud of him, like he's been here since the dinosaurs."

Nick wasn't anxious to get out in gator land anyway, and those biting fire ants had been mentioned more than once. While Bronco and Stan walked a short distance, he and Grant shot the breeze, as his dad used to say. It felt amazing to be out here on this immense stretch of land with open sky. Even if someone didn't hunt, the trophy here was feeling free.

Nick could see Stan talking to Bronco, pointing things out. Bronco wasn't saying much, but shook his head a couple of times and shrugged. Yet he looked intent on whatever Stan was saying. They came tramping back through the sawgrass and got in.

Time seemed unnecessary and almost silly out here, but Nick glanced at his watch. Two thirty, so Claire and Darcy would be in the middle of their lesson with the kids and a few adults. Although she was a big help to him on the Tiger Cage Case, he wished she'd just stick to the Comfort Zone kids for now, at least until she had the baby.

Nick could tell something was really eating at Bronco as he drove them back into Naples. "Did I say something to upset you?" Nick asked.

"Not you. Him. Stan the man, 'Big Cat.'"

He turned more toward Bronco. "What did he say?"

"Actually, a really good job offer."

"Catching gators or snakes?"

"You a mind reader, boss?"

"No, a demented defense attorney. What kind of job?"

"Real lucrative. And with the wedding and us wanting to get a house of our own and all soon…"

"Not a full-time job, I hope. I need you, Bronco. Tell me the specifics."

"Rooting out pythons on the property, but that would take a lot of time. Big pay by the hour, whether I find a snake or not, extra for each one I bring in dead or alive. He wants to put a couple of them on display."

"In cozy captivity—in the same cage or area? Wouldn't that breed more? He doesn't think his guests want to hunt them, does he? I hope he doesn't want to show people how they eat deer. Gross and cruel. Listen, once you're working that vast spread, I might never see you again, or Nita either. Not meaning a python would get you, but it would be a time suck. He offered a lot of money?"

Bronco quoted the offer. It was double what Nick paid by the hour, and he was paying Bronco at almost consultant levels.

"I should have realized he had an ulterior motive," Nick muttered.

"An altered motive?"

"Never mind. I know you're skilled at that, Bronco, as much as catching gators. You did a great job helping to head up that massive hunt with six hundred others earlier this year. I can't afford to lose you, but I suppose you can't afford to turn down that much money. Still, maybe this is a blessing in disguise since I don't trust Stan Helter. Until we get all this figured out, maybe it's a job you can take—if you're willing, and if he'll let you do it half-time. And, since you're getting married soon, you'd better learn to ask your future wife. Those pythons can be deadly, but, believe me, a wife can be too if you overstep or don't consult."

"Is that a joke, boss?"

"Not if you want a long and happy married life, my friend. I haven't been married that long, but forget your tough man gator-and-snake skills when it comes to a woman. Got that?"

"Sure. Thanks. I thought you'd be real upset. If I can stay working for you, and I can keep an eye on that place too, then I'm game."

"Don't say you're 'game' if you're going to work on that hunting ranch."

"Okay. I'll keep my eyes open there and my mouth shut. Bet you're going to say that's another good marriage move, right?"

The hand signals and pool party had been a big success. The kids had taken to Sean well, and they'd all learned "scuba talk signals." Several of them, however, thought that made them ready to dive with the mask, fins and tank, but Sean had said that was for another day and he'd love to come back.

After Darcy walked Sean to his truck and paid him, Claire and Darcy, as cosponsors, said goodbye to everyone. They waved them away as they pulled out of the driveway while Heck and Gina were kind enough to stay out back to start to clean up. Only Marta and Duncan, as well as Lexi and Jilly, remained.

"I'd like to swim like that," Duncan said with a hint of a smile. "Like a fish, breathing underwater."

"Maybe you can learn, since Sean's coming back," Claire said, happy he seemed content, even hopeful. Smiles were rare from Duncan.

"Because," he went on, looking suddenly serious again, "it would be a great place to hide."

Marta put in, "You don't need to hide anymore Duck—Duncan. He's not here."

The boy shrugged. "I just think he is sometimes."

Claire and Darcy exchanged quick glances. Claire was tempted to say something comforting, but she wasn't sure what. The child had lived with fear and pain so long that it might take his father being caught and imprisoned to really make him feel safe.

"Well, gotta go, and thanks again," Marta said, and opened the squeaky truck door so that the boy could climb in. It was an old truck with a dented side door. Claire assumed it might have been Irv Glover's.

They pulled out, honked and drove away. Darcy hugged Claire and Lexi, and went around the side of her van while Claire opened the door for Jilly and made sure she fastened her seat belt. Sometimes lately, Claire wished she could strap herself into one too.

"See you soon!" Lexi called as Jilly rolled down her window. "I like the game where we name the baby!"

"What game—and baby?" Claire asked, as if she didn't know.

"If you would just find out from the doctor and tell us if I'll have a brother or sister, it would be way better," Lexi scolded.

"From the lips of children," Darcy called out. "Our children."

Claire pulled Lexi back a step and Darcy backed out just as Claire saw Bronco's new truck approaching down the cul-de-sac. As she turned to wave, she heard a *thump-thump* and Lexi screamed.

Claire turned and screamed too, jerking Lexi back so hard they almost fell. Darcy, halfway down the driveway, hit the brakes. Under her van—huge, run over, maybe dead—a long brown and beige mottled snake lay coiled with several dead rats near its fangs.

# CHAPTER SIXTEEN

Claire pulled Lexi farther away. But it was dead, wasn't it? The snake was run over—in pieces.

Darcy and Jilly stayed in their vehicle. Bronco slammed his truck to a stop on the street and jumped out with Nick right behind him.

"What in—" Nick said before he saw what it was.

"It—we didn't see it!" Claire called to him. "Darcy ran over it. Are those rats it was eating?"

Nick leaned forward to study it but didn't step closer. Claire stayed frozen where she was with a hard hold on Lexi.

"Even if part of it moves, it's dead, boss," Bronco said. "It's been dead awhile."

"So it was killed, then planted here, like the gator in the pool," Nick said. He turned his head to look at Claire, a steady, wide-eyed stare, as if he were in shock. She tore her gaze away. Three of their neighbors were hurrying over, the Blakes and Mrs. Nelson.

"Cover that with something," Nick told Bronco.

"Got a tarp in the back," he said, and jogged toward his truck.

"Hey, that's one of those Everglades pythons, isn't it?" Tony Blake, their neighbor on the north side, asked. "Man, that's one way to get rid of them. But in our neighborhood?"

Nick was punching numbers into his phone, but told him, "We don't think it just crawled in, so don't worry. Part of the price I pay for being a criminal lawyer."

"Oh—oh, yeah, thank God," he said, and hurried back toward his house, hopefully not to bring more gawkers. Bronco spread a bright yellow tarp over the corpses. But Mrs. Blake stayed on the curb, taking pictures or video with her cell phone. Claire could tell Nick wanted her and Mrs. Nelson, who was talking on her phone, to go away too. He turned his back to them and spoke to someone on his phone; she assumed the Fish and Wildlife Conservation Commission officers.

Wildlife—would her marriage to Nick always be that? If so, he was worth it. She moved herself and Lexi into the line of Mrs. Blake's vision, and she got the message and backed off too. But what would she do with the pictures on her phone? At least there was nothing but a tarp to photograph right now.

When their neighbors left, Claire and Lexi came closer to stand behind Nick, who was off his phone now. Though Claire just stared at the tarp, she could still picture what was under it. Stomach-churning, but no blood, which might mean, like the gator, the snake had indeed been dead before being placed here. And the dead rats—a warning for someone not to be a rat, not to squeal, as the Mafia lingo went, or else? But to squeal about what? Were they the rats or the dead snake? What exactly was the message? And from whom?

Nick was hoping the same two Florida Fish and Wildlife Conservation Commission officers would not come back, but they must have specific areas they covered, because here they were. He knew they'd see a pattern and be suspicious, but then word would probably spread anyway. Though Bronco had covered the gross corpses, the neighborhood was coming around in a growing crowd, including parents with little kids. This was not a good way to make local friends.

Nick had been hoping to keep this contained, but he figured now it was like Pandora's box. Questions and answers would link him to the BAA, to Ben's death, and blow it up in the papers again when they needed to protect Ann and Brit. Then too, he had some other hot cases going at the firm, so he couldn't be positive this was tied to investigating Ben's death. But the use of animals—killer creatures—could be a link.

"Same MO," the older FWC officer—Andy Kurtz—said when he lifted the tarp and peered underneath. "Another dangerous animal, dead on arrival, but not cut up this time—though it musta been dead when the car wheels mashed it. Man, the rats are a strange touch. What the heck can it mean, other than you got someone with a sick sense of humor or real ill will, Mr. Markwood?"

"Yeah, I got that message too."

"You being a lawyer and all might explain it. Some folks resent those big per-hour fees, you know."

Nick's gaze snagged Claire's again, and he didn't answer. She'd sent Lexi inside with Darcy and Jilly, but she looked as if she were going to dry heave. She'd insisted on staying, on helping—par for the course. He loved her for her support and tenacity, but this was getting dangerous. Someone was desperate enough to risk being seen dumping dead animals in broad daylight, though the neighbors had evidently noticed nothing suspicious or even unusual.

"By the way," Wayne, the younger of the two wildlife officers, told him, "we did a necropsy on the gator. It was killed with a gig—a sort of spear point in its small brain. And whoever did it was skilled. It hardly showed the spot on the head. The slashes on its throat were done postmortem—not much blood—with a large knife."

Nick just nodded as he and Claire exchanged another quick look. Were they both thinking of Gracie Cobham's sons slicing into that possum?

Bronco kept hovering, and Nick was grateful for that. If anyone knew gators and pythons, it was his right-hand man. He hadn't said much, but he spoke now when the officers finally removed the tarp to a murmur from more neighbors who had gathered when word spread.

"See that little dark point on the back of the snake's head, boss?" he said, pointing. "Gigged too, I bet. Same bastard at work, even if both gators and Burmese pythons in the Glades are legal kills now."

Officer Kurtz told Bronco, "You got that right—and

good for you for spotting that gig mark. I'll put that in my report."

"I hope you can take all this away like you did before," Nick urged them. "You did a great job with the gator and—"

He saw a police car coming. That's all they needed, a police report, questions, the newspaper or TV finding out about this, especially if it went over the police radio. What if Mrs. Blake had already posted pictures who-knew-where online? All he needed was this going local, let alone viral.

Nick was sorry he didn't recognize this Naples PD officer or he would have asked him for a favor, but no such luck. This was most definitely not his day.

Bronco pointed to Nick as "the man," the homeowner here. The policeman, Officer Scott, introduced himself, then squatted to look at the carcass.

"Not seen one of these big babies in person," he said. "Well, shouldn't say baby. Are those three things, one partway in its mouth, rats? This some kind of hate crime, Mr. Markwood?" he asked, straightening to turn back to Nick. "Saw a report from FWC says you got a dead gator tossed in your pool. You got any enemies?"

"I'm a criminal attorney, so I'd have to say yes," Nick told him, keeping his voice down in the growing crowd. "But I don't know who would do this. If someone thinks this is going to make me back off cases I'm on, no way. I've dealt with snakes and rats before, the human kind, and, in more ways than one, this hits too close to home."

Claire had stuck close again after he'd introduced her

to the officer. Nick saw her biting her lower lip, tears in her eyes, but she still nodded in silent, stalwart agreement. What would he ever do without her?

That night, when everyone had gone and Lexi was finally asleep, Claire and Nick huddled, sitting up in their bed with their backs against pillows and the headboard.

"I asked every neighbor who showed up if they'd seen anything unusual in the way of vehicles," she said. "Carol Blake had seen a pool-cleaning van, so it could have been that. I'll need to find out if anyone had their pool serviced or cleaned. Carol didn't recall what it said on the side, so if none of the neighbors can attest to its presence, that's probably a dead end."

"I've thought it a hundred times today, but I don't know what I'd do without you," he said, and reached out to lift her hand to his lips and kiss her palm, but she wasn't finished.

"Nick, it would have taken more than one person to shove that big snake under Darcy's car, and then arrange it that way. Coil it up, place the rats and all. And someone with access to wild territory."

He just shook his head. He'd made a sketch of the positioning of the snake and the rats, trying to discern if there was a hidden meaning besides the apparent threat.

Ironic that he and Bronco had so recently discussed the job offer from Stan Helter about catching and killing snakes. Helter had access to snakes on the ranch, but why would he intentionally link his wanting to kill pythons to one being on their property? And it was unlikely he could have beaten them back here to leave this one on their driveway, though he could've just ordered one of his staff to do it. Could it be just chance, a threat from another case Nick was working on that had nothing to do with the BAA? He couldn't think of one that fit, so he'd bring it up in a staff meeting.

"Life goes on, right, sweetheart?" he asked. "Dead gators and snakes aside, we'll have the wedding here next weekend anyway."

She sighed. "Yes, and pray it goes well. The plans are set now, and Bronco and Nita are still willing after all of this, and so excited."

He saw she still had the plastic-covered note Ben Hoffman had written on her nightstand, and he was going to protest if she spent much more time staring at it. They'd been discussing whether they were holding back possible evidence.

Nick saw the time on the digital clock next to the letter read nearly midnight. They had to settle down and get some sleep, Claire especially since she'd taken her sleeping meds a while ago. But like him, she was revved up. How in heck had a kiddie visit to a petting zoo morphed into all this?

"We're not going through that stack of mail tonight," she told him, as if she'd read his thoughts about needing sleep, but he dumped the mail on his lap from his nightstand anyway. It had come in the late afternoon, and they hadn't had time for it or anything else but calming Lexi and each other.

"But what if there's a note here—a message to go with the snake?" he insisted. He sat up straighter, shuffling through the pile of letters and tossing the magazines on the floor.

"Anything?" she asked, with a huge yawn almost obliterating her words.

"Well—something from Lane Hoffman. I can't believe Ann would tell him about that letter his dad wrote, and he's not shy about verbal attacks, but a letter? It doesn't look like a legal document, a cease and desist order, anything like that."

He tossed the envelope onto Claire's lap, and she opened it with a fingernail under the flap. "Darn," she said. "One of those paper cuts that hurt and never heal. What a day!"

As she pulled out a folded note, a thin swipe of blood from her finger smeared across it. Two smaller, stiffer pieces of paper fell on her lap. "Oh, Nick. Lane has sent us tickets for two loge seats at the symphony for the Sunday evening performance, the day after Bronco and Nita's wedding. They're playing Gershwin's *Rhapsody in Blue*. So maybe he wants to mend bridges with us. Maybe he feels guilty for being so brusque and rude. And there's a note with it."

She opened it and gasped.

"A threat?" he asked, leaning toward her and taking the folded paper. "No," he said, skimming it, "nice enough, saying that he's been hasty and upset and apologizes." He looked up at Claire. She'd gone as white as—as the sheet she had pulled up to her growing stomach and was gripping with both hands.

"Sweetheart, are you nauseous? I thought you were over morning sickness, and we're far from morning."

"No—look there," she said, loosing the wadded sheet and pointing at the note.

"You mean that it's printed?"

"I mean *how* it's printed," she insisted, and grabbed the plastic-covered letter from her bedside table. Her hands were shaking.

"Nick, look! Lane wrote this suicide note, not his father!"

# CHAPTER SEVENTEEN

The next day, Sunday, six days before Nita and Bronco's wedding, Claire had no time to find a way to corner Lane. Seeing him after the concert would have to do so it didn't look like they were onto the fact that he wrote his father's letter. She had compared more of the printing and was sure it was Lane's. They needed to know when and why he wrote what now sounded like a fake suicide letter, but they had decided not to tell Ann or Brit, or especially full-steam-ahead Jace, until they got some answers. But this afternoon, their house was in chaos.

Bronco had gone to the Trophy Ranch to sign a part-time work contract with Stan Helter, though he wouldn't start until a week after the wedding. Nita was overseeing the professional cleaning of the driveway from the mess yesterday. Pictures of it had been trending online, but their avid neighborhood photographer had not mentioned the exact site of the gruesome array. So far, local news had not picked it up.

This afternoon, Nita and Claire went over the RSVPs for the wedding and rechecked their numbers for the cake and catered food to feed thirty people. With Claire's help, Nita tried on her wedding dress again in the guest bedroom. It was made by their friend Liz Collister, who usually designed corsets, the woman Gina worked for as a caregiver for her father's Alzheimer's disease. Chairs for the outside ceremony and rented card tables for the reception leaned against the wall in the Florida room along with a box of white folding-chair covers and tablecloths.

Claire was proud to have come up with another idea to help Duncan and Marta. The wedding was on Marta's day off from her job at Taco Bell, so they had hired her to help serve and clean up for the wedding so Claire and Gina could just be guests. That was a Saturday they would not meet with the Comfort Zone kids, but Marta had arranged for Duncan to go to a friend's house.

Lexi, thank heavens, was at Darcy's, because she'd been driving Claire crazy with practicing being a flower girl, not to mention coming up with name after name for a new sister or brother. When the doorbell rang, Claire thought Nita might need help with the concrete cleaner, so she hurried to answer the door.

The cleaning man was gone. Nita stood there, but so did Gracie Cobham with one of her "boys," and both of their arms were full of orchid plants in baskets.

"Oh, Gracie," Claire said, "I didn't know you were coming today."

"Don't have a phone," the old woman said. "Don't like

them. Cost too much. We got us a few more plants in the truck."

"They're beautiful."

"Claire, you ordered these without telling us, didn't you?" Nita said, tears in her eyes. "It's going to be so beautiful."

"Of course it is," Gracie told her.

"Ah, rather than bring those through the house," Claire said, stepping out, "let me go through and unlock the gate, and we can bring them straight into the backyard that way." She was thinking Nick would have a fit if he came downstairs from going over some casework and found Gracie and her son. She wasn't sure of his name. And had he been the one with the knife or the hatchet at the BAA? She hoped Nick was wrong that she was out of her mind to befriend these people.

Claire closed the door and tore through the house, unlocked the gate with the combination lock and hurried out to the front to help carry orchids.

"We're certainly going to pay you for these, Gracie. We're having a special event here soon, and we want the backyard to look lovely. Friends of ours are getting married. As a matter of fact, this is the bride."

"Outside's best place for that," Gracie said from behind a massive blooming white Vanda orchid. "Got hitched outside myself, way back when."

Everything was shaping up, Claire thought with a sigh—until Nick came out on the patio. But he shook hands and thanked the Cobhams. Nita brought out iced tea and scones, and, though Nick sat at a table to keep an eye on things, he had a nice chat with Ronnie—what a too-cute name for a hefty six-footer. At least Claire felt relieved. The old woman had the three interior sides of the new fence abloom in no time.

"Oh, Gracie," Claire said to her as they worked in the back corner to hang the last of the orchids, "I meant to ask you something." She figured if she didn't ask this now when everything was going well, the chance might not come again. "You said at the BAA something about you were tired of looking through the fence at Thunder. But which fence? I didn't realize you could see his cage except through the Trophy Ranch's fence—not a public one."

Gracie snorted. "You think I didn't climb trees for years when it was still legal to snatch these plants out of 'em? Hangin' high, most of 'em."

"But the ranch is all fenced off, and around the BAA there's a second fence. Wasn't it dangerous to climb a tree? As for the fence, the twisted cross wire is hardly big enough to get a foot in."

"Ladders, my girl."

"You mean you went over into the ranch land?"

"Then come across near the BAA. Crossed the ranch fence, not the BAA one, but I could see the cage from there."

"But the ranch has a gate you could have used and—"

"Thought of that, of course, but they control it inward somehow. They got some touchy guards, even one, I swear, lives near the front gate. Prob'ly rained it all off now," she went on, hands on her hips, "but there was mud caked on the fence footholds some of those places where you can get a ladder in a tree, then get over the fence, have the ladder pulled over to the other side. Someone climbed it afore me—I saw ladder holes in the mud. I watched my baby Thunder, but not close enough he could hear me or I could get proper food to him. Now, don't you go tellin' those ranch guards or that zookeeper Jackson that stays there all night that an old woman outsmarted them."

Claire finally remembered to close her mouth. Gracie had not been afraid that she'd meet a ranch hand or a wild animal because she wanted to see her own wild animal. And she'd seen evidence someone had climbed that way before. But was that all true? And could they really trust, since fences were no obstacles, that Gracie or her sons had not climbed over, then hit and pushed Ben into Thunder's cage?

Before Bronco arrived to pick up Nita, he phoned ahead to tell Nick he wanted to see him outside before he got to the house.

"You okay?" Nick asked on his phone. "Something happen at the ranch or are you getting cold feet?"

"What?"

"Nervous about the wedding?"

"Naw, I got warm feet and other parts too. I just want to tell you something alone."

"I'll come out to meet the truck down the street a ways. Hope you found something out about dead gators and snakes."

"Five minutes, boss."

Nick told Claire he was going for a short walk. Was there something Bronco didn't even want her to know, let alone Nita?

Bronco had parked down by the Crossing Danger sign.

That, Nick thought, as he stretched his strides to meet him, should be the name of the entire street—of his life.

"Hey," Nick greeted him, and got in the passenger side. "Just tell me. What did you learn?"

"There's girls there, boss. I mean, kind of for the taking. One Latina woman, she came on to me. I overheard one of the Japanese guests telling Mr. Helter it was better than the comfort girls his grandfather told him about during the war. I thought what if Nita found out so I—well, I can guess what a comfort girl was."

"Okay, hold on. A girl—a prostitute—was part of the deal for you? Like a job perk or something?"

Hands gripping the steering wheel as if he were still driving, Bronco nodded and exhaled a hard breath through clenched teeth. "And right before the wedding. I mean, I said no thanks and no way, but what if they meant to kind of blackmail me with that—with her—like take a picture and hold it over me to bring in snakes, or who knows what else?"

"I'm thinking that may be what Helter's hiding—the women, to make sure you don't rat him out—tell on him. Didn't mean to mention rats."

"This woman wasn't hidden, boss. And there was more than one of them around. I mean they may serve meals or clean up, and make beds, but the way they were acting, they're in beds too."

"I'm thinking those may be illegals, and that's what he has to hide, why it made him nervous to have the BAA owners and guests so close. He could be bringing them in to work for him from Mexico, or they could be Cubans he's picked up. I just hope they're not forced into that.

And that would make him and the ranch illegal. Before, I was thinking it might be he'd brought in exotic animals he had to hide, but it might be humans. You just make it clear you're getting married soon—"

"He knew that. Remember, when I met him I said that right away?"

"Yeah, I do. Maybe he thought you'd go for a final fling, a private bachelor party. Look, you don't need to go back there if you think there's a problem, too much pressure, a trap. I don't want you going to a place on my account if it seems risky, but I'll sure like to get evidence to fry Helter—including, maybe, prove he killed Ben."

"I know you were hoping I'd find things like that out," Bronco said, loosing the steering wheel at last. His fingers had gone white. "I owe you and Claire a lot, damn right I do. And I'm glad to help. We all been through worse. So I signed on to work half days three days a week, flexible hours to catch Burmese pythons—live ones. Course I didn't mention I'd just seen a dead one," he said, and forced a little snorted laugh.

Nick turned more toward Bronco and squeezed his shoulder. "If you think there's anything dangerous, you get out of there and come tell me. Stan's for sure not the only one I'm thinking might have urged or helped Ben commit 'suicide,' but he's still my number one."

Bronco nodded. "I'm not gonna tell Nita, not right away. If you tell your partner in crime—well, didn't mean it that way about Claire—make sure she don't tell Nita. I'll tell her my own way in my own time."

"Deal," Nick said, and they shook hands.

"Oh, yeah, one more thing," Bronco said, starting up

the engine as Nick braced himself for what bad news surprise was coming next. "That place might look backwoods, but I parked behind the lodge and glanced in a window. They got banks of TV screens monitoring the hunting areas, clear to the fences, including those two back tree house places. Lots of screens, like inside a TV studio. A couple guys had headphones on too."

Nick's thoughts started spinning. "I wonder if they make promotion videos or souvenir movies for hunters to take home with the heads of the mounted game. Maybe to keep track of the herd movements, so they can take their wealthy guests for a good hunt. Or, of course, security. Thanks for all that info, Bronco. It doesn't mean Stan somehow was responsible for Ben's death, but if not, we may get him on something else. Stay safe, but keep your eyes and ears open there. Now let's go see our women and talk wedding."

The house had finally settled down after dinner when there was a knock on the door. Nick, Claire and Lexi had just started playing the board game called Chutes and Ladders, though Claire kept thinking about that old woman climbing ladders to get a glimpse of her pet tiger—and the fact she'd said someone else had been using a ladder too.

"I'll see who's there," Nick said, getting up. "After all the excitement, we don't need any more."

It was Lexi's turn, so Claire trailed along behind Nick, preparing herself for something bad. But it was Marta Glover at the door, still in her black Taco Bell shirt and slacks. Her old truck was out in front, but Duncan was not in sight.

Nick unlocked the screen door. "Are you all right?" Claire asked, drawing Marta in. "Where's Duncan?"

"Still at the sitter's. I should have called first, but didn't think to. Did you say something about you used to have nightmares, Mrs. Claire?"

"Come in and sit down," Claire said, urging her toward the front library room rather than taking her back where Lexi would overhear. Claire clicked on a light, and they sat on the leather couch, facing each other.

Nick told them, "I'll go make sure Lexi doesn't manage to win the game with neither of us there. If you need any help from me, just let me know. Lexi has nightmares too, Mrs. Glover. Part of growing up."

"But not like this," she whispered when she and Claire were alone. "Your house—so pretty and big," she added, looking around the room.

"We just moved in a few months ago. More room for the baby," Claire told her, but again, she wished she could help Marta get out of that trailer. "So—yes, I've had nightmares for years, partly from a disease I've had since my early teens. It's called narcolepsy. I still have to take my medicine, and I also use some herbs to be able to stay awake, to sleep on time and avoid weird, bad dreams where I really lose reality."

"Well, you think Duncan can have that disease?"

"I haven't seen signs of it in him, Marta. He seems alert during the day, when I used to practically sleep standing up until I got treatment."

"It's the same bad dream. Well, I can understand it some. He thinks he sees his daddy watching him."

Claire's head jerked. "In his bed in the trailer? While he's sleeping?"

"Says when he sleeps he remembers being watched. Says he hears noises outside. He opened the curtain by his bed more'n once and thought he saw Irv watching, even through the trailer-park fence."

A picture of Gracie watching her dear tiger through the fence shot through Claire's mind, but she steadied herself. "Marta, you realize how much it traumatized—that is, shook up—Duncan that his father was such a violent man. To him, to you and to others."

"A killer too. You can say it."

"Let me ask this. Are you sure that your husband—"

"I want to divorce that man! I'm saving money to get rid of him!"

"All right, but let's stick with Duncan now," she said, taking Marta's trembling hands in hers. "Are you certain that Duncan's father really is in Tennessee? Could he have come back, be hanging around, watching you or the boy?"

"I'd be out of here, living in the woods or anywhere if I thought that. Those checks are postmarked Tennessee, and he's even been spotted there, a positive ID the sheriff said. I pray each night the police there will haul him in and put him away for good—for being so bad."

Nick knocked on the open door and stepped in. "Sorry, but I was coming back and heard what you said, Marta. Do you have a restraining order on Irv?"

"It run out about when he took off. He don't pay no heed to something like that."

"But I think I'll get you one anyway—get your old one renewed. If he's spotted anywhere around, it might help to get you police protection, and we can arrange for an officer to drop by now and then, in case he does show up—and, if he's watching you, to keep him away."

"I was telling Mrs. Claire here the boy's having bad dreams over that, but I swear it's all in his head. If I could, I'd take him to a fancy shrink."

"Well, I'm not a fancy shrink, not even a shrink," Claire told her, loosing her hands, "but I am a psychologist, and I'd be happy to have you and Duncan here to use our pool, because he seemed to really love that. And then I'd have some time to see if we can settle him down and assure him he's safe."

"But you got that big wedding next week."

"Then how about midweek, some evening after you get off work, under the patio lights? I could tell he liked our big, solid fence, so he'll feel safe here to have fun and to talk. Just talking can help," Claire tried to assure her.

"It sure does," she said with a decisive nod, even as she blinked away tears. "It sure enough does."

# CHAPTER EIGHTEEN

Monday morning, Nick called his secretary to say he'd be in late, and after they dropped Lexi at preschool, he and Claire drove out to the BAA to see Ann. She'd told them she was keeping regular hours there but, when they arrived, Jackson said she wasn't on-site.

"Had a migraine headache and stayed put at their—her—house," he told them with a heavy sigh as he scattered cut-up vegetables and shrimp for the flamingos. He had mud on his jeans and had stuck a shovel in the soil near the moat. "She's kind of losing it, and I don't blame her. Folks mourn in their own ways. Brittany's here, though, brought by your friend Jace. They're back in the trailer mapping strategy. We gotta reopen soon, but we been threatened with more than one group picketing out front if we do."

Claire told him, "But you're doing what's important,

taking care of these beautiful birds and the other animals here in honor of Ben and for Ann and Brittany."

"Sure am, though Brittany's totally in charge of that tiger now. Two of these birds here getting ready to nest," he announced with a grin, as if he were a proud grandfather. "Not only are they pretty, they're smart." He came a few steps closer and leaned with both muddy hands on the handle of the shovel. "Monogamous—mate for life. Don't lay a whole bunch of eggs, so no hatchlings get ignored. In a nest of mud, feathers, a few stones or shells, they lay only one egg that hatches after thirty days, then they take good care of the chick. Believe in marriage for life, myself. Just missing my wife, Pearl, real bad now and then."

"I'm sorry for your loss," Claire said. "I'm sure you had a happy marriage."

"Funny to say this, but so do some of my pink pets here." He nodded at a pair of flamingos who were actually billing and cooing. "So today, I'm working to dig them a little canal on the elevated spot on this small island back in there." He nodded at the elevated islet, heavy with foliage and surrounded by the shallow, three-sided moat. "It's the highest spot not only on this property, but for miles around, far as I can tell. They can nest real private back in there, build on dry ground, not be gawked at, though they seem happy enough to be admired the rest of the time."

Nick said, "They're lucky to have you, and Ann and Brit are too. See you later."

As they walked back toward the trailer, Nick told Claire, "Since Ann's not here, why don't you stash the Ben/Lane letter in your purse? Let's try talking about Lane without letting Brit know we have it, especially since Ann doesn't seem to have told her."

"I wonder if they're a family that kept secrets from each other," Claire mused aloud. "Serious ones."

When they knocked and called out, Jace came to the door.

"We thought Ann would be here and we'd see how she's doing," Nick explained as they went in and sat across the messy desk from where Brit and Jace had been working.

"Paying some bills Dad used to tend to," Brit told them. "Which makes me realize, like I said before, I'll never afford lawyer's fees."

"I told you I'd help," Jace put in.

"As my grandmother used to say," Brit went on with an affectionate pat on his arm when he sat back down next to her again, "we don't like to be beholden."

"I understand," Nick said, "but there's something to be said for be-holdin' on. Jackson says you need to open soon, but there are problems, outside pressure. At least it looks like you're not going to face a legal problem, so I can certainly advise you pro bono. I have a discretionary fund for that."

Claire and Jace exchanged a glance, but since Nick did not elaborate, neither of them brought up Nick's dedication to his South Shore clients.

Brit sighed and blinked back tears. "Pro bono—defending something good for free. I have no clue what I would do without you and Claire stepping up like this—Jace too, of course."

Claire saw her chance. "Because your mother's grieving and Lane is—well, really, what is Lane feeling?" she asked, looking directly at Brit.

"Eternally hurt," she said. "Bitter. Overly pompous and music-possessed to make up for and hide out from all that."

Claire was stunned at how honest and perceptive that was. "Who hurt Lane, would he say? Would he blame your father or mother?"

"Both, and me, I suppose. Head in the clouds, that's Lane, but don't get in his earthly way. Our parents just didn't get it that someone could live off his musical talent if he wasn't some rock star. A classical music major in the family? What a shock. No way that could make sense to practical, hardworking people."

"Did Lane avoid them or clash with them?" Claire asked, trying not to sit forward in her chair or sound too eager. If she glanced down, she could see the corner of the plastic-covered, so-called suicide note protruding from her purse at her feet. And if there were any chance at all that Lane could have arranged for his father to be hurt, that paper was legal evidence, at least of possible fraud if not much more.

"He clashed with Dad," she admitted with a sigh. "Sulked. Threw each performance, each great review in Dad's face, though Dad said he was proud of him and went to lots of his performances, at least these last few years. Why? You don't think Lane would do something to hurt Dad? He was miles away when Dad died, and he'd want nothing to do with Tiberia or this place."

"Lane's wife didn't seem too hard hit by the loss," Nick put in.

Jace said, "I've met her. She's an airhead. Sculptured,

sprayed hair. The perfect tan, the perfect nail polish job, a husband who is an ar-teest, kids who behave."

"Which they don't," Brit said, raking her fingers like a huge comb through her hair. "What's that about the sins of the father can be spread to the children? But listen, I do have something to tell you. I've already explained it to Jace, something I should not have done but I thought it would work out. About two weeks ago now, I approached Stan Helter on neutral ground to see, since the BAA is in my name, if we could work out a deal where he bought the land but didn't take over or even let on until my parents were both gone."

"Damn," Nick whispered. "I mean, not that you did that—risky as it was trusting him—but I'll be damned if that doesn't give Helter even more of a motive for possibly hurting your father—to hurry things along before Ben could step in and mess up his plans. You ever hear that saying, 'Lord, give me patience, but give it to me right now'? That's the way I read Stan Helter. No one crosses him for long."

Tears filled her eyes. Claire felt for her. She too had lost a father, even much earlier than Brit did, and it still hurt. Her dad had intentionally deserted them, and sometimes, when she and Darcy were young, they blamed themselves rather than him.

"I'm glad you told them, honey," Jace said, and put an arm around her. "The three of us are going to help you through this. And I'm glad they're here, because I've got to go fly. Remember what I told you about pilots needing to have situational awareness? You do too. Just keep on a steady course until you see which way to turn the wheel, okay?"

Brit walked Jace outside to see him off. Claire touched Nick's arm. "Speaking of that, maybe Jace can drop you off at the office, and I can stay here with Brit for a little while. Since Jace drove her here, that way, I'll have your car to bring her back into town on my way home—if she's not staying here."

"Sounds like a plan, because I should get going. I'll catch Jace. Besides, I see that I-can-learn-more-from-her look in your eyes. Let me have the Ben/Lane letter then," he said, and she handed it to him. "As for situational awareness, just be careful driving out on this narrow road."

"As Bronco and Heck say when you give them an order, will do, boss."

"And if she says anything else about meeting with Helter, take mental notes, but don't go near the ranch yourself. I wouldn't even trust him on so-called neutral ground."

He kissed her quickly and went out to explain to Brit and go back into town with Jace.

In Jace's car, Nick said, "I was thinking maybe you could fly over the Trophy Ranch, scope things out there. I've seen it on the ground but not way back in the private hunting area. Jace?" he prompted when there was no answer. "I'll pay for the flight."

"It isn't that. I already did it. Took Brit up a couple of months ago and went up myself since Ben died. There's nothing unusual I spotted even far back in, except for what looks like a couple of roofed buildings."

"Actually, tree houses for the highest-paying guests.

Helter doesn't make a secret of that, and I can't see it relates to any of this. But you didn't want to mention that
second flight?"

"You and Claire aren't the only ones who want to help
Brit. If I'd have seen anything off, I would have told you."

"I can tell you're serious about her."

"I am, but things are a little delicate lately so I'm trying
to be understanding. But it really ticks me off she went to
Helter behind her father's back—actually, behind mine.
How can a bright woman do something so damn risky
and just plain dumb?"

"I think I've finally got that message through to Claire.
She's taking fewer risks, not to be bullheaded, at least
lately, but we've all made mistakes, some dangerous."

"She's got to not only put Lexi first, but her—your—
baby," Jace went on, his voice rising. "I know she's always
been a bleeding heart for others' problems over her own."

"So, in this case, you think it's Helter behind all this
too?" Nick asked. He trusted Jace's opinion, but he could
get overly emotional at times, when you'd think the guy's
combat training would make him steadier.

"Let's just say he has the most to gain."

"How about someone who has motives for revenge?"

"Lane setting a score with his father, you mean?"

"You're starting to think like a lawyer, Jace."

"Or like someone in love. The woman I want is obsessed with a tiger and a petting zoo! Her dad had some
kind of hold over her from when she was young, I can
agree with Lane on that much. And Ann, of course, went
along with Ben's pipe dream. Oh, hell, now a certain
criminal attorney's going to think I parachuted in and

shoved Ben in that cage just because I have negative feelings toward him mixed in with hero worship, father figure stuff. Ten to one, Claire's got that all psyched out."

"Look, I have father issues, and so does Claire. Let's all keep calm."

"Nick, I thought the world of Ben Hoffman. He *was* almost the father I didn't have! But the most important person for me here is Brit. I hope Claire can help her. She's not sleeping much, of course, is obsessed with losing Ben and maybe with losing the BAA too. Why can't life and love just be simple?"

Nick had no answer to that. He thought of Jackson's faithful-to-each-other flamingos as they left the lonely, narrow lane road behind and merged with the two-lane traffic heading south into Naples.

"You didn't say you had to go to a meeting in town," Claire told Brit. "I was hoping we'd have more time to talk, that you could even show me behind Tiberia's cage, maybe where an intruder could get in."

"Look, sorry, but I wasn't thinking straight when Jace drove me here today. I forgot I'd accepted a speaking engagement and want to keep it—they're paying me an honorarium I can use—but if you could just drop me off there, I'll get a ride back home. It's at the main library on Orange Blossom."

"Sure, no problem," Claire said, deciding she'd just question her more in the car. She'd tread carefully, because she'd already upset Brit when she told her about Gracie Cobham's claims she had scaled both the ranch and BAA fences to get a glimpse of Tiberia. "I'm still working on preparations for a wedding at our house this Saturday anyway."

On their way out to Nick's car in the parking lot, they stopped by Flamingo Isle again. "Jackson!" Brit called. The birds shifted and scattered, though they never did that when Jackson raised his voice. "He's such a bird person," she told Claire. "And absolutely irreplaceable here."

He appeared from the foliage with his shovel again. "Tree roots to cut through," he called to them, "but I'm making progress. You ladies leaving? I was about to take a break, go get me some coffee back at my place."

"I forgot I had a paying gig at the main library today," Brit explained. "I'll get a ride home from there to check on Mother and then be back out midafternoon. You, dear man, are king of all you survey while I'm gone. And you've been working too hard since Dad—Dad left. Take as long a break as you want."

He gave them a one-handed wave and waded back through the moat toward the isle rather than his apartment back by the fence.

Claire really didn't like to drive Nick's car, a large, black sedan—like a hearse, she'd teased him more than once—but it ran beautifully. They headed out on the long, narrow, dirt road. This time of year started the dry season, and the car kicked up a cloud of dust behind them. No doubt, visitors to the BAA or Trophy Ranch thought they were really out in the backcountry here.

After some small talk, Claire was just about to ask more about her meeting with Stan Helter when Brit's cell phone sounded, and she grabbed it out of her big purse. The library wondering where she was? Jace checking in already?

He was surely protective of Brit, but then that was his nature—which could turn a bit too possessive, almost obsessive at times.

Yet Claire had to smile despite it all, because Brit's ringtone tune was "Talk to the Animals" from an old movie she and Lexi had watched on Netflix not long ago, *Doctor Dolittle*.

"Oh, Jackson, I see it's you on caller ID," Brit said. "Did I forget something? Is anything wrong?"

Claire could hear Jackson's voice raised but not quite what he was saying. He did sound upset, though, maybe panicked. Claire slowed the car.

"He found something," Brit said. "He wants us to come back right away, not tell anyone." She spoke into the phone again. "Jackson, is it about Dad? Just tell me. All right. All right. On our way, only about ten minutes down the road."

She turned back to Claire. "He won't say what it is, don't know why. Says we have to see it to believe it."

With difficulty since there were no driveways or turn-offs out here—the ranch lay behind them, beyond the BAA—Claire carefully turned the car to head back. Then she went faster than she wanted to.

"Does Jackson have any medical problems?" Claire asked as she leaned closer to the steering wheel. "Maybe he fell and hurt himself. Did he sound delirious or in pain?"

"Nothing I know of. It doesn't sound like he's hurt, just that he saw something, I think. He should have said what it was. Maybe he's called the police or the paramedics. I just hope it's nothing about Tiberia."

"Despite saying he was going for coffee, he was heading

back toward Flamingo Isle when we left. Do you want to try calling him again? Do we want to run into a situation that might be—well, surprising? We need to know more. Nick would say we need to be careful."

"Okay, okay," Brit said. "I suppose Jace would have my head too. I'll call back and tell him to sit tight, and we're just a few minutes away. Darn. I'm going to be late for that library talk. It's all just too much right now."

"I know, believe me, I do. I'll be right there with you," she promised as she did a quick turn into the BAA parking lot and drove as close as she could to the gate instead of going into the parking lot.

But, Claire thought, when Jackson didn't answer his phone and they jumped out of the car, she could only hope she wasn't tempting danger and disaster again.

# CHAPTER NINETEEN

They couldn't find Jackson anywhere. Claire even waded through the shallow water onto Flamingo Isle, calling his name. The flamingos peered at her and shied away as if she were an alien being. On the edge of the small raised island, she could see where he'd been digging to make an inlet for the nests. But he'd evidently decided to just cover up what he'd done, heaping soil back in. He'd even thrown some palmetto fronds across it. His shovel was nowhere in sight.

Claire hurried toward where Brit had gone to check the trailer and his apartment attached to the supply building, but she came running toward her.

"He's not back there. No coffee cup out or anything." They hurried toward Tiberia's cage. The tiger was restlessly pacing and glared at them, but Jackson was nowhere around, including in the work area behind the cage.

"Tiberia's upset about something," Brit said. "Someone's

been on the grounds, besides Jackson or us, that is. God forgive me, but I was scared we'd—we'd find him here. Let's walk the whole perimeter of the fence before we call the police. After what you said about the crazy Cobham woman and her sons climbing fences—well, maybe she came back and Jackson chased her off and one of her bruiser sons slugged him."

Claire wanted to defend Gracie, but she knew now was not the time. Yet how would Brit feel if someone took the tiger from her and gave it to someone else? She scolded herself for always getting emotionally involved with people. It was one of the pillars of forensic psychology that you had to learn to stay objective. Not doing so on an earlier case had almost cost her her life, and now she had another life she needed to protect too, she thought as she pressed a hand to her belly.

Claire was soon out of breath at the pace Brit set around the perimeter. But at the back turn toward the ranch, probably near where Gracie had said they'd scaled the fence to see the tiger, they saw Jackson on the ground on this side of the fences, turned away, sprawled in an awkward position.

"Jackson!" Brit screamed, and fell on her knees beside him.

"Don't turn him over! He may have hurt his head or his neck, even his spine. He's obviously unconscious."

"He didn't fall. There's no ladder here, and he couldn't climb that without one!"

Claire noticed a piece of snagged denim high on the fence, then bent over the prone man to feel for his neck pulse.

"He's alive!" she told Brit. "A pulse and he's breathing. But there's blood on the back of his skull, like on your dad, so maybe he wasn't meant to be. Call 911!"

Brit was already punching it in. She was right that there was no ladder, but imprints of one were on both sides of the fence. And, as far as Claire could tell, no piece of denim was torn or even snagged from Jackson's jeans.

"I'll go to the front gate to guide them in," Brit said once the paramedics were on their way.

"I'll call Nick and stay with Jackson."

"Stay safe… I'm scared to death there's a curse on this place," Brit gasped out and, despite breaking into sobs, took off running.

"I called Jackson's oldest daughter, Sarah, and she'll go to the ER at Naples Hospital to meet them," Brit told Claire. Claire was certain she could still hear the screech of the ambulance's siren, even though the paramedics with their unconscious patient had been gone for almost an hour. She felt like screaming herself.

Brit punched off her latest call, then muted the sound on her phone. It had been playing "Talk to the Animals" ever since the word got out about more trouble at the BAA. Newspaper reporters wanting a statement, the local TV Channel 28 news, friends of Brit's and Jackson's, and calls from Jackson's daughters.

She collapsed next to Claire on a picnic bench behind the BAA's supply building. Claire had called Nick to explain, and he was on his way. Because of Jackson's cryptic phone call, his small apartment and the shed had been cordoned off with POLICE LINE DO NOT CROSS yellow tape until the officers could obtain a search order and examine it. Officers were scouring the area between Flamingo Isle and the fence, looking for his cell phone, even wading through the water and annoying Jackson's precious pink pets.

An officer had taken the ripped piece of denim as evidence. Had Jackson tried to chase someone over the fence and been shoved back? Maybe he'd found a ladder there and tried to climb it and had fallen. The fence had no signs of blood, though the forensic team was on the way. So had he been assaulted? To Claire's dismay, Brit had told the officers about Gracie Cobham spying on the tiger from that area of the fence.

But the police had found something Claire had missed. At Flamingo Isle, someone had tried to scuff out drag marks of something heavy.

"He was always dragging big bags of feed and shrimps for the flamingos," Brit had told them. "He was feeding them earlier today, so it could be from that."

Finally, Nick arrived and was brought back by an officer. "Jace just called me because he couldn't get you," he told Brit. "He heard the news from someone at the Marco Island airport. He'll be here ASAP and insisted I tell you this had to be the last straw for your passion for this place—his words not mine.

"Claire," he said, turning toward her, "you're the eyewitness to the fact Brittany was not on the grounds when Jackson got hurt?"

"Yes, I can vouch for that. Are there—are there going to be charges against Brit for something? Jackson was fine when we left, then he called to say he'd found something he wouldn't explain over the phone, and we came back to find him unconscious."

"Comatose," Nick corrected, cell phone in hand. He was way ahead of them now, in what Claire always thought of as his "lawyer mode." "The hospital had to put him on life support, even before any brain scans. And, no, no one is being charged with anything, but the Backwoods Animal Adventure is to remain closed."

"Indefinitely?" Brit asked, blowing her nose and wiping under her eyes.

"For now, at least. Will you take your attorney's advice—and Jace's—on not fighting that?" Nick asked.

Brit nodded and put her head on her crossed arms on the picnic table. "He's won, you know. He saw I was vulnerable, and he won and it's all my fault—my dad, Jackson—this place being closed and cursed."

"'He' meaning Stan Helter?" Nick asked, keeping his voice low.

"Satan, one and the same," Brit said, her words muffled.

"Listen to me, Brittany," Nick said. "I'm going to sit with you again when the detective arrives to question you while things are fresh in your mind and then later, if you get called in. Claire will be a solid eyewitness when she makes her statement. But do not make any claims that you think you know who did this or your version of why. Stick to the facts of what happened today. Volunteer nothing else. Do you understand?"

She sat up, wiping under her eyes again. "Yes, but please make sure Jace doesn't do something crazy—like confront Helter, buzz their compound or something. He's like that, literally flying off, losing his temper now and then."

"I know," Claire told her, putting an arm around her shaking shoulders.

Nick crouched by the picnic bench between Claire and Brit. "And don't say anything like that about Jace to anyone but us," he said. "He admitted to me earlier today he was really upset with Ben for tying you so tight to this place. He loved Ben too but felt it might be time for you to let go here."

"Let go here and just hang on to him," Brit whispered, her voice bitter. "That's him—all or nothing."

Nick and Claire exchanged a wide-eyed glance, then both looked away. Feeling she needed to beat off a terrible thought that hung between them, Claire blurted, "Brit, you'd better call your mother back. Make sure she doesn't come out here today. It would just remind her of the other day—the other tragedy."

"You're right, but I hate to turn on my phone. It's like everyone's lurking there, waiting to pounce and rip me apart."

Claire and Nick exchanged yet another look. Her choice of words like *lurk, pounce* and *rip me apart* showed she was still obsessed with her dad's death. He frowned; she shook her head.

"Use my phone. Here," Claire told her and dug it out of her purse. She saw her narcolepsy meds there and the herbal substitutes she'd been trying to take lately—narco med lite, she thought of them compared to her subscription meds. She handed Brit her phone and grabbed the small bottle of water in her purse—and though she yearned to take the hard-hitting meds, she reached instead for the herbals.

★ ★ ★

Two days later on Wednesday evening, Duncan Glover perched on the side of their pool, gently kicking his feet in the water. Marta sat in a lounge chair with burritos and a soft drink, worn out after the day of work at the restaurant. Both Claire and Lexi were in the shallow end of the pool near Duncan. Though they had offered him an inflated whale, he'd opted for the child-sized, orange life preserver and still wasn't in a hurry to get in. Without his scuba diver friend Sean here right now, the boy had developed a big case of what Darcy would call "the yips."

"We won't go anywhere near the deep end," Claire assured him. "You'll be able to stand up right here."

"I don't know how to swim, not really."

"That's why you have the life jacket on, just like the one that makes Lexi float, see?"

"My dad threw me in once. Said learn to swim that way, but I didn't. I sank and swallowed water."

"Your father is not here," Claire said, her voice steady and almost stern. "Your mother and your friends, Lexi and I, are here now. Hold my hands and come on in, either just slide off the edge and I'll catch you or come down the steps."

The boy nodded, stood and went around to the steps, holding on to the aluminum rail with both hands as he descended. Claire waded over to meet him, and Lexi paddled close. When he was almost hip deep, Duncan glanced around at the fence, as if he were studying the hanging orchids, but Claire knew better. The poor, damaged child—despite a solid wood fence—was looking for his father.

"Duncan, did you understand that Mr. Nick has arranged for a police order that your dad must stay away from you and your mom, even if he would come back in this area?"

He shrugged. "Sure, but he doesn't pay no heed to that. He said so when—the last time he came back."

Such residual pain, spreading out like the ripples of this water. She thought of today when she'd left Brit with both her upset mother, Ann, and an angry Jace. Claire had asked the trembling Brit, who had insisted on making sure the tiger had calmed down from his pacing, "Could Tiberia have heard Jackson yell or seen an intruder and that's what set him off?"

"He's mostly been that way since Dad died. Paces until he's exhausted, licks himself as if he needs to get clean and falls asleep," she whispered back. "I just feel I'm losing someone else dear to me."

Claire remembered one of the snippets of a million things her mother had once read to them, things that had given her an English major education before she even declared a psych major or set foot in a university. She told Brit, "Hemingway wrote once something about not losing someone you've been really close to. You'll always have your father in your memory and heart, and we'll all pray Jackson pulls through." That had seemed to comfort her, however much Ann had looked puzzled and Jace had frowned.

But that seemed to be little Duncan's problem now. His horrid, hateful father was still and might always be in his head and heart.

Claire had high hopes that Bronco and Nita's wedding day would go well, though not much else had this week.

Jackson was still comatose—as a matter of fact, in a drug-induced coma until his brain swelling went down. The police had gone out to Gracie's house and found it deserted. The BAA was closed, and the police had not figured out who might have come over the fence to possibly harm Jackson.

Since the abutting land was the Trophy Ranch, an officer had spoken to Stan Helter and two of his guides—who evidently knew nothing about anyone climbing ladders or leaving telltale marks. Helter had said he'd assign a perimeter guard, though. He said the guy who guarded the front gate was on vacation. Meanwhile, Claire and Nick had racked their brains about whether Gracie and "the boys" could be involved and planned to question her themselves even though the police had found that they weren't at home.

But today, in preparation for a house wedding, background music was playing—one piece had too much violin in it and Claire fast-forwarded past it. Guests would soon be arriving, and both the Florida room and back patio area looked lovely. Once she made sure that Marta and two hired helpers reporting to her were under control in the kitchen, Claire went into the guest bedroom to see how Nita looked in her gown. Nick was out on the patio, hunkered down with Bronco and Heck as if they were laying battle plans.

"Oh, Nita, you look so beautiful!" Claire exclaimed. She saw Lexi and Jilly had wormed their way in here, Lexi toting her flower girl nosegay around already, though no way she was getting the rings tied to the little silk pillow until later. Gina was here too, fussing with the wisp of a veil Liz had made for Nita to go with the gown. Liz and Gina both were living, breathing proof that people could survive tough times, Claire thought, trying to buck herself up.

"People will be here soon, and Nick's going to play doorman!" Claire realized she had almost sung that out as if to cheer them all up. "Bronco's with Nick and Heck, and looks great too," she told Nita in a calmer voice.

The gown really was special. Since Liz usually designed corsets, the bodice was a close-fitting shimmering pale blue.

"Gina," Liz said, "do you plan to catch the bouquet when she throws it?"

"If I don't, Heck will," she said with a little laugh. "But the only thing I'm eloping with in the near future is American med school!"

"I will try to catch it," Lexi piped up. "I will keep it for my Barbie doll because I'm not sure she's really married to Ken or not. Is she, Mommy?"

"Still dating after all these years, I think. Now, how about you and Jilly come with me until Nita comes outside? And don't bother Marta in the kitchen, asking for mints or punch. Come on."

And so it went, a whirl of business and happiness for their dear friends Charles, aka Bronco, and Juanita, who exchanged their vows without a hitch, repeating carefully after the guest priest. After they were declared husband and wife, Mr. and Mrs. Gates, there were hugs and kisses all around, and Nita threw her bouquet right into Gina's stomach, so she had to catch it. Heck loved that.

Claire tried hard to put away, just for a while, thoughts

and worries about Jace, who was mostly brooding in the corner and left early. Like the bride and groom, Claire and Nick as host and hostess circulated among the decorated tables while guests ate. Nick led a toast, and everyone lifted their champagne glasses and enjoyed the cake. Then, as was custom in Nita's Mexican family, the bride and groom opened gifts with everyone still there. Nita looked radiant and Bronco, so proud and happy.

Claire could only hope they would accept the gift from her and Nick.

Meanwhile, Jasmine Montgomery Stanton, the woman who was at the center of the first murder-suicide case Claire had worked with Nick, had sent a $500 Home Depot gift certificate from St. Augustine, since Bronco used to work for her and "'I know you'll be fixing up a lovely house or apartment for your family to come.'" Bronco proudly read that note out loud.

"Wow!" Nita cried when she opened the envelope from Nick, Claire and Lexi. Bronco just stared at it. "We were going to just drive south and stay somewhere for a few days! Three nights at the Ritz Carleton here in Naples from the Markwoods!"

Crying, she hugged Claire and Nick and kissed Lexi, who was practically hanging on her skirts anyway. Liz's gift was, of course, a sexy, pale green brocade corset everyone applauded while Nita blushed and Bronco grinned. Gina and Heck gave them a laptop Heck had revamped with all sorts of user-friendly features.

"One more thing left," Bronco said, picking up a large white envelope from the gift table. "Thought we'd seen them all from you friends, and we can't thank you enough, 'specially Claire and Nick for this great gift of our honeymoon as well as the wedding."

He handed the envelope to Nita, and she slid a polished fingernail under the flap. Claire wondered who had brought that in, but then some things had been mailed. Yesterday, setting up, Marta had answered the door for a UPS delivery truck.

"Oh!" Nita cried as she drew out a large photograph. "A pretty house!" She looked back into the envelope but that was apparently all.

Bronco leaned over her shoulder to stare at it.

"There's writing on the back," Claire told them.

Nita flipped it over. "It says," she said, wide-eyed, reading the large hand printing, "'This house in East Naples is yours if the bridegroom will work for the Trophy Ranch full-time. It will be fully insured by Florida Gulf Coast Life Insurance. Also, Bronco will be given a full life insurance policy. I know a good man when I see one and an occasional out-of-control gator and too many snakes are not my friends. Let me know when you want to see the house. Stan Helter.'"

"So, a well-baited hook," Nick whispered to Claire, who finally remembered to close her mouth. "A hook fully insured by Helter's buddy and mine, Grant Manfort."

# CHAPTER TWENTY

Though the last thing Claire wanted to do was attend the symphony since she was so tired the day after the wedding, they did want to talk to Lane. And they'd had a message on their answering machine in which he had said if they were coming to the concert, he'd like to take them to a nearby musician hangout for a drink afterward.

Without Nita to babysit, they dropped Lexi at Darcy's for Sunday evening and drove to Artis, as the philharmonic hall was called. It was a beautiful building, lighted to show off its architectural grandeur. Claire realized she hadn't been here in months. Their seats were in one of the elevated boxes to the right of the stage, in a short first row with a fabulous view.

"He didn't skimp on good seats for us, did he?" Nick asked as they settled into the plush chairs.

"Good. I'm going to study him, though Brit said when he's lost in his music, he's in another world—not himself.

Which is good, as far as I'm concerned. His 'self,' at least as we've seen it so far, leaves something to be desired."

"Do you really think he'd hire someone to sneak into the BAA to hurt—to kill—his father?"

"Incomprehensible, I know, especially to those of us who lost our fathers early and miss them still. But I know he wrote that fake note and stashed it where it would turn up at some point. Ann finally remembered that it was Lane who suggested she look in Ben's Bible for a reading he might have underlined, and voilà—there is was, in print when Ben never printed. Lane may be talented and brilliant, but he's not smart."

"We've still got Gracie and Helter as possibilities, and I'd sure rather it turns out to be one of them. The idea of a son betraying his father, even if they didn't get along—and who would he hire to have done that?"

"Let's just hope Lane realizes he's made a fool of himself with us and does better tonight. I know he'll be excellent in performance, but I mean afterward."

"And there's always that possibility I don't want to accept—that maybe Ben did make the mistake or intentionally walked in that cage himself. But if Lane's guilty, he still may be giving the performance of his life. Look—speak of the devil," he said, leaning forward to gaze down at the audience on the mezzanine.

"Who? Lane's not out on the stage yet."

"Grant Manfort, and do I have a big bone to pick with him over offering all that free insurance coverage to Bronco in Stan Helter's buyout scheme. But tonight's hardly the time. Tomorrow, I'll try to face him down on that, so— Wait, you know who he's with?"

"I don't recognize her, but I remember seeing him at Ben's memorial service," Claire said, squinting to see at that distance through the lights. Grant and an attractive woman, perhaps in her fifties, were about a third of the way back on the main floor, dead center.

"Remember I told you that Grant's mentor and the man's granddaughter—his name was Steve Rowan, CEO of the insurance company Grant now owns—drowned at sea and their bodies were never found?"

"I remember the newspaper coverage of it too, the search by the coast guard and their finally calling that off when their yacht washed ashore empty."

"Yeah, well, the woman with him is Margot Rowan, daughter of Steve and mother of Leslie, who drowned. At least he's still making an effort to support their family."

"Could they be romantically involved?"

"Can't say, but I think he's a real loner. Passionate about his adventure treks and his vision for zoos of the future without bars and cages."

"I'm starting to like him better already. So maybe that's how he got hooked up with Stan Helter. The animals roam there without bars and cages, though they're endangered in another way—namely, of being shot dead in a setup orchestrated by Stan Helter."

They stopped talking as another couple came into the box and sat behind them. They nodded in greeting just as the penetrating sound of the oboe to tune the other instruments cut through the buzz of the audience. Lane, as first violinist, made an entrance on stage, then took his prominent place to more than polite applause.

★ ★ ★

After the concert, they met Lane and his wife, Sandra, at Brick Top's Restaurant in the nearby outdoor mall called the Waterside Shops, though the place itself wasn't waterside. It did, however, have pools that reflected the sliver of autumn moon in the dark night sky. Lane's wife, as Jace had said, had fabulous makeup and not a hair out of place to complement her sleeveless, glittering black sheath. Claire, in the only dressy black dress that still fit her and had a jacket, felt both overdressed and underdressed.

Sandra had preordered crab cakes, blackened fish tacos, spicy tuna sushi, and they all had wine. The place was abuzz with regular concertgoers who called out comments or kudos to Lane, and he seemed to drink it all in in more ways than one as he raised his glass. He had, at least, arranged a booth for them out of the mainstream so they could hear each other talk.

"So, did you stay awake through the most sweeping, soothing parts?" Lane asked Claire. "She's with child, Sandra, though she hardly shows it in that dress," he told his wife, and smiled at both Nick and her.

What a change, Claire thought, as the suddenly ingratiating man talked about Gershwin composing the symphony, about how his tastes were actually a bit more classical. "I always go back to Bach," he said.

But, Claire thought, either Brit or Ann must have told him she was pregnant, because men usually weren't that observant, and she'd been dressed in loose shirts the several times she'd been near him.

Small talk mingled at first with the generous appetizers

and the wine. Lane said he never ate before a concert, so he was putting food away now and didn't seem to have a care in the world, nor did Sandra, just as at Ben's funeral.

But, staring into his glass of white wine, Lane said suddenly in a lull in the conversation, "*Rhapsody in Blue* was the perfect piece for me to practice lately and play tonight. I try to carry on, but I'm mourning not only my father's loss, but the loss of what we could have had if he'd just understood me."

Sandra nodded, overly long, Claire thought, but here was the opening she'd wanted. "Your mother and even Jackson said he was very sad and depressed lately," Claire said. "They were actually worried about his state of mind. I guess he left some sort of note in large print, regretful, perhaps a little despondent."

Claire realized she'd just broken another forensic psych rule: even if you do some leading in an interview of a suspect, do not lie. Well, she hadn't, exactly, but she felt the steady, increased pressure of Nick's leg against hers under the table.

"Really?" Lane said, sitting up straighter. He started to stroke his immaculately trimmed beard. "Like—like he'd try to hurt himself? He didn't hurt easily, I'll tell you that, so it's—so dreadfully terrible what happened—how he did it—if he did it."

Lane stared into his goblet again, frowning. Sandra put her hand on his upper arm and gave it a squeeze. Those broken comments just now, the remorse that seemed false… Funny, Claire thought, but he'd said earlier he was sorry he'd given them the wrong impression and wanted to make up for that tonight. Yet the reflection of his lower face in his wine made it look as if he were smiling. And if he believed tonight would ease their opinion of him as unsympathetic toward Ben at best and bitter at worst, he was so, so wrong.

"Nick Markwood to see Grant Manfort," Nick told the receptionist in the lobby of Grant's four-story insurance office on Monday morning.

"Do you have an appointment, sir? I don't see it here."

"Please just let his secretary know Nick Markwood is here."

"Have a seat please, and I'll tell her."

Nick knew this was a gamble, but he was starting to feel this so-called Tiger Cage Case was too. He was banking on Grant's seeing him if he was here, not just putting him off via phone or email if he asked to set up a meeting. He didn't want another lunch date; he wanted to see him right now.

Nick tried to get hold of himself. That end-around trick of Stan Helter's trying to steal Bronco with the house bribe had really teed him off. Of course Bronco and Nita had stars in their eyes over it, even though they said they didn't want to stop working for the Markwoods and would take time to think about it.

It was obvious to Nick that he'd do better bargaining with Helter through Grant than arranging a head-on collision. Of course, in the end, it would be Bronco and Nita's decision, but he didn't like dirty tricks and he didn't like that Bronco, who had been upset by the earlier attempted trick of the seduction at the ranch, was being invited to sell his soul to someone like Helter. The ranch owner was a take-no-prisoners kind of guy, and that was trouble. Maybe it had been trouble for Ben too.

"Oh, yes, of course," he heard the receptionist say into her mouthpiece as she shifted her gaze toward him. He steeled himself. Maybe he'd made a mistake, but he felt he'd built a bond with Grant in the past.

"He'll see you now, Mr. Markwood. Please follow me, and I'll take you right in."

He followed her down a carpeted corridor with individuals working in glassed-in cubicles, most staring at large screens, some on the phone. This entire fourth floor was laid out much like the law offices. He found Grant in a corner office with walls of windows overlooking Venetian Bay. He was standing at one of those desks you could elevate. It annoyed Nick to go through the usual what-brings-you-here, glad-to-see-you-again formalities, but he did.

"Sit," Grant said, gesturing at a chair for Nick but ignoring one himself. "I don't always stand, but I like to keep in shape. I swear, I'm heading back on a climbing trip or safari soon. So what can I do for you?"

"I'm here about the house Stan Helter offered to Bronco. Gratis, in East Naples, insured by your company and with a life insurance policy from here thrown in for good measure—as an added bribe."

"Whoa," he said, holding up both hands. "Yeah, I signed off on the policies, but I thought Bronco had agreed to work for the ranch—"

"Bronco agreed to work part-time three days a week. Look, Grant, the guy is not only a friend but his wife is our nanny."

"Then aren't you happy for this really sweet deal he's been offered? And I admit, I didn't think it was a—"

"Bribe, I said."

"Buyout, I'd say. So your wife is upset too, of course."

"As I recall, you've never been married, so maybe you don't get the impact of that, but frankly it's Bronco and his bride we're worried about."

"Meaning you don't trust Stan to keep his word or your guy will get hurt doing that dangerous work?"

"I really think Stan's playing dirty. I'm sure there's a clause somewhere to get Bronco completely under his thumb with no freedom, and the guy needs that." Nick almost blurted out that Stan had a strong motive to be happy Ben Hoffman was dead, but he finally fought to stop the accusations and calm down.

"I've known Stan a long time," Grant said with a shrug. "I admit he goes for the jugular to get things done, runs the ranch without guardrails sometimes, if you know what I mean."

"I know he'd like to get his hands on the BAA property when he's already sitting on massive acres."

Nick noted, for the first time, Grant showed his frustration in his face as well as his voice, but he had to admit he'd come on pretty hot and heavy—not like him, more like Jace. Grant's cheeks and forehead reddened and a vein stood out, beating madly at the side of his neck before he turned away and looked out his sweeping windows to the glittering bay lined with buildings.

"Whatever Stan's faults—and we all have some," Grant said, his voice unsteady now, "I have to admire his ambition. Always have. He came from next to nothing and now hobnobs with the internationally rich and famous. And I admit, I'm still tied to him, because some of his clients have become mine. Many of them are movers and shakers, lots of them wealthy, and they need to protect their financial and family assets."

"Helter borders not on ambition but aggression. You heard the BAA overseer was hit on the back of his head much like Ben Hoffman was."

"I read about it. A tragedy," Grant said, turning back to face him and finally sinking into the other chair. "But you're not accusing Stan, are you? They don't think the guy could have fallen from trying to climb the fence? And Ben Hoffman's demise is your concern too, isn't it?"

"I can't discuss that case further."

"So it is a case? And I can't discuss this wedding gift matter until I check with Stan. Look, Nick, you and I had kind of an understanding from way back over losing the men we both cared for, the ones we pattern ourselves after, right? I was devastated by that loss—and that of Leslie too. Beautiful girl, red hair, green eyes..."

Nick nodded, but he was thinking of his own red-haired, green-eyed girl. He and Claire had been round and round about what was so damned important about the few acres of the BAA. Meanwhile, Claire was getting emotionally sucked into a case that looked more dangerous all the time, when he didn't want her to go farther than their orchid-covered backyard wall and a trip to her sister's right now. Damn, was he losing it. Should he just let all this—and Bronco—go?

No, because he owed it to his dead father, who was murdered by an evil man who wanted it to look like suicide. He'd sworn to help others who might have been caught up in such evil, whether the motive was greed, revenge, hatred...

"Tell you what," Grant said in the sharp silence between them. "Stan owes me from way back for supporting the ranch in more ways than one. I saw it as a refuge for animals, even if there was hunting there. I'll see if he'll go back to the half-time deal for Bronco and maybe let him buy the house cheap, reduced rates, and I'll throw in the insurance until he gets on his feet, so you can have his service half-time."

Nick remembered to exhale. Grant extended his hand, and they shook. Maybe he had done the right thing to come to Grant.

"Your new wife must be a hell of a woman if you finally settled down," Grant said, leaning back in the chair, seeming calmer now, though his foot crossed over his other leg bounced. "Saw you two at the concert Sunday. She's a beautiful woman. Maybe I should try marriage sometime. That was Steve Rowan's daughter I was with, if you noticed me. I like to keep in touch with her, squire her around once in a while, since she's divorced and alone now. I'm just as driven as you to make something good come from tragic losses in the past."

"And more recent ones," Nick told him. "That's my focus too."

Grant nodded, frowning, and went to look back out at the panoramic scene again. Nick stood and gazed out too.

"A beautiful view," Nick said.

"But it's not this I want that money can buy," Grant said with a sigh. "Give me the sweep of the raw, great outdoors with exotic animals, even if it's bred in them to attack each other, even if running free means facing death from human hunters. Sometimes, sadly, that costs human lives too, the price we pay for paradise in peril."

Nick realized that was Grant's manifesto. Admirable but—was he justifying Ben's death? Jackson's injuries? No, it was just that Claire's obsession with finding guilt had rubbed off on him, surely that was it.

# CHAPTER TWENTY-ONE

After Nick settled down from his conversation with Grant, he went home for lunch to talk to Claire. Thank God he did! A police car followed by an unmarked vehicle had just pulled up at the curb in front of the house, and Claire was already opening the front door to step outside. After the dead gator and python were dumped on their property, the police said they'd drive by more, but this must be something else.

Nick pulled in the driveway and jumped out. He raised a hand to keep Claire from coming out farther, but of course she paid no attention. They faced two Naples police officers and one man dressed in plainclothes—oh, yeah, Detective Ken Jensen, who had investigated Ben's death at the BAA. Nick didn't know the policemen.

"Officers. Detective," he greeted them. His pulse started to pound. "I've been keeping tabs on how James Jackson is doing. Is he—"

"The same," Jensen said, stopping partway up the front lawn. "Life support until his brain swelling goes down. Hope he remembers what happened to him if—when—he regains consciousness."

"It's not—someone else hurt?" Claire asked. "Our daughter...she's at school."

"No, ma'am. No problem with anything like that."

"Let's step inside," Nick told them with a sweep of his hand.

"Actually," Jensen said, holding his ground, "we're on our way out to question Grace Cobham, since she just evaporated into the wilderness the first time I went to see her. We understand from talking to her son Ronnie, who works at Home Depot here in town—"

Nick and Claire exchanged a wide-eyed glance. That sounded so homey, so normal, when Gracie's boys seemed far from that.

"We figured out the hard way," Jensen went on, "that she's an old Florida cracker who doesn't like visitors unless they've been invited. Believe it or not, she has no phone out there in the boondocks, halfway down the Tamiami Trail, and we weren't about to chase her into the swamp. Ronnie says she has a good relationship with you, Mrs. Markwood, and we wanted to ask if you would do a ride-along with us."

Nick almost wondered if his clever Claire had set this up. She'd been wanting to go see Gracie on her own turf, question her more about the day Ben died. At least he was here to head this off, and he tried to get a word in before Claire did.

But he failed, as she turned to him and said, "Nick, you

didn't want me to go out there without an armed escort. He was just kidding, Detective Jensen, but what could be better than this? Yes, I have begun to build a relationship with her, which I would not like to see harmed by the company I keep, if you'll excuse me from looking at your plan from her point of view. Perhaps the officers could hang back a bit, and you and I could talk to her."

Nick managed to get out, "Claire, I don't th—"

"I understand," Jensen said. "Actually, I don't like to involve civilians, but I know you're a trained forensic psych, and part of their gig is interviews. I'm thinking we'll more or less need a cultural interpreter once we get near her—if we do. We've picked this time frame because Ronnie Cobham's at work and Lonnie Cobham drives a delivery truck for an exterminator, and he's on the road in Fort Myers."

Lonnie and Ronnie. Sounded like cute kiddie TV characters, not overgrown men with hatchets and knives, and Nick didn't like the idea of one of them being an exterminator. Hell, they dealt with poisons. But with a police escort, maybe they could find out more about Gracie as a possible exterminator of Ben Hoffman. And since someone had evidently climbed the fence to hurt Jackson, Gracie and the boys could be considered prime candidates for that too. But wouldn't Jackson have been more specific on the phone to Brit about what he'd seen? Both Claire and Brit had said he sounded not only scared but shocked. Well, maybe an old woman scaling the fence back by the tiger cage would do that.

"You mean now?" Nick asked Jensen as Claire, looking pleased and excited, tore into the house to, as she put it, *get her stuff.*

"We heard the old lady sells orchids on the roadside along the Trail, so we may not even have to drive back to her place again," Jensen said. "Okay, Claire and I will go in together, with the police officers nearby as backup. We don't expect any problem if we can just get the old lady snagged for a talk."

"Not to arrest her?" Nick clarified as, despite it all, his lawyer instincts kicked in.

"Just question her," Jensen said. "We'll be careful, Counselor. Forensic psychs are trained for tough interviews, and we can really appreciate that. I remember when Claire was shot at the courthouse after testifying and then that Marco Island murder case where she fought the killer—"

"Exactly," Nick interrupted as Claire hurried out with a jacket, a purse and a notebook. "And we don't need anything like that ever again, so please—" he lowered his voice "—keep a good eye on her."

She kissed Nick on the cheek and got in the front passenger seat of Jensen's car. Just to steady himself, Nick stared at the holstered pistols the officers sported. Jensen no doubt was also carrying, so she was well protected. Why was it always that way with Claire, into the thick of things, pregnant or not? It was bad enough to lose some of Bronco's time but, after what Jensen had just said about Claire, all he needed was the police trying to hire her, even as a part-time consultant.

Jensen turned to him before he got in his car and, resting his arms on the roof, called to Nick, "Appreciate the help, Counselor. By the way, the thorough search we did of Ben Hoffman's office on the BAA grounds after his death turned up two hidden listening devices—strictly audio surveillance, not visual, but state-of-the-art. Mr. Hoffman's death has been ruled accidental, but it does sound like a suicide, since he must have known what he was doing, going in that cage. Anyway, the case will remain open for a while. No decent prints or DNA on the bugs, which is what took us so long before we got the word on it today."

Nick's mind raced. Someone was spying, overhearing BAA conversations? Lane? Stan? Hardly Gracie, though they seemed to want to question her further anyway.

Jensen went on, "The deceased's wife and daughter say they didn't know the bugs were there. But if foul play is ever indicated in Hoffman's death, and if you were preparing a defense case, you'd read about the bugs in the police report for fair disclosure anyway. Actually, Brittany, hard as she seems to be taking this, looks like the one with the most to gain, right, other than Stan Helter? She said her father actually forbid her to leave the BAA for another job. The place was in her name but not really in her control, and she had some kind of an argument with her father shortly before he died—she admitted that to us. I hate that we always have to look at family first."

Jensen got in and closed the door. Damn, but the guy should write scripts for *NCIS* with that kind of timing for dropping bombs. Nick tried not to look upset. The police were thinking Brit was a person of interest? Jace would go ballistic, probably Claire too. Sitting in the car, she'd no doubt heard all that.

The vehicles circled the cul-de-sac and headed out. Nick tried to process everything he'd heard here and at Grant's earlier today. And there went his wife, however well protected, off to battle without him.

Jace left work early and decided he needed some time alone to think. Besides, he was starving. He pulled into the Carrabba's restaurant on the trail, sat in a booth alone and ordered a burger, even though it was a decent Italian restaurant. Man, no one ever made burgers like his mother used to.

He wanted a beer but ordered a soft drink. He checked his email, texts and voice mail. Lexi had left him a voice mail saying that Dad was there instead of Mommy when Aunt Darcy brought her home from school. That was weird, he thought. Big criminal lawyer, senior partner, home from work early and pregnant wife out. Maybe she and Darcy had gone again to take something to that Glover kid Lexi had talked about.

Jace practically tore into his burger and fries when they came. He should probably not have left flying early, considering he kept going in late, but his FBI contact trusted him and knew his girlfriend had problems right now. He'd get back to spraying fruit trees soon—as if that was his primary purpose instead of electronic recon of local criminals. The Stingray surveillance was a good enough gig to keep a steady salary coming in right now, but no match for his paycheck when he'd been an international airline copilot. That had kept him away from Claire and Lexi too much, though it had sure paid the bills, even after they split up and had two households. Right now there were more important things, such as saving his own skin, let alone Brit's.

Because that argument he'd had with Ben right after Brit and her dad had argued over the future of the BAA still haunted him. Ben was both shaken and despondent over the place. Jace wished he and Ben had not argued that night too. He felt guilty that he'd had a near knock-down, drag-out with a man who might have killed himself shortly after. And when Jace, despite how much he looked up to Ben, had sided with Brit, the roof could have blown off the Hoffman home. Damn good thing Brit had left and Ann wasn't there. He could hear Ben's voice, his hurt, angry tone even now.

"Well, hoo-yah, fancy flyboy! Siding with Brit when she's not the one who founded the BAA, not the one who put her sweat and blood and college-smart brains into it. Here I thought this old marine grunt and you had an understanding, a friendship going."

Jace realized right away Ben had been drinking. His words were slurred, and he smelled it on his breath. Four empty beer cans and a half bottle of scotch sat on the coffee table. Worse, this was starting to remind him of more than one dressing down he'd had from his own father when he was young. And more than once, he'd wanted to kill his dad. Damn, but Jason Britten Sr. had always treated his marine recruit classes better than he did his own kid, who was named after him.

"Sit down, Ben," he'd tried to calm his friend that night. "I know Brit just left. I just think she's too talented and dedicated to helping and saving wildlife to be tied to that little zoo. She's put in a couple of years with you. She loves big cats and wouldn't be near one if Tiberia hadn't more or less fallen into your lap."

Ben kept prodding Jace in his breastbone with the tips of his fingers, hard enough that Jace either had to step back or hit back, so he gave Ben a little shove. He wondered if he'd order him to drop for twenty-five push-ups the way his dad had more than once, standing over him, yelling. Either the booze or an argument with Brit, who had not seen Jace when she'd stormed out, was making this guy into a Frankenstein. And he'd regret it in the morning when the bad buzz wore off. Who knows, but maybe Ann took off for somewhere when he got crazy like this.

"Ben, look. Let up, man. Both of us love Brit. And Brit and I care about the BAA and y—"

"You'd like to take her away, wouldn't you? Not only marry her, but get her into some fancy zoologic—zooey, whatever—professorship or working for a big-time zoo?"

"That's not true, unless it was here. I'd like to stay in the Naples area because of my daughter—so we both love our girls, right?"

"Let's drink on it, then," he said, finally stepping back and making a lunge for the bottle of scotch. He knocked it off the table onto the tile floor where it shattered.

"Ben, I think you've had enough and—"

"I have had enough!" he said, rounding on Jace again. "Even Ann wants to sell my BAA to that bastard Helter from hell! Brit goes to see him behind my back, and Lane would be happy to play the violin and dance at the sale of it. Helter owns half the county, so what's so damn special about my little place to him?"

The memory, Ben's strident voice and angry expression,

faded but Jace's own anger boiled up again as he sat alone in the restaurant booth. "Helter just wants what he wants," he whispered as he doused his french fries with ketchup, gripping the plastic bottle so hard it dented and the bloodred sauce splattered. "Damn, but don't we all?"

"I heard what you said to my husband about Brit being a suspect," Claire said to Detective Jensen en route to Gracie's home.

"Mrs. Markwood—"

"Claire."

"Great, thanks. Claire, I didn't say she was a suspect."

"That was the subtext."

"I got a temporary partner who's a forensic psych, that's right. Luckily, one with nine lives."

"I'll admit I've been in the *Naples Daily News* a few too many times."

"Your website, *Clear Path*, is a good one, but you ought to consider consulting for the NPD."

He'd been researching her. She sat up straighter. "For the immediate future I'm consulting with motherhood, present and future. But I do not read Brittany Hoffman as someone who would have her father harmed. Like Lane, she has multiple eyewitnesses, including me and Nick, that she wasn't there to hit him or push or drag him into that tiger's cage. She loved her father and that tiger."

He heaved a sigh. Heading south on the Tamiami Trail, he stopped at the red light near the road to Marco Island. "Yeah, I know. Everyone I'd pursue if this was going further has alibis, except Grace Dixon Cobham."

"So Stan Helter was in full view—of whom, his paid staff who probably think he walks on water?"

"If he's your hit pick for Ben Hoffman's death, it wasn't hands-on for sure. He's got a staff of about thirty people at the ranch, and at least half of them saw him during that time period."

"I'll bet it shook him up to even be a person of interest. And Gracie only has her boys, Ronnie and Lonnie, to work with. We told you about the loud and crazy possum party. Do they seem the sort to you to get in and out fast and quietly without leaving any evidence behind if they killed Ben?"

"You're starting to sound like the attorney you're married to. Well, that happens. I know more about Skye Terriers than I ever thought there was in the books from my ten years of wedded bliss. Okay, I'm blinking my lights to let our escort behind us drop back. I'm keeping my cell phone open so I can bring them in, but getting Grace to not take off into the Glades is in your hands now. I'll keep quiet and let you do the talking at first."

"I'm just hoping she doesn't think I've betrayed her. Once again, Detective Jensen—"

"Ken."

"Ken. I don't think Grace Dixon Cobham hit anyone on the back of the head or murdered anyone, even if she had a revenge motive. I know Gracie can climb a fence and has two big bruisers at her beck and call, but my training and instinct say no."

"You play hardball, Claire. I do too, so glad to have you along for more than the ride."

# CHAPTER TWENTY-TWO

Claire saw Gracie under a trellis dripping with orchids behind a ramshackle table along the roadside. Behind her lay a crooked path back into thick foliage, but no house was in sight, though there was a dirt-and-stone driveway just beyond.

"Don't pull off right in front of the table so she feels blocked in," she told the detective.

"Gotcha, Dr. Freud," he said. "I suppose we'd better move slow too. Don't want to spook her. You know, speaking of that, she disappeared in less than a minute when I tried to approach her little house to talk to her last week. I swear, she just evaporated into the Glades."

"Yeah, well, she grows ghost orchids, so you never know," Claire kidded him back. Surely he was kidding.

Claire got out first and led the way.

"Why, you done found me!" Gracie called out. "But you changed your man."

Claire moved right up to the table and leaned over to take Gracie's hand in both of hers. "I'm just going to level with you, Gracie, because you have with me."

"Sure have."

"I knew the police had to talk to absolutely everyone who ever had anything to do with Tib—Thunder, so I said to this officer, let me go along with you because I know Gracie and how generous and helpful she is."

"Doesn't look like a cop," she said, slanting a narrow-eyed look at Jensen. Claire let go of her hands—steady hands for an old woman, no apparent nerves of quickening pulse. "The same one been talking to my boys?"

"The same, Mrs. Cobham," Jensen said. "They've been very helpful."

"Hmph."

"And I'm astounded at how beautiful these orchids are. I'd like to buy one or two for my wife. She breeds dogs, so we'll have to hang them high. Darn critters eat stuff they shouldn't. None of these would be toxic, would they?"

"Nope, but hang 'em high—sounds like some old Western. Used to have a TV and phone before my Sam died. Hang 'em high, like a lynching. So let me just say, though you can maybe get me for trespassing, I had not one danged thing to do with Thunder harming someone crazy or dazed enough to get in his cage. Just climbed a ladder once or twice to see him and say hi."

"You weren't checking on the tiger that morning, were you?" Jensen pursued.

"Nope, and wasn't anywhere near when their overseer got hurt. Read it in the paper Lonnie brought home."

"Okay," Jensen said, "that's clear enough."

"Do have something bad to confess, though. It's gonna get out. It hurt me too, but it's the worst for the best."

Claire held her breath. Gracie looked up at Claire and stood, shoving back her old wooden chair. She unhooked two orchids from above her head and handed them to the dumbfounded Jensen, then plucked two more and thrust them at Claire.

"You can call that down payment for coming out here, so I could warn the both of you. Now Brittany Hoffman is going to know how it felt for me to lose my boy Thunder."

Fears crashed through Claire. Gracie had decided to poison the tiger if she couldn't have him? Poison Brit? After all, one of her sons worked with poison as an exterminator. Surely she didn't mean Jackson. But could he have eaten something strange meant to harm Brit, then fell and hit his head?

"I reported that Thunder should not be in that crummy cage in that little petting zoo," Gracie said, crossing her arms over her chest. "Why, can't pet a beautiful beast like Thunder, so he shouldn't have been there!"

Claire exhaled in relief, but Jensen asked, "Reported to who?"

"Why every wildlife group I know of, local, state, even national. And those people in Tallahassee took Thunder away from me in the first place. I know the BAA got a general not-their-fault ruling, but that tiger should not be there. I admitted in the letters I shouldn't have had him—which hurt—'cause I should have. I got a letter just couple days ago that Brittany Hoffman would receive a legal order he's to be moved to the Family Friendly Zoo up by Tampa, where they can take care of him proper. I'll save up my money, go visit him, though probably now without a possum dinner."

Ken Jensen, who had no doubt seen and heard a lot of things in his career, seemed speechless. Claire didn't know whether to laugh or cry. To have Thunder moved, even farther way, was wise and took bravery and concern. But that would be the last straw for Brit at the BAA. At least the old woman had not shot or hurt the tiger because she didn't want someone else to have it.

"I see," Claire said, cradling the orchids after she paid for them.

Jensen had put one of his down and was thumbing two twenty-dollar bills out of his wallet. "It took a lot of courage and honesty to tell us that, Grace," he said as he handed over the money.

"I know Claire here has a kid, but do you?" she asked Jensen, squinting up at him.

"Yes, ma'am, two teenagers."

"Well, I have three boys. My Ronnie is not quite right in the head, but a hard worker and never married. Lonnie, he was married once, but she took off. And the third was that baby tiger I nursed and loved."

Claire blinked back tears, amazed that Jensen kept nodding and didn't ask one more question. It was as if good old Gracie had cast a spell on him, on them both.

"Claire," Gracie said with a nod as she stashed the forty dollars in her jeans pocket, "you take good care of that baby you're carrying now. Just stay out of all this, 'cause someone—don't know who—still must have some big bone to pick and best you not be in the way."

They thanked her for the orchids and placed them on the floor in the back seat of Jensen's car.

"That's twice that old cracker woman's got the best of me," he muttered. "Gotta call our backup and tell them to head to Naples. I still say someone that street-smart— well, swamp-smart—could have hurt Ben Hoffman and Jackson, if she had a mind to do it."

"She's put one over on Brit too," she said as he made a U-turn and they headed back to Naples, driving past the police car that followed them. "I don't know how many blows Brittany Hoffman can take, losing what and who she loves. And here, you did sound like you suspect her of something."

"I think she's wanted out of the BAA for a couple of years, and either couldn't hurt her dad to tell him or wanted to hurt her dad by telling him. Maybe the influence of her fiancé or—"

"They're not formally engaged."

"I guess you'd know since you share a child. But listen, the tiger being moved is for the best, really. I read up on that breed, and they're really endangered."

Claire nodded. She did not agree with Jensen's thinking that Brit wanted out of the BAA, especially not so badly that she'd harm her father. Of course, it was fairly new information too that Ben had been rough and violent, and Brit could have resented that. It seemed this case she and Nick had been drawn into was getting more complicated, not easier, to solve.

On their way back into Naples, Claire called Nick and filled him in on everything, except how annoyed and upset she was that Detective Jensen still seemed to be suspicious of Brit. She told Nick she was going to the BAA with Jensen to break the news to Brit if she hadn't heard about the legal decision to move the tiger, maybe comfort her.

Nick said, "Glad you're with the police, but that doesn't mean you don't have to be careful. Lexi and I are playing Chutes and Ladders again, but call me if I need to come out there. The officers are still with you?"

"He sent them back downtown."

"Claire, be careful!"

She guessed she could hardly argue that she always had been. Too much water under the bridge for that. But when they arrived at the BAA, they found only Ann and not Brit. And Ann, as well as Brit, had heard the news of Tiberia's new home.

"Brittany and Jace left for somewhere when the letter was delivered to her," Ann told them. Her voice was froggy either from crying or from the fact she was still grieving. When Claire's father had left—though he was not dead—it took her mother weeks to even get out of bed.

"Can we see the letter?" Jensen asked.

"Took it with her. One week and she has to surrender the tiger, that's what it said. Tiberia's going to a special facility near Tampa. Broke her heart, mine too, but it is for the best. It will kill me to close and sell this place—well, it's in Brittany's name—but I suppose it has to be done. We'll find good homes for all the animals first. Somehow." She glanced around, her eyes resting for a moment on Jackson's beloved Flamingo Isle. "She and Jace were having an argument they've had before. He says apply to work at the Naples Zoo, got tigers there and a blind Florida panther someone took a shot at. Jace told her, 'See, big cats need you there too, especially that one got shot.' Scared me more what she said then. 'Things are so bad, I might as well be shot.'"

Nick was glad to see Claire come through the door in one piece. She was cradling two more beautiful orchids when the backyard had already turned into a jungle of them. She put them down on the foyer tile and walked into his arms.

"What would I do without you?" she said, holding him tight, as if to assure him she was safe. "All's well that ends well with Gracie, at least, though Ann says Brit's distraught. At least Jace is with her, though I guess they were arguing too."

"Lexi fell asleep in the back room, but I fed her some early dinner—mac and cheese, of course, which the microwave and I can handle. Did you take your meds or herbs? You need some rest. Heck and Gina are stopping by soon, because I had him ask his NPD contact about the bugs Jensen says were in the BAA office."

"Heck and his sources," she said, stepping back and looking up into his face. He kissed her nose, her cheek, her mouth. "I'll just run to the bathroom and be back out to see them. Mac and cheese will do for me, master chef."

Nick hustled to reheat more of that, adding a slice of avocado and tomato. Claire had barely finished it when the doorbell sounded, and he went to let Heck and Gina in. It was only Heck.

"She's nervous again," he told Nick before he could ask.

"Rereading some of her med school books, but they're in Spanish, and who knows if the medical training there is anything like here—her latest worry. I know you got worries too, boss. I couldn't find out much. I know you—and my contact—both said the audio surveillance devices were state-of-the-art, but I doubt it. You know you been complaining about how your cell phone CPU runs everything slow lately? Let me see your phone a sec."

They sat in the front living room, and Nick turned on lights, explaining that Claire had to wake up Lexi to get her into her own bed. "The demands of beginning school," he told Heck as he handed over his phone. His tech genius always amazed him by the way he buzzed and punched around so fast on electronic devices.

"Whoooaa," Heck told him. "You think the BAA office is bugged? I was thinking that with how someone's risked a lot to give you a dead gator and snake, you're maybe being bugged too."

"You know I'm so paranoid from the past, I have the house swept every couple of weeks, and I did it after the gift of the dead gator. But you mean maybe my location is being traced by my phone, like Jace does in the sky with the FBI's Stingray program?"

"Nope. Bugged, right here, but I just disabled it so that this phone isn't spying on you anymore. Maybe you'd better get me Claire's phone too."

"What are you talking about? A spy bug has been inserted into my phone, which has not been out of my possession?"

"Yep. Cell phone spying. Someone downloaded—probably just through a simple phone call to your number

where the phone didn't even ring—a monitoring and re-
cording program on your phone. It also acts as a microphone during any call you make. Whoever did this can
receive remote alerts when you dial. Anyhow, you saying
it ran slow—which means too much CPU used—was the
tip-off. That and you and Claire seem to make enemies
everywhere you go. This is getting sticky, boss. Someone
really values that little acreage of the BAA."

"What would I do without you? Are you sure it's disabled now?"

"Yep, but go ahead and get me Claire's phone. You said
she was with the police today, so someone might know
that now too."

Nick swore under his breath as he went into the master bedroom and took Claire's phone from the dresser.
As he headed back toward Heck, he could hear her and
Lexi's voices in the hall bathroom, even over the running tub water.

"You know, boss," Heck said after he had disabled the
listening device on Claire's phone too, "someone could
make a mint selling software to shut this kind of spying
down. Might take it up myself—in my spare time. Get
some money, a nice house, impress my lady."

"I can't believe it—the phones, the extent of the spying, I mean. Or that someone is clever and powerful—and
scared—enough to toss dead, dangerous animals in our
yard one minute, and the next be savvy about something
like this I hadn't even heard of. Once again, my friend,
you are worth your weight in gold. This case is getting to
be a damn dangerous swamp, with some sort of human
animal lurking in it. If we can just figure out the why,

maybe we can get to the who. My money's still on Stan Helter, so maybe I'm going to have to rattle his cage."

"Pretty funny, considering this case."

"Yeah, but I don't think any of this is funny. We're missing something, Heck, just like I was missing that cell-site simulator right on my phone that was in my jeans or suit-coat pocket. And now our enemy will know we're onto that, and that we're not going away. So what will he—or she—do next?"

# CHAPTER TWENTY-THREE

Claire joined them and was annoyed—and scared—to hear their phones had been bugged without even being out of their possession. Heck was just getting ready to leave their house when the doorbell rang.

"I'll get it," Nick said, jumping up. "It's dark—almost nine."

Claire darted to the library window. "Jace's car. He's on the porch with Brit."

"I'll be on my way, boss," Heck said, getting up to follow him out.

"No, Heck," she called after him, "don't leave. You'll need to check both of their phones too."

"Right," Nick said, hitting his forehead with the palm of his hand. "Sweetheart, without you and Heck—and Bronco—I'd be more distracted than I already am."

He opened the front door with Claire behind him. In the foyer she nearly tripped over the two orchid plants she'd brought from Gracie's earlier. And what was wrong with her too, she scolded herself, that she hadn't moved them out of the way for hours? Their lives were in chaos, but, she prayed, not really in danger. So far, dead animals and phone bugging—methods of a hands-off coward. For Lexi's sake and the baby's, maybe she should try to sit this case out. But she was probably in too deep now. She really cared about Brit, Ann—Gracie too. And, of course, Jace.

Claire could tell Brit had been crying and Jace had been arguing. Brit's hair was a mess as if she'd been running her hands through it. Jace looked flushed but grim.

"Come in," Nick told them. "Brit, we know about the court order to have Tiberia moved to a facility near Tampa. We went to see you at the BAA, but you'd just left. I don't think there's any legal way to stop that, considering everything, and maybe the environment will be better for the cat. If there's another attack at the BAA, someone might hurt the tiger too."

Brit and Jace said nothing as they stepped in. Trouble between the two of them too? Claire wondered.

"You don't know the half of it," Jace finally said.

Claire steered them toward the library instead of the back room. Out there, they could be watched through the glass if someone scaled the fence. The BAA fences, even the ones along the ranch's border, had not stopped even an old woman, let alone a possible attacker and murderer. They were better off huddled here in the enclosed library.

Jace and Brit sat on the couch. She moved a bit away from him, but he scooted nearer and threw his arm behind her but not around her. They exchanged greetings with Heck, who was perched on the big ottoman near the chair Nick took. Claire sat in the upholstered one facing Brit and Jace.

"Claire," Brit said, "Mother told me she had a feeling you already knew about Tiberia being forcefully removed in a few days when she saw you."

"That's true. I went with the police to question Gracie Cobham today and—"

"This legal tiger kidnapping is all her fault, isn't it?" Brit exploded, leaning forward as if she would vault off the couch. "The letter mentioned her complaint against me, and I don't need that on my record! I'm not an idiot—I know the tiger shouldn't be kept at the BAA with all that's happened—but I should control the animal's destiny, not her!"

Nick said, "Brit, you must realize that Tiberia going to a good, safe place is the best thing for—"

"But I had a deal where he was going to the Naples Zoo, and I was going to work part-time there, a fill-in if they needed help with the Malayan tigers, other large cats and the Florida panther they have that some idiot shot in the face and blinded. I was going to have my foot in the door there, and we'd either sell the land to Helter or hire someone to run the BAA for me and Mother. But now, with this legal letter about a Tampa-area zoo taking him— well, I know they're an excellent facility..."

When she broke into tears, Jace patted her back, and Claire got a tissue for her. She wiped her eyes and blew her nose while everyone waited.

"It was Dad's dream, his and Mother's," Brit choked out, "but I—I was so glad to help, and then Tiberia seemed like a gift from heaven—for me, and to bring more visitors in. But if I moved on in my life—if I stayed here with Jace, like he wants—I would have to work at the zoo here. There's nothing else—no other place for me to work with big cats nearby."

Nick said, "So you and Jace are planning to marry and stay here?"

She shrugged. "We were. But now that damned letter that old woman sent screws everything up."

Jace said, "Unless you can get that zoo job here without Tiberia to hand over, I guess I'm second place and you'll move on from Southwest Florida and away from me. Brit, you know I have commitments here, at least for now."

"I told you it doesn't have to be that way," Brit said, her voice nasal.

They'd evidently argued this out before, Claire thought. She turned to look at Jace.

"Husbands move for their wives' jobs sometimes in this enlightened day and age," Brit plunged on. "We can have Lexi visit in the summers and some weekends."

Claire didn't speak or move, but her eyes widened and her nostrils flared. She gritted her teeth. One of her worst nightmares of the many she'd faced in her life was that Jace would try to take Lexi half-time. And if he wasn't even in this area...

"Nick," Claire said, turning toward him, "are you sure there's no way to arrange for Tiberia to stay here? To counteract that order if the Naples Zoo is willing to take him—and Brit?"

"I can't promise, but I'll look at the letter and make some calls. Now since you two are here, Heck has something to explain to you about the search for Ben's killer—if there was one. He figured out that Claire and I have had our phones bugged, tapped, whatever you want to call it, and I'd like for Heck to examine your phones too. It just takes him a second."

"But it hasn't been out of my possession," Jace said, digging his out of his shirt pocket. "And the FBI checked it a couple of weeks ago before I started flying Stingray."

"Doesn't matter," Heck said, reaching for it. "This is done by the bad guys with a simple phone call you don't know about and a quick download, the ultimate in malware."

Brit was getting hers out of the purse at her feet. "Since all the media hoopla over Dad's death and then Jackson's injury, I've hardly had mine on. Too many crank calls, media, etcetera."

"*Caramba*," Heck said, "it's here on yours, Jace, and I'm going to kill it. 'Course whoever's doing this can get right back on, so you, Nick and Claire gonna have to change your numbers ASAP. Hello, you evil SOB out there, if you're listening now," Heck said as if he were holding a microphone. "Just kidding. I knocked it out before I said that."

"What about mine?" Brit asked, stretching to hand it to Heck. "Like I said, I might not have that bug since I've tried to ignore the phone. I've changed Mother's number but didn't have time to do mine. This is diabolical, but doesn't it mean someone really did kill Dad and that Jackson's injury is not some freak accident? Someone has a huge stake in all this, if he—or she—is willing to go to all this time and high-tech expense."

"Too much is still undetermined or circumstantial,"

Nick said, "but lawyers and the police always check out circumstantial."

Heck finished with Jace's phone and handed it back to him. Staring at the monitor, Jace muttered, "And I thought the way the Feds track criminals with my flyovers was state-of-the-art."

"Too many people know about Stingray," Heck said, starting to work on Brit's phone. "Media coverage. I haven't seen much public info on this cell-site simulator, but it works kind of the same as what you do, Jace. Still got to have a real expensive analyzer."

Pocketing his phone, Jace said, "Yeah, well, the equipment I fly with is around four hundred thousand dollars for a suitcase-size brain."

"So," Nick said in the sudden silence, "whoever did this to our phones—whoever thinks we're a danger—is probably rich. Another vote for Stan Helter over someone like Gracie Cobham."

"Or over Lane," Brit added. "Like I said, I know that they were not only looking at him, but at me too lately. But I'm barely making ends meet. So, is it on my phone too, Heck?"

"Nope," he said, shaking his head. "Of the four of you, yours is clean."

"Well, it must be, like I said, that I had it off for a while. Besides, whoever is behind this obviously thought it was enough to use those—those physical surveillance bugs in our office. I'm going to have Mother's house and my apartment swept for bugs. The police gave me a good person to call."

She leaned back against the couch and crossed her arms

over her chest protectively, much closer to Jace than before. Claire wished she could be objective about all this, but she could draw several conclusions. First, Jace must have proposed marriage and that they stay in Naples. If Brit had agreed before, she'd changed her mind now, because she desperately needed a job and wanted one working with big cats. And, especially with Tiberia as a bargaining chip, she'd thought she'd had an in with the Naples Zoo. Had she gone behind Jace's back on that as she'd gone behind her father's to deal with Helter?

Second, it was strange—especially since Brit had obviously had her phone on sometimes, including when Jackson had called her right before he got hit—that hers had not been tampered with, since she was at the center of this case.

Third, it made Claire sick to admit it, but when it came to why Brit's phone was clear, she thought *the lady doth protest too much*, expounding on reasons it might be clear before Heck even checked it—as if she knew it would be but couldn't refuse to hand it over. It was one of the forensic tech ten tips for an interview: a guilty person will give many nervous, verbose reasons for their innocence, perhaps even before they are accused or caught.

Interestingly, that *doth protest too much* line from *Hamlet* that Mother read long ago to her and Darcy was about a young man whose father had been murdered. And here sat Brit in tears again, yet still looking defiant—or guilty. But who could she have set up to do the murder for her, and why then, with the place loaded with children? Claire knew she'd been wrong about suspects before with nearly deadly results. And poor Jace. Could he have fallen for a killer?

★ ★ ★

Jace hated the silence in his car as he and Brit finally drove toward the BAA. They'd stopped at Brit's place to get some clothes for her, then at his place too, where, exhausted, they'd fallen asleep on the couch. It was late, after 2:00 a.m. He really did want to comfort, not confront Brit, but she was making it hard. Besides, he was furious with himself too. Damn, what kind of a father was he? Was he so obsessed with Brit that he hadn't even asked to tuck Lexi in bed, before Nick had said he'd carried her upstairs? What if Lexi learned he was there and didn't even try to see her?

"Thanks for insisting on coming along, but I can't ask you to keep spending nights there with me." Brit picked up their argument.

"I've already said yes. Once the tiger's gone, we'll hire someone. You've said you're not thinking straight, so try listening to me."

But he was starting to think she actually was unstable, not that losing her father, Tiberia and probably the BAA wouldn't be enough to shake anyone. But she'd flared up so fast at him more than once today that he'd feared she could lose her temper, go over the edge. And she hadn't told him anything about her dealings with the local zoo at first, though he liked the fact that she was trying to stay here. It reminded him she hadn't told him she'd gone to Stan Helter until well after she'd done it. So what else was she hiding, he fumed as they left the lights of the city behind and headed out on the highway toward the BAA.

"Look, honey," he said, trying to keep his voice steady,

"you can't be staying there alone where your father was killed and where Jackson was attacked."

"*If* dad was murdered, *if* Jackson didn't fall."

"Don't you think Jackson ending up that way is proof there was foul play with your father?"

"Yes, but Dad could be unstable. The drinking, for example."

"I know he was bad that last night we both talked to him, but, believe me, I've seen men with his training and toughness not crack under pressure. He had not only physical instruction years ago, but how-to-be-tough mental training too. I don't think he walked in that tiger cage on his own because he was drunk or despondent. He'd been through worse in the corps, serving his country for big stakes."

"Now you're sounding like Claire with all her analyzing. But fine, at least for tonight. I can sleep on Jackson's couch and you can have his single bed. The police have searched the place for signs of someone else inside and found nothing."

"If it gets to be too much at night for us, I'll hire a guard so we can get some sleep."

"Ha—who would want that job in the dark where two people recently met disaster in broad daylight? If only Nick Markwood can get some sort of order to keep Tiberia from being shipped to Tampa," she said with a huge sigh.

Jace kept his gaze straight ahead. It was black as pitch out here as they turned onto the one-lane road that led to the BAA and the ranch. He turned on his brights and drove slower. What if he hit some sort of animal on the road at night? Thank heavens he hadn't seen that big snake smashed under Darcy's car, but he could imagine it.

"You know," Brit went on, "I can ask the Naples Zoo director to write a letter to the Family Friendly Zoo, saying the tiger was promised to them first—but he might not want to get involved. My tiger is Siberian, not Malaysian, though I was trying to make the point to the Naples Zoo that they could then have two distinct areas of the world represented—if the tigers would just get along all right."

"Are we getting along all right?" he asked, still keeping his eyes glued to the dark road ahead. "I know you've been through the wringer. I want things to work out for us. I know men follow their women across the world these days if she has a good job offer, but with Lexi here..."

"Just as Claire has moved on to have a future family with Nick, you and I could do the same."

"But if I can understand that you don't want to lose a tiger you love, even though you could visit him, you must see that I could never stand to move away from Lexi, even if I could visit her or she could visit us, so—"

The car hit something in the road, something he hadn't seen. A bump, more than one. Did he hear gunfire? No, the bangs of flat tires, then their flopping sound as he hit the brakes and lost control of the car. It spun sideways. The rear tilted into the ditch at the side of the road, nearly upending them. They jerked forward in their seat belts, then slammed backward.

The headlights of the car went straight up, through a cypress tree, shooting into the black heavens overhead. He quickly killed the engine. Then silence screamed at him.

"You okay, Brit? We've got to get out, get down."

"What happened—did we hit something?"

"Spike sticks, I think, like the cops use to stop fleeing fugitives. I hope it's not a setup, but if it is, who did it? Unfasten your belt, and I'll open my door, and we'll go out—and down that way. Hurry, before the hydraulics lock up."

"But there could still be someone out there, waiting to pick us off."

"Then we're sitting ducks. But this may just be another warning—a threat like the dead animals for Nick and Claire. Considering the ranch beyond, maybe this wasn't meant for us. Come on. Quiet. I have a gun in the trunk, but it's probably not going to open in the ditch. The BAA can't be far. The dark is our friend, but if you see a light, hit the ground. Brit, damn it, give me your hand and climb over the console! Make sure you have your phone, and let's go!"

# CHAPTER TWENTY-FOUR

Something dragged Claire from heavy, dark sleep. Some-one was touching her, pulling her arm. A distant voice. Her mother's? Or was that Darcy's voice as a child, and she had to get up to care for her? Daddy had left them. Mother was sick. The doctor said Claire was sick too—falling asleep in the day, nightmares both night and day…

"Mommy, I had a bad dream," the silvery whisper slid through Claire's exhaustion and her meds. "Dad said there's a blind Florida panther we can go see at the zoo, but I dreamed he got shot—the panther, I mean, not Dad."

Claire awoke with a jerk. Somehow, Nick slept on, but then he was exhausted too. Lexi. Lexi was here in the darkness, looking like a little ghost in her white nightie. The clock read 2:30 a.m.

Claire fought to summon her senses, to face reality when she'd been deep in narcoleptic dreams. Yet if she went without her meds, her nightmares became reality.

"Shh!" Claire whispered. "I'll come in your room with you."

Trying to shake off sleep, she got up carefully and followed Lexi out and across the hall. She suddenly felt cold, as if a chill breeze was blowing, but no—that had been in her dream. She had been trapped in a cage with tall fences as a storm circled in.

"I was having a bad dream too," she told Lexi as they crawled into the child's bed together where the sheet and blanket were twisted. Claire covered them both and put her arms around the child, who snuggled close with her back to Claire's chest.

"Like dreams you had when you were little so you had to take pills and that bad-tasting stuff you still have?"

"No, not that bad. Everyone dreams, you know, and sometimes bad ones sneak in. Do you want to talk about yours? Sometimes that helps."

"Well, I love Dad but I was missing Daddy."

"That's okay. It just means you love Daddy too."

"But the bad dream wasn't about him. It was about a poor Florida panther like the one we saw on our street, only it's blind. Its name is Uno, and it's a sad story, but Brit said she is going to help it."

Claire tensed up. "Brit told you about that? When?"

"Last time I talked to Daddy on the phone, she got on it and told me all about it, but said it was a secret from Daddy for now, so I guess he wasn't listening to her then."

"You didn't tell me she said all that."

"She said it's a secret, so she'll tell him later. Tell him she wants to help it because he already knows it's blind."

"Oh. I see. Well, tell me what she said about Uno."

"He's at the Naples Zoo. Some very bad person with a gun shot at him and made him lose an eye and got blind in the other one. Uno couldn't see but he lived on road-kill—that's dead animals that get hit by cars, maybe like the snake Aunt Darcy hit, only that was in the driveway. But Uno got saved, and he's at the zoo, and I was going to tell you and Dad too when she said it's not a secret any-more, so don't say I told you now. So can we take Dun-can and the other kids there to see Uno, even if he can't see us?"

The child's voice trailed off, and Claire gave her a hug.

"The zoo trip sounds like a good idea."

"Yeah, if no one gets killed when we're there. But like I said," Lexi went on, though her voice was slowing, "when I dreamed about poor Uno who can't tell if it's dark, I had to tell you. 'Cause Daddy said once if you share a bad dream it won't come back again."

Jace's version of pop psychology, Claire thought. She had nothing to add to that. It was sweet that Brit had shared that animal story with Lexi, and that it had a good ending. And that Lexi had realized it would be a good visit for the Comfort Zone kids. But did any child, even one as cherished as Lexi, really live in a comfort zone anymore?

Maybe this was a sort of warning that she should steer clear of all this right now, stay home, be safe. But with the threats that had been thrown at their front and back doors, were even adults safe these days?

Jace's car wasn't completely on its rear, but it was at such a slant they had to drop a ways to get out of it. Re-membering that, if your car went into a ditch with water, you had to get a window down fast or a door open before the electronic system seized up, he had his window down. It would be almost impossible to shove the door open at this angle.

Going out his window feetfirst, Jace held on to the sill, then dropped to the ground, about eight feet down. He landed crooked on the side of the ditch and twisted his left ankle, but not bad—he hoped. He looked up. If it wasn't for a quarter moon and stars, it would be totally black here. Brit had one leg and her upper body out the window.

"I'll catch you," he called quietly up to her after a quick look behind him and then up and down the deserted road.

"I wanted to call 911 first."

"No! Get down here. The car could shift. It seems rocky. And we've had a phone tapped recently—I have anyway—so maybe that was the plan, to get our location when we call for help. Now, Brit!"

She squirmed free of the window and let go. Her purse came off her shoulder and fell a few feet away. When he half caught her, they tipped off balance to the ground. Pain shot through his ankle.

"You okay?" he asked. "I hurt my ankle, don't know how bad."

"I'm all right—just shaken. Are you going to check what did that to us?"

"I'd hate to have that happen to someone else, but I don't want to do the obvious or get out from this tree cover."

"We need it for evidence," she said, and darted out into the road before he could grab her.

"Brit—damn it, get back here!"

If his ankle wasn't starting to throb, he would have yanked her back, but here she came, dragging a metal thing with big teeth that looked like some prehistoric dinosaur jaw.

"It's too heavy to carry far," she told him. "Let's hide it in the brush somewhere and get going."

"Yeah, then let's go a ways on the other side of this ditch before we try to call," he said, tugging the spike stop off the berm with her. It wasn't as heavy as he thought. He remembered he'd heard officers could even heave spike sticks out into the road just before a vehicle approached. Was someone near watching them now?

"Brit, you know this area better than me. How close are we to the BAA?"

"I'd say a half mile. This road is hardly traveled at night except by ranch traffic."

"We won't be flagging anyone down for help, not if it's Helter's people."

"But this may have been meant to hurt ranch traffic. If those pro-wildlife groups can picket and threaten a petting zoo, surely they'd hate the idea of a hunt ranch, so they could be behind this and we just happened to come along. Do you agree with Nick that Stan's probably behind everything—even when I told him I'd sell under certain circumstances?"

"Possibly him behind it with the help of his guide and guards."

They shoved the spike stick under some leaves at the foot of a big palmetto and started off, Jace limping and swearing under his breath. She moved closer so he could put one arm over her shoulders to take the weight off what he hoped was only a sprained ankle. It was uneven ground, but he was not going out into the road. They picked their way slowly along the fringe of the trees, mostly palmettos and spectral melaleucas, silvery with road dust. Their path was middle ground between the road berm and the darkness of the deeper wilderness.

"You're keeping calm," she said. "Lately, not like you."

"I've been through worse, including a plane crash into shark-infested water," he told her through gritted teeth. The pain was spreading. Surely he hadn't broken a bone.

"Do you think human sharks are after us? Even if someone was following us, they couldn't rush ahead to plant the spike sticks, but they could call ahead to give our position to someone waiting."

"Sadly, you're starting to think like me. And I just hope we're out here alone."

They stopped under a big fica tree and sat on its twisted roots. Jace took out his phone, but covered its light with his hand as he punched in the number.

"You're calling a longer number than 911," she said.

"Calling in a favor from my FBI contact. You want a good, armed guard at the BAA tonight—and I can hardly walk—this is our man. I'm gonna ask him to chopper in, and then I'll call for some tow truck help."

"What's his name? Indiana Jones? James Bond?"

Despite it all—his damaged car, their precarious position, his damned ankle and the fact Brit was just as bull-headed as Claire had always been—Jace had to love her nerve and spirit. If he could only trust her all the way to level with him, she was for sure the woman for him.

"'Lo?" a sleepy voice on the phone said. "Mitch here. Oh, it's you, Hawk. In that case, Falcon here. What?"

"Hawk needs your help. Personal but possibly dangerous."

"Right up my alley anyway. Give me your coordinates so I don't have to track you, and read me your recon."

Claire jolted awake and sucked in a quick breath when she saw a tall figure looming over her. Oh. Nick. Wearing only the boxer shorts he slept in. She was in Lexi's bed, and faint light from the hall sifted in.

"You two all right?" he whispered.

She nodded and slowly, carefully extricated herself, put the covers back over Lexi and followed Nick out of the room.

"She had a nightmare," she told him as they headed for their own bed.

"That's the name of this game lately."

It was early yet, barely 3:00 a.m. They got back in their bed and cuddled, Nick embracing her this time. "Nick, Lexi said Brit told her about the blind Florida panther at the zoo and not to mention it to Jace, though—excuse me for putting it this way—the cat is out of the bag since she told me."

"Brit's good at going behind people's backs, but I don't think we should read too much into that. She's an independent woman, desperate to get her life back on track. Listen, I didn't want to get anyone's hopes up, but I'm going to contact the Tampa area zoo, and perhaps something good may come of it, though they may still want the tiger."

"'Oh, what a tangled web we weave.' I agree with you that Brit does things on her own. She didn't tell her father she was talking to Stan Helter, then didn't tell Jace what she's up to with the Naples Zoo. But I'm glad you agree she's probably not guilty of plotting against her father or Jackson. No way."

He gave her a little squeeze. "*Probably* is a pretty big word. Let's not have that happen around here, going behind the other's back."

"Of course not, but I've been thinking."

"Uh-oh."

She gave him a little elbow punch in his stomach, then said, "Actually, I was thinking that I'll let you and Bronco, even Heck, lead the way in investigating this tiger case. The police have looked at both Lane and Brit. I think I've proved that Gracie was not a suspect. I know you've been waiting for Bronco to get back from his honeymoon this afternoon—their three days have gone fast—to see what he can uncover about Stan at the ranch."

"I'd love to have you just advising from the wings, concentrating on Lexi, the baby—me, of course—and your Comfort Zone kids, especially poor Duncan. I think you're making progress there."

"I do too. I'll just act as a sounding board—consultant—but please keep me up on everything. Maybe staying objective will help. But I do think—really—that Brit cannot, absolutely cannot, be guilty of more than frustration and ambition. And she has Jace to take care of her."

"And you have me. I love you, Claire. You know how people say, 'You've made my day'? Well, my sweetheart, you've made my life."

★ ★ ★

"This seemed a lot farther than a half a mile," Jace gritted out as they approached the BAA gate. His ankle felt like it was on fire.

"You should have had your friend pick us up where we were. Men, when they are hurt or sick, are babies not to let someone else take care of them, if you ask me. Here, I'll get out my gate key."

"Why is it so damn dark here? Has the entry light gone out—or been put out? Maybe we are being followed and set up."

"No, it's been that way for a while. I think some of the nastier picketers hit it out with stones. The security gate camera up in the palm tree was damaged and isn't working either."

"You should have told me!"

"I don't want to keep asking for money! I know this place is on borrowed financial time. I don't want our future relationship to be based on that, and you've been playing finances close to the vest too."

"Not the same salary as I was used to, but I'm not paying child support anymore. Which reminds me, I've got to support Lexi more with my time. I'm still 'Daddy' but am now in competition with 'Dad' Nick. Brit, can you unlock that? I can't stand on this ankle! And we're getting the light and camera fixed!"

She fumbled with the lock and popped it open. They went in and relocked the gate behind them. Jace had told Mitch he could land just inside the entrance to the BAA, and they'd clear the area and light it. He figured the chopper was about twenty minutes out and hoped it wouldn't freak out the animals. At least the landing site that Brit hurried to clear and light with four battery lanterns was not near the larger animals, especially the tiger.

Bless her, she made an ice bag for his ankle from an old feed sack. They waited, scanning the sky, listening for the *whap-whap* of the rotor blades. It reminded him of the night he'd spent on the ground in Iraq after he'd had to bail out, but they'd found him, come in a helo to save him, given him a second life he was trying to get in order now.

"Here it comes," he said. "Hear it?"

"Yes, I do."

"But it's coming from the wrong direction."

"Maybe he circled around."

"It doesn't sound like the one he uses to fly the Stingray recorders to his contact. That sound—too big. And it's coming from the east, maybe the other side of the state. Brit, turn those lanterns off. Now."

"But he probably just got in a bigger one and—"

"Now!"

Jace dived for the nearest lantern and turned it off, despite his ankle.

"Have you heard choppers here before at night?" he asked as they huddled under the overhang roof of the ticket office in the now dark area.

"No, but I don't think I've ever been here this late— like, nearly 4:00 a.m."

"Jackson ever say anything?"

"No, but he said he was a sound sleeper. Jace, what are you thinking?"

"I'm not thinking, I'm just reacting. Look, look, there it is," he said, pointing at the sudden blaze of lights above the tree line. A sharp searchlight swept the area where it was evidently going to land, just across the fence, on ranch land. It slowly descended to the ground.

The noise from the rotors upset some of the birds, especially the vocal one who squawked and screeched *Who— are—you?* Exactly, Jace thought. Who the hell was landing a big chopper just over the fence on ranch land in the middle of the night and why? He jumped again as two flamingos, looking like gray ghosts in the darkness, ran across the open patio in panic.

"I'll get them back later," Brit said. "The helicopter is going to the ranch."

"Exactly."

"Meaning what?"

"Meaning maybe nothing, like maybe it's just a jumper flight in from the Miami or Fort Lauderdale airports, new high-paying guests here to live it up and shoot game for a few days. Or maybe something sneaky that needs to be brought in at night."

"Exotic animals to kill?"

"Or illegals that work there. It's a big chopper. Nick mentioned that as a possibility, something Helter maybe had to hide—who knows, maybe something your dad or Jackson were on to. And here we are, waiting for our own guest. Since that chopper's down, let's light up here again."

"Jace, I do want to marry you," she said, tears in her eyes as she hugged him hard. "But I still want to work with lions and tigers, not bears—oh, my."

"I like the want-to-marry part, but is that from some kid's song?"

"The movie *The Wizard of Oz*. You never saw that? What am I ever going to do with you?"

"Love me—and tell me the truth up front, when it happens, before you do something dangerous, not after. Promise?"

"Till death do us part."

# CHAPTER TWENTY-FIVE

"It may be broken, man," Mitch, alias Falcon, told Jace when he looked at the discolored, swollen ankle. The FBI contact he seldom saw for security's sake wore a blue denim jumpsuit and had shaved his blond hair so close he looked bald. Jace had been told never to contact "Falcon," that he would contact him, unless there was an emergency, and Jace had figured this was. He huddled with him and Brit in the trailer office.

"I told him it could be broken, but he's a tough one," Brit said. "He'd be no help if he stayed here, and he needs the ER, so I hope you can fly him out. I usually have a vehicle and our guard used to be here at night, but no one and no car right now."

"My car's being towed," Jace said.

"That strands you out here, so you better both come with me," Mitch said. "I can fly you both to the chopper pad, then drive you to the ER if you want to keep things quiet from the cops, which is always my option of choice. Look, Jace, I read about the problems here at this place, but what's the latest? Someone taking potshots at you, Ms. Hoffman? No offense, but I have to keep an eye on my guys in the sky, like Jace."

"I understand," Brit said. "But those spike sticks could have been planted by picketers. Some radical pro-wild-life groups have been protesting our little petting zoo, and some have been after the ranch next door where they shoot animals."

"Brit, I don't think there are picketers out here in the boondocks in the middle of the night," Jace protested.

"Copy that," Mitch said. "But I understand multiple suspects. You know, Jace, this attack could have been aimed at you. Stingray really annoys the big drug import-ers. Maybe they're on your six for being with me. There have been a couple cases in other states where the Sting-ray pilots were located and attacked."

"My phone has been hacked, but then so have some of my friends' cells. I can't help but think this has to do with the BAA's problems."

"I'll have to report to my superiors what happened to your car tonight, but first things first. I get you don't want Brit to stay here alone or to leave the animals un-guarded, but I got to go. You both with me, or not? You got a weapon on-site here?"

"Not on-site," Jace said. "There's a Glock in the trunk of my car. I couldn't get to it so—"

"I have both a pistol and a rifle here," Brit interrupted. "One's in the small apartment next door, and the other's locked in that filing cabinet in the corner. Neither have ever been fired on-site as far as I know."

Jace frowned, not from ankle pain this time. Brit should have told him. Again, what else did he not know about her or this apparently harmless place?

"Brit," Jace said, "I know you're worried about the animals, but you'll have to come with me. Guns or not, I can't leave you alone, not with all that's happened here."

"Guns or not? I've never shot anything more than a tranquilizer gun anyway. Those weapons were for Dad or Jackson. I—I was so panicked when Dad was attacked, I didn't run back to the trailer to get it, then the Naples Zoo people used their tranquilizer on Tiberia when they got here. My—my fault for panicking when I saw Dad—that way," she stammered. Hugging herself and blinking back tears, she turned away from them.

Behind her back, Mitch rolled his eyes, and Jace shook his head. "Let's get out of here," Mitch said. "From the ER you can call someone, Brit, get back here ASAP after daylight to tend to the animals. Jace, next time so much as your phone gets hacked, let alone your car slams into spike sticks, call me fast, and not just 'cause you need a lift, okay? I repeat, this could be about your work with Stingray."

Jace nodded and kept quiet for now, but there was something else he had to know. He waited until Brit went to the shed with a flashlight to get a wheelbarrow to roll him to the chopper, since his ankle was starting to look as big as a grapefruit and he couldn't put any weight on it now.

"Listen, Mitch," he said, speaking fast, "there's a lot going on here at this Backwoods Animal Adventure that has nothing to do with me, even stuff that the media hasn't covered. I'll fill you in later. But do you know anything about a large helo coming from the east to land near here, across the northern fence line, at the Trophy Ranch next door? A big one came in there just before you arrived."

"Saw it on radar, but have no idea about it. I don't make it a habit to fly over wilderness and the Glades this hour of the night, man. Maybe you should ask the owner of the ranch."

"Yeah, right," he said as Brit rolled the wheelbarrow in. Feeling like an invalid and furious he wasn't going to be much help, he shifted his big frame into it.

Claire tried to keep her promise to Nick about staying on the sidelines of the Tiger Cage Case. All afternoon she tended her *Clear Path* website, gave some advice about fraud to an independently owned women's clothing store client and sent out a newsletter to a sponsor list she and Darcy were assembling to help support some of the Comfort Zone kids. It wasn't the same as doing things for others up close and personal, but it helped some.

Yet she couldn't just let things go at that. She decided to check out several items she hadn't had time for lately. First, she researched Irv Glover's road rage assault trial where Nick and his team had sent Duncan's dad to prison. A mug shot of him filled the screen. She downsized it so it wouldn't seem so threatening. The man seemed to leap at her with that defiant glare. He was clean shaven and not bad looking but still seemed sinister. She could see Duncan in his older features, especially the mouth and eyes. She prayed that was all the boy inherited from this man.

She read about the assault trial, then, after his release

from prison, the murder he'd committed, about how it was assumed he had fled and was living incognito out of state. The man was still missing, but how much were poor Marta and Duncan missing—peace, reputation, decent financial support, happiness—because of this horrid man?

She read up next on Stan Helter, but he seemed to have no past. Oh, one bio said he came from Montana where he had worked on and inherited part of a cattle ranch when the owner had died in an accident. The original newspaper coverage of the Trophy Ranch opening mentioned that there were several local, wealthy investors, and she found Grant Manfort's name among them. She followed a link to corporate news about Grant taking over the Florida Gulf Coast Life Insurance company when its founder and CEO Steve Rowan was presumed drowned in a storm with his granddaughter, Leslie. They'd been out in Rowan's small yacht fishing just off Marco Island nearby.

She skimmed the story about the Coast Guard's searching for the boat. It had washed ashore on nearby Keewadin Island, but their bodies were never found. Claire enlarged the photo of the missing pair. It was in color, first page of the Sunday paper. The grandfather was very tall. Another picture of him, a close-up with the girl, showed he had a gap between his front teeth, so unusual today with orthodontists, but he was probably not one for modern ways. And the girl, Leslie, was pretty, her smiling face framed by straight, long red hair that fell past her shoulders.

A kindred soul, Claire thought, fingering her own red tresses, though her hair was shorter and naturally curly, the bane of her early years before she learned to appreciate it. She skimmed the article. Leslie Rowan had been just twenty-one and loved to fish with her grandfather. She was his only grandchild and, with her mother, his heiress. Claire recalled seeing Leslie's mother, Steve's daughter, at the symphony.

One more thing she'd wanted to do. She searched for the Tampa area Family Friendly Zoo that was supposed to receive Tiberia/Thunder. It was privately owned too, like the BAA. She checked to see if they had tigers and they did, but a link came up to an article about a "tiger escape."

She checked it out and gasped. A tiger had been shot and killed on the grounds there! No, not exactly on the grounds. In 2002, an escaped Sumatran tiger had gotten out of its cage and wandered through an unlocked gate into a reconstruction area. They had tried to tranquilize it, but that had provoked it, and he had charged at a person standing nearby. So they had shot it—killed it.

She reached for the phone so she could read that to Nick, then recalled he'd be in a partners meeting. She glanced at the clock. It was her turn to pick up Lexi and Jilly from preschool today, and she had to go now if she didn't want them waiting. Anyway, Nick had said he'd be home early. This tiger death had happened a long time ago, yet, knowing Nick, he could probably make something of it, something to help keep Brit's tiger in Naples.

Claire picked up Lexi and Jilly from preschool, listened to their chatter, dropped Jilly off and made her own chatter with Darcy. So normal, so calm, though her thoughts were still on the case—both tiger cases now.

To her surprise, Nick phoned at about four to tell her he'd be there in an hour—early for him. "I need to drop something off at the courthouse, but I need to tell you what happened to Jace and Brit after they left last night. Lexi isn't right there, is she?"

"She ran to her bedroom to change clothes. Are they all right?"

"Pretty much." She gasped as he told her Jace and Brit had had an accident, but were okay and were rescued from the BAA by a pilot friend of Jace's. He had called Nick since Claire had said she was trying to stay out of things a bit more. "I wanted you to know so you wouldn't hear it somewhere else first," Nick explained.

"Like on the news?"

"They kept it quiet, but you never know. Anyway, his car was taken by a tow truck, and he's getting the tires replaced. He hid the spike sticks that caused the damage."

"Those things the police use?"

"Right. And he'll need to stay off his own tires, so to speak, because he broke his ankle and is in a cast. His pilot friend got him to a walk-in Urgent Care—not that he could walk in."

"At least they weren't seriously hurt, but it gets worse and worse! Can he fly?"

"Not until he's in a soft cast instead of a plaster one," Nick said. "Right now he's on crutches, so he won't be much help for Brit at the BAA at night. Wish Bronco wasn't a newlywed who is going to start working for Helter soon. Did you hear from Bronco and Nita? They probably had to check out of the Ritz around 11:00 a.m. today, so I thought they might stop at the house."

"No, but I hope they're still on a honeymoon high, so why

would they want to see me or us? Oh, you mean to give us their decision on the house bribe Helter offered them?"

"Which I hope has now, thanks to Grant, been reduced to a reasonably priced place they can pay for. Lexi have a good day?"

"I swear, she's always obsessed with something new, but at least she's off her name-that-baby kick. They were playing some memory game today in school with items hidden under cups, and she says we should do that for the next Comfort Zone meeting instead of playing freeze tag."

"Hmm. Now where did she ever get that tendency to organize things her way?"

"I hear you. But I have some news of my own. The Family Friendly Zoo that is supposed to get Brit's tiger had to shoot an escaped tiger there years ago, and the reviews of the place were bad, and not just for that."

"Whew. This is why you're still on my personal payroll. Yeah, their lawyer's being sticky, but that could help. Great job. I'll have Heck call you to get more details for me. See you soon, sweetheart—and partner."

"Just be prepared for a memory game. And I do hope to talk to Brit later about maybe going to the Naples Zoo with the Comfort Zone kids, but I don't want her to know Lexi spilled the beans about Uno."

"Okay. I've got to go."

"Nick, I hope that tiger info helps. Brit deserves some good news after everything she's been through—and so do we."

Nick and Claire had a late dinner and were just getting ready to head for showers and bed when the doorbell rang. Claire looked through the peephole.

"It's Bronco and Nita. You're psychic," she told Nick as he joined her. She put her arm around him. They were in a great mood because this afternoon Nick had convinced the Family Friendly Zoo lawyer that their zoo didn't need a resurrection of the earlier tiger-death publicity, which might be rehashed when they took in Tiberia. That made Claire feel she'd contributed.

"Well, hello to the post-honeymoon newlyweds!" Nick greeted them as he opened the door. But Claire saw the glow was gone.

Was there some sort of curse on this house, the way Brit had claimed there was on the BAA? Brit and Jace had been barely speaking when they showed up here yesterday, and they'd gone on to disaster. Now Nita and Bronco looked—well, upset and even at odds.

Claire was going to invite them in and finesse the tension, but Nick blurted, "What happened? Are you two okay?"

Bronco shuffled his feet but didn't budge. "We're here to say that I—we—decided I wouldn't work at the ranch full-time. Nita doesn't want me to even do it part-time, but I already signed on to help you out, boss. We want the house, but don't need strings attached—at least not to someone else. Each other—remains to be seen, I guess."

"What happened?" Nick repeated.

Claire knew he was relieved about Bronco not leaving his employ completely, so maybe the newlyweds had just been arguing about that. But she sensed this was something deeper.

"Come inside," she said, tugging Nita in and gesturing

toward the library, though that room was getting to be bad luck too. "A problem or disagreement?"

"First fight," Bronco said, perching on the edge of the couch while Nita sank on it with a sigh. "Not my fault, 'cause I was just leveling with her. Trust, all that."

"He didn't think I should know it till I had signed on the dotted line!" Nita erupted. "I thought he just agreed to work where we could get a pretty house. But there are girls there for the taking! Why did he not tell me before?" She produced a wadded-up tissue from her jacket pocket and blew her nose.

Nick said, "You mean at the Trophy Ranch?"

"Oh, yes," Nita said, her voice surprisingly flippant. "Some trophy for him!"

"But he did tell you he didn't do the taking, didn't he, Nita?" Nick asked. He sat in the closest chair and leaned forward, elbows on his knees. "Didn't he?"

"You mean *that* kind of girl at the ranch? Like prostitutes?" Claire put in, sitting on the arm of Nick's chair. Nick was way ahead of her on this. Why hadn't he told her either?

"Free ones! Fits Bronco's budget!" Nita cried, blinking back tears again.

"I guess I'm learning not to tell the truth, 'cept to you, boss," Bronco muttered.

"Now wait a minute," Claire insisted, holding up both hands, palms out as if to halt a crash. "Nita, Bronco told you that when he went to his interview at the ranch he was offered a woman?"

"Turned that down right away," Bronco put in. "Could

lead to blackmail, but more important, only one woman I want, sitting right here and damn mad at me for nothing."

"Nick," Claire said, turning toward him, "you knew about this?"

"He told me right after."

"Oh," Nita burst out, "of course, he told you, man to man, but didn't trust me! So can I trust him? And if Nick knew and didn't tell you, can you trust him, Claire?"

Claire glared at Nick. Hadn't they just been happy to be working together again, hadn't he promised to tell her everything about this tiger/trophy ranch case if she kept her physical distance from it all? And had the fact he'd from the first tried to steer her clear of Stan Helter, "a womanizer," meant he knew all about the women there—and maybe hadn't kept his distance? Had he kept her in the dark because he'd availed himself of those freebies earlier, before she knew him—or even after?

"No, Nita, I didn't know that," Claire clipped out. "I believe it slipped my husband's mind to tell me. I don't know how I can help out, or even advise, when I don't really have a clue what's going on, what's at stake. Now, I can see why Bronco didn't want to spring that on you at this time, and he was committed to work at the ranch to help out Nick and me—that is, to help Nick, since I obviously had no idea about anything. I'll take you to the guest bathroom so you can wash your face, and tell me—I hope—that you had a lovely honeymoon at the Ritz before that bombshell dropped. Come on, we'll leave these men to figure out how to make that big secret, which we're apparently too fragile or foolish to understand, up to us. At least Bronco finally told you!"

"Sorry, boss," Claire overheard Bronco say as she and Nita hurried out the door.

"Yeah, me too," Nick said. "I may be a hotshot criminal lawyer, but there are obviously different rules when you're married. We'd both better forget innocent until proven guilty around here."

# CHAPTER TWENTY-SIX

"I would have told you what Bronco learned at the Trophy Ranch, Claire," Nick said as he came into their bedroom after his shower that night. She was already in bed with her back to his side of their king-size mattress.

"Oh, really? When were you planning to do that? Just before it appeared in the *Naples Daily News*?"

She hadn't been speaking to him when he first came in, so this was a start, he thought. It felt cold enough in here you'd think the air-conditioning was on full blast, but he wasn't about to give up.

"Bronco had to settle it with Nita first," he went on, keeping his voice calm. If they went to bed angry, it would be worse in the morning, and he had to get in to the office early to keep working on helping Brit settle Tiberia's destination and her future employment problems. He had to admit Claire had given him a great idea on how to proceed with that.

"So," Claire said, her voice still deadly calm, "either you couldn't trust me not to blab to Nita, or you had some personal stake in my not knowing. And don't say, 'Objection, Your Honor.'"

He smiled at that, despite it all. Clever Claire. He risked walking around the bed and sitting on his side with his back to the headboard. She shifted farther toward the edge of her side.

"Claire, it's Grant I've known, not his friend Stan Helter. You know I had my first tour of the ranch recently. I hope you also realize I—as a moral person and a lawyer—would never take advantage of women like that, if that's what you mean by 'a personal stake.' I'd have a personal stake in anyone being abused, as you should know by now. One thing I'm going to do is be sure Helter's not using illegals as cheap help or sex slaves, but we've got to learn whether he's a murderer first. If we turn him in on suspicion of trafficking illegals or for running a house of prostitution, the murder mess will be swept away in the sensational coverage of that."

She sat up and turned toward him. "Maybe both Ben and Jackson had hints about the women, were onto that. So he had to get rid of both men and make it look like accidents. Meanwhile, Lane's trying to make it sound like a guilt-ridden suicide."

"That's my girl. What would I do without you?"

"You are not off the hook yet, my boy."

"Then I'm really going to be in trouble now, because there's something else I have to tell you that may support the imported women theory," he said. "Something that tied to Jace's undercover work. Speaking of undercovers, will you not freak out and scream for help if I get under the covers with you?"

"It's a big bed, though maybe right now not big enough," she said with a dramatic shrug as he lifted his corner of the covers and got in. "But what does Jace have to do with the women at the ranch?"

"He told me that last night at about 3:30 a.m., a large helicopter landed just over the BAA fence at the ranch. It seemed to be coming from the east."

"But that's wilderness and Everglades."

"Unless you fly over all that, coming from the east coast—Lauderdale or Miami."

"New paying customers coming in and looking forward to hunting game and bedding girls?"

"Or the ranch importing the girls themselves? I don't know how to go at that but to let Bronco keep his eyes open—his eyes, Claire, not his zipper."

"All right. I—I know that. You and I can declare a temporary truce, but right now I'm exhausted. Maybe we'll have some good news soon. We've been playing too much therapist like Dr. Phil to arguing couples, and then we turned into one."

"So let's just play matchmaker for ourselves," he said, and reached way over to stroke her shoulder.

"Nick, we're arguing. We're having a fight," she said, but her voice was suddenly as warm as honey.

"I know I try to overprotect you sometimes, but after all we've been through—and since you and the baby you're carrying are two key people in my life—give a guy a break. Let's not waste any of our time together, the two of us or our family, especially after the tough times we've been through."

"You're always so persuasive, Counselor," she murmured, reaching out to circle his wrist with one hand. "But I want to be part of your professional team, even if I'm pregnant and domestic for a while."

"You're always an in-house forensic psychologist and fraud examiner. The tip you gave me about the dead tiger at the Family Friendly Zoo may keep Brit here, may mean she and Jace can get their lives together—together."

"All right," she said, "here's the deal. Unless it's about a wonderful, expensive, surprise present you have purchased for me, please don't keep things from me."

He scooted closer and cupped her cheek with his hand. "Deal. Absolutely."

"Oh, no," she said. "I was so intent at being mad at you I forgot to take my night meds. The bottle's in the bathroom. Be back in a sec."

"Don't get up. Be right back with it."

What would she do without him, on little things and big things too? She sat up a bit and turned to face him as he came back with the bottle and a spoon.

"Ouch! Damn! Stubbed my toe, maybe cut it on something under the bed!" he cried, hopping on one foot on her side of the bed. He put the bottle and spoon down to sit and examine his hurt toe.

She was instantly up, bending close to check out his foot. "Wow, you actually cut it on something—that metal piece that holds it up, I think. I'll get a washcloth and bandage. You men have to learn to be careful!"

She meant him and Jace, he realized. Weird, he thought,

but his cut big toe wasn't the only part of him that was throbbing. He loved and wanted this woman so much. Vulnerable, yet capable. Strong yet soft.

She tended to him and took her medicine, then they tended to each other as if they'd never had cross words. Finally, both tired, she turned her back to him in bed and he scooted close again until they were lying like a pair of spoons. Her body fit perfectly against his, which really turned him on again, but then, she always had since the first day he saw her, testifying against him in court, and she'd managed to make him lose a rare case. But he wasn't going to lose the Tiger Cage Case, and he wasn't ever going to lose her.

By late afternoon the next day, Jace was going stark raving crazy not flying, not driving, hardly walking, but getting around on a pair of damn crutches. All he'd been through, basic training, flight school, combat, he'd never broken a bone before. He'd bailed out of planes but couldn't handle bailing out of his own car. And tough-as-nails Brit had done it just fine.

The apartment walls were closing in. He decided to call a cab and go out to the BAA for the rest of the day.

True, he'd be no help manning the gate if those picketers or the media showed up again, but at least he'd be there for advice and support, could order a new gate light and get the surveillance camera repaired by a phone call. He could find some sort of project where he could sit in one place. Besides, then he'd be with Brit.

He was nervous too that Falcon might be right about him rather than Brit being the target of the spike sticks, though he had figured earlier that his phone being tapped was more likely to have to do with Ben Hoffman's death or even the attack on Jackson.

He called a cab but then decided to stop at Claire and Nick's to see Lexi, so he called Claire to be sure they were home and it was okay. She sounded really worried about his ankle and the car accident.

"Too much going on," he told her. "Like an idiot, I hadn't even asked to see Lexi last time I was here." He didn't say so, but he was thinking that, maybe in this downtime, he could spend more time with Lexi, at least on the weekends, but he couldn't drive her anywhere for now. He liked Nick, but when he arrived and Claire led him out to the Florida room, he felt a stab of regret that his child wasn't really a big part of his life anymore.

"Daddy, sorry you hurt your foot! Can I sign your cast and draw a heart on it?" Lexi cried and ran to give him a hug that nearly knocked him off balance. Nick, sitting next to her on the couch, got up too.

"Ah, yeah, sure, Lex."

"Daddy, I beat Dad two times at this game."

"We're playing by flexible rules—her rules," Nick said, raising his eyebrows, as they shook hands. "I'm sooo glad I came home early today. I don't care what everyone says, it's a woman's world, at least around here. Listen, I'll let you and Lexi have some time, and escape for a few minutes. Stay for dinner."

"If you're partway through a game, finish it and I'll watch to catch on. Then Lexi can put a heart on my cast, okay? Any news on Brit's tiger being able to stay in Naples?" he asked as he sat awkwardly on the couch with his leg stretched out to the side. He leaned his crutches against the arm but one slid to the floor.

"Claire came up with something from online research and Heck's expanded on that—and I played bad lawyer today to the Family Friendly Zoo in Tampa and good lawyer to the Naples Zoo. Decision to be made tomorrow."

Jace realized that he smiled for the first time in quite a while. "So there's hope. Animal lovers of the world, rejoice!"

"Which means me," Lexi put in. "I love my pony Scout about more than anything—except the people in this house and the ones in Aunt Darcy's. Okay, now Daddy, here's the rules. Important stuff like silver dollars and a bracelet are hidden under these cups, but you close your eyes and they get switched around."

"It's a unique filing system," Claire said, coming into the room. "And you never know what you'll find or if it has magically moved under a different colored cup when your eyes were closed."

"That's it," Nick said, hitting his forehead with the palm of his hand. "How could I have forgotten that?"

"What?" Claire asked.

"When Jackson took me out to his big storage shed so he could give me that letter, he told me his system was to put important things under the supplies out there, paint cans and all. And I bet the police never looked there, moved all that, when they had their warrant."

"So," Jace said, "we should. I can call Brit about it."

"Let's just eat here, then all go out there. It will still be dark. You can ride shotgun and look for spike sticks. With four adults searching, it won't take as long, though he's stashed tons of stuff in there. I have no idea what we'd be looking for but—"

"If I go too," Lexi put in, "that's five people. We could teach Brit this memory game too, because I know she wants to remember her dad who got killed."

The two dads in the room looked at each other. "That's right," Jace told Lexi and reached out to stroke her hair. "Claire, some of your observational talents are rubbing off on your daughter."

"Yes, I'm always proud of her. I'll set an extra place for taco salad, and then we'll head for the BAA."

Brit brought in a baby lamb for Lexi to "take care of," while the four adults worked with big flashlights to look under each paint can and bag of feed in the BAA storage shed. Claire, who hadn't seen the interior, was amazed at the length and height of the aisles. She wished they had left Lexi at Darcy's because this could take a while, even with four of them.

"Is this the lamb on the BAA signs?" Lexi asked, petting the little animal.

"Not now, Lex," Jace said.

"It's the daughter of the one on the sign," came Brit's voice from the end of an aisle. "Her name's Wooly."

Claire appreciated that Brit could be considerate to answer that, even though Jace had already spoken. There was no way in the world Brittany Hoffman would have harmed her father or anyone else, and perhaps she would be a good stepmother to Lexi. If Jace did marry her, Claire could more than live with that. Although it was probably not good to be friends with an ex-husband's new wife, rules were made to be broken.

Nick said, "We should get Bronco, Nita, Heck and Gina in here tomorrow too. This could take a while, but it could be a wild-goose chase."

"Whatever happens here," Brit said, her voice muffled, "I'm just praying that Tiberia can go to the Naples Zoo and me too."

As Claire unstacked then restacked cans of varnish, she said, "Nick might know tomorrow. We're hopeful."

"And," Brit said, coming out of her aisle, looking both sweaty and dusty, "Nick was right that Jackson stashed some things of import here at least." She opened the end of a large, brown mailing envelope to display rubberbanded piles of cash within.

While everyone gasped and gathered to take a look, Claire had the same thought again: Brit was to be trusted. She was in financial trouble, but she came right out with this money, rather than pretending she'd found nothing and then using it for herself. "Wait until Jackson's daughters get this!" Brit said, and laid it on the worktable.

They soon realized it wasn't nearly as much as it had looked like at first, because it was all in small denominations. "You know," Brit said, "he told me he didn't trust banks. I guess he meant it."

At that, everyone went back to their search with renewed interest. No talk now, unless they could count Lexi's singing "Mary Had A Little Lamb" to Wooly.

Nick said, "Can someone help me move this big bag of feed?"

"Let me," Jace said, hustling over on his crutches. "It's my ankle that's broken, not my arms."

Claire stretched her back and watched as the two men managed to slide out a big bag from the first shelf up. She gasped, Jace swore and the others came crowding in as a flurry of photographs spewed onto the concrete floor.

# CHAPTER TWENTY-SEVEN

"These pics are all blown up so large," Claire said, stating the obvious as she helped Nick scoop them off the floor. Each was 8 by 11 inches and printed on regular paper.

"I knew he had a camera, but those look like pictures of just random foliage—and the fence," Brit put in, as she stood over them, shining her lantern down at the mess.

"I see a couple of his pink pets," Claire said, now on her knees on the concrete.

"Is it pink pigs?" Lexi asked.

"It's flamingos," Claire said. "Stand back with Wooly, hon, till we get these picked up."

Although so much of the shed was yet to be searched, they crowded into the office trailer, including Wooly in Lexi's arms. They stood around Brit's desk as she fanned through the pictures, then laid some of them out.

Nick said, "You're right, Claire. They have lousy definition since he—or someone—has enlarged them. I think they were done on a copy machine. So you have no idea about the why of these, Brit?"

"Not even that they existed. Look! This one has a face blurred on the other side of the fence. Is that a bearded man?"

They all looked and agreed. "A daylight shot," Nick said. "But what section of fence? Brit, can you tell from the foliage the guy's looking through where this was taken? It's not a picture of Lane, is it?"

Frowning, Brit stared at it, then squinted. "I don't think so. No—no way. His beard is more trimmed. It's ridiculous it would be Lane, anyhow, since His Musical Majesty would just walk right in. It's getting dark outside right now, but tomorrow, I can try to make a match of the place this was taken, walk the fence line looking for the site. Why didn't Jackson capture one of the animals' cages in this photo, so we could tell where it is?"

"Because he wanted to photograph the man," Claire said. "Maybe he felt—rightly so—the BAA was being watched, probably from ranch land. And, for some reason, he didn't want to show these to you at the time. Maybe he thought they would worry you when you were grieving, but I wish he'd shown them to Nick. Look—we can tell where this one is, but it's still just mostly fence and foliage."

"The corner of Tiberia's cage shows," Brit said. "And look—look at this one! I can tell who this is! I told you she's out for revenge."

She kept slapping her finger on a photo so it took a moment for Claire to tell who it was, though she was afraid she already knew. Gracie was peering through the double fence—the ranch's and BAA's. The blurred rungs of a ladder were barely discernable too.

"She's already admitted to climbing to call to the tiger," Claire protested. "But let's think more about why Jackson took these and didn't tell you, even about Gracie."

Brit said, "When the police got the warrant to search his things, they said they found his camera but it had nothing on the memory card."

Nick said, "Of course, he might have emptied it, considering all these pictures he took. Or it could mean, if someone did attack him, that person also knew to erase the card themselves."

"But then to place it back in his apartment, and be sure there were no fingerprints but his on it?" Claire asked.

"You know," Brit said, when they'd scrabbled through the photos, about thirty of them, "Jackson did mention that he had some pictures to show me, but he'd shown me some before. I just assumed, as usual, they would be of the animals and endless ones of his flamingos."

"The thing is," Claire said, "where are the originals of these that would be clearer, even if smaller?"

"He didn't have a computer that I know of," Brit said. "Unless he used Dad's and, once again, the police found nothing of interest on his laptop while they had it."

"It's getting late," Nick said. "We've got to get Lexi home to bed. Jace, I can run you home after that, unless Brit can take you. But I'd like, as your lawyer, Brit, to take these photos with me to study more closely, let Claire look them over too. Jackson was obviously taking pictures of a person—persons—watching the BAA from the ranch, and that could be key in your father's case."

"Yes. Yes, all right. Key in Stan Helter being behind everything after all, even though that's hardly him in that photo. I think Helter looks like that rugged Marlboro Man they used to use to sell cigarettes before the tobacco companies had to admit those things cause cancer. Helter's a cancer too, and I should have realized it. Sorry I'm such a downer right now."

"'If Winter comes, can Spring be far behind?'" Claire said quietly.

"Mommy, it's October, so winter's coming soon," Lexi put in.

"It's a quote from a poem by someone named Percy Bysshe Shelley. I meant it in a kind of special way," she explained, pulling Lexi to her and petting the lamb's head. "It means if times are hard, something good could be just around the corner."

Jace said, "Let's hope so. Like pilots under fire have been known to say, 'Sometimes there's nowhere to go but up.'"

That night, after the house was quiet, Nick and Claire studied Jackson's photos until their eyes were as bleary as the photos.

"We'd better hit it," Nick muttered. "All these photos but only two faces, Gracie and the bearded guy."

"So many men are wearing beards these days. You'd think we're back in Civil War times. It really hides their faces, and most men look better without them."

"I'll remember that, Your Honor," he said, patting her rear as she got up from the kitchen chair.

They turned out lights and headed down the hall to their bedroom. While he went ahead, Claire peeked in at Lexi. She had dug an old stuffed animal of a lamb out of the back of her closet and had her arm around it. The petting zoo had certainly done a lot for some kids. Duncan still talked about the pig he had befriended there. If things just worked out with the Naples Zoo, that would indeed be the place to take the Comfort Zone kids, especially if Tiberia was safely living there, a good lesson about hard times getting better. She hated to admit it, but the BAA animals would be better off at a different facility, certainly one with better funding.

She quietly closed Lexi's door and went into their bedroom. Nick was lying in bed already, hands behind his head, staring at the ceiling.

"I can't believe I'm slipping," he said. "It took that memory game of Lexi's—and your mentioning that it was a unique filing system—before I recalled that Jackson had told me he had a so-called filing system in the storage building. Worse, I'm thinking he also told me it was his best hiding place. Talk about Lexi's memory game—my brain's wired wrong lately."

She sat down beside him on the edge of the bed. Her weight rolled him a bit toward her. He took his hands from back of his head and put one arm around her waist, one on her thigh.

"Nick, you have so much going on, and some of it means life or death for your clients, so you can't keep everything straight."

"Yeah, and here I was relieved Brit didn't get accused of anything, so that didn't turn into a court case. And then I end up playing middleman between two zoos, when I have other big-time cases pending."

"As well as family life—for the first time in your life."

"Which I don't want to screw up, and sometimes do," he said, tugging her down into his arms. "First things first—you and family. After all the years I was out for justice, even revenge, against the man who murdered my father, here we are, the target of someone who fights with dead animals and—maybe—dead people. And then those weird pictures Jackson took. Mostly thick foliage, as if he was obsessed with someone watching there, hiding. It's like some nightmare..."

"I know about those. Which reminds me, time to take my pill. Nick, I'll study those pictures again, and I can take Heck and Bronco out to search for more in the storage shed—maybe Nita too, if they're speaking now. Jackson used that place like a bank and a file drawer."

"You're right—what you said earlier about that memory game," Nick called after her as Claire rose and went to get a drink of water to take her pill. "Memories are hidden, but you lift the cup or something, and out they come. Then what you do with them is what matters."

She swallowed her pill, went back in, removed her robe and turned out the lights. "I'm interested in making new family memories," she told him as she got into bed. "I think it's great that Lexi has animals to love, beyond Scout. Maybe animals can help the Comfort Zone kids, even someone as damaged as Duncan," she said, through a yawn.

He reached for her in the darkness, and they held each other tight.

The next morning, Claire was back out at the BAA, searching the shed with Jace, Bronco, Nita and Heck. Even though she and Nick decided she wouldn't be hands-on anymore in this case, he'd agreed to this. After all, she figured, there was safety in numbers.

While Brit was feeding animals, they'd come up with two more stashes of photos, but ones of Jackson and his family from way back to the present. When Brit joined them, she said, "I called Jackson's daughters about the windfall of money, and they'll be thrilled to have these family photos too. Actually, I hate to just give everything to them as if he's dead already. The doctor said he may pull through, though he can't discount brain damage. And here, I couldn't even afford decent insurance for him, though he had some of his own."

She sat down on a bag of feed and started to cry. "It's best this is all over. I've got to let go of this, Dad's dream, no matter where Tiberia and I have to go."

Jace hobbled over and managed to sit on the sack next to her, with his crutches on the floor. "We'll make it, Brit. We'll find a way to work it all out. If Gina can go study in Miami and she and Heck can stay together…"

Claire saw Heck's stricken look at that. Oh, not him and Gina too! Did she have to give up her forensic training and just go into a couples' counseling business?

And did she hear Nick's voice, calling her name outside or was she losing it too?

But Bronco's head jerked up, and he started for the door with Claire right behind him.

Nick was coming at a sprint past Flamingo Isle, with his white shirtsleeves rolled up and his tie flapping. And—in his hand—a magnum of champagne?

"I'm going to have to fire myself for missing too much

work lately," he called to them as the others waited with Claire. The sun popped out of a cloud as Nick stopped and lifted the bottle. "We'll have to give a dish of this to Tiberia too," he told them, out of breath. "Brittany Hoffman, you and your tiger, as well as the other BAA animals, are going to the Naples Zoo! The small Tampa area zoo has decided that will be best for the tiger—best for them too, I persuaded them. Are you crying already?"

"Oh, Nick," Brit shrieked and the others exploded in cheers. It thoroughly annoyed the tropical birds, especially the one that always screeched *Who—are—you?*

Brit hugged Nick; Claire hugged them both. Brit fell so hard into Jace's arms she almost knocked him off his crutches. Heck grinned, for he'd had a part in this too, and, thank heavens, Bronco and Nita embraced.

"Hope you have some crystal goblets around here!" Nick told Brit when everyone calmed down.

"Paper cups in the snack booth! Oh," she said, breaking into tears again, "Dad would be so happy to hear this, and Mother will too! The animals will be well taken care of, and I can stay here too," she added with a teary smile at Jace.

Claire had to laugh through her own happy tears of relief. Nick might be over programmed and forget things at times, but the man was usually amazing with details.

This was a huge victory, she thought. For Nick, for Brit and Jace too. And the next victory was going to be finding out who came over that fence, possibly to kill Ben and hurt Jackson. Surely nothing else bad could happen now.

# CHAPTER TWENTY-EIGHT

Just before noon the next day, Claire heard a car door and got up from working on her laptop in the library to look out in front. Nick was home in the middle of the day. Why hadn't he called so she could have lunch ready? She hoped something wasn't wrong.

Maybe he was trying to make it up to her for wanting her to "stay domestic" until the baby was born. Or because he hadn't told her about the women at the Trophy Ranch. Surely he wasn't ill. But he hadn't pulled into the garage, so he must not be staying for long. And, thank God, she saw a smile on his face.

She met him at the front door with a hug. "What's happening?" she asked.

"I love to tell good news in person. And we have a lot of work to do between now and Saturday afternoon. Part of the deal I just finished negotiating with the zoo."

"Which zoo? An interview? An event?"

Smiling even more broadly, he took her hand, closed the door and tugged her down the hall toward the back of the house. With his free hand, he dug a folded piece of paper out of the inside pocket of his suit coat and opened it as they went into the brightly lit Florida room.

"Don't keep me in suspense, you tease!" she protested. "I'll pour you a cup of coffee, but you'll explain before you get one bit of food."

Still playing it to the hilt, he picked up an apple from the bowl of them on the table and bit into it. "Actually," he said with his mouth full, "I proposed something like this to sweeten the deal, and it's worked out." He put the apple down, sat and skidded the papers toward her across the corner of the table. "You're right, an event. The BAA and the zoo here are inviting the media, the mayor, zoo board and other special guests to the donation of the BAA animals to the zoo this Saturday. It will include Tiberia being moved into a travel cage, put on a truck and taken to his new digs."

"Oh," she said, skimming the second page after the copy of the press release. "I'm glad he'll have his own cage for a while."

"A necessary period of quarantine for disease."

"And who knows how he'll react around the tigers they already have? I'll bet they socialize them gradually."

"I think you'd be a good animal psychologist too. The problem is, of course, that this is happening tomorrow, and we have a lot to do to prepare for a crowd at the BAA. But it will be great for zoo publicity and to have the BAA dissolved on a good note, so to speak. I called Brit, and she's so happy things worked out she'll agree to any-

thing. Except when she told Lane, he insisted on bringing a string quartet to play, which probably won't fit the
hoopla atmosphere."

"I wonder what poor Gracie will think."

"She may not have a phone, but the word's out here in
town and on local news. I thought, if you had the noon
news on, you might see it before I got here. Brit is worried that Gracie might try to spring the tiger before the
zoo can get him protected. So the zoo management—
Brit's ecstatic about this too—is assigning two of their
guards to spend tonight at the BAA, tending and guarding the animals."

"This will be another huge shock for Jackson when—
if—he recovers. But a happy ending to a sad case for the
animals and for Brit," she said, pouring him a cup of coffee and setting it next to him on the table.

"For sure. Except, she says, for two things worrying
her, besides Gracie. One, that zoo visitors won't get over
Tiberia's reputation for having killed a man. And two—
like me—she doesn't want this Disney-happy ending to
mean we won't still pursue the foul play possibility in her
father's death, especially since the police are accepting the
accidental death autopsy report."

"That makes me feel better about Brit. I believe in her,
I believe her, yet occasionally I realize she, and Lane much
more so, do have reasons to have been angry with Ben. Is
Ann okay with all this?"

"I talked to her this morning too. She was with Brit.
She's sad yet relieved. It was a financial burden for her, and
the BAA just depresses her now. Despite losing Ben, she's
glad to see Brit happy—and maybe ready to settle down."

"With Jace."

"He proposed once before, and Brit said they had to wait."

"Oh. Didn't know that. At least they won't be leaving for parts unknown where they'd want to have Lexi with them sometimes."

"I know that worried you—me too. But here's the deal," he said, finally stopping talking long enough to sip some coffee. "Brit needs help to plan the event at the BAA. Ann is helping, of course, apparently so is Sandra, Lane's wife, who usually won't set foot in the 'dirty' place."

"I'll see if Nita wants to go out there with me, since Bronco's working at the ranch starting this afternoon. I told you I won't go out there on that road alone, and I won't. I'll call Gina too. I'll be glad to help Brit, and I'll call her right now."

He snagged her wrist as she got up, then tugged her onto his lap. "Just look ahead on the road for spike sticks and don't drive too fast. Sweetheart, I don't know what I'd do without you, though I suppose I'm repeating myself. I actually came home to tell you in person not only because we both deserve some great news, but because I thought you might be interested in a little private celebration. Lexi's at school, I'm taking a long lunch and you're not exhausted or on your narcolepsy meds. The truth is, I can do without coffee or lunch right now. I'm really only hungry for a little R & R with my beautiful wife."

"Good news and flattery will get you everywhere."

"Including in our bed, Mrs. Markwood?"

"I thought you'd never ask."

They kissed so long, right where they were, that Claire

was certain she could float down the hall. All they'd been through, since their lives had been endangered—well, she'd never felt so happy.

"Jackson would have hated all this," Brit told Claire as the six women sat around one of the BAA picnic tables late that afternoon to plan transition day, as Brit was calling it. Not only would Tiberia be departing, but the other animals would be following soon after, all heading for new homes at the Naples Zoo.

It had also been announced that the cleanup and dismantling of the BAA would begin soon, sponsored by the zoo as part of the deal. The Trophy Ranch, which was buying the property, had insisted they would take the land with the buildings as is, but Brit wanted it "buried." The work crew would leave the trees, but the foundations and contours of the razed buildings would be bulldozed to smooth the surfaces out rather than leaving things to rot, derelict and sad.

Ann sat between Brit and her daughter-in-law, Sandra. Lane's wife looked as if she should be modeling for Saks Fifth Avenue casual wear rather than sitting at a wooden table in a petting zoo. On the other side of the table, Claire sat between Nita and Gina. Gina was leaving next week for med school in Miami. They had quickly divided up duties to welcome nearly one hundred guests tomorrow afternoon for the grand farewell.

Ann would oversee phone calls in the BAA office. Brit was the media liaison. Claire, Nita and Gina were figuring out supplies and food to offer a light buffet and drinks for the 3:00 p.m. event. Besides insisting on Lane's string quartet, Sandra kept talking about tying welcome balloons near the gate, pink ones around Flamingo Isle and black and orange ones on the fence around Tiberia's cage. She'd also brought a huge plastic bag of various colored ribbons, so "this plain place would look pretty."

But after their meeting ended and they each went their own ways in the BAA, Claire had not been prepared for Lane's appearance as he came striding toward her.

"I hope you're not going to side with Brittany on my part in this," Lane told her as he cornered her near the exotic bird cages.

"Your part in the welfare of the BAA?" she asked, instantly regretting she was goading him. "Brit won't change her mind about closing the BAA, though I suppose you'd like to keep it open."

"Very funny. Hardly. You know what I mean. A string quartet will add some class to the event. We can play appropriate music, of course, something lively and triumphant, not calm and soothing."

"Lane, your beautiful music should be for people who are going to stop and sit and listen to really enjoy it. With guests and the media here—"

"Exactly."

"—things will be busy and a bit noisy with the focus on moving the animals into vans and trucks. You certainly aren't thinking you need the publicity?"

"It never hurts. And it's—it's the best I can do to honor Dad's dream of this place," he added in a rush, suddenly sounding sincere instead of snide.

She stopped walking back toward the business trailer,

just as, you might know, the familiar screech of *Who—are—you?* filled the air close by.

Her gaze locked with Lane's. He demonstrated that nervous habit he had of stroking his beard. But that bird's question was one she desperately wanted to ask him. Was he just a hurt son who wanted back in his family's good graces? Was he a fraud, a forger of more than that letter he'd written? She was tempted to ask him that now, but she didn't need him going ballistic on her. It suddenly bothered her too, standing here with him, the fence and line of thick tropical foliage nearby, that, on second thought, Lane did remind her of the bearded man in the photo peering through the ranch fence. The outsider looking in—to the BAA, to his family—was that Lane? Had Jackson recognized that and so not shared those blown-up photos with Ben's family to make their agony worse?

"Talk to Brittany about it for me," he said, still speaking fast as if to fill the awkward silence. "The beginning of this place—Dad's pipe dream—was not a family affair, but the end of it can be. Tell her we'll be here to play and keep the music light and—and triumphant."

He turned and strode away toward Sandra, who was down the way already tying ribbons on the railing of the bridge that led toward Tiberia's cage. Lane had used the word *triumphant* twice just now. Was that the way he felt about getting rid of the BAA? About getting rid of his father?

She knew she'd have to tell Nick her continued fears about Lane. Here she was involved again, but she really didn't feel she could accuse Lane any more than she could accuse Brit of setting up their father's demise. They were his children. Surely it was one of Stan Helter's men, just across that double fence, and Bronco said he'd report to them right after his afternoon of work there.

Nick and Claire were worried that Bronco didn't appear when they thought he would. Surely he wasn't doing overtime on his first day at the Trophy Ranch—and in the dark. Nick debated whether to call him but said he didn't want to in case he was still on ranch property.

But Bronco phoned Nick at about 8:00 p.m. and said he'd like to come over and bring Nita with him.

"Here's how he put it," Nick reported to Claire. "He and Nita wanted us to see they are happy together, not like last time they were here."

"Good," she told him, and met his smile with hers. "Everything is looking up. Even Lexi fell asleep without the usual questions about visiting Tiberia after he's moved. I had told her, yes, for the tenth time, we will take the Comfort Zone kids to the zoo just as soon as Tiberia's settled in and on display. And Marta says Duncan wants to see his favorite pig there too."

Bronco, when he arrived with Nita, seemed both relieved and nervous. "That ranch—what a place, boss, even behind the scenes," she heard him tell Nick the moment he was in the door. "Those tree houses way back on the grounds are really something! Really open-air. Big and fancy!"

"You got a tour of them already?" Nick asked as the four of them sat in the formal living room they seldom used, but, after dark, because of the gator incident, they preferred not to be in the lighted, glassed-in Florida room out by the pool.

"Not a tour, but went up the steps to peek inside one. Mr. Helter wanted me to start hunting pythons and stray gators in that back area. He had a guy drive me in a dune buggy. I pointed out a couple places there were fire ant colonies too. Those things can sting a man nearly to death—least you wish you was dead. Those babies bite hard."

With a playful punch in his ribs, Nita put in, "Harder than an upset wife?"

"Not quite that bad," Bronco said with a grin. "Boss, there's Russian guys there now, that's what my driver said, though I thought they were still talking German. I think they're leaving tomorrow. I caught one pregnant python who was in an old deserted gopher tortoise hole."

"You killed it?"

"He doesn't want the first couple killed. Wants his guests to see them, 'specially one gonna have little snakes."

"Ugh. To impress them?" Claire asked, realizing she'd put her hand on her rounded belly.

"That, or—" Bronco hesitated, frowning now "—Mr. Helter just likes to see things dead and dying, I swear he does. And—he was gonna feed the python a couple of rats he got somewhere."

"That snake in the driveway—the rats," Nick said.

"My thinking too," Bronco added.

Claire said, "Bronco, you can't trust Stan Helter. You have to be very careful of him, careful there."

"Promised Nita and the boss I would be."

"Anything else important?" Nick asked him.

"They talk a lot about preserving animals on the ranch, saving them for the future, not just killing them. Wanted me to hear that, I think. Mr. Helter said something about a guy that stuffs and mounts them—taxi something..."

"The taxidermist, Drew Hewitt?" Nick asked.

"Yeah, him. 'Course, what he does is preserve dead things. That big back area at his shop might be a kind of private museum where certain folks can see the remains of special projects he does."

"I remember that back area of his shop," Nick said, "the exterior of it anyway. He said the only thing in the back room was storage and a freeze dryer unit. The place has no windows, so no way you can peek in."

"I guess the only folks who have the key to that place are Mr. Helter, Hewitt and that nice insurance man that's your friend."

"Grant Manfort?" Nick asked. "Doesn't sound like his style, but he is big on preserving animals—live ones running free, I thought. So glad you're keeping your eyes and ears open too."

"And," Bronco said, reaching for Nita's hand, "anything Mr. Manfort does or says is okay with Nita and me. 'Cause we're gonna start buying that house at a real good monthly rate and can move in soon as the papers get signed. Would really appreciate it if you'd look them over first, boss."

"I'd be glad to," Nick said with another quick, proud glance at Claire as if to say, *Everything's coming up roses.*

Yet, she thought, they still couldn't let go of the earlier evil events. Dead animals, the dangerous, frightening kind, had been thrown in their yard as obvious threats to steer clear. Jace and Brit could have been hurt in his car, and he was temporarily out of action. Jackson was comatose and critical, and Ben was dead. At least the BAA saga was ending tomorrow, so that might make everyone safer at last.

# CHAPTER TWENTY-NINE

The Saturday of the big event at the BAA dawned bright and crisp. Although Claire and Nick were going early to help oversee things, and it would be a long day, they took Lexi with them, after she promised to always stay with her mother or Nita. Gina helped them set up a long buffet table for the food, which would be arriving at about 2:00 p.m. They'd ended up ordering from Wynne's, Claire's favorite grocery and deli store in Naples, but she'd packed sandwiches, potato chips, apples and sodas in an ice cooler to get them through until then.

The entire area was awash with fluttering ribbons and bows and balloons Sandra had arranged. Claire thought she'd gone overboard with helium animal balloons tied here and there, but at least Sandra—hopefully Lane too— would feel a part of the petting zoo as they had not been part of its short run so far.

Claire hated to admit it, but this dissolution of the place

today was probably for the best for the Hoffmans as well as the animals. But she'd had the most unsettling dream last night that both Ben and Jackson had been peering through the back fence in their yard and gesturing to her. And, in the dream, both of them were bearded.

"Glad it's Saturday so I can be here all day, help keep an eye on things," Bronco said as he hurried past carrying a pail of smelly shrimp. "Brit said to empty this back on the flamingo island, last time they'll be fed here. Zoo's gonna move them last, 'cause they have a nice habitat, she said."

"Jackson loves them. I'm sorry he's not here today, yet it would have really crushed him, not to mention the fact he's been living here and would have to leave. Brit said she'll have to get a U-Haul to move his things to his oldest daughter's house before they raze the buildings. Well, don't let me keep you with that stuff. The way the shrimp advertises itself," she said, fanning the air in front of her face, "I'm sure the pink pets will be able to locate it right away."

"Mrs. Claire—Claire," he said, turning back as he started away, "we're hoping Nita gets pregnant too, soon, 'cause we kinda got a late start on getting married. She loves to help you and Lexi—I know you'd help her through that too."

"I would be honored to play nanny for her, and we can rear them together, just like Lexi and her cousin or like my sister and I grew up, tight as could be. You know, Darcy finagled an invitation here today representing that Save Our Wildlife group she's in."

"Clever as you, getting what she wants," Bronco said with a grin and headed for Flamingo Isle.

Jace had planted himself at the front gate where Brit would welcome visitors when they started arriving. But the *Naples Daily News* reporter and photographer came early and a wildlife officer too, followed by two police officers, one who was manning the front gate, one who would circulate inside. Claire noted that the older officer had been here the day Ben died.

Time and people blurred by. An hour before the program would begin, Nita kept Lexi tight to her so that Claire could lie down for a few minutes. She had the choice of either the bed in Jackson's apartment or the one in the back room of the trailer, which she picked. But she was too excited to sleep and could hear Ann's voice on the phone in the attached office as she fielded phone calls.

At one of them, Claire came wide awake. "Yes, Lane, people are already here, but I don't think your musicians are. You're on your way right now?... I don't like it that you use the phone and drive. Now I know I sound like a mother, but people get hurt and worse with distracted driving... No, no picketers, not yet, at least, and we have a police officer out front... Yes, some TV people. I know your music is a gift today, but listen, I want you to support your sister. I don't want another rehashing of the argument you had with your father right before he died... Of course he told me. Look, my dear, I can't tie up this phone right now, but... What?"

Her voice went on, her words more muffled now. Claire got up and tiptoed to the door to hear better. She hated spying on Ann, but she still could not let Lane's forging his father's letter go. "No, of course, I never told them— not even Brittany—that you threatened him. I know you didn't mean the things you said, and he should not have thrown you into the wall, but you've never been able to keep your temper in check either… Of course, *of course*, I know you didn't want him to die. Now, I have to go, so thank you for the music later today and don't get in a huff if people don't stop to listen. The tiger is the focus today, not you, dear… Yes, I—"

She said something else, and Claire scurried back to the narrow bed. She would never sleep now, but she couldn't go right out so that Ann might think she'd overheard the call. The possibility that Lane had dirtied his hands to hire someone to hurt his father—and maybe silence Jackson too—had just gone from being a long shot to being a much shorter one.

The zoo truck, with a cage inside for transporting large animals, had backed up to Tiberia's enclosure. Claire could tell the crowd made the big cat nervous, so she was glad the zoo would be gradual in its introduction of the animal to the public. In the waiting crowd, more than once she heard the whispered word *killer*. They no doubt meant the cat was the killer—or was she getting so obsessed with finding who killed Ben and hurt Jackson that she was imagining things? She was still tired, emotionally on edge, and should take one of her strong pills to stay alert.

The guests had nearly wiped out the food and drinks, and were standing behind the low fence barrier to watch the transfer. Again, Claire scanned the small crowd, looking for Gracie or one of her sons. She even studied the nearby fence line where Gracie had climbed to watch her dear Thunder. Shifting a bit more to the side and moving to the periphery, she scanned the fence, wondering if the bearded man would appear. There were several bearded men in the crowed she studied, but the photo had just been too blurred to tell if any of these men bore a resemblance.

Since she wasn't in the press of people, she took pictures with her phone camera, though she knew the ones the professionals were taking would be much better. Brit had asked Nick to stay near the front of the audience in case there were any last minute legal questions. He held Lexi so she could see as the zoo representatives spoke, then Brit. Jace was sitting somewhere up front, invisible from here. Claire had had a brief chat with Darcy, but she was also lost in the crowd, taking notes for her committee. Bronco and Nita, Heck and Gina were somewhere on the periphery.

Claire saw Lane with Sandra standing close to his mother in front. His group had performed for over an hour near the food table, so everyone who came by for a bite could see them, even if no one stayed long to watch. The wild birds and other animals got more attention, which probably had not gone over well with him. Claire hadn't found time yet to tell Nick what she'd overheard from Ann.

She was getting tired from so much standing after an active morning and lack of a nap, but if she left the area, she needed to tell Nick. She was tempted to take some herbal meds or even one of her hard-hitters, but decided to wait to see the entire tiger transfer. The other animals would be leaving with much less fanfare.

She edged closer to Nick. Brit was explaining in a loud voice that she was going to hand the program over to the zoo director, just as she was ready to hand Tiberia and the other animals over. She said she hoped they would continue to help children love wildlife, but on an even bigger stage than her father had first envisioned.

*I'm going to sit down back there a minute,* Claire mouthed to Nick with gestures.

"Mommy," Lexi said, "Tiberia doesn't want to leave here."

"He'll like his new home just as we like ours."

*You okay?* Nick mouthed back to her.

She nodded. *Just tired.*

The crowd applauded, and Claire saw Tiberia react, stopping his pacing and glaring at them. He hissed, then showed his fangs with a low roar. A hushed murmur went up from the crowd as the tiger slunk back to sit in the corner of his cage, still glaring at everyone.

Perhaps this public program was a mistake, she thought, as she made her way to the end of the same bench where she'd ended up the day Ben died. If they had to tranquilize the big cat—as they had that day—it might make him more than restless. The tiger who had escaped from its cage at that facility near Tampa had gone berserk when it was tranquilized, and that's why they'd shot it.

She felt as upset and restless as poor Tiberia. She had to go to the bathroom, and the closest one was back of the bridge Sandra had decorated so elaborately that it looked like a parade float. Had she had too much lemonade at the buffet? No, it was just another sign her pregnancy was progressing.

The crowd had pressed in even more around Nick and Lexi. Bronco and Nita had edged closer. Jace, balanced on his crutches, had moved toward the back edge of the crowd, where he wouldn't be jostled. He'd said earlier he didn't want to get in Brit's way anyhow.

Claire decided she'd just go to the bathroom and hurry back, hoping the tiger would be in his transfer cage by then. And that would be the end of Ben's dream and Jackson's love for the BAA.

"If anyone's missing me, I'm just going to the restroom," she told Jace, since she could get to him. "I'll be right back. There's still a policeman at the gate."

"Poor Brit," he told her, looking back toward the tiger cage. "I don't think the cat's going to cooperate. It's like Tiberia's not leaving until he clears his name from jumping poor Ben. Brit's speech was good, but she's jumpy too—afraid something's going to happen to screw things up before she can clear things up."

"You don't mean she wants to clear herself of harming her father?"

"No, my fave amateur psych detective girl," he said, turning to look at her again. "She just wants answers about who set Ben up, and it wasn't her."

"Right. Of course," Claire said, and hurried away.

When Claire left the deserted restroom and headed back toward the action, she noticed a police officer was still at the gate. She'd seen the other one watching the crowd as the Naples Zoo personnel were preparing to move Tiberia into the truck that had backed up and was almost touching the back bars now. It was a blessing that none of the picketers—or Gracie, the boys and the possums they brought for the tiger—had appeared today.

As she walked toward the beribboned and balloon-laden bridge, she noticed the flamingos were running amok again as they had one other time she'd been here. What if one of them ran out the gate? What if Tiberia looked up and saw running game? If a tiger ever ate a flamingo, it surely wouldn't be more than a few bites—poultry lite.

She waved her hands and flapped her purse at one of the loose birds. It made a U-turn to head back toward Flamingo Isle. Amazing any of them stayed where they were with that low stone fence and shallow water, though they knew well enough when they were going to be fed. In their new home at the Naples Zoo, would the flamingos have room to run like this?

She paused a moment, watching yet another graceful bird nearly sprint from the isle they called home. Its spindly legs barely stirred the shallow water in the moat. She shooed that one back too.

Oh, maybe that nesting pair Jackson had been so proud of were running the others off. Or what if the female had already laid the egg or hatched their single chick, and something was threatening it? Brit had said that occasionally raccoons got in there.

She took off her loafers, held them in her hand, rolled up her jeans nearly to her knees and waded into the moat. She'd just peek through the thick foliage as she had before when Jackson was trying to dig a nesting spot for the pair. She didn't want to startle them, but what if that distant tiger roar just now or the applause of the crowd had set them off?

She sneezed and jammed her finger under her nose to stop a second one. They didn't need to be scared off by her.

The palm fronds Jackson had left behind where he'd been digging had been moved. Evidently Brit, or maybe one of the zoo workers who had stayed here last night, had seen what he'd been doing and picked up where he'd left off.

It was beautiful here. Serene. Private, special and Eden-like. She'd just take a quick photo, then head back. She pulled her phone out of her purse, touched the camera icon and zoomed in. *Click. Click.*

Still holding the phone, she looked closer at what was in the picture. No nesting pair but, with the zoom, she saw a shovel thrust into the mud near the hole.

She stared at the tiny frame, then enlarged the photo with a stroke of her finger on the screen. Laid out on a black piece of plastic, in the thick shade of looming foliage, were what appeared to be bones. Bones! Soil-stained, discolored bones! Thick bones, long ones. Too large to be from the delicate birds here. No skulls, but a large animal must be buried there or—

Humans in some sort of shallow grave.

She gasped and turned to flee, dropped one shoe. Would Nick be able to hear her phone call in the crowd? Despite the noise, she'd call him, tell him. Just in case, she'd run back, get that policeman at the gate.

As she lurched away, palmetto fronds slapped her, seemed to snatch at her.

Someone grabbed her from behind. Everything she held went flying. She was lifted off her feet, and a big, muddy hand clamped hard over her mouth.

"Well, lookee who I caught," a strange voice whispered, the man's lips in her hair.

# CHAPTER THIRTY

"Where's Mommy?" Lexi asked, craning her neck while in Nick's arms.

"Your dad said she went to the bathroom. She'll be back soon. Don't tell me you have to go."

"Nope. I can see better up here. Daddy can't hold me if your arms are tired, because of his crutches. He doesn't like them."

"Shh, they're ready to move Tiberia to his traveling cage now."

The zookeeper in charge explained briefly what he planned to do. They had baited the travel cage with fresh meat and backed it up flush to the opening of the tiger's current enclosure. The tiger would make his own transfer, they would drop the gate to the travel cage behind him and lock it, be sure it was safely stowed, then drive slowly out through the front gate.

It seemed to Nick the cat scented the meat but maybe

scented danger too. Tiberia hesitated, crouched, then sprang at the exit.

"Bet that's what happened when he killed his owner," someone behind them said. Nick didn't turn around and hoped Lexi hadn't heard.

Tiberia roared, as if bidding the cage and everyone goodbye. The trap was sprung. With a clang, the door descended. Hemmed in, Tiberia roared again while everyone cheered or applauded. Nick saw Brit crying.

He looked back to the bench where he figured Claire would be but didn't see her. He scanned the crowd. She wasn't back yet. Maybe she had intentionally wanted to miss the tiger's departure. He hoped she wasn't feeling upset or nauseous. As soon as the zoo truck drove away over the narrow, decorated bridge, he'd go look for her.

"He was pretty mad he got tricked, got took," Lexi said as he put her down and took her hand.

"Got taken, honey. Yeah, he was fighting mad."

Claire fought fiercely. The attacker had pinched her nose shut and completely covered her mouth. With his other hand, he pinned her arms at her sides. She tried to kick, but he must be standing with his legs apart and she hit nothing but air. He was strong—too strong.

Getting out of breath. Furious. Fearful. Struggling, going limp. She'd done that once before, pretended, then fought back. When was that? Somewhere in drowning water...

So dizzy. Should have taken her meds. Exhausted now—the baby. Strength wearing out. Out... Would he put her in the grave with all those headless bones?

Then—but it must have been later—she was bound and gagged and laid out faceup on that tarp near the bones. No, the bones were gone, the shallow grave filled and covered with fronds. How long had it been? Mere minutes? Were they looking for her now?

The man moved back into her view, towering above her. A bearded man. A man she couldn't place except for Jackson's photo.

"Mmmph!" she said through the gag stuffed in her mouth. She thought she would throw up. Who was this madman to do this with so many here today, visitors, zoo staff, wildlife officers, police? If only they would turn their attention to Flamingo Isle. The birds must have run from this man. Why didn't someone bring them back here and find him? They were all focused on the tiger cage.

She felt caged now, trapped by her bonds, by the high double fence that loomed almost overhead. She'd seen no ladder this intruder had used, but it must be hidden in that thick foliage by the fence. Maybe he thought he had to move the bones before the flamingos were moved or this area was bulldozed. But whose bones?

Dear Lord, was he planning to take her with him so she wouldn't tell? When he bent over her, she feared an attack, but he only leaned close to gather the edges of the tarp around her. To be buried alive? She remembered Jackson saying this little isle was the highest piece of ground for miles around in the Glades. How long had those bones been here, barely above the waterline?

He dragged the tarp with her on it back into the thicker foliage by the fence, where palms and other plants ran riot. She prayed he was going to just hide her, leave her.

But she could ID him, even if she didn't know him. She realized her purse was gone, her phone too, though she felt her shoes on her feet. And something big was wedged under the curve of her back. That could be her purse, but she hadn't had time to put her phone back in it. She'd dropped it somewhere, hadn't she?

He loosed the edges of the tarp. She lay in thick leaves that seemed to reach skyward forever. Her head hit the BAA fence, just about a foot from the ranch fence. If he tried to climb the fences with her, she'd fight, try to roll off, be dropped—but no. Jackson might have done that, but she had to think of the baby.

Through her gag she muttered, "Huh-uh, huh-uh!" hoping he would get the message to stop, to just leave her.

"You talk too damn much," he muttered. "Shut up or I'll shut you up better'n that. More'n once, I seen you yakking to Marta and Duck."

Irv Glover! He had a beard now, not like in the picture of him she'd seen online, but it was him all right.

He must have spied on Duncan. The boy's nightmares were real—hers too. But what was Glover doing here with buried bones? She nearly dry heaved in fear but was even more terrified when she saw a good-sized hole dug under the fence, and on the other side, a pile of plants that must have been stuffed inside to hide the opening. They lay, exposed roots and all, just across the two fences that the hole spanned. Was he going to put her in a shallow grave and then just walk out into the crowd?

But Glover belly-crawled through first, then pulled her through on her back, inching her along, wrapped in the black tarp like a pall. She remembered that a piece of denim had been snagged on the fence where they'd found Jackson. Maybe he had found the shallow grave and had been seen— had to be stopped and silenced. On the phone call Jackson had made to Brit in the car, he'd sounded panicked when he said he'd found something. Maybe he was being watched through the fences again or his phone too could have been bugged the way theirs were. Maybe he'd stumbled on the bones but didn't want to panic her and Brit then, wanted them to come back so he could show them the bones.

Claire knew she was almost halfway under the fence of the Trophy Ranch grounds. Suddenly it seemed a fearful place, a place Nick had not wanted her to go. She had to leave something behind—if people searching for her were ever going to find this hidden hole under the fence—but her hands were tied and she couldn't rip at her shirt, nor reach her watch to leave it either. She turned her head, again, again to try to rub an earring loose, even though that tore at her earlobe. She was sure her left small hoop gave way, but it was probably snagged under her in the tarp.

When the twisted wires at the bottom of the second fence snagged the plastic and scratched her forehead, she turned her head to the side and saw the pile of bones already on the ranch side. Irv Glover used to work at the Trophy Ranch, so he obviously knew the territory and maybe hid out here when he sneaked back from Tennessee. And was she some kind of a trophy for him, someone he blamed for turning his wife and son against him—just as he had blamed the social worker he had killed?

Nick was in a total panic. Where in the hell was Claire? She seemed to have vanished into thin Everglades air.

Both of the officers who had been here had moved into the parking lot to conduct the sudden glut of traffic onto the narrow access road, then left without knowing of the situation. No one still here had seen her.

He passed Lexi off to Nita to take home, while he, Bronco, Heck, Gina and Brit scoured the now deserted area. Gina had been back to the ladies' bathroom over and over, looking for clues. Ann had searched the trailer, the storage areas and Jackson's apartment.

Jace paced on his crutches, back and forth over the bridge. Nick, Bronco and Heck walked the perimeter of the entire BAA fence where it was not absolutely obscured or overgrown by rampant foliage.

Nick had the sickening feeling that Stan Helter was somehow behind this, and he had to check that out before he called in the cops. He'd get Grant to help him.

"Wait!" Brit said, smacking her forehead with the heel of her hand. "Those flamingos we saw running around. Now that Jackson's not here, if they're disturbed, they leave their area. Let's look there again, even though we scanned the fence. Maybe she went in to corral them and slipped in the mud."

She and Nick jogged toward the shallow water surrounding the heavily leafed isle on three sides while Jace, swearing, came along on his crutches behind them.

They waded through the shallow water. The birds nearby scattered again, fluffing their feathers, but didn't flee. Nick and Brit walked through the moat, then climbed the higher ground of the little island.

"Claire! Claire!" he shouted for the hundredth time. His voice kept breaking. This could not be happening, not after everything, not after how well things were going. And the baby.

"Look!" Brit cried, pointing, just as Bronco and Heck ran up behind them. "Drag marks! They look fresh."

"And someone's been digging," Nick said, pointing. Raw fear clawed at him.

Brit said, "Jackson used to dig shallow holes on this high ground for nesting pairs. This was his bailiwick, and I almost never came back here, but if you look around the fringes of this little islet, you'll see other depressions. It looks like he—someone—covered this one over. And it's bigger than the others."

Nick stooped and moved one palmetto frond, then a second. In a sudden spot of sun through shifting trees above them, his gaze snagged on a piece of white-brown plastic. No, not plastic. A bone. Part of a finger bone? He thought he would be sick to his stomach.

"Don't touch that!" he ordered Brit when she reached for it.

"But it can't have anything to do with Claire. These birds have small, delicate bones. Maybe Jackson buried some of them back here."

From near the fence, Heck called to them. "The drag marks continue over here, near the fence. Like—I mean—heading for the fence. But there's nowhere to go."

"Just a sec!" Nick called to him. "We'll be right there and get a ladder to go over."

Scared to death he'd find more bones, even if they couldn't be Claire's, he moved a few other fronds away from the site. He'd glimpsed something white under one sharp leaf and thought it might be a bigger bone. He half wondered if Jackson had used this high spot at the BAA to bury all kinds of dead animals, maybe ones who weren't well cared for, ones that Ben or Brit didn't want outsiders to know about. He could not trust anyone, could not get his mind around the fact this wasn't a nightmare.

They all stared at the small piece of white paper he'd uncovered, as if it were directions to a treasure trove. It was just a piece of wrinkled, smudged and lined notebook paper, folded in two, standing with the fold upright. He pulled out his handkerchief and picked up the card with it, just as Jace sloshed through the water, coming closer on his crutches.

"If she's not here, let's call the cops," Jace insisted, almost slipping as he climbed the mud and soil of the small islet.

Nick looked down at the note, written in pencil in big, shaky printing. His voice shaking too, he read aloud to them the crudely printed words: "'1ST SIGN OF COPS SHE DIES.'"

# CHAPTER THIRTY-ONE

Once Irv Glover had dragged Claire far away from the two fences, he told her, "Be right back. Gotta stuff loose leaves back in that hole."

He was quickly back, muttering something about the posse on his trail. It made her think of an old man who had dementia, who thought he was a cowboy from out west. Now who had that been? She was so dizzy, the trees above her spinning into the sky.

He picked her up and carried her deeper into ranch land. She fought to keep her head clear, to reason things out through her fear and desperate need for her medication. Could he have a car waiting nearby? But wouldn't the guard near the ranch gate Nick had mentioned see them?

He hid her under some pygmy palms surrounded by a thick patch of crotons and left her, heading back toward the BAA.

Maybe she could roll away or find something to saw

her wrists free. There was a patch of sharp-sided sawgrass in sight, but that would take forever. Could she rub or snag her partly protruding gag against a tree trunk until it pulled out?

But he was back fast, with another tarp, dragging the bones on it. He went past her with a narrow-eyed scowl. Despite the lack of skulls, surely, those were human bones. If she could only talk, could reason with him—if that was possible with a murderer. Maybe she could sympathize with him, play on his love for Duncan—Duck. She would have to call that poor little boy Duck if she had a chance to speak.

The sound of the other tarp being dragged and his footsteps swishing through the sawgrass faded. If only she could scream. Maybe someone inside the BAA fences could hear her from here, or she could attract the guard at the ranch gate. Surely Glover didn't mean to just leave her here until dark when he could move her again.

Or bury her here.

Nick was sweating but felt ice cold. "Grant, thank God you answered."

"Nick, you okay? You sound upset."

"I need your help, friend. Claire has disappeared from the crowded gathering at the BAA today."

"Disappeared? Like how?"

"I don't know, but there are—are signs—she's been abducted and taken onto ranch land, which scares me to death."

"Damn, man! You sure?"

"Not exactly. Can you come to the BAA now? In case

I need to confront Helter about information or a search, I need your help, but no cops, at least right now. We found a note."

"I'm walking out the door right now. A ransom note?"

"Not so far. We found drag marks and a threatening note saying no cops. Grant, maybe we can figure this out together. I'm scared to call in the police. I might need to bargain with whoever took her—if they contact us."

Nick heard a door slam. Thank God some kind of help was on the way.

As soon as it got dark, Glover was back again. By then, Claire had managed to rub and hook the gag out of her mouth, though she'd scratched her cheek and chin against rough, ragged bark. She'd just gotten it out, was gasping for breath when she heard his quick footsteps coming through the patch of sawgrass.

He shone a flashlight beam in her face.

"Well, lookee you," he said.

"It's been out for a good hour," she lied, "but I didn't scream. I know you plan things out so well it wouldn't have done any good. I just couldn't breathe well—for me or my baby. I'm sure you understand my worrying about my unborn baby, what with you being a dad. It's really clever how you came back to Naples and kept an eye on Duck."

"I think Duck knew it was me watching sometimes, but the beard fooled him. Fooled a lot of folks, that and my new name."

"A new legal name? That took some doing."

"Got a few connections. Keith Morrison, that's me."

She'd been hoping he'd brag that Stan Helter had helped

him get an alias, but the fact he'd offered her his new name scared her even more. He didn't plan to let her go.

"No one had a clue you were here," she plunged on, trying to use positive interview techniques she'd learned long ago: get the suspect to trust you, like you. Build him or her up, because they often have abused, damaged psyches. "You know," she added, "Duck said he dreamed you were back. Fathers are very important to their children."

"So you're pregnant?"

"Yes. I'm hoping to have a boy half as good and courageous as your son."

"You try to turn him against me?"

"Irv—or Keith, if you wish—I never said a word against you to Marta or Dun—Duck. I lost my father when I was young, and I know how that hurts. Even if you've done some bad things in the past, it's important that he looks up to you for things you do now."

"Yeah, well, sorry you're hatching a baby like those pink birds, 'cause that makes all this harder. Sorry too I had to knock out the black guy, but he kept digging around there, was turning up the bones. But being sorry don't keep me from doing what I have to, and don't give me that sob story about my son. Once I clear this place for good, I'll take him with me and we'll get along fine then."

Worse and worse, she thought. But she was getting dizzy just lying down. Trying to keep her voice steady, she said, "I can feel my purse under me. I have pills in there I need to take or I get very sick."

"Thought they was drugs—kind I could sell. Stashed 'em back a ways, buried to get later."

Her stomach went into free fall again. Without her narcolepsy meds, she'd begin to have hallucinations, nightmares. But then, this was a nightmare right now.

Instead of stuffing her gag back in her mouth, he shoved it between her jaws and tied it around and across her open lips. Could she think that was a slight kindness, a concession? If he let her talk again, she needed to continue to get him on her side, make him trust her enough so she could get away.

He picked her up, tarp and all, and plodded through grass and past trees toward a small, lit building. She could barely make out a narrow road beyond. A truck came in—a large, black one—illuminated by the rising moon. She remembered Stan Helter had a vehicle like that. Its headlights swung across the tropical terrain, and with a *honk-honk*, headed down the road deeper into the ranch. Its lights had hit the silhouette of the guard building, but not them.

"Big Cat's back," he muttered, starting to sound out of breath. "Only a couple of 'em have the opener, 'cause I control the gate."

Despite starting to feel that terrifyingly weird sense of losing reality, Claire jerked alert. Irv Glover must once again be working here. As the guard and gatekeeper! So he not only could be doing all this on Helter's orders, but maybe that shallow grave had something to do with the sex trade or illegal immigrant women working at the Trophy Ranch. Maybe that's where they stashed women who had gotten sick or—or were killed for not obeying.

And it meant Glover had the run of the entire ranch to dispose of her.

★ ★ ★

Bronco came bursting into the trailer where Nick was waiting for Grant to arrive. Nick was also keeping an eye on his cell phone in case Claire called or texted. They hadn't found her phone or purse so she could have those with her, though she wasn't answering her cell.

"Nick," Bronco said, gasping for breath. "I swear, Heck and me just spotted what might be Claire's earring. Left it where it is, 'cause you say to do that with evidence. Come see!"

Nick tore out right behind Bronco. Jace, crutches and all, was at the scene with Heck.

"It's hers, right, boss?" Heck asked, pointing.

Nick got on his hands and knees. Between the two fences the small, golden hoop, minus its pin, lay amid fallen leaves.

"Yes. That's what she wore today. Maybe it came off when she was carried over these fences. Any marks of ladders around here?"

"No," Jace said, leaning in too. "Brit," he called over his shoulder, "we need those lights we had the other night! Brit! Where the hell did she go now?"

"I'm over here!" Her voice came from behind thick foliage. "The cops will be furious, but maybe they'll understand we had to do some things on our own when they see that note. I think we need to cordon off this whole area and search for any other clues. Nick," she said, joining them at the fence, "you're right, that's what she wore today."

Nick's voice broke, and he cleared his throat. "Her sister gave them to her. What about Darcy? She'll have a fit I didn't tell her, let her help, but we can't get her in this too."

Heck said, "Gina told me Darcy went home a long time ago. Had to write up notes about the success of the event."

"Damn," Nick whispered as tears filled his eyes and he looked away. "I'm going to call Ann to have her bring Grant right here when he arrives. I can't believe I'm telling all of you to tamper with evidence at a kidnapping site, crime scene, but let's search every inch of this place. We've already tramped our footprints all over it."

"I'll get the lights," Brit said. "They're bright ones Jace and I used when that chopper friend of his landed."

"That's how I can help," Jace said. "He has access to a thermal imaging infrared camera. From a low-flying plane it can pick up the heat humans—or animals—give off in total darkness. You can even see the shape of the image, like of someone running."

Nick said, "A low-flying chopper or small plane flying over the ranch might panic her abductor. But we may need all the help we can get. Can you call him? But no flyovers until I talk to him."

"He was in the corps. Never leave a marine behind, and we're not leaving Claire out there." He turned and lurched away as he tried to maneuver his crutches on the soft ground.

"Okay," Nick said, "let's get those lights in here. Soon we'll have two—I hope—lifesavers here to help us, Grant and Jace's pilot friend."

He blinked back tears. Claire. Their baby. Lexi. It was like his entire life needed to be rescued too.

The outside lights were on, but inside the small guard building, Glover only turned on a flashlight. It made his features look like a fright mask. He took the gag out of her mouth, so that gave her hope he had some kindness in him, and she had to tap into that.

He had been working here as a ranch guard under an assumed name for—for how long? What month was this?

Reality was getting wavy, drifting as it sometimes did if she was off her strong meds too long. She hadn't even taken her herbals in the rush of events. When was all that? Oh, yes, today, but it was nighttime now.

She saw she was sitting on the floor with her back against a cot. He had a tiny fridge and hooks with extra clothes in this small space. And tacked to the wall a faded photo of him with a much younger Duncan. So he could and did live in this guardhouse, at least some of the time.

"We're not staying here," he told her. "We're heading in."

"Into the ranch?"

"Know it like the back of my hand."

He swigged water from a big plastic bottle, then— maybe there was hope!—put it to her lips. She drank greedily.

But when a voice came in over an intercom or radio in the next room, he stuffed the gag back in her mouth, went around a corner and took the call, something about a helicopter coming in later with a load.

In the middle of the night? she wondered. It was night, wasn't it? She had to get Lexi to bed, see what Nick was doing. If only her mother would stop reading that story to her and Darcy...a tragic story, one that scared her so she might not sleep... When was Jace coming home from another flight to Hong Kong? He was gone too much, but he loved flying. Was he flying a helicopter now and bringing in another load? A load of what?

She heard her captor take a second call. Even in here, she could hear a man's voice, very angry on the other end of the phone. A man's voice asking if he had the phones. Or had he said *bones*? And where were those bones? Had he buried them again?

She had to concentrate, to hang on. She never forgot to take her meds. But it was worse in middle school before she knew she was sick, when the kids called her Sleepy Creepy and Crazy Claire. And then things got better, but she was so scared they weren't going to get better in the school she was in now because this teacher didn't like her at all.

# CHAPTER THIRTY-TWO

Nick was relieved when Grant arrived. Since he'd helped Nick out a couple of times with Helter and his ranch, he was desperate for his advice and assistance now. Grant took one look at the lighted flamingo isle and, frowning, hunkered down close to Nick where they'd just turned up another piece of bone near where the earring had been found.

"Thank God you're here," Nick said. "Whoever took her left a note that said if we bring in the cops, she dies." Again Nick blinked back tears. He had to hold on here, stay steady.

"You think she's been taken onto ranch land?" Grant asked as the others backed off a bit to give them some room. "It's a big place, but I'm sure we can get Stan's staff to search for her. That wouldn't be calling in the cops, at least."

"We found fragments of old bones here, which I can't

figure out. Human ones, I think, not from these birds or other zoo animals."

Grant looked really alarmed, even stunned. "Human bones here? Could that be a warning too? I mean, the bones wouldn't be from here, but maybe planted as part of the threat for you not to pursue Claire? Can I see those?"

"We left them where they are, but you can sure look at them," Nick said, leading him over to the islet. "See, the digging here, the depression. This little place is high ground in flat Florida. We think someone was buried here in a fairly shallow grave, maybe years ago as the bone pieces look discolored, maybe leeched in by the soil."

Grant leaned against a palm tree, closed his eyes and squeezed the bridge of his nose with one hand. Nick was moved and impressed by how much Grant cared about a woman he didn't really know, but then the man had known tragedy.

"Unbelievable," Grant whispered. "But we've—we've got to find her." He looked down at the ground, then followed Nick back to where they'd found the second bone piece and Claire's earring.

"So," Grant said, "exactly what would you like me to do? Tell Stan or not? Ask for help to search or not? Despite the moon, it's damn dark over there in hundreds of dangerous acres."

"And," Nick said, frowning toward the thick foliage near the fence where Claire had evidently been lifted up and over, "even if someone took her onto ranch land, it doesn't mean she's there now. But I've got to try that."

"Okay," Grant said, "let's go. I'm sure Stan will help."

Nick heaved a huge sigh. He'd really wanted to ask Grant

if he knew of any illegal immigrants coming in to work at the ranch, even about foreign women for a sort of private sex trade, but he had to think of Claire first. Focus on that now, and pray Stan did not have something to hide.

"I'm grateful, Grant."

"Nick, I'm so sorry this happened. But if that's been a human grave over there, it might have been a pioneer burial or even a Seminole Native American interment. Don't lose hope." He squeezed Nick's shoulder.

Nick turned toward Jace, who was hovering. "So you're in charge," he told the man he'd been through so much with, both bad and good. "Do what you can through that friend of yours."

"What friend?" Grant asked. "If we're going in, no one else does unless we call for help."

"Agreed," Jace told him. "I have a pilot friend coming with a recon plane, but we'll wait for the okay to move from you two. Find her, bring her back. For Lexi, for all of us."

Claire was gagged and the man was moving her again. She wondered if she was in St. Augustine where she'd been in a dark dream like this, or maybe this was Cuba. But where were the sugarcane fields she'd run through? She wanted to run away.

The man carrying her—it wasn't Nick—put her in the back of a golf cart. Oh, they must be on a golf course. Jace had liked to play golf but almost never had time unless he had a layover in Hawaii or California. But he was only flying little airplanes now, at least she thought so. He was spying for the government. That was a secret. She needed to wake up. She had a feeling that she was supposed to be spying on someone too.

The golf cart purred right past a cluster of buildings, a big lodge, a swimming pool lit at night, other buildings. It was quite a golf course. Or maybe they were at a resort, because under the pool lights she glimpsed pretty, dark-haired girls with lovely tans—oh, the women were top-less—mingling with men who didn't look Latino.

Maybe one of the buildings was a smokehouse as she smelled a rich, meaty scent. Her driver said, "Bet you were scared to see that gator in your pool. No clue how it got there, right? Then that big, dead snake. Didn't get the message, though, did you and your bastard lawyer husband? Lay off! Don't meddle with that kiddie zoo. Wish I had my hands on him, 'stead of you. Sent me away for years, lost years, and now you're gonna be lost to him."

Did this man know Nick? She should know who the driver was but she'd forgotten. Anyhow, she did remember the dead gator and dead snake. She would have liked to lecture this man about scaring children, if she could figure out who he was. Oh, that's right, he was the one watching and scaring Duncan and his mother too. And he was scaring her now.

The man pulled the golf cart around behind a square wooden building with an air conditioner humming in back. Was it warm enough for AC? She felt sick, shaky. Ice cold.

The driver stopped the cart, dug in his pocket and produced a key. He went to the narrow back door of a building and unlocked it. Wan light slanted out from inside. He hadn't brought her home because the place was not big enough to be their new house. She still had an urge to call for Nick or Lexi until she realized she had a gag in her mouth.

That was not right. None of this was right! She had to fight to clear her head, not to drift off. Something was very wrong here, very bad.


"Now listen up," Jace said to the assembled group after Grant and Nick had left. "I'm gonna call my pilot friend to land here again, this time to bring the thermal imaging infrared camera. But we won't do a flyover of the ranch unless I get the word from Nick or Grant."

"It's true that a low-flying plane might panic who-ever took her," Heck said. "Like, her captor thinks it's the cops."

"Still, time's of the essence when someone's been kid-napped," Jace muttered, frowning. "So, we'll light the way for my friend to land here, even if we don't go in, which, damn it, I'm dying to do."

He hobbled off on his crutches and fished in his pocket for his phone. This was a freaking horror movie. After all they'd been through, after Nick had said Claire would stay out of things at least until the baby, stay home, take care of Lexi.

Furious at himself, at the world, he leaned against the fence near where she'd been lifted out of here to make his phone call. He hit at the fence with one crutch. The entire length of it shuddered. But something gave way, a clump of low bushes, sod, even a small, dead-looking palmetto tree.

And that exposed a good-sized hole under not just the BAA fence but the ranch fence too.

★ ★ ★

The driver had carried Claire into the building and put her in a chair. A sort of refrigerator—or was it a special kind of oven or even a washing machine—sat above her on the counter. It had a control panel and a sort of grate on the front. Was this another hideout where the driver stayed sometimes?

What terrified her was that various cutting tools, knives, things that might be scalpels, were displayed in a rack on the wall. Tacked to a kind of pegboard were furs or hides, one maybe of a fawn. One pelt had been scraped clean and looked more like stretched skin. A strange, sharp smell permeated the area.

Maybe this was an operating room. She fought to clear her foggy, back-and-forth thoughts again. These weren't doctors' tools, were they? She knew it wasn't time for her to have her baby.

Her driver—no, this guy was her captor, she remembered, and that's why she was tied and gagged. Oh, he had pulled her gag out, but she was so sore from having her mouth forced and held open that she still felt gagged. Her throat was so dry, so sore. He'd tied her wrists and ankles tight, and even her earlobe hurt.

But she had to get up and reach one of those knives to cut herself free. Then she could run for help back to those people at the swimming pool. Yes, her mind was clearing now, but if she only had her meds. He'd said he'd buried them, and he must have buried people too.

She tried to rise, to balance herself with her legs still tied together. She stood on her feet. Dizzy. And without the light her captor had, she might cut herself or make a knife drop reaching for it in the dark. But she had to try.

If she could just grab one of those knives, hide it under her...

She tried to knock one loose with her head. The rest of them bounced and swayed at her clumsiness, but one fell to the countertop. She dropped it on the floor, but her elbow hit a big glass jar of marbles or balls of hard candy on the counter. The jar tipped, but she lunged for it, shoved it back onto the countertop with her shoulder, trying to lean on the edge so it wouldn't fall, but the contents spilled out, rolling, bouncing. At least her captor didn't seem to hear that over a phone that was ringing.

In the other room, through the open door, she heard that man—that's right, it was Irv Glover—answer his phone.

"You're kidding," his voice carried to her. "You told them pioneer or Indian bones? Fifteen years ain't that long ago... Yeah, I still have her... Because she saw what I was doing and she—or Markwood—would put it all together... Yeah, okay. The tree houses are empty right now, so meet you there... He's gonna be with you!... Yeah, I know we have to. It's been my longtime dream to get my hands on him. Let's clean this up, get it over with, so we can rebury the bones, and I'll get out of here for good. I know you're a climber, but my idea of digging under was a lot smarter."

Again, Claire fought to clear her head, to remember what Glover said. Did he mean Stan Helter was with him? Or was he talking to Stan? It kept jumping through her mind that Glover hated Nick for sending him away to prison. She knew she had to get and hide the knife until she could use it. Use it to cut her bonds, use it to stab him if she had to. Marta and the boy would be better off without him. And she had to protect herself, protect her unborn child.

She nearly slipped on the marbles on the floor. Only, now that her eyes were adjusting better to the dim light, she realized that she was in a taxidermy shop on the ranch, not a golf course. Terror poured through her.

Besides those skins on the wall, she saw—under her and all around, on the counter, on the floor—the gazes of dead, glass eyes of every size and color. Even green, like hers.

# CHAPTER THIRTY-THREE

"So much for the she-was-taken-over-the-fence theory," Jace told Bronco and Heck. He carefully got on his knees and leaned down to peer through the hole. "Bronco, see if Nick's gone yet. He and Grant should see this before they head out."

Brit brought him one of the electric lamps. "Damn, damn, damn," she muttered under her breath. "We kept looking over the fences but they came under them, at least here. Took Claire out this way too, I'll bet."

Bronco rushed back in with Nick behind him. Brit left the lamp but moved back to give Nick room. Bronco hunkered down to look. "For sure a grown man could crawl through there, and a woman—well, could be forced to—or dragged."

Jace cleared his throat. He'd seen Nick crying earlier, and he was about ready to. Had Claire been conscious? Alive? At least the intruder had left Jackson's unconscious body behind after attacking him, so maybe she was at least in better shape than that.

"Grant should see this before you guys leave for the ranch," he told Nick.

"I'll tell him because we've got to get going. He asked for a little time to make a couple of calls so people don't think he's—he's missing."

Nick helped Jace to stand and handed him his crutches. They grasped hands. No more to say. They'd both loved Claire, and Jace knew he'd lost her through his own stupidity and temper. He just hoped Nick wasn't going to lose her too.

As Nick hurried away, Brit stepped back and put her arm around Jace's waist. He tipped toward her. As he touched his broken foot to the ground to keep his balance, pain shot through him, but a broken bone was nothing. A broken heart was something.

"They'll find her, get her back," Brit whispered.

"She's pregnant. She's on meds for narcolepsy."

"Jace, as soon as you call your pilot friend, I know what we can do to help. It's what Claire would do."

"What?" he asked as they started slowly out of Flamingo Isle.

"Analyze that threatening note. Nick left it in the trailer office—under the glass on the desk."

"We'd need fingerprints or DNA."

"Which he has in mind if we have to call in the police. But, I mean, we can at least assess that big, awkward printing."

"You're right. Let me call Falcon again, then we can try to psych out that note. Thanks, honey, for propping me up in more ways than one, for understanding and helping."

"Understanding you still love her in a way? I knew that. I still want you anyway."

Before they waded through the moat, he put both crutches in one hand and pulled her to his side. "I love you, Brit. I really do. I—I keep trying to put this all together in my head—to be strong, strong like you've been through losing your father and then what happened to Jackson—losing the BAA and the tiger."

The lamp she held illuminated several flamingos nearby, a couple of them asleep, standing on one leg, just like he was, two of them acting lovey-dovey. They'd be leaving here soon too.

"It wasn't easy to stay strong, but you helped," she said. "Claire and Nick did too, so I'm all in to help them."

"Any crisis, in the air, or here—like this," he told her, "I make myself go back to what I learned in flight school. My dad used to drill me on it. I hated his guts—shades of Lane and your dad, right? But Dad was at least proud of me for wanting to serve my country like he had."

"Drilled you on what?" she asked, turning to him as they clamped themselves tighter together in a hard embrace. The top of her head fit perfectly under his chin. He could feel her breasts rise and fall.

"Okay, the so-called Four C's for emergencies in flights are, first confess the predicament to ground control. Second, communicate with them. Third, climb in altitude if possible for better radar and direction finding."

"I like that one. Go high, not low when things get tough. What else, my man?"

"Comply with advice is the fourth C, but I always add a fifth to myself—keep calm."

"We're doing all that, right now, aren't we?" she said, lifting her face to his. Tears gilded her eyes in the reflection of the lamp, but she looked at him strong and steady. "You tell your friend Falcon to bring that chopper in case we need it. But maybe Nick and Grant will find her and bring her back. And you and I will stand together to welcome her."

He hugged her hard, desperate for her strength. He knew for sure he loved her, wanted her in his life. But he had to help get Claire back—for Lexi, for Nick and himself—or he was going to ignore those four C's and crash.

"You clear everything with the people you were going to meet tonight?" Nick asked as Grant drove them the short distance to the ranch entrance in the dark.

"Yeah. Didn't tell them why. Then I called Stan to say you and I were stopping by," he muttered as his headlights illuminated the sign and tall double gate to the ranch. Nick realized his friend was really nerved up too.

Grant reached into the well between their seats and pulled out something that looked like a garage door opener. He held it up and clicked it once. The gates opened inward, and they drove forward. Nick saw in the side rearview mirror that they automatically closed behind them.

"I knew you were the one to call," Nick said. He blew his nose, which kept filling up, even though he'd managed to get hold of himself. His eyes were red and prickly; he fought hard to steady his shaking hands. They had no choice but to come to Stan, so he hoped they could trust him on this. No way he'd want bad publicity for his ranch.

And words his father had written once, which had inspired him then and that he'd held on to since, kept going through his head: *I will be safe on the south shore forever more.* He'd always figured his father meant in the afterlife, and he'd named his private charity firm South Shores after that quote. Now all he wanted was to keep Claire safe.

"Sorry for bringing this up," Nick said, "but did you feel desperate like this when you couldn't find Steve Rowan and Leslie, when they were missing at sea—and then were never found?"

He saw Grant's hands tighten on the wheel. "Yeah. They were both close to me, my mentor—and my girl-friend. She was beautiful and special. She was just twenty-one. I've had plenty of female companionship, but maybe that's why I never risked marriage, because I knew the pain of losing ones I loved."

That hit Nick right in the gut. He and Grant had the agony of loss in common. Dear God, he couldn't lose Claire.

"The guard's not on the gate after dark?" he asked as they drove farther in and he leaned forward to look out the front car window. A pale moon, half covered by ropes of clouds, was rising amid a scattering of stars.

"I guess not," Grant said with a frown and a shrug. "No one usually comes in after dark unless it's Stan or a shift change—regular staff."

"I'm figuring the hole under the fence I told you about would come through to the ranch near the guardhouse. That's why I asked."

"Still, some of that distance we drove on the road, maybe a quarter to half of a mile, would be between those fences and this road. You aren't thinking the death of the BAA owner by that tiger attack could be tied to someone wanting to take Claire, are you? I mean, like a bargaining chip or something to make you quit investigating that?"

"I don't know, but right now, all I want is to get her back. Good—there's the lights from the lodge and pool area. You're driving really slow."

"On this narrow road at night, I don't want to hit any of the nocturnal animals. Besides, if swamp buggies go out at night, their lights are terrible to spot. If we go back into the ranch—which I hope Stan will let us do—we'll take one of those. Look, Nick, it's obvious that someone brought her onto ranch land, but who knows if she's still here? I think the best place to look would be the so-called tree houses way back in. Stan said they're between guests right now and, if someone knew the ranch well, that would be an obvious hideout. Stan would know if something was going on in the compound area. You aren't thinking he's behind this?"

Nick almost admitted Stan had been his longtime number one suspect, but he didn't dare. He needed and trusted this man, but Grant had so much at stake here too. "I'm just clutching at straws," Nick said, knowing that was a cop-out, but if Grant had to choose between helping him or Stan, which would it be?

"Look, I know Stan. He's squirrelly at times, but he knows he's got a good thing going here, and I've seen him toe the line more than once not to screw that up. He's not into abducting women, believe me, nor burying bodies on BAA property, if that's what you're thinking. After all, he has hundreds of acres here to do that."

"And plenty of women around anyway."

Grant's head snapped up, but he said nothing else. Nick

wondered if he'd just said too much. How far could Grant be trusted since he was close to Stan? But it almost didn't matter since this long shot was all he had right now.

The appearance of the lighted compound near the lodge made Nick feel better. At least he could see farther than the distance of Grant's headlights.

Stan greeted them and invited them into the lodge. The place was either deserted or it had been hastily cleared out, though Grant had mentioned they were between visitors, and Bronco had said something about a transition between German and Russian guests.

But the acrid scent of cigarette and cigar smoke still hung in the air in the main room as if ghosts were here. No ashtrays, though. No empty glasses or beer bottles. He saw wet water rings on a table where glasses might have been sitting—and two that had been missed in the cleanup, both with lipstick marks on them.

The skin on the back of Nick's neck crawled. Well, of course, they wouldn't want a lawyer to know there were women here to please the guests. It was even possible that they were girlfriends of workers here or guests. After all, women hunted, came with men here from time to time, no doubt. Yet, something seemed off here. Grant was totally uptight—well, he could understand that. Nick realized he might have made a mistake to walk into the lion's den, but that note about not calling in the cops had really scared him. He and their friends had been watched through a fence, glass patio windows and their phones. He had to trust Grant and risk this.

"The truth is," Grant told him as Stan poured them straight scotch from a bottle in his office, "I had to tell

Stan we needed his help and why. I thought it might take too long to explain it here."

So that was why he was so nervous. Grant must trust Stan. At least that meant they could get down to business. However much he wanted a drink, he turned the scotch down.

Pouring himself a slosh of whiskey, Stan said, "Grant and I have worked together for a long time—trust each other. You don't want the cops or any media loudmouths to know what's happened till you find your wife, and we don't either. I swear, we'll get to the bottom of this, call in staff, search the grounds, whatever it takes to recover her for you—if she's here. I swear, I didn't have a damned thing to do with her disappearance or whatever bodies you found on BAA land, right, Grant?"

"Absolutely. I know Nick's on edge, and I am too, so let's get going."

Nick hesitated, however good that all sounded. Because suddenly, his lawyer instinct for spotting liars kicked in, and he didn't believe Stan. Something about his nervousness, his not looking him in the eye now, and probably even more signs Claire would have picked up. But Stan didn't dare do anything to harm him since so many knew Nick was here. Still, he didn't like that these two seemed to have an aura of not only friendship but collusion.

"Hit me again," Grant ordered, rapping his glass on the counter, then getting up to stretch while Stan poured him more scotch.

Stan told Nick, "I've got a swamp buggy with lights ready, so we'll head out."

Then something hit Nick in the back of his head, and black night descended.

★ ★ ★

The man in the other room who had been on the phone, then was quiet for a while, came back into the room where Claire was madly kicking the glass eyes on the floor out of his way. She didn't want him to know she'd spilled them trying to grab a knife.

But he slipped on some of them anyway and slanted his flashlight beam onto the floor, then into her eyes.

"Oh, great," he said. "Look, this taxidermy guy's an artist, and he'll have my head for that. That's a joke around here. Wanta see some of his heads on the walls? Hey, I got something even better to show you 'fore we end all this."

She smelled liquor on his breath, though she hadn't before. After his phone calls, he'd been drinking. Had someone fired him as a driver on the golf course? He'd been told off for something, that was sure.

He yanked her to her feet and dragged her into the next room. Heads of stags with huge racks of antlers stared down at her. Also mounted heads of a bear, a wolf and so many alligators with their jagged jaws open.

He shoved her into the single chair in the room and dug into his pocket for a short chain of keys. He lifted them out, rattled them, eyed them, then chose one. "Mr. Brilliant got no idea I have this one. But got to protect myself and the man, case Mr. Brilliant ever tries to turn us in. He was so excited to get these samples to work on 'stead of a bunch of animals, so he'll keep his mouth shut or else."

She wasn't following his stream of talk. Just words, words but she wanted to put them together. As he unlocked a cabinet in the back corner of the room behind the cluttered work counter, Claire fought to clear her head.

She had to pay attention, remember what he said and did. If they went outside again, and he didn't leave her here, she'd have to know the way they went on the golf course to bring others here later—no, not a golf course, but that animal ranch.

He opened both doors of the cupboard. He came back to her, pulled her to her feet. Oh, she remembered who he was now, the man in a photograph she'd seen looking through a fence. A man who had terrified his wife and son, but she had to keep him from scaring her.

He put the gag back in her mouth, then pushed her close to the cupboard and slipped his flashlight beam inside.

She felt her baby move, punch at her as if to say *Stay alert.* But how could she not? Because there, staring at her with glass eyes that reflected the light, were two heads of—of people. Real people. Dead people, mummy heads with parchment-like skin stretched over their skulls. Surely they weren't real, but reconstructed masks of missing persons this man was trying to scare her with. She'd seen the work of forensic artists who re-created what someone missing looked like when just their skulls were found, even years later.

But from the depths of her being, she wanted to scream because—because she knew who they were, didn't she? And why the skulls of the bodies in the shallow grave were missing.

The preserved head of the white-haired man had front teeth with a big space between them. And the much younger female had a face Claire had seen in a photo too, and she still had her long, lovely red hair.

# CHAPTER THIRTY-FOUR

Nick jolted awake, bouncing along in some vehicle. His head hurt like hell, but his screaming thoughts seemed clear and awful. He and Grant had been talking to Stan about searching the ranch for Claire. And then someone—Grant?—hit him, knocked him out.

He saw he was in a swamp buggy, and Stan was driving through the pitch-black night. Grant sat next to Stan, and Nick lay on the back seat. He tried to move. Tied, wrists and ankles. Damn, he'd been played for a sucker, so desperate to find Claire he'd ruined everything. Grant had to be in it with Stan. But no—Grant must have been the enemy all along.

Nick tried to test and stretch his bonds. He was not tied tight. That gave him hope he could roll off the back of this swamp buggy, hide and get loose somehow. But maybe they were taking him to her. And for the wrong reason. Maybe Stan had taken her because she'd found out something about him. Maybe her phone had been monitored again. Or else someone Stan worked for just wanted to make them back off investigating the goings on at the ranch or even Ben's death.

Thoughts poured through his brain. He'd tried a case a couple of years ago in which the killer had admitted to the cops that he didn't tie his victim tight so when the corpse was recovered, there would be no marks of restraint, so it would look like the victim killed himself. Could that be their play here? He was terrified for himself but nothing mattered if he couldn't find Claire.

His captors weren't talking much, as if they were angry with each other. Could he use that? An odd pair, but partners. Partners in crime.

Stan drove the swamp buggy past an area Nick recognized in the wan moonlight. It was the entry to the verboten "back forty" area of the ranch. In the darkness, he couldn't read the words on the sign they passed, but he recalled what it said: STAY OUT. No wonder Stan had let slip they should check out the tree houses where high rollers stayed. His hopes rose they must have Claire stashed there, but who had taken her from the BAA?

They drove into a stand of what looked like huge fica trees with their massive twisted roots and trunks. He saw lights on in the one tree directly overhead. The tree houses?

They came to a halt. They must be getting out here. He didn't think either man had looked back at him, so he'd try to be deadweight, pretend he was still unconscious. Just before he shut his eyes when Stan killed the motor and climbed out, he saw the glint of a gun in Grant's hand.

He closed his eyes and prayed hard, that Claire was here and that she was alive.

And that he'd find a way to save them both.

"It's gonna take you how long to get here?" Jace asked Falcon on his cell phone. He didn't like what he'd just heard.

"Look, man, you want the helo for something like this, I said almost an hour, give or take. I'm not near the airport, but I'm pretty sure the helo's gassed up. Tell me more. You think your ex-wife was targeted, so per my earlier theory, maybe it could be someone wanting to get to you?"

"Someone wanting to get to her, not me, I swear it. She and her husband—a friend of mine, really—are investigating a murder case, but let me fill you in when you land. I swear I'll pay anything for fuel, your time, anything."

"*Semper Fi*, man. I'll be there as fast as I can, but have those landing lights ready. And, like they say, keep your head down."

Jace ended the connection. His head was already down. He was more than depressed and scared.

"He's coming?" Brit asked, breaking into his thoughts.

"Yeah, but ASAP isn't soon. We need to put the electric lamps out again. I don't know, just don't know," he said, glaring at the dark screen of his phone in the dim light of the BAA trailer, as if he could read something there.

"Don't know what?"

"What I'm gonna do. Nick said to lay off, wait for him to call, but if they go back too far into the ranch, it's blackout land for phones." He hit his forehead with his fist. "I may just get in the chopper and have Falcon take me in. We need a miracle, and the thermal imaging just might be it."

"Here, coffee, remember?" Brit asked, pointing at the cup she'd poured him either a few minutes or ages ago. Time was fading, terror was growing. Combat had been easy compared to this.

Claire was still tied, though Glover finally pulled out her gag again. He'd put her in a rope hammock high in the tree, a mere step from the upper floor of a wooden tree house. As far as she could see, this open air room held a large bed, a small chest of drawers and a table and two chairs. Rolls of mosquito netting were tied above, since they weren't needed this time of year.

Glover amused himself by sitting on the edge of the floor, telling her things like, "Don't look down," and "Don't rock the boat," and swinging her hammock with one foot. It would be a beautiful place if she wasn't terrified, a room where someone could eat and sleep cradled in the massive limbs of the trees with leaves rustling all around.

Irv was obviously waiting for someone. She figured Stan Helter. Somehow Stan—maybe with Irv's help—had found the bodies of Grant Manfort's lost mentor and his granddaughter. Maybe Irv had killed them, but how did Grant fit in? Could Irv be blackmailing Stan or Grant? Stan must have wanted to get Grant away from his mentor, get him to invest in the ranch and not just the insurance company he had joined.

In the moments when Claire's head cleared and she didn't hallucinate, she figured out that Irv's cell phone did not work out here. And that she probably did not have long to live. Irv was not only killing time until Stan Helter came but probably planning to kill her.

"Irv," she said, her voice shaky, "you could end all this right now by just getting out of here. You said you know this place like the back of your hand. My husband will pay you a fortune to bring me back, and then you can just keep going. And make your son proud that you didn't harm his friend, because I am that."

"Sounds sweet, darlin', but I already got me a fortune coming. Besides, it's gonna feel like a fortune to settle with the lawyer who sent me away in the first place, and he's coming here now—know who I mean?"

Shock shot through her when she was sure nothing could get worse. "Nick? Nick is coming here? You told him he had to come here to get me back? Is that what this is all about, to trap him?"

"Naw, that's just a bonus. Honest, I wasn't expecting you to find me digging up those bones. Overheard on the spy phone they rigged up for me that the land would be searched and maybe bulldozed, so had to cover my tracks. Hey, I hear voices, someone close. Party's on," he told her and gave her hammock another shove with his foot that rocked her hard, so hard she thought she might spill out. At least he left her.

She too heard voices and looked down through the web of hammock rope. She saw no people but noticed another hammock like this one right below, no doubt for the ground-floor level. She hadn't had much time to look around when he'd carried her up here. She'd tried to stop remembering her mother reading to her and Darcy from that old story, *The Swiss Family Robinson*, where the ship-wrecked family lived in a tree.

Again, she heard voices below, men's voices. But she didn't hear Nick's. She felt so scared and so very alone. But then, once more, her baby moved as if to say *I'm here with you*. But if she died, her little one died too.

Nick still pretended to be out cold. Stan slung him over his shoulder and struggled to carry him upstairs to the top level. Nick was glad the bastard was grunting and groaning. Were they going to throw him off the second story? Bury him in this wild area Bronco said was full of gators, pythons, fire ants and who knew what else? It was survival of the fittest out here in more ways than one. And where was Claire?

Stan dropped him on a hard wooden floor and pulled out his gag. He smacked him on both cheeks, thinking he had to bring him to.

"Careful, or you'll roll off the edge, Markwood," he told Nick, so he must have realized he was conscious now. Damn. That might have given him an edge.

"You got about five minutes," Stan went on, "then you're both outta here for good—for parts unknown. Just be grateful I'm not letting a guy who works for me at you—yet. I could just fly you out to where we get our girls, but no can do. Your wife's in that hammock out there. One wrong move and she's going down two floors and you with her, but Grant says to give you two some time." He snorted. "After he got rid of Rowan and the girl, funny he's getting soft. Irv says your wife's a little looney, off her rocker. Like I said, make it quick."

Irv? Irv Glover? He'd come back and kidnapped Claire to get his son back? Nothing made sense. Stan left him, and Grant wasn't in sight.

"Nick, is he gone?" Claire's quiet voice came to him as if from a dark, vast space. "Are you there?"

He rolled closer to the edge, lifted himself up on one elbow. Her voice came from a spiderweb of white ropes suspended just out of his reach. A dim light shone from across the room and more ricocheted in from downstairs. Rolls of mosquito webbing hung from the ceiling above her, but he figured they'd never reach the ground, hanging on that.

He managed to find his voice. "Sweetheart, yes, I'm here but tied."

"Me too."

"Thank God you're all right. We saw where they took you under the fence."

"Just Irv Glover. He hates you. He's working for Grant. I think Irv helped Grant kill his mentor, that insurance CEO, and the girl. The bones—I saw their heads—preserved heads in the taxidermy shop. I keep going in and out of dreams since I don't have my meds, but I'm trying hard."

She saw their heads? She must mean their skulls. He'd seen her like this before if she didn't take her meds. "Keep talking, sweetheart, and I'll respond. I think they're downstairs deciding what to do with us."

"And, hopefully, keep Irv away from you. He hates you for sending him to prison."

"Talk."

He had an insane thought, but they were goners if it

didn't work. That time he'd stubbed his toe and cut his foot on the metal frame under their bed—maybe there was a similar frame under this bed. Such a big bed for a tree house, but he had no doubt there had been women imprisoned here, warming it for guests for a price.

Yes, reaching underneath now he could feel a piece of metal that held the frame to the leg of the bed had a thin edge. He tried to concentrate on sawing it across his wrist bonds while Claire's trembling voice went on. He loved her—so much.

"Nick, I know we said we wanted to be surprised, but I swear I'm carrying a boy. He's been trying to help me through this, giving me a little punch now and then when I went—went off too far, off the edge. He gives me strength. I love you. You're so good for Lexi, but together— Nick, they're arguing downstairs."

He couldn't believe that this minimal exertion had made him break out into a huge sweat. The wind up here was chilly for autumn in South Florida.

"I can't believe I screwed this up—trusted Grant," he called quietly to her.

"I've done that before, all my training and still I've done that. Darcy will take Lexi and love her if I'm gone."

"Don't—talk—think—that way."

"What are you doing?"

"Loving you no matter what happens. There—ah…"

He'd sawed loose one of the several cords around his wrist. He yanked his wrists apart, tried to slide a wrist free. Sweat, desperation…

The ropes burned his skin, but one wrist popped free, then the other. He pulled his knees up to his chest and reached for the knots around his ankles. Big mistake that they hadn't wanted rope marks on his corpse. But how to get Claire free, get her past them? Grant had a gun and who knows who else was down there. Damn, he'd made mistakes, but Claire had not been one of them. And just when he'd told himself they were safe, out of danger... dead gator in the pool, snake in the driveway, but neither could have prepared them for the criminals planning their deaths below.

To avoid making noise he didn't get to his feet, but rolled to the edge of the open-air room.

"Nick, what are we going to do?"

"Keep talking a regular conversation. Pretend to cry a little. I think I can unhook one end of your hammock, and we can ride it down to the ground. Hang on. I know you're tied, but hang on to some of those woven ropes, because we're going to swing free."

"I wish we could get away, but they have us trapped," she said, maybe a bit too loudly. At least voices were raised below now.

He was amazed at the weight of the hook that fastened the foot of the hammock to a post. But he'd carried her before, over the threshold, to their bed...

When he freed her, the weight of the hammock almost yanked him over the side. Claire clung to the webbing, swinging back and forth. He lunged for her and the hammock. Crazy, but he pictured Tarzan and Jane in the jungle from some old movie.

Claire, her tied wrists thrust through the webbing, held to him with both hands. They went one way, then the next, and finally snagged in the other hammock on the lower level.

He had to get her feet untied so they could run. But he'd carry her away first, get a little distance.

But they must have been seen or heard already.

"No!" someone shouted, a man's voice he didn't recognize. "Stop! Don't! You need me!"

A gunshot. Another, one, two more, *bam, bam.*

But he didn't think the shots were aimed at them—yet. He picked Claire off her feet and ran for the thick blackness of the trees.

# CHAPTER THIRTY-FIVE

*You need me…you need me*, the man's panicked shout circled in Claire's head after the gunshots rang out. She needed Nick, and he needed her.

She would have jumped and screamed at the sound of shots, but she was hanging on to Nick with all her might. Had someone shot at them? Dim light from the tree house windows chased them as Nick ran, bouncing her.

She fought her dazed confusion. It must be time to take her midnight meds. So hard to wake up to do that. Her phone must not have buzzed to remind her, so Nick was trying to wake her up. But her head was always clear when she had to take that bad-tasting stuff.

She heard a shout behind them, a man's voice, upset. But who else would be in the house but Nick and Lexi?

Gasping for air, Nick sloshed through shallow water. Were they back at Flamingo Isle?

"Listen to me," he told her, his voice ragged. He gave

her a little shake. "This is not a dream. We're in danger. Stan Helter and Grant are working together. They knocked me out, must want to kill us. One of them may have shot the other, but we have to run and hide."

Her head cleared. Fear fueled the remnants of her energy. "Nick, I know the voice that shouted 'You need me.' That's Irv Glover, Duncan's dad. He dragged me under the fence. He's the gate guard there—here. He hates you."

Nick swore under his breath as he put her down behind a thick tree with protruding cypress knees. Despite the blackness, wan light from the tree house cast hanging moss and vines in twilight. The water came just above her ankles as he propped her up against the rough bark of a tree trunk.

"You sound clearheaded again," he said as he reached down to fumble with her bonds in the water. "You come and go, but you have to concentrate. We have to get out of here, get help. If they shot Glover, they've decided to make a clean sweep of witnesses, and that means us. Maybe they're bringing in exotic animals—sex trade women too. But I still don't think they killed Ben Hoffman."

Untied at last, her feet tingled from the ankles down like when a foot fell asleep and tried to wake up...she had to wake up. Nick said this was real. They had to get away, save their baby.

"Nick, it's not just that," she said. She leaned hard against the tree as he fumbled with her wrist ties. "I think Irv either murdered Grant's boss at the company, the guy's granddaughter too, or knows that Grant did. They were the ones in the shallow grave, and I caught Irv finally moving them."

"But Stan and Grant would get the grave back when the BAA is sold to Stan—no, that's right. It was going to be surveyed and leveled. Maybe they knew that."

"Yes, Irv said it was going to be bulldozed. Maybe one of them has our phones tapped again. It could be that's how they knew Jackson had to be shut up or stopped too—they overheard his call to Brit when I was with her."

"If the bones belonged to the lost pair, that means Grant must have paid Glover to get rid of them, probably to get his hands on the company. He'd somehow gotten himself in Steve Rowan's will, so the company would have been his, but he must have not wanted to wait until Rowan's natural passing. I—I can't believe it, that he hid their bodies all these years. Terrible he killed the girl too—he was supposed to love her—but either she was onto him or else he was just using her in the first place to get close to Rowan. You'll have to testify what you heard, even if it's hearsay. But are you sure the bones in the grave were the Rowans?"

"No, but I recognized their detached heads from seeing their pictures during my research. The preserved heads are in the taxidermist's cupboard at the ranch. Irv showed me—horrible."

"And we're next on those maniacs' list. Can you run?" he was asking, his voice rough and shaky as her wrist bonds fell away. "Once they get rid of Glover, they'll be hunting us."

"If we go deeper in, they'll trap us against the fence. What are you doing?" she asked as he bent to lift her discarded ropes.

"Stringing these between two cypress knees. If they

run in here, maybe it will trip them up, or they'll at least think that's the plan, and that we're hiding deep in this cypress swamp."

"But it's so far to the road. We could go under the fence where Glover brought me through."

"That's miles away too."

"To get out of here, I can run." Words tumbled from her as he finished with the ropes.

"We'll head toward the road and hope there's a lot of darkness left, and that we don't panic or stampede nocturnal animals. And that Jace figures I've been gone too long and brings his friend to look for me."

He took her arm and they started away, wading, trying to avoid cypress trunks and knees.

A sharp shaft of light stabbed the darkness, then swept across them. They jumped behind a tree, snagging themselves in hanging Spanish moss.

"They gotta be out here," Stan's voice came to them. "I'm going back to the tree house for that infrared hunting gun that picks up animal heat in the dark. Just a sec."

Trying not to make noise in the knee-deep water, they felt their way from tree to tree, stumbling toward what Claire prayed surely had to be the way out to salvation.

And there it was—a wooden walkway elevated above the swamp. They climbed onto it. It had a railing and was not in good repair; even a tree trunk had fallen on it to partially block their way.

"Don't know where that goes, but we're taking it," Nick whispered.

Their feet thudded like muted drums along its rough surface. But another beam of light skittered across the low water, probing the night, searching for them. Nick pulled her over to the side after him where a piece of railing was broken. He sat, then got down into the mire as another light beam swept their way.

Thank God he didn't disappear into the muck. She sat on the edge of the rough wood too; he lifted her down with him. Cool mud and water came up to her thighs, but what if snakes and gators were in here? No choice—maybe no chance now.

Until Falcon brought the helo in, Jace had paced despite his crutches.

"So what's the plan?" his friend asked when he got out, even before the rotors stopped revolving. The two of them huddled away from the others standing around.

After he brought him up to speed, Jace added, "I swore I'd wait and not rush in, but my gut's telling me not to sit this out. Nick said not to call him, but he should've called me by now."

"You sure cells work over there?"

"As far as the compound part, yeah, but probably not way back in," Jace said. "Without being able to recon the area, it would be damned dangerous to go in but..."

"Yeah. I'm game if you are. A flyover?"

"It may be survival of the fittest at the hunting ranch, but we're the fittest, man."

"You need help getting in the helo with that bum foot?"

"Hell no. Bronco, we're going in!" Jace called to those standing outside the circle of landing light.

"But Nick's the boss in this, and he said wait!" the big

man shouted before the *whap-whap* of the starting rotors drowned him out.

Jace pretended he didn't hear him. He thought Brit would try to hold him back, but, bending low, she ran close to hug him hard and then released him. "Bring them back!" she shouted.

He nodded and turned away. Damn sure, that was the woman for him, and he'd propose again soon as he got back. Though pain sliced through his ankle, Jace climbed in and threw his crutches behind his seat. When they lifted off, in the square of landing lights below, he saw the little crowd covering their faces from the swirl of dust and debris: Bronco, Heck with his arm around Gina, Ann and his beloved, bold Brit. He belted in as the helo rotated its nose west and lifted over the double fences as if there was nothing there at all.

They both put headphones with mics on. "You fly, and I'll work the FLIR ground surveillance radar," Falcon told him.

"I basically know how, but give me an F-35. I don't do helos."

"You do now, flyboy. I been missing combat and, from what you said, this just might be it. We just got to find them first."

Claire was instantly exhausted, though she didn't want Nick to know. They slogged out through the swamp, slipping, fighting for footing. At least the voices of their pursuers faded.

Once they staggered out onto dry land, he'd tried to carry her. Her legs felt numb, her wrists aching. Her entire body hurt. She could only hope that their baby was not being hurt through all this. She prayed he was safe in his own little sea inside her. But she insisted on running on her own, praying they were going in the right direction.

Nick had her pinned to his side, so he was running for both of them, half dragging, half lifting her. Leaving the cypress swamp behind, they headed through a prairie of sawgrass that snagged at their pants and could cut their skin. Thank heavens the moon didn't throw much light, but their pursuers evidently had not only wheels now, but night-hunting gear.

"We don't dare—follow the road," Nick gasped out. "Not sure if a cell phone would work here, but they've got mine."

"Mine's long gone. Should we try to double back—get a vehicle? There has to be at least two there since Glover had one."

"We can't chance that, and daylight will not be our friend. How are you—the baby?"

"He's a trooper. Remember, his nickname is Trey for Nicholas Markwood the third."

Claire could sense that Nick's strength was flagging, and she'd just made him cry. But they pressed on. She put out her hand to wipe his cheek. "Nick, darling, whatever happens—"

"Shh! I want to hear what you have to say, but I hear an engine."

"Helicopter?"

"Swamp buggy."

He was right. And they stood in the middle of what must be an open field with no cover.

"Down," he said. "We have to get down."

Hoping there were no fire ants or worse, Claire lay flat beside him in the blowing grass. Nick threw an arm over her.

"Heat source over here, maybe thirty feet!" a voice she didn't know called out not too far away. "Got 'em!"

That must be Grant. They had her and Nick pinned down. And she supposed raptors would clean their bones if these men didn't put them in a shallow grave. At least Irv Glover would never give poor Duncan nightmares again.

Then another sound, a roar. Claire pictured Tiberia angry about being caged, then sweeter scenes tore through her terror. She pictured Lexi cuddling next to her in bed. She and Darcy were children, both in bed, and their mother was reading to them from Kipling's *The Jungle Book* about an evil, man-eater tiger.

"Chopper too," Nick said in her ear. "It may be theirs but..."

She looked up. Not a big one, coming fast, sweeping the ground with a big beam of light.

"It's Jace!" she shouted through the roar.

She lifted her head to see Stan running at them, keeping low, big rifle with a night-vision scope in his hand. But the chopper swooped fast, landed between them and him. The chopper's lights made the area bright as day.

"Stan's down—helicopter's landing skid hit him," Nick shouted. "I see Grant running away from their vehicle! Stay down!"

"No, Nick..."

But he leaped to his feet and tore after Grant. She saw the rotor blast tear at his hair and shirt. The chopper lights blinded her, and the grass around her whipped wildly. She tried to get to her feet, then just stayed down.

The wind from the rotors was still fierce, but Jace came hobbling out of the chopper. Keeping low, he helped her to her feet.

"Nick chased Grant Manfort!" she screamed. "Can you help him?"

"He tackled him, and Falcon's helping him drag the bastard back. Claire, come on. Just do what I say for once!"

Bending low, blown by the fierce wind, with Jace limping so she had to help him, they headed for the chopper. For one moment she was afraid he might have told her Nick was safe to get her to come, but no, there was Nick with a battered-looking man who must be Grant. And Jace's pilot friend had the unconscious Stan Helter, bleeding from a head wound, and was tying him to Grant.

Nick got in back of the helicopter with the bound men and pulled Claire in from the boost Jace gave her. Sitting on the floor behind the pilot seats, Nick tugged Claire to him as the chopper lifted, tilted and flew. Nick put his feet on the two trussed men—Stan unconscious, Grant bruised and bleeding.

"Party's over," Nick shouted to Grant above the roar of the engine. "Your life's over too. And ours, you lying, murdering bastard, has a new beginning!"

# CHAPTER THIRTY-SIX

*Four Months Later*

"I can't wait to see Tiberia in his new home!" Duncan told Claire with a big, bright smile. "He's gonna be so happy here!"

Marta, holding her son's hand, when he didn't tug it away, whispered, "You bet! He's gonna feel safe here at the zoo. Claire, no matter if life *is* a zoo, I'm right with him on that—feeling safe and happy too."

Standing near the expansive tiger enclosure at the Naples Zoo, the two of them smiled over the heads of their excited children.

Irv Glover was in a deep, not a shallow, grave. The police in Tennessee had finally traced and arrested the ex-con who was sending Irv's monthly checks to Marta.

Grant and the ranch taxidermist had been charged with two counts of abuse of a dead human body.

Those horrible preserved heads—it turned out when Irv Glover was supposed to just bury the bodies, he had decided to sell Hewitt the heads, to make a little extra on the job. Grant had finally admitted that he'd had Glover commit the Rowan murders and hide their bodies so they were presumed drowned and so that Grant could be out of the state that day to have a solid alibi.

The two preserved heads of the murdered Rowans were temporarily being kept as evidence. But Drew Hewitt, the taxidermist, had disappeared, so somehow he must have gotten wind of the discovery and was on the run.

Grant would stand trial next year on murder charges. Bullets from a gun still in his possession had caused the deaths of Steve and Leslie Rowan, though he'd hired Glover to do the killing. One bullet had shattered the back of Mr. Rowan's skull and was still lodged there, though taxidermy work had smoothed the dried skin over. Stan had been complicit in those crimes too, even blackmailing Grant to help fund the Trophy Ranch or he would testify against him.

Although Nick would testify at both trials, thank heavens he was not prosecuting. It had been a huge international scandal that the ranch had been importing women for prostitution, then passing them on to the West Coast in a sort of sex slave ring.

The ruling for Ben Hoffman's death remained an accident, not suicide, so that had helped Ann, and settled Lane down too. Nick and Claire kept quiet on that ruling, but Ann had told them privately that she had finally accepted that Ben had intentionally entered Tiberia's cage.

"I'm telling myself, though, that he changed his mind

at the last minute—that he didn't want to leave me," Ann had insisted to Claire. "Maybe he changed his mind, turned away, fell, hit his head in his panic when he realized he was wrong—that there was a better way than taking his life."

Wanting to comfort her, wishing she believed that, Claire had tried to assure her. "That's very possible, Ann. Besides, the medical examiners, even psychiatrists are not always right. I've seen that time and again."

But when it came to Brit, Claire realized she had accepted that the once strong man she knew as her father had simply caved in. What Lane really thought, Claire had no idea at first, until Nick talked to him, and, for once, she didn't want to psych Lane out up close and personal. How well she knew that family life could be more complicated than any crime investigation, and she vowed to focus on her own family for now at least.

Brit did say that her father had probably hoped that his insurance policy would kick in to save the zoo. And it was true that he deeply regretted his ruined relationship with Lane. When she had shared all that, Nick had vowed to have a good, open relationship with his yet unborn son.

Nick had had a long talk with Lane, trying to use some of Claire's I-care-you-can-talk-to-me strategies, and they now believed Ben had actually written that hand-printed note, hinting at suicide, then hid it and just hoped Ann would find it someday. Too many deaths—including the alligator and even the snake Irv had admitted to Claire he had put in their yard because he hated Nick and wanted him to quit investigating the Trophy Ranch.

So, finally, Claire was concentrating on nothing but being pregnant and healthy.

She'd grown so big lately, but she would not have missed this event. Neither had Gracie Cobham and her sons. The old woman had donated several dozen orchids to the zoo and had a permanent entry pass. "Took my boy Thunder coupla months to get comfortable living here, but he'll be fine," she'd assured Claire and Darcy a few moments ago.

But best of all, Jackson was with them today. Granted, he was in a wheelchair his oldest daughter was pushing, with Ann Hoffman hovering over him, but he was much better and was expected to make a full recovery. That and Jace and Brit's engagement were two other good things to come out of a terrible time. Looking happy, they stood together, waiting for the moment Tiberia would appear.

As the crowd, including Lane and his family, gathered around the tiger compound—Tiberia was finally not going to be living alone—the magnificent animal stepped out into view, seeming not a bit wary.

"Looking confident, just like us," Claire said, squeezing Nick's arm.

"Life is never dull, is it?" he asked, and laughed so loud Claire startled. He pointed to the side as Claire saw one of the flamingos from the BAA race past as if it had permission for the run of its new home.

"Never!" Claire agreed, and, as Tiberia stretched his back haunches and roared to his new audience, she felt more than her baby kick. She sat down on a bench fast, but not before her water broke.

"Nick, sorry to cut this short," she told him, "but I've been through this before, and it must be baby birth time."

He looked shocked and scared. "Should I get Darcy? Now?"

"Now!"

Nick had never felt more out of his element. Even arguing a case before the Florida Supreme Court had never scared him as much as being with Claire as she went through labor. The nurse who had been with them off and on had just sent for the doctor in a big hurry. Something about a "double footling birth" and a "pulsating cord where it shouldn't be."

Nick felt helpless and panicked. "What does that mean?" he demanded of the doctor as he appeared and Claire was quickly wheeled out. "Why is she going to the operating room instead of a delivery room?"

"Emergency C-section," Dr. Summerhill told him. "Once the baby is this far down, it can't be turned, and we need to get the baby out now. We'll keep you posted—send for you soon."

As the doctor too disappeared, Nick banged his fist against the wall. He had expected to be with her, be strong for her. They'd gone through classes to prepare for this day. He'd give anything to help her, be there.

And his son... Of course he'd be a fighter, of course he'd be all right. But there had been such haste, and all because of a throbbing umbilical cord? Damn, what did that really mean?

But Claire was strong. Very. From the first, even when she was fighting her disease. A great mother, a great partner. After all they'd been through, nothing more could go wrong now.

He paced. He prayed. He paced, he prayed.

"Mr. Markwood, you can come in now," the nurse at the door to the operating room told him. "You have a fine son, and Claire's conscious and doing well. It was a bit of an emergency for a while."

*A bit of an emergency for a while*—the story of his life with Claire Fowler Britten Markwood!

He hurried down the hall behind the nurse, tears nearly blinding him. But not so much that he couldn't see the squalling, kicking little boy who was minutes old and needed a bath. He bent to kiss Claire on the other side of a drape that hid her lower body.

"Told you it would be a boy," she said, and promptly went to sleep.

Lexi sat on the side of Claire's hospital bed and occasionally patted her new baby brother on the little knitted cap he wore. "I hope he grows up fast," she told Claire. "I want to teach him to ride a pony. And I'll tell people when they meet him, his name is spelled *T-r-e-y* and not like a tray with food on it."

"We'll all teach him a lot of things," Claire said with a smile at Nick, who hovered on the other side of the bed.

Nick held Trey, walked him briefly around the room before the nurse came in to put him in his little bassinet just down the hall under what Lexi called "grow lights" because he had a touch of jaundice, but he looked just beautiful to Claire.

"Here's some cards, Mommy, that came to the house,"

Lexi told her, and dug them out of her pink backpack. "And wait till you see all the orchids that tiger lady sent to you at the house—a couple dyed blue for a boy."

"Everyone has been just wonderful. Okay, before I take a nap and Bronco and Nita get here so Nita can see her new charge, I'll open just a couple of cards."

"This one's got a pretty stamp on it," Lexi said, plucking one out.

Claire looked at the foreign stamp and return address and gasped. She opened it with her fingernail. "Kristen Kane! She must still be living in Europe. We've been so out of touch. Oh, it's not a baby card but a letter. It's been forwarded to me from my old address."

Nick sank on the side of the bed, tipping her slightly toward him. He looked beat, she thought. Just wait until the baby woke up several times a night to be changed and fed. He would finally be able to grasp what narcolepsy was like—sleeping on your feet during the day, nodding off, then waking up the moment Nicholas "Trey" Markwood made a peep.

"Oh, you won't believe this, Nick," Claire said as she skimmed the handwritten note. "Kristen was my Florida State roommate, who went on to do grad work in forensic archaeology. She's studied and worked in Scandinavia. She's coming back from Denmark, and read about what happened at the BAA, our finding the Rowans in a shallow grave years after they disappeared, all that."

"Do I know the Rowans, Mommy?"

"No, honey. But, Nick, here's the thing. Kris and I were

especially close since I was fighting my disease and she had hers. Face blindness. Ever hear of that?"

"Yeah. It's got some long clinical name. I read Steve Wozniak, the guy who helped found Apple computers, has it."

"The last card I got from her said she was 'all bogged down.' She's been studying prehistoric peat bog burials and says there's one that's been discovered not far from here, at the edge of the Glades, similar to the one they found up near Disney. Can you believe it? And she wants to talk to me about consulting, but says to keep it secret for now."

"You just told Dad and me about it," Lexi scolded, "but I won't tell."

Folding his arms over his chest in a classic "no way" posture, Nick said, "Lexi, honey, pick Mommy out another card, a baby one this time."

"Well, of course, I wouldn't consult right now anyway," Claire assured him. "But isn't that fascinating? Studying bodies hundreds—thousands—of years old to try to find out about the culture and individuals? No villains or complications from that. I know, I know," she said as Lexi thrust another card at her, "I'll be too busy, I have another life now, but I'll certainly read up on that. Imagine!"

Nick sighed. "I guess that's the best kind of clients to have—long gone, silent and beyond law suits or leaving gators in a pool or shooting guns. Reading up on it is fine, but..."

"And visiting the new local dig," she said, still reading. "Amazing."

Nick sighed and leaned in to kiss Claire. "I vote a definite maybe, if you just consult—after Lexi and Trey are off to college," he added with a little smile. He pulled both of them into a one-armed embrace.

Claire managed the last word. "No bogging down, indeed! Not us! It does sound exciting but very safe, so we'll see. We'll just see."

★ ★ ★ ★ ★

*If you enjoyed SHALLOW GRAVE,*
*don't miss the next suspenseful story in*
*Karen Harper's SOUTH SHORES series,*
*SILENT SCREAM,*
*available soon from MIRA Books.*

# AUTHOR'S NOTE

Thanks as ever to my editor Emily Ohanjanians and my agent Annelise Robey for their advice and support for this series. And to publicist Shara Alexander, part of my great MIRA team. As ever, to my husband, Don, for his proofreading and business manager roles. With doctor questions, our ob-gyn friend Dr. Roy Manning comes to the rescue.

The problem of indigenous animals fighting for their space in South Florida, as in other places on the planet, is real and sobering. Signs near highways warning of Florida panther crossings are frequent near Naples where my husband and I wintered for thirty years. Estimates for these solitary, elusive predators are that only 120 to 160 remain in the wild. Nothing like endangered animals and an endangered heroine for a suspense novel!

And, sad to say, some invasive animals have been released and thrive in that region, especially the dangerous Burmese pythons, which are hatching hundreds of eggs in the Everglades. Wildlife experts are asking the public to report any sightings of these large snakes through the IveGot1 app or hotline. Python hunters like Bronco do go out to catch and kill.

The Naples Zoo at Caribbean Gardens is in a lovely setting. We have enjoyed watching it grow from "Jungle Larry's African Safari" to the great facility it is today. The BAA is fictional, as is the Trophy Ranch; however, such entities do exist in South Florida. There are legitimate hunting ranches without the likes of someone like Stan Helter.

A Big Cat Public Safety Act is a bipartisan bill being considered in the US Congress, which would ban the possession and breeding of lions, tigers, leopards and other big cats by private individuals or unqualified exhibitors at "roadside zoos." Bill supporters say that thousands of big cats are being kept in people's backyards and basements or in poorly maintained facilities, creating a safety hazard for the public while threatening the cats' health.

As for a tiger killing a keeper, a zookeeper was killed recently by a tiger in the Palm Beach Zoo. The ruling was that the keeper did not follow established safety procedures. In May of 2017, Hamerton Zoo Park, eighty miles north of London, England, also reported a female keeper killed by a tiger when she somehow entered the same area with the animal, which did not escape or threaten others. The Hamerton Zoo blamed a freak accident. Such zoo clashes between wildlife and their human custodians once again emphasize that the closeness of wild animals and humans can go very wrong.

I hope you have been able to read the first three books

in the South Shores series and that you will look for the next suspense novel featuring Claire and Nick Markwood. There is a prehistoric burial bog in Florida not far from Disney World. I love the clash of cultures in a novel, and, of course, Claire's idea that helping with Kristen Kane's dig would be safe is hardly a possibility in a Karen Harper suspense novel.

See you online at www.KarenHarperAuthor.com or www.facebook.com/KarenHarperAuthor

# WRITERS HELPING WRITERS

*P.D. James and Mary Higgins Clark*
*Up Close and Personal*

As a reader, I look up to certain authors. But as a veteran writer, I look up to particular trailblazing authors too. I was blessed to spend time with Mary Higgins Clark (who needs no introduction to readers of suspense) and had dinner with the famous and fabulous British crime writer P.D. James. Time with those two veteran authors has been one of the highlights of my thirty-five years (and counting!) as a published novelist.

In early February of 1996, I was invited to be on the faculty of a three-day writer's conference sponsored by the University of South Florida in St. Petersburg. I accepted happily (we were snowbirds in South Florida) but I was even happier when I saw that famed British author P.D. James was on tour in the US and was also speaking at the conference. I had begun to write contemporary suspense as well as historical novels, and I remember thinking, *If I can just breathe this woman's air, it will help me!*

I attended two workshops she gave and was seated next to her at the faculty dinner. I'm used to being with authors and have met and learned from some of the best, but this was special to me.

Granted, I am a rabid Anglophile in general, but I greatly admired her work. This was five years after P.D. (Phyllis Dorothy) was dubbed by the queen as "Dame James," Baroness James of Holland Park. How well I recall (and still have my notes from) her advice in her workshops and during our meal together.

One thing she shared was that she always began to build a book with a particular setting in mind, rather than a plot or character coming first. This surprised me, since her police procedurals present character and plot so well. Of course, her best known work—the Adam Dalgliesh crime novels—has continuing characters. So perhaps she had those "persons" well in hand, but they did evolve and change within the fourteen Dalgliesh novels that stretched from 1962 to 2008.

I always begin planning my stories with a place that intrigues me but I know I'm in the minority; most authors I've talked to take one of the other two routes to their stories. It gave me a big boost to know she conceived of a new story the same way I did. She told me, "If the place seems real to the reader, everything else should too."

Another piece of advice I've hung my writing hat on for over twenty suspense novels is to keep the suspects (she called them possible villains) to about three, so each one can have the attention he/she needs in the story: character development, motives, unique personalities.

In short, I found the (then) seventy-six-year-old Dame James not only charming but generous with her advice. In addition to meeting and spending time with Mary Higgins Clark when I won her award in 2006, my time with P.D. James was one of the most moving and valuable events in my career.

Mary Higgins Clark also always gives her readers a great suspense novel; she specializes in "woman in jeopardy" stories. I believe one reason I won her award for my Amish-country-set book *Dark Angel* (and was also rewarded with some time and advice from her!) was that I strive for that story structure too. And in the South Shores series, family drama, danger and the love story of a woman with an unusual disease make a great mix for romantic suspense.

P.D. James died in 2014, but Mary Higgins Clark is still going strong with great books. I found both women generous and willing to uplift newer authors. I really appreciated the advice from them about writing great suspense and hope I can "pass it on" through my novels to my readers and other writers.